# BIRTHDAY PARTY PALOOZA

Becky Baines

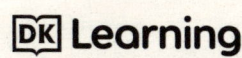

## HOW TO USE THIS BOOK

This isn't your average story. Here, you have the power to decide how the adventure unfolds!

Throughout this book, you will be given choices between two actions. Make your choice, then turn to the page number listed beside it. Once you're there, keep reading to find out how the adventure plays out for the characters in your story.

Each of your choices has an outcome that will take the story in a new direction—some good and some, well, not so good. If you make stellar choices, you'll see a message like this:

> **GREAT JOB!**
>
> With your help, Tami and Sam had the ultimate birthday bash! You have reached the end of this story, but you can go back to the beginning and pick different paths to see where another adventure leads!

Other choices you make might lead to an unhappy outcome. That's OK—this is just a story! Take a second to read about why that outcome might have happened, and think about what you could do differently to change the outcome next time around.

Within these pages, there are 20 different paths you could take. That's a lot of choices! So if you don't like the outcome of a choice you've made, don't worry—you can read the story as many times as you want and change up your choices as you go.

At the end of the book, you'll find questions and activities that will really have you think about all the different decisions you've made, as well as the outcomes.

**Are you ready to start your adventure? Remember:** You've Got This!

## YOU ARE OFFICIALLY INVITED TO TAMI AND SAM'S SUPREME, ULTIMATE, FANTASTIC, AMAZING, BEST-EVER BIRTHDAY PARTY PALOOZA!

**WHEN:** Saturday, October 10

**WHERE:** Fantastic Frank's Fun Park

**WHY:** You only turn teen once!

**RSVP:** Me! (Tami)

"Sam, wake up! Today's the day!" Tami shouted. She was too excited to sleep. If she was awake, her twin brother had to be, too.

"Ugghhh... what time is it?" Sam asked in a groggy voice. Opening his eyes and squinting at the clock, he rolled back over and covered his face with a pillow. "7:30am?! That's criminal! Why are you up this early on a Saturday? Why am *I* up this early on a Saturday?"

"Because. Today is the official start of the one-week countdown to Tami and Sam's Supreme, Ultimate, Fantastic, Amazing, Best-Ever Birthday Party Palooza!" Tami exclaimed.

"Can you please not call it that?" Sam groaned.

"Well, what do you suggest?" she asked.

"I don't know. Sam and Tami's birthday party?" Sam suggested.

"Too late. I already made invitations!" Tami removed the pillow from Sam's face and waved a neon pink piece of paper in front of it.

Sam pretended to shield his eyes.

"Wait—Fantastic Frank's? I thought we agreed to Skateland?" Sam said, sitting up.

"Oh yeah... about that," Tami began.

Fantastic Frank's Fun Park had been Tami and Sam's special family hangout ever since they first learned how to walk. They had dozens of family photos in front of the iconic clown face whose mouth you entered to purchase tickets. Sam even lost his first tooth on a candy apple from Fantastic Frank's candy shop. (Not one to be outdone by her brother, Tami fell running to the carousel an hour later, losing her first tooth as well.)

"Me on wheels? No, thanks! Besides, you love Fantastic Frank's. Remember when you ate four corn dogs and tossed your cookies on the Ferris wheel? Ah, memories..." Tami laughed.

"Fantastic Frank's is for babies, Tami. We're going to be thirteen!" Sam emphasized the word "teen." "Skateland—or no deal."

"Fantastic Frank's, or I tell Mom about your little project," Tami responded.

Sam had been secretly stashing tadpoles he caught at their backyard pond in tanks in the closet. He was documenting their metamorphosis for his science fair project. But their mom hated all things slimy... especially if that slimy thing turned into a jumping slimy thing.

"Joke's on you. Dad already told Mom. She thinks they're cute!" Sam smirked victoriously. "Skateland. And that's final."

Tami puffed her chest. "Fantastic Frank's, and that's final-ER."

**You've Got This!**

Compromise on a new place. → Go to page **46**

← Go to page **61** Let fate (and a deck of cards) decide!

Tami had always been a fan of anything vintage. One of her favorite things to do in the whole wide world was to visit secondhand shops with her friends on weekends. They would find old clothing with plenty of life left and figure out different ways to style it to fit their personalities. A retro party was her dream come true!

"Sounds dope. You know I love eighties music!" Sam said.

"Wait, I thought by retro we meant nineties... you know... boy bands and tie-dye? Like Dad was saying," Tami responded.

"I think the eighties had boy bands and tie-dye, too, Tami," Sam said dismissively. "Besides, eighties... nineties... what's the difference?"

"Uh, EVERYTHING..." Tami was shocked at her brother's lack of historical knowledge. "Hairstyles,

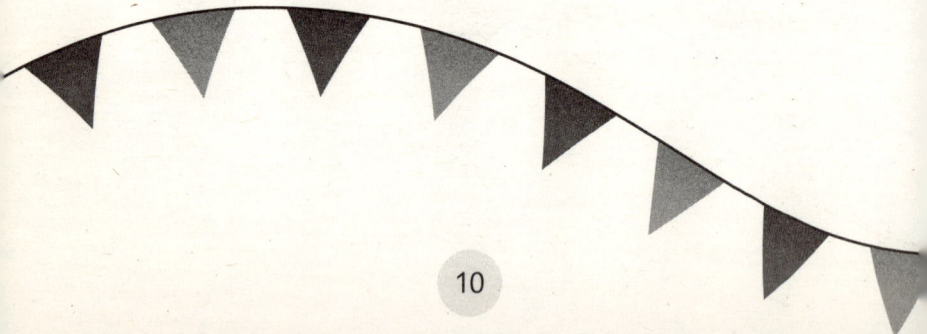

food, music... you really don't have any appreciation for culture! Right, Dad?"

"Don't drag me into this," Dad said, eyeing the exit. "Once the Trouble Twins get going, I'm out." He held up a peace sign and ran out of the room.

Tami slapped her palm against her forehead. "Peace signs... so seventies."

"Ahem," Sam cleared his throat. "You and your friends were doing peace sign selfies yesterday!"

"No, those are modern peace signs, Sam. Not one of dad's vintage peace signs."

"What's the difference?" he asked.

"The age of the person," Tami explained.

"Whatever." Sam laughed. "If I have to dress up, I'm wearing a big rock-and-roll wig."

"That's eighties!" Tami shouted. "Or early nineties I guess," she corrected herself.

"Hey, wait—I have an idea," said Sam. "What if we had all the decades at our retro party? That way you can go nineties if you want. I could go eighties. Mom and Dad can dress twenties or whatever decade they're from."

"I heard that!" Dad yelled from the hallway. He popped his head back in the room and gave them an accusing look. Then he held up another peace sign and left. Tami rolled her eyes.

"We can have music and food from all sorts of eras!" Sam exclaimed.

Tami's face lit up. "Oh, I am gonna have some fun with this!"

Go to page **107**

"I think..." Sam looked at the ceiling. He thought back to all the happy moments he and Tami had shared over the years. He remembered how cool she had been for supporting him at all his games, and all the times he needed her and she had been there for him. Sure, she may not be the first person he called when he needed someone to practice his free throws with. But if his school project was ruined, she would help him pick up the pieces and come up with a new one in five minutes flat. She never let him down, and he wasn't going to let her down now. "I think I'm not ready to give up," he said.

Tami's face lit up. "Me neither!" she exclaimed. "You know, Sam, I know we're different these days but... who wants to be the same? The same is boring. Different is good!"

"That's exactly what I was thinking," said Sam.

Go to page **100**

"I don't know... boy bands and eight-bit video games sound a little too exciting," Sam said sarcastically. "Maybe we should save that for our sweet sixteen party."

"Your loss," their dad said with a shrug. "I'll leave you masterminds to it then."

Sam began moving aquarium tanks out of the closet and lining them up on the dresser. "Guess these can come out of hiding now."

Tami leaned down to examine the tadpoles as Sam was plugging cords into outlets. Each contained aquarium gravel, a couple of bigger rocks, some fake plants, and water. Inside, the tadpoles were just doing their tadpole thing—swimming and being slimy.

"Hey, this one's already got legs!" Tami said, pointing to the tank with the biggest tadpoles.

"That's Ned," said Sam. "He's definitely growing the fastest. But his buddies in the red tank aren't far behind!"

"Red?" Tami asked. "This tank is black. They all are."

"No, I mean the red light tank... see?" Sam walked over to the dresser and flipped on the light above Ned's tank. It glowed red.

"Cool! Do they like that?" Tami asked.

"Yeah, from what I can tell. I did a lot of research on raising tadpoles, and herpetologists—that's what frog scientists are called—say if you put them under different kinds of lights, they'll grow faster," Sam explained. "That's my science project this year."

"What kind of lights are over the other tanks?" Tami asked.

He flipped on the other two. "This one is a UV black light. And this one is just a regular white light," Sam explained. "They're growing at about the same speed, much slower than the red light frogs."

"Oh yeah! These other guys are tiny by comparison," Tami said, tapping on the glass.

"Ahem." Sam scribbled something on a piece of paper and taped it to the wall. It said: NO TAPPING THE GLASS.

"So many rules around here," Tami said, shaking her head. "What are you gonna do when they go full frog? I can't imagine Mom would be cool with having more mouths to feed."

"No, she made it very clear she would not!" Sam laughed. "I'm going to put them safely back in our backyard pond where I found them. Their own little private paradise."

He flipped off the lights. First, the red, then the white. Before he turned off the black light, Tami pointed to the stars on his ceiling.

"I didn't know you still had those!" she said. "I remember when we put them up. Man, they look cool under black light."

"I started to take them down but they left marks behind. I figured it was better to have a starry ceiling than a mad Mom, so I left them up," Sam said.

"Oh my gosh—Sam. I think I have a brilliant idea. Close the curtains!" Tami instructed.

Sam did as he was told. Tami went to Sam's closet, selected the brightest white shirt she could find and pulled it over her head. With the blackout curtains closed and the door shut, there was no natural light coming in.

"Look!" Tami said. Between the illuminated stars on the ceiling, her white glowing outfit, Sam's neon soccer shirt, the collection of posters with neon graphics on the wall, and the lava lamp going in the corner, Sam's bedroom was instantly transformed into a certified party room.

"I think I have an idea..."

Go to page **104**

Tami thought this whole situation was silly. Sam couldn't tell her who she could and couldn't get lessons from. If she was going to make a fool of herself in front of all her friends, she wanted the best teacher to help her look like a fool with style and grace.

Tami went to the skate park after school while Sam was at soccer. She was sure she'd find Alan there. As expected, he was at the top of the half pipe, getting ready for a jump. Tami stared on in amazement.

Alan skated to the bottom of the ramp where Tami was waiting. Much to her surprise, when she told him she was Sam's sister, he eagerly agreed to help her.

"I've always admired Sam!" Alan said. "He's an incredible athlete. I try to hit him up every time I see him, but he's always too busy to talk. Seems like he's got a lot going on."

And Sam thinks Alan's the snobby one! Tami thought to herself.

"Let's start with stance," Alan began.

Two hours later, Tami was skating with ease.

"See? You're a natural," Alan said.

"Hey, Tami," said a cold voice from behind them.

Tami turned around to see Sam in his soccer uniform, skates in hand.

"Hey, Sam. Thought you had practice," she said innocently.

**You've Got This!**

Sam is cool with Tami's decision. → Go to page **56**

Sam is **NOT** cool with Tami's decision. → Go to page **68**

Mom overheard the commotion from the kitchen. "Hey, you two, get in here," she yelled.

Tami and Sam knew that voice.

"Matt and Allison, you can have a seat, too," their mom said in a much softer tone. "I'd love for you to see this."

The four kids sat. The kitchen table was filled with photo albums and boxes full of junk—buttons and ribbons and bows, key chains and patches, old cards, ticket stubs, even a whistle.

"What's all this, Mom?" Sam asked.

"This, Sam, is your box of birthday treasure. I've been keeping it since you guys were babies," she explained.

"It looks like trash to me," Tami said coldly, scooping up an old candy bar wrapper preserved in a plastic bag.

"To me that's a memory from your first birthday," Mom said. "Your dad gave you a candy bar, even though I told him not to, and it melted everywhere. I had to bathe you in a sink at Fantastic Frank's. See?"

Tami laughed at a picture of herself covered head-to-toe in chocolate. Sam was behind her, clapping and giggling his head off.

"Sam, this is a button you won from Peter Pepperoni's for becoming the top scorer in Skee-Ball on your fifth birthday. They couldn't believe it. Just a little thing nailing shot after shot!"

"Sounds about right," Sam said confidently.

"And guess who was there waiting to steal your prize?" Mom asked.

"Tami?" Sam guessed.

"And guess who was there to lick chocolate off your cheek, Tami?"

"Gross, Mom," Tami said.

"That's right—Sam. You guys have been at each other's sides since the day you were born. You really want to let this silly party thing get in the way?"

Tami and Sam looked at each other. "Guess not," they said.

Go to page **92**

"They've got a point, Tam," Sam said after reconvening the twin conference in the privacy of his room.

"Okay, well, uninviting them is out, but we can't run the risk of our friends seeing that dance!" Tami said.

"I've said it once and I'll say it again: this could all be resolved if we could just go to Skateland," Sam responded.

"Yeah, it could also be resolved if we just go to Fantastic Frank's Fun Park," Tami retorted.

"You can't skate at Fantastic Frank's Fun Park, remember? I tried last year and they confiscated my skates for the whole day!" Sam reminded her.

"Well, you certainly can't ride bumper cars at Skateland," Tami said.

"I hate bumper cars. Everyone gets stuck in a big old jam. Now car racing—that's a different story. There's a clear winner and a loser. That's more my speed," Sam said.

"What's with you always needing to win?" Tami asked. "Can't you ever just have fun?"

"Winning is fun. You should try it sometime," Sam snapped back.

"Are you Trouble Twins arguing again?" their dad interrupted.

"Hey, Dad. No. It just seems like we have very different ideas of what fun looks like these days," Tami responded.

"I thought that might be the case," he said. "I just saw an ad I thought might interest you." He placed it in front of them.

"'Action Zone! Greendale's first indoor action park,'" Sam read aloud. "Cool! It says it has laser tag, mini golf, bowling, SKATING, a ropes course, an arcade, and BUMPER CARS."

"Are you serious?" Tami asked. "DAD, WE NEED THE PHONE!" She turned to her brother. "Sam, I think we just found the answer to all of our problems. Action Zone will make everyone happy!"

Go to page **112**

A few hours later, they met up at Sam and Tami's house. Allison, Sam's best friend Matt, Alan, and both twins were gathered around the kitchen table. Matt looked at Alan, then over to Sam. Sam could tell from Matt's face he was silently communicating, "I thought we didn't like this guy." Sam shot a look back to say, "I'll explain later."

Tami rose to her feet, as if she were leading her team into a new battle. "All right, guys. This is Operation Party Palooza. You have each been selected as a member of this team because you bring something special to the table. Alan: skill. Allison: wit. Matt: snacks..." She pointed to the bowl of chips in the center of the table. "Sam: Matt, who brought snacks... and me: organization. Now, our mission is to save this party. First order of business: how do we get Skateland to reopen?"

"Ohhh, me," said Allison, raising her hand.

"Allison?" said Tami, calling on her friend.

"We complete the renovations ourselves!" she declared excitedly.

"Exactly," said Tami. "Now let's put together a list of what we need—"

"Whoa, whoa," Sam interrupted. "As interesting as that idea is, there's no way we are equipped to handle industrial-scale renovations, guys."

"Not within a week, at least," said Matt, chomping down on a chip.

"Hey, I have an idea," Alan chimed in. "Why don't we open our own Skateland right here at your house?"

Go to page **72**

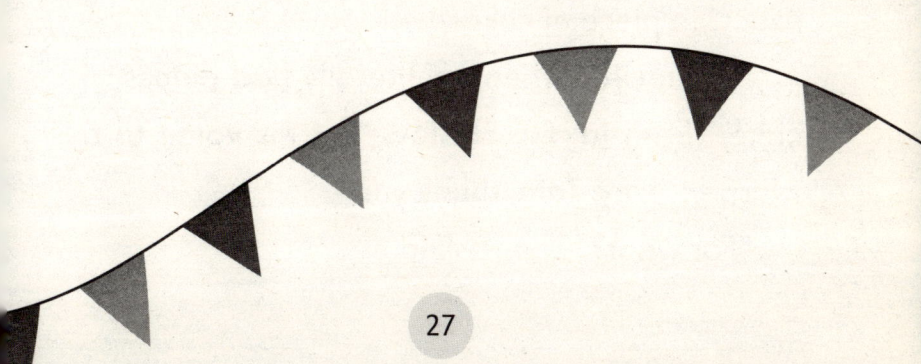

The glow party was a HUGE success. Kids at school couldn't stop talking about it on Monday.

"Did you see Sam's outfit? It was so cool! I wonder where he got it?"

"I asked my mom to try to find me the same one online!"

"Those glowing drinks were killer. I wonder how they did that?"

Tami smiled to herself as she overheard the conversations. At lunch, Sam was smiling, too. "Tami!" he shouted when he saw her. "Our party is the talk of the WHOLE school. Even some eighth graders came up to me and asked if they can be on the invite list next year. And they'll be in high school by then!"

"Let's not get ahead of ourselves," Tami cautioned. "It's not like deciding this one was exactly a piece of cake."

"Except for when we literally had pieces of cake," Sam joked. He lowered his voice to a whisper. "Hey, Tam, thank you."

"For what?" Tami asked.

"Being the best sister ever. You always have my back and you have the best ideas," Sam said.

"You're welcome, but why are you whispering?" she asked.

"Because I don't want anyone to hear me getting gushy," Sam responded.

"Aw shucks, Sam!" Tami yelled loudly for everyone to hear. "I KNOW I'M THE BEST SISTER IN THE WHOLE WORLD BUT YOU DON'T HAVE TO LAY IT ON SO THICK!"

"Okay, okay!" Sam said hushing her. "I deserved that." He laughed. "But you really are the best sister. And that was the best birthday ever."

## GREAT JOB!

With your help, Tami and Sam had the ultimate birthday bash! You have reached the end of this story, but you can go back to the beginning and pick different paths to see where another adventure leads!

Tami and Sam headed home and announced their plan to Mom and Dad.

"A throwback glow-in-the-dark party?" their dad asked. "Sounds fun—as long as we can still dress seventies!"

The family got to work. Tami called all their friends to announce the change in venue. Sam and their parents got to work clearing the furniture out of the basement. Dad covered the walls and windows with black craft paper. Mom called around to neighbors and friends to find a couple of black lights that would illuminate the room. Dad and Tami went to the hardware store for fluorescent paint. Mom and Sam went to the party store for glow sticks, necklaces, highlighters, and face paint so kids could do their own glow-in-the-dark makeup.

Inside the room, they painted fun shapes and symbols like happy faces and peace signs all over the walls with fluorescent paint. Outside the room, they made a fun and funky photo booth with silly signs and accessories where people could show off their costumes, but only if they wanted to.

When it was done, the family gathered to admire their handiwork.

"Ready?" Dad asked.

"Ready!" Mom, Tami, and Sam said in unison.

He flipped off the lights and turned on the black lights. The room lit up like fireworks.

"Hey, Sam, you look like a neon ghost!" Tami said, pointing to Sam's white glowing shirt.

"Hey, Tami, you look like a floating set of teeth!" Sam remarked as Tami's grin glowed eerily in the lights.

"Do you want to go put on our costumes now?" Tami asked. "Might ease your mind to give it a trial run," she suggested.

"Okay..." Sam hesitated. "But be gentle."

Moments later, Tami emerged from her room wearing an unexpected outfit: cutoff jean shorts, a baggy band T-shirt, and loose oversize flannel. On her head, she wore a backward cap, and on her feet, chunky skater shoes.

"You of all people should be able to recognize the nineties grunge look," she told her parents when they laughed at how un-Tami her outfit was.

"Ah, yes," her mom said, nodding. "An iconic era of fashion. How could we forget?"

As for her mom and dad, they were decked out in matching velour bell bottoms and silky button-down tops with big collars. Both were weighed down with fake gold jewelry.

"Disco is back, baby!" Dad said, one hand on his hip and his index finger pointed to the sky.

But it was Sam's outfit that blew everyone out of the water: a hot pink color-changing shirt tucked into black parachute pants covered in geometric shapes. With white high tops on his feet, his hair slicked back, and sunglasses on his face, he looked like he had stepped right out of 1988.

"SAM! You did it!" Tami said. "I'm so proud!"

"Our little boy is all grown-up and dressing like our most embarrassing decade," their dad said, arm around their mom, embracing her in a jokingly proud parent moment.

"Yeah, and if you thought that was cool—check this out!" Sam touched a button on his sunglasses and the shades transformed into a screen that spelled out words. FRESH appeared over one eye and FUNKY over the other before changing to a flashing combination of peace signs and smiley faces.

"Well, so much for going unnoticed," said Tami. "You do realize LED lights glow in the dark, right?"

"Take a chill pill, Tam. I don't know if it's these dope duds, but I'm ready to party," Sam said while sliding down the banister.

"You've created a monster," Dad told Tami, handing her an armful of glow sticks.

Go to page **28**

"Mini golf. So cool!" Tami whispered to herself.

She quickly saw the source of the commotion: Sam surrounded by a group of friends. His name atop the leaderboard—he was about to make his fourth consecutive hole-in-one.

"Tami!" Sam shouted enthusiastically. "Check out my score! An Action Zone record!"

"I thought you were camping out in the skate section all day?" Tami asked.

"Skating? Nah—that's old news. Mini golf is my thing now," Sam said with a shrug.

Tami sighed. Same old Sam.

"Hole in one!" someone shouted.

"And that's that," Sam said. "I officially get my name on the wall. Race you to the cake?"

"Why does everything always have to be a competition?" Tami demanded. "For once can't we just have a good time without—," Tami interrupted her own rant. "Uh-oh... someone just took your first-place spot..." She pointed behind Sam's head to the leaderboard.

"Where?" Sam whirled around. "No, they didn't, my name's still there—"

But Tami had taken off running. "First one to the cake is the winner for life!" she yelled.

### GREAT JOB!

With your help, Tami and Sam had the ultimate birthday bash! You have reached the end of this story, but you can go back to the beginning and pick different paths to see where another adventure leads!

The next day, Tami headed out to "T.C.O.B." as she called it—Take Care of Business. While she was away, Sam used the opportunity to talk to his mom and dad about the glow party. Surprisingly, they were on board.

"You make a mess, you clean it up, mister!" his mom said.

"Aye, aye, Cap!" Sam responded.

"Wait, does Tami know about this or is it a surprise?" Dad asked.

"No, she knows. I just want to surprise her with some fun decorations!" Sam explained.

"Cool beans," Mom said.

"No one says that anymore," Sam said, shaking his head.

"I do!" Mom said.

"I'll be back in a bit!" Sam yelled as he ran out the door. "Devon is buying my skates so I can buy a black light from Marcus!"

"Be safe, sweetie," Mom yelled.

As Sam ran out, Tami walked in. She was carrying a bag in her hand.

"You were off bright and early this morning," her dad pointed out.

"Had to T.C.O.B., Dad!" Tami responded.

"What kind of 'B' exactly?" Mom asked.

"I was selling my light-up shoes to Kira. You know she's always loved them," Tami said.

"Um, why's that, honey?" Dad asked.

"So I can afford some skates for the Skateland party. Mine are way too small," Tami explained.

"Tams, your birthday this week... is that the Skateland party you're talking about?" Mom asked.

"Yeah, Mom, Sam and I finally agreed on the party yesterday," Tami said.

"I see..." her mom replied.

Go to page **128**

Sam and Tami decided that keeping track of all their friends in a busy amusement park was going to be too much trouble, so they invited their two BEST friends, Allison and Matt.

They mapped out the park beforehand to make sure they were going to hit the hottest spots first thing in the morning and during lunchtime when most people were busy eating.

"First, we gotta knock out Roller Coaster Coast, because the longer you wait in the day, the longer the lines get," Matt said.

"We'll hang out in Arcade Alley during the peak wait times, then when things die down we can do the swings, Terror Tower, and Franky's Freak Out," Sam strategized.

"Think we can hit it all?" Tami asked.

"Only one way to find out!" said Sam.

The morning of their birthday, Mom and Dad surprised them with a gift: skip-the-line passes.

"We were so touched by your generosity toward each other, we wanted to get you something we knew you'd love," Mom said.

Tami and Sam had the time of their lives. They rode everything twice, except Terror Tower, which they rode THREE times. "My legs are all wobbly," Tami said that night. "Like I'm still on a roller coaster."

"Not me," said Sam yawning. "I could ride it all again right now!"

"I guess you don't think Fantastic Frank's is for babies anymore?" Tami asked.

"Super cool babies, maybe," Sam joked. "Hey, Tami, I have a question."

"What's that?" she asked.

"Can we do this for our birthday again next year?" Sam said.

## GREAT JOB!

With your help, Tami and Sam had the ultimate birthday bash! You have reached the end of this story, but you can go back to the beginning and pick different paths to see where another adventure leads!

An hour later, Tami was suited up and raring to go. Luckily, they lived on a cul-de-sac, smooth and flat, perfect for a beginner skater.

"Okay, remember what I told you? Head up. Feet shoulder-width apart. Bend at the knees. And don't show the skates that you're afraid," Sam instructed.

"Don't show them I'm afraid?" Tami asked.

"Yeah, they can sense fear."

"That's about the dumbest thing I've ever—whooOOAAAA!" Tami's feet slipped out from under her body. She landed hard on the ground.

"Told ya," Sam said with a smirk.

"That's because you distracted me!"

"Okay, up on your feet. Now remember how I showed you to glide? There you go!"

Tami was making slow strides around the cul-de-sac, pushing off on one foot, gliding, then switching and pushing off on the other, until she slowed. Back and forth, slow and steady.

"Hey, this isn't so hard!" Tami shouted.

"Exactly! As long as you don't show the skates any fear!" Sam shouted back.

"WhoooaaaAAAAA!" Tami said as she landed on the asphalt again. "STOP doing that!"

Sam laughed. Good thing she was wearing a helmet and pads! But all in all, Tami wasn't half bad for a beginner. As he sat back and watched his protégé hard at work, she was gaining speed and doing self-congratulatory fist pumps.

"Easy there, speed racer!" Sam cautioned.

"What are you talking about?" Tami retorted. "I'm a natural. I'm taking this skill straight to the Olympics bayyy-bee! WhoooaaAAAA!"

"Famous last words," Sam shouted back as he watched her crash. "But seriously, you're good!"

"In front of you, maybe," Tami said as she skated back home. "In front of our friends? The whole school? That's too much pressure."

"Hey, I have an idea," Sam said.

Go to page **123**

"Tami! I haven't seen you in over a week! I was worried something happened," the shopkeeper at the secondhand store joked. Tami was a frequent visitor. She was always worried she would miss something good that had come in. That was the thing about shopping vintage. Everything was one of a kind!

"Yeah, I've been kind of busy. We're planning our big birthday party for this Saturday!" she replied.

"I heard about that from your friends. They were in here shopping for their retro costumes! What a fun idea!" the shopkeeper said.

"That's what we're here for," Tami responded. "My brother needs a costume. He's dressing up eighties."

"Well, we've got plenty. Especially boy's clothes. I haven't had any boys come around for their costumes yet!" the shopkeeper said.

Sam felt his stomach drop. What if his friends weren't dressing up? What if he was the only boy in costume?

Tami gathered an armload of clothes and pointed Sam to the dressing room. He tried on a cool acid-wash jean jacket, a shirt that changed color from the heat of your hand, several pairs of parachute pants, an authentic eighties tracksuit, and a Members Only jacket. Each item was awesome in its own way, but now when Sam looked in the mirror, all he could see was his friends making fun of him.

"Everything okay?" Tami called from outside the dressing room.

**You've Got This!** → Go to page **121**

**No, I can't do this.** → Go to page **121**

**Yes, just looking at my options!** → Go to page **94**

"All right, team, we've got less than twenty-four hours to pull this party together. I'm gonna need focus! I'm gonna need energy!" Drill sergeant Tami called together an emergency meeting. "I think I have an idea for replacing the decorations without doing any work."

"What's that?" Sam asked.

"A paint-yourself party!" Tami said.

"Wait—a paint-yourself, or a paint-it-yourself party?" Allison asked.

"Well... both!" Tami explained, "Since we don't have time to do much more than dry the floor and rehang paper, we'll put out more fluorescent paint so people can paint on the walls. But—we'll also put out fluorescent FACE paint, so they can paint themselves. Why not go all out?"

"That's an amazing idea, sweetie!" their mom said. "Also, I have to show you a little trick I came up with." She pulled a glass out of the cabinet and poured in a mixture of tonic water, lemonade, and sparkling water. "Lights, please!" Sam turned off the light and turned on the black light. The drink glowed in the dark.

"Whoa," they all gasped. "How'd you do that?" Tami asked.

"Tonic water!" their mom said. "It has an ingredient that glows under black light."

"Speaking of glowing," Sam said. He ran out of the room and returned a minute later. He had changed into a hooded tracksuit. "Check this out!" He reached inside the hood and pressed a button. Lines in the shape of a stick figure illuminated down his arms, legs, torso, and around his face. "Imagine this in the pitch-black room. I'll look like a glowing stick figure!"

"This is going to be the best party ever," said Tami.

Go to page **28**

"I think we need to seek the input of an impartial third party," Sam said.

"English, please," Tami replied.

"Let's get another opinion," Sam explained.

"Knock knock!" their dad announced, knocking on the door while simultaneously opening it. "How are the Trouble Twins today?"

"Oh, good. Dad can settle this!" Tami said, ignoring the question.

"Noooo, not Dad. I meant we ask someone cool!" Sam whined.

"Hey, I'm cool!" their dad protested.

"Uh, sorry. I meant someone under forty," Sam clarified.

"He's gotcha there," Tami said with a shrug.

Their dad slumped his shoulders and clutched his lower back mimicking their granddad getting up from his easy chair.

"Daaaaaaddd..." Tami laughed.

"Fine, you win!" Sam said, cracking up. "We need birthday party ideas."

"That's right—the big ONE-THREE is this week, huh?" Dad scratched his chin. "Boy, do I remember those days. My thirteenth birthday party was one for the books! We went cosmic bowling—video games, tie-dye T-shirts, boy bands on the radio. Those boys could harmonize!"

"Don't forget the horse and buggy rides!" Sam said, taking another jab at his dad's age.

"That's it!" Tami clapped her hands. "A retro bowling party!!"

**You've Got This!**

That sounds fun! → Go to page **10**

Ew, that's too cheesy! → Go to page **15**

Sam and Matt carried Ned's full tank down to the basement and placed it on top of the washing machine. Ned's tankmates, Ed, Fred, and Ted, came along for the ride.

"I'm not sure tadpoles understand your art, Sam," Matt said, giving his buddy an odd look.

"I know, but I wanted Ned to see why I haven't been around as much the past two days. Besides, they're not tadpoles anymore. Ned and the other -ed's are froglets now!" Sam explained.

"What's a froglet?" asked Matt.

"It's the final stage in between tadpole and frog," Sam continued. "They still have a tadpole tail, but they also have legs and lungs like a frog. I think I can let them out of the tank at this point, but I'm nervous. Being a tad dad is tough."

"Sounds like a lot of pressure, man," Matt said as he put his hand on Sam's shoulder to reassure him. "Hey, wanna go see if there's still pizza before Tami and Allison scarf down the leftovers?"

"Yeah, but we better run!" Sam joked. "Ned and the gang can hang down here for the night. It'll be like a vacation!"

Upstairs, Tami and Allison were each on their fourth slice, leaving one left for the boys to share.

"I knew they'd be back up for round two," said Allison.

"You snooze, you lose," Tami said with a shrug.

Go to page **88**

Sam had to admit that he wasn't surprised Tami wasn't into skating, but she had given it her all. Now it was time for him to return the favor.

"Tami, I think we need to rethink this whole Skateland thing," Sam said.

"I'm SO relieved to hear you say that," she responded. "I think it's time for a signature Tami brainstorming sesh!"

Sam jokingly rolled his eyes as he followed his sister upstairs.

"Clean slate!" she announced, wiping down the large whiteboard that hung on the wall. "We'll write down every activity we can think of, until we find one we BOTH like!"

"Sounds fun," Sam said sarcastically. "Don't put brainstorming on the list."

"Fine, but it works." Tami said. "You're up first."

"Skating," Sam said.

"Well, duh," Tami responded, but she wrote it on the board, anyway. "Okay, I like gaming!"

"Well, duh!" said Sam mimicking her.

"How about bowling?"

"Sweet! Bumper cars."

"Eating."

"Well, that's a given."

"Oh, laser tag!"

"Tami—wait!" Sam shouted enthusiastically. "Guess what they just opened next to the mall?"

"What?" Tami asked.

"Action Zone!" he shouted.

"What? No way! That's so cool!" Tami said. "Uh, what's Action Zone?"

"It's like a huge giant warehouse with all of this stuff! Skating. Bowling. Mini golf. Laser tag. Huge arcade. Pizza. EVERYTHING!" he said.

"You're just telling me this NOW?" Tami asked.

"Sorry, I didn't think about it. But—we can have the Supreme, Ultimate, Fantastic, Amazing, Best-Ever Birthday Party Palooza, Tami."

"I told you the brainstorm would work!" she responded.

Go to page **112**

They showed up to the bowling alley ready to show off their outfits to the world. Sam had made a very unexpected choice: an eighties power suit. Big shoulders, piano-keys tie, slicked-back hair, and shiny wingtip shoes.

"You look like a stockbroker!" their mom said.

"That's the point, Mom," Sam said. "I'm an eighties business tycoon. I drive a Lamborghini. My mansion has tennis courts."

"Love the creativity!" Their mom laughed. "And what about you?" she asked Tami.

"Mom, don't you recognize this dress?" Tami answered. "It's only the iconic dress from the most iconic nineties movie of all time. I mean, I know it's not the original but I can't believe she had an exact replica!"

"Oh, THAT dress..." their mom said, pretending to know what Tami was talking about.

The bowling alley was packed with their friends and family, and every single person was dressed in costume. Sam was relieved. And everyone loved their outfits.

With the music pumping and the snacks going, Tami and Sam sat back and relaxed for the first time all week.

"Hey, Tami, thanks for always thinking outside the box and pushing me to be different," he said.

"Of course, Sam. What are sisters for?" she asked. "Oh, by the way, I put you on my bowling team. And you're up first!"

Sam looked up at the big board above their lane. The team name, TAMI'S TIME TRAVELERS, appeared at the top. Below it was a picture of Sam at the vintage store dressed in a leopard jumpsuit and giant wig.

"TAMI!" Sam laughed.

"Best sister ever, remember?" she said.

## GREAT JOB!

With your help, Tami and Sam had the ultimate birthday bash! You have reached the end of this story, but you can go back to the beginning and pick different paths to see where another adventure leads!

Not only did Mom and Dad agree to be on "Team Glow," they were thrilled with the idea.

"A party at home? Well, that sounds cheap... er—I mean exciting," their dad said as their mom elbowed him in the ribs.

Matt and Allison were in as well.

"Put us in, Coach!" Matt joked.

Allison even had the idea of challenging their friends to come up with the best glow costume they could—the brighter, the better!

"I know exactly what I'm going to wear," said Sam as he clicked on his laptop.

They created their list of ideas, assigned duties, and agreed that the biggest challenge would also be the one to make or break their party atmosphere. How do they make the entire basement glow? Dad had an idea: "Let's cover everything—the walls, the floor, the ceiling, the windows... everything... in black craft paper. That way it'll feel like you're walking into an empty abyss, and it will make everyone's outfits pop!"

"I can bring home rolls of paper from work!" Mom offered.

"I have an idea," said Sam. "What if before we hang the paper on the walls, we decorate it with fluorescent paint? We can use old tennis shoes to create trails of footprints everywhere. The floor, the walls, the ceiling..."

"It'll be just like the school dance, only times one hundred!" Tami said. "You're a genius, bro!"

Everyone got to work. A few days later, they were finally finished.

"Man, I didn't realize how big your basement is. We're completely out of paint," Matt said as they wrapped up the final night before the party.

"Yeah, but it'll be worth it. This place is gonna light up like a Christmas tree!" Sam said. "Hey, will you help me carry Ned down here? I want him to see all our hard work!"

Go to page **48**

"I did. It ended early so I came by to see if you and Allison needed help, but I can see that my services aren't needed," Sam said flatly.

"Hi, Sam." Alan gave a friendly wave. "I'm not sure if we've ever—"

"I know who you are," Sam said coldly, cutting him off midsentence.

"Sam, Alan was just telling me what a great athlete you are. That he's tried to talk to you on the field before but you're always so busy coming and going," Tami said, gesturing and emphasizing in their secret twin code to get across the point that maybe Sam was in the wrong on this one.

"I don't remember you ever trying to talk to me," Sam said.

"Last year, after your team beat my team for first in the junior state series. You almost pitched a no-hitter! It was unbelievable. I came over to congratulate you, but you were signing baseballs for the peewee leaguers. I didn't want to interrupt," Alan explained.

"Oh... well... uh..." Sam seemed at a loss for words. "You could've said hi."

"Yeah. I didn't think you knew who I was or I would have talked to you about that basketball thing," Alan said. "I was shocked when they didn't pick you for first string. I know I'm a year older and all. It's my last year of eligibility so I think the coach was cutting me a break."

"Oh, I didn't know that," said Sam. He suddenly realized he had gotten Alan all wrong. After all—who gives up their entire afternoon to teach his clumsy sister—a stranger—how to skate? Sam had an idea. "Hey, it's Tami's and my birthday this week. We're having a big party. Do you want to come?"

"Oh yeah, that would be sweet!" Alan replied enthusiastically. "Where is it?"

"Skateland!" Tami and Sam said in unison.

**Go to page 109**

"Mom and Dad will never let us paint the basement, Tams," Sam said.

"Well, you'll never know unless we ask," Tami responded.

"Nah, I don't want them up in my business. I'd rather have it at Skateland," Sam said.

"Enough with Skateland, Sam!" Tami had reached her boiling point.

"I don't understand why I can't celebrate where I want to celebrate for ONCE!" Sam yelled back in frustration.

Just then the doorbell rang. It was Matt and Allison—Sam's and Tami's best friends.

"Hey, guys," Matt said. "I was coming to see Sam, and I ran into Allison."

"I was coming to see Tami," Allison said.

"Well, duh," the twins said in unison. Matt and Allison exchanged confused looks.

"Sorry," said Tami, "you just caught us at a bad time."

"Uh-oh, sounds like trouble in Twinland," Matt said.

"You guys go through this like once a week!" Allison said. "What is it this time?"

"Birthday drama," Tami said coldly.

Allison rolled her eyes. "Look, you two. I don't think you understand how lucky you are! Not only do you have a sibling, you have a twin—I would give anything for a brother or sister!"

"Me too," said Matt. "My brother's only three, so he doesn't count. If I had someone to watch movies with... throw the ball with... share my chores?! Dream come true, man!"

**You've Got This!**

I've never thought about it that way.
Go to page **22**

I'm sick of sharing everything.
Go to page **67**

"Why'd you sell your skates? You love to skate!" Tami asked.

"Because it was the only way I could buy the black light for YOUR party!" Sam shouted.

"I thought this was OUR party!" Tami raised her voice back.

"It stopped being our party when you were so stubborn about getting your way!" Sam insisted.

"Me?! That's a joke," said Tami. "I'm the only one who's been trying to work together."

"That's it. I give up," said Sam, slumping off to his room. He knew they were both out of line, but he needed to let off some steam.

## NICE TRY!

When something frustrating occurs it's easy to play the blame game, but mistakes happen. Before you point fingers, take a moment to reflect on the situation and decide if that is going to help resolve it or make it worse.

**Go back to page 58 and try again!**

"Let's settle this," Sam said as he grunted his way over to the dresser.

"You might want to see a doctor about that," Tami joked.

He rolled his eyes. "Har-har. Very funny. We had double soccer practice yesterday."

Sam played practically every sport and made every team he tried out for. Baseball, basketball, ice hockey—even skiing and surfing. Tami liked to surf, too, but her surfing involved the Internet. She loved building websites, coding, and even creating her own online games.

Sam opened his top drawer and pulled out a deck of cards. "Okay, here's the deal: I'm going to shuffle the cards and spread them out face down on the bed. Then we each select one. Whoever has the higher card gets their choice of party location. Got it?"

"Got it," Tami responded.

"But!" Sam went on. "All decisions are final. No complaining. No crying to Mom and Dad."

"No cheating," Tami interrupted, examining the cards to make sure it wasn't a trick deck.

"No cheating." Sam held out his hand.

Tami held her hand parallel to his. They clapped four times, then crouched down to mimic a pair of praying mantises—their version of a secret handshake. The tradition was born out of a school assignment where they were tasked with making an anagram of their names: combining the letters and mixing them up to form new words.

Turns out there wasn't a lot you could do with Tami or Sam, so the teacher let them join forces. Sam said it was a shame Tami's name wasn't Tin, because then they could spell M-A-N-T-I-S, his favorite insect. It made Tami laugh hysterically, and from that day on, the praying mantis became the secret symbol of their twin bond.

"Okay, let's do it," Tami said. "On the count of three, flip. One... two... three... flip!"

Tami's card revealed a ten.

"Yes!"

Sam slowly moved his hand. A queen.

Go to page **97**

Before she could finish her sentence, Tami's foot slipped over the edge and she was flying backward down the ramp at an alarming speed. Sam watched in horror... and amazement. Even though it lacked the grace of his skilled ramp session, Tami's panicked and unintentional drop had great form: her body positioning, her balance, even the way she delivered the return were all that of a seasoned skating pro. Of course, the screaming definitely detracted from the show.

There was stunned silence from the crowd as her skates slowed and she came to a halt at the bottom of the ramp. Suddenly, everyone erupted in applause.

"Where in the world did that come from?" someone shouted.

"Wow, Tami, can you teach me how to do that trick?" Alan Thomas asked.

Everyone pushed and shoved to congratulate Tami on her amazing feat—no one had ever tackled the ramp backward before. In the process, they pushed Sam right out of the way.

For the next half hour, as Tami's adoring fans lined up for tips, Sam sat there confused. He was the athlete in the family, the one that people normally sought out for advice. Tami was the clumsy one. His friends were pushing him aside to ask *her* for tips on *his* sport?

**You've Got This!**

No way, skating is my thing. → Go to page **84**

That's my sis! Way to go! → Go to page **90**

First things first, Tami and Sam drew up plans for their party. Sam took the whiteboard off Tami's wall and they propped it up above the kitchen table. At the top, Tami scribbled "SUPREME, ULTIMATE, FANTASTIC, AMAZING, BEST-EVER BIRTHDAY GLOW-PARTY PALOOZA!" Below it, she wrote out a to-do list. Assemble team. Brainstorm ideas. Design event layout. Make shopping list. Assign jobs.

"Who should be on our ultimate party planning team?" Tami asked.

"Obviously, Matt," Sam said, referring to his best friend. "And I guess that means you'll want Allison," he said, referring to Tami's best friend.

"Duh," Tami said. "That's a given. Who else?"

"I guess Mom and Dad," Sam said. "We'll need someone to drive us around. And, you know, someone with a bank account."

"Very true," Tami agreed.

Go to page **54**

"You guys want a sibling? Take this one!" Tami shouted as she nudged Sam forward.

"Oh yeah?" Sam shouted back. "I'd trade you for either one of them any day!"

That one stung. Tami knew they were both angry, but it was starting to feel too personal. "You know what, Sam? I think twelve years is enough sharing. Let's just have separate birthdays this year. You go to Skateland, I'll go to Fantastic Frank's Fun Park, and we'll both be happy," Tami said, fighting back tears.

"If that's what you want, fine with me," Sam said stubbornly.

## NICE TRY!

Arguments between siblings can be a normal part of growing up. Always take time to cool down before working through a situation so you don't say something you don't mean.
**Go back to page 46 and try again!**

"I did," said Sam coldly. "I just... thought I left something here." He was lying, but he wasn't about to help out Tami now after seeing her with Alan.

"Sam, wait up!" Tami yelled, running to catch her brother as he walked away. "I think there's been a misunderstanding. Alan is actually—"

"I don't want to hear it, Tami," Sam said. "I told you how I feel about him, and you came here, anyway."

"You can't tell me who to be friends with," Tami responded.

"Fine. This party's off," Sam said, hopping on his bike and riding away.

## NICE TRY!

Judging someone without getting to know them can mean you'll miss out on meeting some really great people. And in this case, a really great party.

**Go back to page 97 and try again!**

"Maybe," Tami said sadly.

Tami didn't know when she and Sam had become so different from one another. They used to do everything together. They would wake up at the same time and eat the same breakfast together.  Now Sam liked eggs, and Tami preferred cereal. Sam liked classic cartoons; Tami preferred anime.  On weekends, they used to ride bikes, hang out with the same friends, and talk and play for hours. Now Sam was always off playing his sports, at the skate park, or with his buddies.  It felt like he never had time for Tami anymore.

From Sam's perspective it was the opposite. Tami seemed like she just wasn't interested in his stuff, even when he really tried to take an interest in hers.

He loved his sister's cool and funky style, and the fact that she could creatively take anything old and make it new. He even sometimes volunteered to be her dummy as she pinned and buttoned things on to her creations. And he wished they could hang out like the old days. But every time he invited her to throw the ball, she would just shrug and say, "No, thanks." Maybe they were just too different to find common ground anymore.

"What do you think?" asked Tami.

**You've Got This!** Let's skip the party this year. → Go to page **111**

Go to page **14** ← **Embrace your differences.**

"I can't believe I've trusted you for thirteen years of my life, and you've just been gathering evidence to destroy us!" Tami said.

"That's a bit dramatic, sweetie," their mom said. "Your dad and I keep these memories because we love them. And we want to remember every moment of your childhood, even the not-so-glamorous ones."

"And one day, we'll show them at your wedding," Dad joked.

"Not funny," Sam said, crossing his arms. "If these get out, they could ruin us."

## NICE TRY!

Remember that parents are human, too. Some decisions they make may not make sense now. Some will when you get older, some won't. But when you don't agree, try talking your feelings out. Approaching a situation calmly will always get you further.

**Go back to page 46 and try again!**

"Now that's an idea!" said Sam. "But how?"

"Well, people go to Skateland for three things," Alan replied. "One: the skating. Two: the nachos. And three: the arcade. We can make all of those things here!"

"Hate to burst your bubble, Alan, but I'm pretty sure our parents won't let us roller-skate inside the house. Mom gets mad when Sam dribbles a basketball indoors," Tami explained.

"Not inside! Outside!" Alan said. "You guys live on a cul-de-sac. The flat, round asphalt is a perfect skating rink. All we have to do is ask your neighbors if it's okay that we block it off from cars for one evening. Then we add a DJ booth, some fun lights and decorations, and ta-da! Skating rink!"

"What about the video games?" Matt asked.

"Hmm... how many TVs do you guys have?" Alan asked.

"I think four," Sam said.

"Would your parents let us move them into one room?"

"I think so."

"Do you have gaming consoles?"

"Want me to show you my whole collection?" Tami asked.

"I'll take that as a yes." Alan laughed. "So if we have four different consoles on four different TVs—that's four video games in a mini arcade," Alan explained.

"So cool!" Allison exclaimed.

"And nachos, well, those are the easy part," Matt said.

"What do you think, Tami?" Sam asked.

**You've Got This!**

Sounds like a blast! → Go to page **102**

Go to page **106** ← At-home parties are boring.

"Sorry, kid, you're gonna have to tough this one out. I already told the guys," Sam said.

"Okay, first of all, I'm fifteen minutes older than you," Tami shot back. "So, I'm sorry, KID, you have to UNTELL the guys." She didn't understand why her brother was being such a jerk.

"That's not the way the world works, Tami. You lost the draw. You can't go back on the deal," Sam fired back.

"Well, you lost the considerate brother award. Congratulations!" Tami shouted.

They both stormed into their rooms and slammed the doors.

## NICE TRY!

Planning an event is hard work, especially when people don't see eye to eye. Instead of approaching every situation as black-and-white, try to find a compromise.
**Go back to page 130 and try again!**

"I guess you guys have the seventies covered," Tami said, watching her parents with a mixture of amazement and horror. She turned to her brother. "Sam, if you are going to dress up in a certain decade, you have to at least know something about it. I think I need to put you through eighties bootcamp."

The next three days, the twins watched all the classic movies from the eighties. Tami played her brother the top hair metal bands, hip-hop classics, and love songs. They watched clips of eighties TV, and Tami quizzed Sam on pop culture.

Finally, Tami gave Sam the eighties fashion 101—big shoulder pads, spandex, geometric prints, and lots of denim. "I think you're ready," Tami said. "It's time to go shopping."

Go to page **42**

"Why is it that everything we try ends up a mess, even when we're doing something nice for each other?" Tami asked.

"I think I know," said Sam. "Even when we stopped thinking about just ourselves and started considering each other, we still weren't doing a great job of working together."

"You're right," Tami admitted. "I mean, we weren't exactly clear yesterday when we thought we were on the same page. I just thought it was our twin telepathy doing its thing."

"Not this time!" Sam laughed.

"So what do we do now? Should we make a final decision between the glow party and Skateland?" Tami asked.

"But I just sold my skates and you sold your light-up shoes." Sam laughed.

"Oh yeah, I forgot about that," Tami said. "We could try to buy them back."

"I think I have a better idea," said Sam. "I've been thinking... Mom's walk down memory lane reminded me of all the fun times we've had at

our birthdays over the years. This has been such a headache trying to figure out what we want... and make all our friends happy. We've got extra cash from selling our stuff. What would you say to keeping it simple and going back to our roots?"

"Wait... Are you thinking..." Tami couldn't believe it.

"Actually, yeah, I think I am." Sam laughed.

"Fantastic Frank's Fun Park?!" Tami screamed.

Sam couldn't be sure, but he thought maybe he even saw a tear in her eye.

Go to page **38**

For the next hour, the girls followed Tami's notes to a T. They scooted, they squatted, they crouched, they pushed off, and finally, they glided. Sort of.

"I don't think we're doing this right. We're laid out on the ground more than we're on our feet, Tams," Allison finally said.

"I think my whole body is just one big bruise," Tami said, examining her scraped-up pads. "I'm not sure skating is for me. I'm just not coordinated enough."

"Well, practice makes perfect!" Allison said cheerfully.

"Yeah, that's one option," Tami responded.

"Well, what's the other?" Allison questioned. "The party's only a few days away!"

"Simple. I go back to Sam and say sorry, bro, I tried. I failed. Back to the drawing board!" Tami explained.

"But you lost the draw!" Allison said.

"You know Sam. He's a pushover. I just have to do my sad sister face," Tami said as she quivered her bottom lip. "He'll cave."

"I don't know, Tami. You sure you're ready to just throw in the towel?" Allison asked.

Truth be told, Tami was more on the fence than she sounded. The last thing she wanted was to be known as a quitter. But she was nervous—all those people watching her try to skate? Nightmare fuel.

"What do you say, give it another shot?" Allison asked encouragingly.

**You've Got This!** → Go to page **82**

**Try, try again!**

**Ask Sam to reconsider.** → Go to page **118**

"Well, Samuel," his mom began. Sam knew that tone. "If you ever bothered to do a load of laundry, you would know that our washing machine is Bluetooth enabled. And I often start loads at night from my phone so we don't use up hot water during the day. I guess now I have to check to make sure no one has placed an aquarium full of frogs on the edge of the washing machine before I run it!" his mom said angrily.

"Now, honey," their dad chimed in. "No one was hurt; the frogs are okay. Sam's going to clean up the rest of this mess... right, Sam?"

"Uh, yes, right," Sam said, examining the makeshift home his dad made for the tadpoles. "Guess I'm pretty lucky these guys have fully developed lungs!"

Sam scanned the rest of the room for damage. His eyes settled on a wet mess of black paper piled up in the corner.

"Yeah, that's the other thing," Tami chimed in from the staircase. "When the aquarium fell, it knocked the hose off the side of the washer and the floor flooded. So all of our decorations are ruined."

**You've Got This!** Better get to work! **Go to page 44**

**Go to page 125** All this work for nothing!

When party time finally arrived, Tami felt both anxious and excited. Skateland was decked out in balloons and streamers, strobe lights, and a huge HAPPY BIRTHDAY banner. The nachos were flowing and the music was vibing.

Allison ran up to Tami. "Are you ready?"

Tami had skated every day that week. Each day, she improved. Regardless of what happened, she was proud of herself for working so hard and overcoming something that scared her.

"As I'll ever be," she said. She and Sam laced up and skated to the rink. Tami started slow, but soon she was in the zone. Everything she had learned was coming together as her limbs worked in sync with her brain. But when she went to stick one foot out, a familiar feeling came flooding back.

"WhooooOOAAAA!" Tami wobbled and bobbled... and fell flat on the floor. There was a stunned silence for what felt like an eternity. Until...

"WhhhoooOAAAA!" Sam dramatically flailed his arms and shuffled his feet. He came crashing down next to her. Everyone laughed.

"Did you just..." Tami began. Sam winked.

The crowd began singing "Happy Birthday" as Sam and Tami's parents carried the cake out to the center of the rink.

"You didn't tell me about that hilarious surprise ending!" Allison said.

"Always keep them guessing," Tami responded, looking at Sam with admiration. They might not always see eye to eye, but he always came through for her. And as long as they celebrated together, it would always be the most supreme, ultimate, fantastic, amazing, best-ever birthday.

## GREAT JOB!

With your help, Tami and Sam had the ultimate birthday bash! You have reached the end of this story, but you can go back to the beginning and pick different paths to see where another adventure leads!

Sam kept his distance while Tami tried to escape a group of fourth graders who were following her every move.

"Phew—that was close," she told Sam as she caught up to him on the bike ride home. "I had to sneak over to the playground and hide until they thought I had left."

Sam said nothing.

"Um... hello?" Sam continued to ride in silence. "Is something wrong?" Tami finally asked.

"Nope, not a thing," Sam responded.

"You're not mad at me because I learned how to skate, are you?"

"No, I'm mad because you were a show-off."

"Wait... do you mean when I accidentally fell down the ramp that you dragged me up? And instead of crashing to the ground and breaking all my bones, I decided to save myself by using proper body position like you taught me—you're mad at me for that?" Tami asked.

Sam was silent.

"Sam—" Tami continued. "Do you know how

much time I spend rooting for you? How many games and awards and trophy ceremonies I go to for you? And I don't mind! I love that you're great at sports. And I love that you support my interests, but gaming doesn't give out trophies. Can't you be happy that I am actually good at sports for once?"

Sam didn't answer. He was so used to being in the spotlight, he never thought about how it felt to be in the shadows.

**You've Got This!**

Don't budge. → Go to page **99**

Go to page **114** ← Reconsider.

"I know, you're right. I don't want to give up, either," said Sam. "I wish we could just think of an idea that my friends would think was fun and cool but would also make you happy. I would never want you to celebrate your birthday somewhere you aren't comfortable, Tams."

Tami looked at her brother. Sure, they argued like most siblings do, but all in all, he was a really good brother. He always cheered her up when she was feeling down. He had her back when she was feeling picked on. And best of all, he was there for her when she needed anything.

"Thanks, Sam," Tami said. "And I wish I weren't such a klutz. I would go to Skateland for our party in a heartbeat because I know it would make you happy."

Sam knew his sister was one in a million, he just didn't always have a great way of showing it. Maybe it was time he did something for her, and not himself.

That's when Tami made up her mind that she needed to get over her skating fear. "As a matter of fact, I know the perfect place for our party."

"Me too," said Sam, deciding for himself he would cave and ask Mom and Dad about hosting the glow party.

"Hey, are you thinking what I'm thinking?" asked Tami.

"I think we're both finally on the same page," said Sam.

Go to page **36**

The next morning, Sam awoke to Tami cautiously nudging him. "Uh, Sam... I think you need to come downstairs..."

"What's going on?" Sam asked bleary-eyed.

"There's been a teeny-tiny... accident," Tami said. "You might call it a *tadccident*." She giggled to herself. She knew it wasn't the time for jokes. Sam was going to be upset, but she couldn't resist the opportunity.

"My tadpoles!" Sam suddenly shot up in bed. "Is everything okay?"

"I think you just need to come see for yourself," Tami explained.

Sam didn't wait for Tami to finish. One look at the dresser and he knew she was referring to Ned and the gang—his favorite tadpoles—as everyone upstairs seemed alive and well. He should have known better than to leave them outside the safety of his bedroom last night! Tad dad guilt was setting in as he flew down the stairs.

"What happened?" Sam demanded as he entered the basement to see his mom and dad with a mop, bucket, broom and—a shattered aquarium tank?!

"Now, Sam, before you get upset—" their mom began but Sam cut her off.

"How could this happen? How could I be so irresponsible? I'll never forgive myself! Who did this?" Sam threw himself to the floor dramatically picking up an aquarium rock and holding it against his chest.

"Sam, that's what we're trying to tell you—everything is fine. The tadpoles are right here!" Sam's dad held out a plastic container full of froglets and handed it to Sam.

"Oh—" Sam replied, finally pulling himself together. He kissed it. "Wait, what in the world happened here?"

Go to page **80**

"Well, I'll show you how my brother showed me to do it," Sam overheard Tami saying as she corrected the stance on a younger kid. He taught his sister everything she knew and she was actually good. Very good. He should be proud of both of them. Sam decided right then and there he would swallow any feelings of competitiveness or jealousy as he skated over to Tami.

"Tin! That. Was. Incredible! How did you do that?" Sam asked in disbelief.

"Simple," Tami responded. "I closed my eyes, started screaming, and hoped I didn't die."

Sam laughed. "Well, if you're over your trauma, I have a few more tricks up my sleeve that I could teach you!"

"Do I have a choice?" Tami answered, knowing once Sam had an idea there was rarely any chance of backing down.

The pair spent more hours over the next six days on wheels than they did off. Tami continued to get better and better. She learned how to crabwalk, slingshot, snakewalk, and other variations of fancy footwork. By the end of the week, she could even do a mini jump, a sit spin, and a one-foot spin.

"Okay, who are you and what did you do with my best friend?" Tami looked up to see her BFF Allison had come to cheer her on at her final practice. "It's like aliens came down in a little spaceship, abducted my clumsy friend Tami, and replaced her with a new graceful Tami in old Tami's skin."

"Well, that's a weird thing to say. But no, it's just me." Tami laughed. "Maybe new and improved. Let's just hope I don't get nervous in front of everyone tomorrow and totally wipe out."

"Nah, you're gonna be fine," Sam chimed in, grinning. "Tami, this will be our best birthday yet."

"Already is!" she replied.

Go to page **82**

Later that day, Tami and Sam found themselves alone thinking about what their mom had said.

"Mom's right, Sam. Remember last year when we went to the indoor waterpark?" Tami said. "It was just us, our two best friends, Mom and Dad, and an ice-cream cake. Super simple. Maybe we've overcomplicated this thing."

"Maybe," Sam agreed. "There just seems to be more pressure now. The guys from the soccer team will probably be mad if they don't get an invite. And then there's my baseball buddies... basketball... tennis."

"You need fewer friends," Tami interrupted.

"Well, what about you?" Sam asked. "You have tech club, Spanish club, and all your friends on student council!"

"Guess you're right," Tami said as she shuffled her feet. "When did things start getting so complicated?"

"When we grew up," said Sam.

"Sometimes I miss the good old days," admitted Tami.

"Do you think it's time to throw in the towel?" asked Sam.

**You've Got This!**

No, we can't give up! → Go to page **86**

Maybe we're too grown-up for this. → Go to page **69**

Sam thought about the situation. He could chicken out, worried that his friends wouldn't dress up and he would be made fun of, or he could take the Tami approach: worry less about what other people think. After all, he had had a blast reliving the eighties with his sis. He loved everything about it—the music, the movies, even the fashion! It just felt so fun and silly.

"You got more out there, Tams? I'm just warming up!" Sam shouted. For once, he was going to dare to be different.

"Really? I thought the parachute pants would put you over the edge, but yeah... let's do it!" Sam's wardrobe was all track shorts and T-shirts. She never thought she'd live to see the day he got a little wild with his style!

For the next two hours, Tami handed Sam clothes, he tried them on, he did a loop around the store, and she applauded.

"Hey, Tams," Sam said, stepping out of the dressing room in a velour tracksuit. "How cool do I look?" He bent one knee and extended his right leg behind him and his right arm in front while clutching something invisible in his hand.

"On a scale of one to ten, negative five," Tami said with a laugh. "Why are you doing that?"

"'Cause I gotta make sure the outfits look good when I'm knocking down those pins."

"I don't know about bowling, but I'm gonna strike that outfit from the list. Do you have a spare?" Tami laughed at her own joke.

"You need to stop hanging out with Dad," Sam said, shaking his head.

In the end, he chose seven items and told Tami his final pick was going to be a surprise.

As they were checking out, Sam looked at Tami and said, "Hey, what are you gonna wear?"

"Me?" She hadn't thought about that. She had stuff at home, surely she could throw something together.

"What decade are you dressing as?" the shopkeeper asked.

"Nineties," Tami responded.

"I have just the thing!" she said.

Go to page **52**

"Sam, I love this Skateland idea. Really. Brilliant as usual. But I think you're forgetting one thing," Tami began.

"What's that?" Sam asked.

"Me? Skill? Grace? Coordination? As in... I have none?" she said sarcastically. "You remember what happened when you tried to teach me to skateboard!" Tami rolled up her sleeves to reveal the telltale scars of two skinned elbows.

"I'll never understand how you managed to injure yourself wearing elbow pads," Sam said, shaking his head.

"Yeah, a mistake I'd not like to repeat anytime soon!" Tami responded.

"Well, you've got a week to learn, better get started!" Sam said defiantly.

With the party seven days away, and Sam not wavering, Tami weighed her options. Skateland pros: great nachos, sweet party room, neon glow lights. Skateland cons: she could wipe out in front of half the school, on her birthday. But she had a week to prevent that from happening.

"FINE-UH. Let's do it. BUT—because I'm the nicest, sweetest, best possible sister ever, who is letting you have the party where you want... YOU have to teach me how to skate," Tami said.

Sam rolled his eyes. He had soccer practice every night this week, not to mention wrestling tryouts, homework, and basketball...

**You've Got This!**

Seems like a fair trade! → Go to page **40**

Sorry, sis, you're on your own! → Go to page **130**

Sam scowled. So what if she came to all his dumb games? That didn't mean she could take over his turf. After all—he never once tried to one-up her when she was cracking jokes or playing one of her online games.

"Maybe this is a bad idea. Maybe we're too old to share a birthday party," Sam finally said.

"If that's the way you want it, Sam. You do your thing; I'll do mine," Tami conceded.

## NICE TRY!

Jealousy is a tough feeling to deal with, especially when someone shines in an area where you are used to being top dog. But instead of hogging the spotlight, try sharing it. A little competition and fun friends who share your interests? That's a win-win!

**Go back to page 97 and try again!**

"Okay, let's think here," Tami said, tapping her chin. "You want to skate. I'm a lousy skater."

"Inexperienced, Tami. You don't know you're lousy unless you try!" Sam said.

"Okay, fair point," Tami said. "And I want to dance, but you're a lousy dancer."

"Inexperienced, Tami."

"Oh no, you've tried to dance. We've both seen you dance."

"Yeah, but have you seen me dance with the lights off in complete darkness? That's when I really shine!" Sam joked.

"Exactly, which is why I suggested a glow-in-the-dark party!" Tami replied.

"Ohhhh, now I get it," Sam said, realizing that Tami's party idea benefitted him, too. "But that doesn't help with the fact that I don't think there's any way Mom and Dad will let us paint the basement."

"Who's talking about painting the basement?" Tami asked. "I can set up a pitch-black dance spot on the side of the house using tarps, clothesline, and tape, like the forts we used to build as kids. I know Dad will help me. We can borrow some black lights and, bada bing, bada boom, you've got yourself a certified glow party!"

"You think we could actually pull off combining the two ideas?" Sam asked.

"If Mom and Dad let us use the house. The cul-de-sac would make a great skating rink. We just have to clear it with the neighbors!"

"Hey, I heard that Alan Thomas's brother is a DJ. Maybe he could bring some stuff to play music," Sam added.

"Sam, I think we've finally stumbled onto our genius idea," Tami said, wrapping one arm around her brother.

Go to page **132**

"Well... I guess I say that I'm... IN!" Tami shouted enthusiastically. "This is going to be bigger and better than any old Skateland party any day."

"Yes! We better get to work. There's a lot to do. Can you guys come over after school tomorrow, too?" Sam asked. The group nodded yes. "Guess I could miss one soccer practice..."

Tami pretended to faint. "I'm sorry, I thought you just said you were going to miss soccer practice."

"You gotta do what you gotta do." Sam smiled. "Tami and Allison, will you clear the cul-de-sac details with the neighbors, and I'll work on Mom and Dad about the TVs. Then we can all start working on decorations?"

"You got it!"

Tami and Allison went door-to-door to the five other houses on their circle to see if it would be okay to shut down the street to cars for three hours on Saturday evening. Fortunately, it was a close-knit neighborhood, so Tami knew all of her neighbors pretty well.

"Man, am I glad we bake them Christmas cookies every year," Tami said to Allison as they secured the final yes. They arrived back at the house in time to see Mom and Dad carrying the living room TV down to the basement.

"Lift with your knees, Mom!" Tami joked.

Matt, Alan, and Sam arranged basement couches, folding chairs, beanbag chairs, and any other sitting apparatus they could find into a cool "video game café," as they called it.

Back upstairs at the table, Sam had laid out their full array of arts-and-crafts supplies: paint, paper, glue, sequins, glitter, even a few disco balls leftover from Mom and Dad's groovy Halloween party... and lots and lots of string lights.

"Hey, guess what?" Alan announced, hanging up the phone. "My brother is going to loan me his turntable. I can DJ!"

Go to page **132**

"Remember last year how the school spring dance theme was 'Starry Night'?" Tami asked.

"Yeah," Sam responded.

"And the whole cafeteria was lit up with stars and Christmas lights and they gave us all glow sticks?" Tami continued.

"Yeah." Sam listened.

"But then some of the eight graders pushed some tables together to clear space for a dance circle and they crushed a box of glow sticks?"

"Go on..." Now Sam was really curious!

"And before anyone could clean it up, someone walked through the glow-stick mess and tracked glowing footprints all through the cafeteria..." Tami was grinning ear to ear.

"I DO remember that!" said Sam. "Then everyone started walking through the mess and tracking glowing footprints ALL OVER the place. Principal Myers was SO mad. We had to stay thirty minutes late to clean it all up!"

"Yeah, but it was fun while it lasted, right?"

"Of course—how often do you get to walk through glowing paint?"

"Well, what if we did that for our birthday?"

"A walking-through-paint party?"

"No! A 3D glow party!" Tami clapped her hands together in excitement.

**You've Got This!**

Sounds awesome! → Go to page **66**

Not interested. → Go to page **58**

"I don't know," Tami said, folding her arms. "At first, I didn't want to go to Skateland, but then I got really excited."

"We could make it better than Skateland, Tin," Sam reassured her.

"Maybe. I guess I'm just really not in the party mood," she said quietly. "Thanks for trying to cheer me up, guys. You're great friends." Tami left the table and went up to her room.

"She'll be okay," Sam assured them. "Tami just gets passionate about things and then it's hard for her to reset."

## NICE TRY!

Sometimes things don't go according to plan and unexpected obstacles pop up in your path. Instead of letting them derail you, try to go with the flow and embrace new ideas!
**Go back to page 130 and try again!**

Tami and Sam ran downstairs to find their mom and dad staring out the window, binoculars in hand.

"Look, honey, a common grackle," their dad said, pointing to an iridescent bird perched on the windowsill.

"Ohhh, we don't have that one yet," their mom said, excitedly waving their bird bingo card.

Tami looked at Sam. They shook their heads as if to say, who are these people?

"Hey, Dad—guess what!" Tami said.

"You guys are leaving home to join the circus?" he asked jokingly, fingers crossed.

"You wish," Tami said. "No—we've decided to make our retro bowling party a through-the-decades theme. So people get to pick which decade they want to dress up as!"

"Oh. My. Gosh. Sweetie—this is gonna be SO fun!" their mom said. "Honey, remember that party we went to in high school that was a seventies-themed disco?"

"How could I forget? That was the night we first met!" their dad responded. "I can't wait to recreate it!"

"What was that dance we did?"

"The hustle!"

Tami and Sam's parents both shouted, "DO THE HUSTLE!" and hummed along to the same tune while dancing in sync.

Tami's face turned white. Sam's eyes widened.

**You've Got This!**

Embrace it. Go to page **75**

Think again. Go to page **116**

"You know that place is undergoing a renovation now, right?" Alan asked.

"Wait, what?!" Tami screeched.

"Yeah, why do you think there are so many kids at the skate park?" Alan pointed to the hoards of kids, from elementary school through high school, crowding around the various ramps and slopes. "They're closed for the next three weeks!"

"I'm sorry. What? This is a disaster. What are we going to do? I've already reprinted the invitation. I picked out roller-skate toppers for the cupcakes. This ruins everything!" Tami was talking a mile a minute.

"Tami, calm down," Sam instructed. "It's fine. We can just reprint invitations. And I'm sure everyone will still enjoy the cupcakes even if we don't end up skating."

"Don't end up skating?" Tami said in disbelief. "But I bought skates. And I've had two hours of lessons. Do you know how much time that is for a kid my age? I've only lived like 100,000 hours to begin with!"

Tami sat down on the pavement and put her head in her hands. "No, no, no, no," she muttered to herself, shaking her head back and forth.

"She always like this?" Alan asked.

"Sometimes it's worse," Sam explained.

"Any ideas to snap her out of it?" Alan continued.

"I generally just walk away and let her work it out on her own. Her best friend Allison is usually better at crisis management," Sam said. "I'll rally the troops. Sounds like we could use a little help coming up with plan B, anyway!"

Go to page **26**

"We've tried, Tams. Maybe we just need to take a break from the party thing," Sam said.

"Yeah, that's probably for the best," Tami agreed.

"Hey, look, we just agreed on something!" Sam said. They both laughed, but inside, they both felt a heaviness they couldn't shake.

## NICE TRY!

Growing up is hard. Relationships change and grow. As you evolve you will have new likes and dislikes, and so will your friends and siblings. But rather than remembering "the good times," embrace the new you. Appreciate people for who they are now and what they add to your life.

**Go back to page 92 and try again!**

Waiting six whole days for the party to arrive felt like torture. Tami strategized how to pack the most fun into three hours.

"Well, if you need me, you know where I'll be," Sam announced, patting the new skates his parents let him open early.

"We know, Sam," Tami rolled her eyes. Action Zone had THREE skate ramps.

But when the big day arrived, Tami didn't know where Sam was. She had lost sight of him five minutes after they arrived and hadn't seen him in over an hour. He was missing during bowling and laser tag. He didn't even show up for pizza!

"Tami, are you having a great birthday party, sweetie?" their mom asked.

"Yes, Mom, this place is ah-MAZ-ing. But... I can't find Sam anywhere! I'm having a ton of fun with my friends—but I was kind of hoping Sam and I would celebrate our joint birthday party... you know... jointly."

"Well, there's still plenty of party left," their mom reassured her.

That's when they heard it: "Sam! Sam! Sam! Sam!"—the sound of chanting coming from a dark doorway in the corner. Tami followed the voices to discover an area decorated with neon sculptures of ten-foot-tall flowers and mushrooms illuminated by black light. Giant squirrels, bunnies, and raccoons towered over bridges and small streams that created a labyrinth around eighteen small putting greens.

Go to page **34**

"Well, when you put it that way," Sam began, "I guess it is about time we found something you're good at."

"Hey, now—I'm good at a lot of things. For example, I can beat you in a race," Tami said matter-of-factly.

"Oh yeah?" Sam asked. "Name the time and place. I'll be there."

"How about..." Tami took off. Racing her bike as fast as she could, leaving Sam in the dust, she called back "NOW!" when she was safely several hundred feet ahead.

"Cheater!" Sam yelled to her, already out of breath from trying to catch up.

They raced home, Tami holding her lead the entire way. When they pulled into the driveway, Sam was huffing and puffing away while Tami was pretending to polish her nails. She probably didn't need that head start after all.

"Okay, okay. I get it. So I'm not the only athlete in the family. It's just... a tough pill to swallow," Sam admitted.

"It's okay, humility has never been your strong suit," Tami responded.

"But seriously, Tin—I really do appreciate how much you've supported me over the years," he said sheepishly.

"Are you getting gushy on me? Gross!" Tami squinched her eyes and gagged in fake disgust.

"Yeah, I didn't like it either so don't get used to it." Sam laughed.

"Well, while we're being honest, I have something I have to admit," Tami said. "I hate skating. It's terrifying. I mean, the attention was great and all—I'm so happy I stuck that landing. But that was pure luck! I stick by what I said earlier—I'm not cut out for wheels. Give me solid ground any day!"

Go to page **50**

"Excuse us one second," Sam said, grabbing Tami's arm. He pulled her into the stairwell. "Tami, we can't give Mom and Dad free rein to sing and dance and dress how they want! We'll die of embarrassment!"

"Good point. What do we do?" Tami said.

"Uninvite them?" Sam suggested.

"Excuse me, what's this now?" their mom asked, obviously listening in. "You don't want *moi* at your birthday party?"

"Or *poi*?" said their dad, who didn't know a word of French.

"The thing is... you can be kind of..." Tami began.

"You guys are super embarrassing," Sam cut to the chase.

"US, embarrassing?" their mom repeated. "You guys have no idea. Honey..." She looked at their dad. "It's time."

Their dad walked to a cabinet, pulled out a black photo album, and handed it to their mom.

"What's that?" Tami asked.

"This is an album of your greatest hits," their mom explained.

"What kind of hits?" Sam asked.

"Oh, you know... public tantrums, diapers on heads, that time a bird pooped in your ice cream and you—"

"STOP. I don't want to know," Tami said, putting her hand up.

"Are you blackmailing us?" Sam asked in disbelief.

"No," laughed their dad. "We're just saying sometimes we embarrass you, sometimes you embarrass us. It all evens out in the end."

**You've Got This!**

Mom and Dad are right. → Go to page **24**

← Go to page **71** How could they?

Tami found Sam back at home lying on his bed, his muddy soccer cleats kicked off in the doorway.

"Sam?" she asked in her nicest sister voice. "Can I ask you a question?"

"Sure, Tin, what's up?" Sam responded.

"You know how it's our birthday this week?"

"Yeah, you won't let me forget!"

"Did you buy me a present yet?"

"Did you buy ME a present yet?" Sam countered without skipping a beat.

Tami knew that meant no. "Good, because I know what you can get me," she said.

"If it costs more than ten dollars you're out of luck, because I'm broke."

"Lucky for you, it's free!" Tami said hopefully.

"Oh yeah? I'm listening..." Sam leaned in.

"I want a new party," Tami said quickly.

"What? No—absolutely not. I won the draw. Fair and square," Sam said adamantly.

"But, Saaammm." Tami groaned. "You don't understand. You're sporty. You're coordinated. You're good at everything. You won't look like a total dummy in front of all your friends. Allison and I were at the skate park for over an hour today and all I have to show for it is a bruised bottom and a bruised ego!"

Sam looked at his sister sympathetically.

**You've Got This!** → Go to page **74**

**No way.** → Go to page **74**

**Okay, I'm proud of you for trying your best.** → Go to page **46**

"You can be so self-centered, Sam!" Tami whisper-shouted. She didn't want to make a scene but Sam pushed her too far. "I'm trying everything I can to compromise, but you are shooting down everything!"

"You are the one who's self-centered, Tami," Sam shot back. "You don't want to go to Skateland, so you're just trying to find a middle ground to get your way."

"I'm leaving," said Tami. "You can throw your own dumb birthday."

"Not if I leave first!" Sam yelled, racing her to the exit.

## NICE TRY!

Compromising can be difficult, especially when several options meet dead ends. When you're feeling frustrated trying to work together, sometimes it's better to hit pause. Come back a day or two later with a clearer head.

**Go back to page 107 and try again!**

"You have GOT to be kidding me." Tami threw up her hands in frustration. "After I spent the last THREE days pumping you up for this?"

"You don't understand, Tami. These styles are out there. WAY out there..."

"I know, that's what makes them awesome."

"But what if I'm the only boy there who dresses up?"

"It's not going to kill you. In fact, being unique is often considered a good thing."

Sam admired his sister's sense of individuality. He often wished he had the confidence to march to the beat of his own drum. But for some reason, he found it much easier conforming to a team than being the odd man out.

"Tami, you know your friends are dressing up! The lady up front said they've already been here to shop for outfits!" Sam said.

Tami hadn't thought about that. Coming from Sam's perspective, it was a little scary to jump into something possibly alone.

"Hey, Sam," she asked, her wheels turning.

"What are you more excited about—the eighties thing... or going bowling?"

"I did get pretty pumped about dressing up eighties after you put me through eighties bootcamp," he confessed.

"What if I told you there may be a way to have our vintage party, minus the bowling, but WITH the costumes... and you might feel a little more comfortable because... well... it would be dark," Tami hinted mysteriously.

**You've Got This!**

I'm listening... → Go to page **30**

I'm NOT dressing up! → Go to page **120**

Before she knew it, Tami was standing with Sam at the top of the biggest ramp at the biggest skate park in town. A group of kids from school were gathered below.

"Uh, no way. Nah-ah. I just learned to skate an hour ago!" Tami folded her arms defiantly.

"Oh, come on, Tin—the only way to conquer your fear is to go all in," Sam said, giving her a hearty smack on the shoulder.

"Ow! And no! Absolutely not. You must want me dead or something," Tami responded.

"Nah, I'm just kidding. The ramp's not for you. It's for me. Watch and learn!" Sam turned and shouted to his buddies, "And for my next trick—turning this mountain into a molehill!"

Moving to the edge, Sam tightened the straps on his helmet and pads. He positioned his legs shoulder-width apart and bent his knees in a slight crouch position. With one foot leading, he balanced his weight as he dipped his toe over the edge, preparing to drop in. A final body check and WHOOOOOOSHH!—he was flying!

With an unfairly easy sense of style and grace, Sam gently glided up the other side, rotating his skates into a half turn at the top and came back down. Piece of cake.

"Nice form, Sam!" someone shouted.

"Show-off," muttered another.

Sam turned to see Alan Thomas—his school sports rival. Did he say that? Sam wondered. Either way, he was glad he nailed the drop in front of that guy. Turning back to his sister, he yelled, "All right, Tami—your turn!"

"Yeah right—I think you're mistaking me for your other twin!" Tami called back. Turning to find a safe way to the ground, she continued, "The day I go down this ramp is the day that pigs—AAAAAAAAHHHHHHH!"

Go to page **64**

"You mean everything?" Sam asked.

"Everything," Tami said.

"But the party's today!" Sam said.

"Not anymore, it isn't!" Tami responded.

"I'm so sorry, Tami!" Sam said, tears welling up in his eyes. "I've ruined everything." Sam ran up the stairs to his room.

## NICE TRY!

Working hard on something only to have it ruined can be one of the worst feelings in the world. But rather than letting it completely mess up your plans, think about creative ways you can turn a setback into an opportunity. Can any part of your initial work be saved? Can you turn it into something else? Can you think of something else to replace it?

**Go back to page 105 and try again!**

By the time Tami made it to the skate park, Allison was already there. She looked even more unsteady on her skates than Tami, if that was even possible.

"I'm not so sure about this, Tams," Allison said. "If I break a bone, my mom's gonna be really mad at me."

"Relax. We're wearing pads, right? And you've got a helmet. Where did you get that, anyway?" Tami asked, looking at Allison's oversize headgear.

"Oh, it's my bike helmet. You didn't think I had a skating helmet, did you? I'm brand-new to this! I had to borrow my brother's skates!" she said, pointing to the black-and-red monstrosities on her feet.

"Okay, I looked up some video tutorials, and I think I've got the basics down. First, we have to get the position right. Feet shoulder-width apart," Tami instructed. Both girls shuffled their feet side to side until they were roughly the right distance apart. "Okay, now bend your knees." Allison did what she was told. Tami followed. "And finally, squat."

"Squat?!" Allison asked.

"Yes," Tami said matter-of-factly. "Behind backward pointing to the ground."

"I'm much more comfortable standing, thanks," Allison said, dismissing the directive.

"Good luck with that. It says here it's hard to stand in skates," Tami said, reading her notes.

"Let me see that," Allison said, grabbing the notebook. She lunged forward to reach it, tumbling to the ground and taking Tami with her.

"Owwww," they said in unison. "This is going to be harder than I thought," said Tami.

Go to page **78**

That evening, Mom and Dad called a family meeting. Tami and Sam didn't like the sound of it. The last time there was a meeting like this it was because someone broke the TV.

"Solidarity?" Sam asked Tami.

"They won't break me!" Tami said proudly.

"Have a seat, you two," Dad instructed.

"What did we do?" Tami groaned.

"Nothing," Mom said. "We just want to know more details about this party..."

"Yeah, tell us more. Who's coming? What are we planning to do?" Dad asked.

"We narrowed the list down to thirty kids," said Sam. "And before you say that's too many, remember, there's TWO of us!"

"Noted," Mom said with a nod.

"And I think it's pretty obvious what we're gonna do," Tami stated matter-of-factly.

"And what's that?" Mom asked.

"Skate."

"Dance."

"What?" They looked at each other.

"Dancing at Skateland?" Tami asked.

"Skating in the basement?" Sam wondered.

"I think you have some talking to do," Mom said as she and Dad left the room.

"Tami, did you think I meant we should do the party at Skateland?" Sam asked.

"Yes. Did you think I meant we were settling on the glow party?" Tami asked.

"Yes," Sam replied. "And I sold my skates to buy a black light!"

"I sold my light-up shoes to buy skates!" Tami said.

**You've Got This!**

This is a disaster! → Go to page **60**

We can bounce back from this. → Go to page **76**

"Sorry, Tin—no can do! As much as I'd love to spend the week teaching the clumsiest person in the world how to maneuver on wheels, I've got a packed schedule," Sam said.

"Sam, puh-leaseeee? I'll make your bed for a week!" Tami offered.

"I wish I could, Tami, but look at my after-school calendar. I'm slammed!" Sam pointed to some sheets of hastily ripped notebook paper taped to the back of the door. The word OCTOBER was scribbled at the top with a list of locations, dates, and times.

"Hey, isn't Alan Thomas a really good skater? Maybe I could ask him!" Tami said enthusiastically.

"No way. Do NOT ask that guy," Sam said.

"Why, is he no good?"

"Oh, he's good all right. At skating. But as a person he's the worst. Seriously, Tami, stay away," Sam cautioned.

"Is this because he beat you for the last first-string spot on the basketball team?" Tami asked.

"No," Sam said defensively. "He's just a snob and I don't want you hanging out with snobs."

"Uh-huh," she said suspiciously.

"Why don't you get Allison to help you?" Sam suggested, referring to Tami's best friend.

"Allison? Why? She doesn't know how to skate, either!"

"All the better! You can learn together!"

**You've Got This!**

Ask Alan Thomas. → Go to page **20**

Ask Allison. → Go to page **126**

Over the course of the next few days, everyone pulled together to cut, string, glue, paint, hammer, and sequin the best makeshift skating rink they'd ever seen. Tami set up a dance spot with tons of lights and glow sticks.

When the party day finally arrived, Sam and Tami couldn't be more excited to show off all their hard work. And their friends couldn't be more excited to see how they had transformed their house into the ultimate party destination. Balloons and streamers were just the start: with help from their friends, the twins had created dozens of "photo booths" with hilarious backdrops and matching accessories. Dad had placed a garden pole in the center of the street and strung hundreds of lights across the makeshift rink. Alan had borrowed spotlight equipment from his brother's DJ set to project disco balls off the neighbors' houses. The effect of both had instantly transformed the quiet neighborhood street into a showstopping party pad. To top it all off, Mom had created a "grab 'n' go" snack wall out of an old peg board they had hanging in the garage.

When it came to the skating, Sam dazzled his friends and Tami managed to stay on her feet the whole night—which was good enough for her.

As the party wound down and their friends headed home, Sam and Tami walked around cleaning up cups, plates, napkins, and empty nacho bowls. "Looks like everyone had a great time," Tami said, smiling.

"Well, what do you think? Was it the supreme, ultimate, fantastic, amazing, best-ever birthday party palooza you had hoped for?" Sam asked.

"No, Sam. It was better!" said Tami.

## GREAT JOB!

With your help, Tami and Sam had the ultimate birthday bash! You have reached the end of this story, but you can go back to the beginning and pick different paths to see where another adventure leads!

# REFLECTIONS

**Think about one of the choices you made in this book. Then answer the prompts below on a separate sheet of paper.**

1. Why did you make the choice that you made?

2. What emotion(s) did you have when you were making your choice?

3. What did you expect would happen as a result of your choice?

4. How did your emotion(s) change after reading the outcome of your choice?

5. How do you think your choice affected the feelings of the characters in the story?

6. How do you think your choice affects the relationships of the characters in the story?

7. Do you think you made the right choice? Why or why not?

# ACTIVITIES

## Color Compromise

**You'll need:** *red paint, blue paint, a piece of paper, a paintbrush*

Think about a time when you and someone else had different ideas about how something should go. Then grab some red paint and blue paint. Side by side on a piece of paper, place a small glob of each one. The glob of red paint represents an idea you have, and the glob of blue paint represents someone else's idea. With a brush, mix together the two colors. See how they make a totally new color—just like a creative solution that includes multiple perspectives! Think about how the new color "solution" could include both of your ideas.

## Go With the Flow

**You'll need:** *a piece of paper, a glass of water, food coloring, a pen or pencil*

Draw a stick figure on a piece of paper. Then, in a full glass of water, add several drops of food coloring.

Dip your fingers into the water, lift them up, and flick them over the piece of paper. The paper—and your stick figure—will be covered in colorful dots. Now, draw something on or around your stick figure that connects some of the dots. The water is like an unexpected obstacle or setback. You might not know where it will lead, but if you embrace the change, you could make something awesome out of it!

## Embrace the Present

**You'll need:** *scissors, magazines, glue, a piece of paper, a pen or pencil*

Think of someone in your life who you haven't always seen eye-to-eye with. You might have a long list of reasons why you don't get along. But instead of focusing on those things, make a list of five qualities that you appreciate about that person. Maybe you like their taste in music, or how they stick up for their friends and family (even if that's not you... yet). Flip through some old magazines and cut out examples of the items on your list. Then glue them all on a piece of paper and label each one to create a collage.

If you're comfortable with it, you can even consider giving your collage to the person who inspired you. Sharing your appreciation could spark a conversation, and might just bring you closer together!

## Sour Feelings

**You'll need:** *A clear glass jar, a box of gelatin, 4 tablespoons of baking soda, 2 tablespoons of lemon juice, a stir stick*

**Warning: This could get messy!** Start by placing a clear jar on a cleanable surface, such as inside a sink or on a stretch of pavement. Then pour gelatin and baking soda into the jar and stir them together. Now pour the lemon juice into the jar, and watch how the ingredients react. Sometimes super-strong feelings—just like chemical reactions—can bubble up before you see them coming. Before you know it, it's too late, and you've made a mess that's tough to clean up. Learning to anticipate and manage these feelings—whether by taking time to cool down, writing down your thoughts, or finding some other way to reflect on them—will put you back in the driver's seat, and help you avoid future messes!

# RESOURCES FOR ADULTS

## The CASEL Framework

Kids are faced with tough choices every day. To share or not to share? Try something new, or stick with what I know? When I'm angry, should I reflect or react?

Guided by the CASEL Framework, the pick-your-path adventures presented in this book are designed to help children practice making good decisions in their daily lives. Every choice is totally up to them!

Children can revisit this book time and again to choose different paths through the adventures, along the way learning skills and principles to build their social and emotional competencies.

## About the Framework

The Collaborative for Academic, Social, and Emotional Learning (CASEL) provides a framework for schools, families, and communities to develop and apply skills that support children's development as citizens of the modern world. The CASEL Framework, sometimes called the "CASEL wheel," focuses on five interrelated areas:

- **Self-awareness:** Understanding emotions, thoughts, and values—and how these factors play a role in behavior
- **Self-management:** Regulating emotions, thoughts, and behaviors to achieve goals
- **Social awareness:** Developing empathy for people with diverse perspectives
- **Relationship skills:** Forming and maintaining healthy relationships, and navigating interactions with diverse groups
- **Responsible decision-making:** Making thoughtful choices about behavior and social interactions

## HOW IT WORKS

Each choice presented in this book has two options: one that supports a competency in the CASEL Framework and one that does not.

Example:

Good choices are rewarded with more choices, and ultimately a congratulatory message.

### GREAT JOB!

A not-so-good choice is followed by asking the child to try again.

### NICE TRY!

The grid below outlines how the CASEL Framework competencies are covered in the book and includes some questions for discussion.

| CASEL Framework competencies presented | Key questions to ask to relate to the characters |
|---|---|
| **SELF-AWARENESS** Integrating personal and social identities | When Tami was getting attention for skating down the ramp, Sam was upset because he was the athlete in the family. How might his identity as a skater impact how he feels now that Tami has the spotlight for something he is known to be good at? |
| **SELF-MANAGEMENT** Using planning and organizational skills | When Tami had the idea for the Glow Party, she created a to-do list. How might her planning skills help to organize an amazing birthday party? |

# Night Shift

## B.R. Myers

ALSO BY B.R. MYERS

*Butterflies Don't Lie*

*Girl on the Run*

*Asp of Ascension: A Nefertari Hughes Mystery #1*

*Diadem of Death: A Nefertari Hughes Mystery #2*

Night Shift

Copyright © 2016 B.R. Myers

All rights reserved.

This book is a work of fiction. Any references to historical events, real people, or real places are used fictitiously. Other names, characters, and any locales, and incidents are products of the author's imagination, and any resemblance to actual events or places or person, living or dead, is entirely coincidental.

Library and Archives Canada Cataloging in Publication information is available upon request.

*Edited by Penelope Jackson*

*Cover by Emma Dolan*

ISBN 0995044708
ISBN13 978-0995044708

*To Barbara, Tricia, and Shannon,*

*for never wavering in their enthusiasm for this story.*

*LLW*

# CHAPTER ONE

The gray-haired security guard narrowed his eyes, taking in Daniel's faded pea coat over the hoodie, and his worn out backpack. Months of travelling had left its mark; his clothes were dingy, he hadn't shaved in a few days, and even his skin was pale and tired-looking.

Daniel caught his reflection in one of the video monitors that lined the opposite wall, tracking all the movements inside Willard's department store. No one from school would recognize the zombie he'd become.

The man's wrinkled fingers drummed on the antique wooden desk beside Daniel's pathetic, half-page resume. "You left the education section blank," he said curtly.

"I'm a few credits short of graduating from high school." *A few plus some more,* Daniel thought to himself. Then he added quickly, "I'm hoping to finish by correspondence in the next few months." A lie. A diploma was the last thing on his "to do" list.

"You dropped out?"

"No." Daniel's cheeks grew warm. He faked a cough, hoping to disguise the blush. He hadn't anticipated having to explain his circumstances. "I just didn't finish the last semester."

"Any trouble with the law?"

"No, sir."

"You can call me Mr. Oliver," he instructed. His eyes barely stayed on Daniel before his attention returned to the paper.

"Okay…" There was an uncomfortable pause, then he added, "Mr. Oliver."

"Daniel Gale," he read, his finger going over the resume as if reading it by brail. "Not a very common name."

Daniel stayed quiet, unsure how to respond. He didn't think his name was all that special.

The questions started again. "You're a long way from home. Why?"

"I'm eighteen," Daniel answered, slightly put out by the insinuation he was a helpless kid. "I've been travelling."

"But not anymore?" One white eyebrow arched, but Mr. Oliver didn't look up.

Daniel was struck by a heavy gloom. He needed this job; it was his last hope.

The thought of getting on another plane made him sick. Long ago, he'd made a game of trying to guess which of his fellow passengers had someone waiting for them. A woman with an infant would more than likely be embraced by anxious grandparents, waving a new teddy bear. The middle-aged man wearing a baseball cap was always picked up by his brother or sister. And the girl who checked her makeup just before the plane landed was meeting a boyfriend.

But there was never anyone waiting for Daniel.

Before he could put a spin on his situation, Mr. Oliver spoke again. "Next of kin is your lawyer." It wasn't a question, but he paused, waiting for an explanation.

"My parents are, um…gone." Daniel looked down at his scuffed loafers, taken from his father's closet the day he left home.

"Ever work in a department store?" Mr. Oliver asked. Clearly, the fact that Daniel was on his own didn't concern or interest him. Daniel guessed if he'd been purposely going for

NIGHT SHIFT

the sympathy angle, it wouldn't have worked on this tough crank.

"No," he answered.

"Any experience with security?"

"No."

"How long have you lived in the city?" he asked suspiciously, as if trying to catch Daniel in a lie.

"Just arrived." Daniel felt like he was in his school's state hockey championship all over again, but this time, every slap shot was missing the net. His fingers slipped inside his jacket pocket and found the small round object. He managed a half smile—feeling the Magic 8 Ball keychain always made him relax.

"I see," Mr. Oliver said, studying him. He smoothed out his royal blue tie, letting his fingers pause at the golden *W* on the clip.

Daniel squirmed, making the wooden chair squeak.

"Do you believe in ghosts?"

He cocked his head to one side, unsure if he'd heard correctly. "Um, ghosts?" Daniel didn't dare crack a joke; in fact, the old guy was creeping him out. Why was it important for a night security guard to believe in ghosts? He shifted his weight in the chair again, trying to buy time to think. He was totally unprepared for this interview. The silence grew painfully long; he had to say *something*. Daniel took a deep breath. He knew all about the finality of death. "No," he said. "I don't believe in ghosts."

"Good. Willard's has a bit of a reputation—unfortunately. The store goes through a lot of night guards."

"Oh," Daniel said. His gaze flicked around the room, wondering if there was a hidden camera on him. Maybe this was some psychological component of the interview? "Excuse me, but by 'go through,' what do you mean?"

"They quit."

"Oh," Daniel said again.

9

Mr. Oliver folded his hands on the green blotter and stared back. "Why *do* you want to work here?"

Daniel's fist squeezed the keychain inside his pocket. He met Mr. Oliver's gaze and told him the truth. "Because it's just what I need."

Mr. Oliver let out a long breath, and then added Daniel's thin resume to a pile of more substantial hopefuls, making the outcome of this disastrous interview obvious. Daniel's last bit of hope faded, and the disappointment weighed on him like a wet blanket.

"Thank you for your interest in Willard's," Mr. Oliver said, nodding toward the door. "Come to the office tomorrow, half an hour before the store closes. We'll get you fitted for a uniform."

Daniel almost fell out of the chair. "I got the job?"

"Don't be late," he said, then paused, and his voice dropped a few notes. "Daniel Gale."

"I won't. Thank you!" Daniel was stunned for a moment, unable to move. Mr. Oliver frowned at him, and then motioned impatiently to the door again.

Daniel left the security office, shouldering his backpack, suddenly giddy with his change in luck. He leaned against a long glass counter and grinned. He was finally getting closer to finding an answer.

Earlier that morning, Daniel had left the hotel with his little black notebook and a map of the city. He'd passed the bare trees of Gramercy Park, shivering in the light drizzle—everything had looked gray and dead. The feeling in his chest had grown heavier as he crossed the traffic on Broadway, and then Fifth Avenue.

He paused every few blocks along West 18th to consult his map. Bent into the wind, he took shelter under some scaffolding. He stared across the street at the five-storey building of glazed terracotta and rusticated ironwork. Something clicked inside his head, like the tumblers inside a lock falling into place. A large royal blue banner hung over the

entrance. Golden letters spelled out *Willard's—It's Just What You Need!*

He flipped through the little black notebook. It was mostly small notations of his travels, a few doodles from his dreams, and near the back, lists of cities with lines crossed through them. Daniel double checked the last address.

*Willard's.*

He crossed the street and waited under the banner, frowning at the main entrance, still hesitant. The large front windows were covered in brown paper stamped with *DISPLAY IN PROGRESS*. A steady stream of customers bustled by, oblivious to his shaking in the rain. Only when the glass doors had closed and the brass pull handles came together did Daniel finally let out the breath he'd been holding.

With nothing but intuition leading him, he had entered the store and filled out a job application form. The Magic 8 Ball had encouraged him.

*Signs point to yes.*

Human resources had called his cell phone within a few hours to see if he was interested in night-shift duties; the head of security was coming in early and wanted to interview him.

Now, newly hired, he stood, propped against the glass counter, enjoying the sweet victory of pulling off the miracle of somehow impressing the stodgy guard.

"May I help you?" A pretty clerk in a blue vest and white shirt leaned on one hip as if posing for a magazine cover.

Daniel blinked a few times, unable to speak. He hadn't thought of anything sweet like *that* in a long time, either. The idea hadn't even crossed his mind for months. Since the funeral, finding this store had been the only thing occupying his imagination.

She prompted him again by waving a hand toward the glass jewelry counter. "Maybe something for your girlfriend?"

He noticed the playful hint to her question. He grimaced at his loafers, hoping his cheeks didn't look as red as they felt.

"Um…I'm not shopping today," he finally said.

"Feel free to look, then," she flirted, smoothing out her blue vest. Daniel's gaze couldn't help but wander to her strategically placed golden name tag.

Her smile made it easier for him to answer back. "Thanks, Monique," he read. "But I actually work here."

"Really?" She looked him up and down. "I've never seen you before."

Daniel remembered his scruffy reflection in the monitor. "I just got hired," he said, sliding his hands into his coat pockets, desperate to appear aloof and somewhat interesting in front of this slick Manhattan girl.

"Oh yeah?" She smiled and tossed her hair. "Let me guess, a waiter in the Matinee Room or a clerk in Menswear?" She didn't wait for him to answer. "It doesn't matter where they put you, most of the staff are cool. There's a lot of standing and it can be sort of boring, but we get a discount on everything…" She darted a quick glance at this shoes. "Including designer labels."

Daniel didn't feel insulted; he knew how scruffy he looked. He grinned, showing off his dimples. Flirting felt awkward, but he couldn't ignore the lightness in his chest. "Actually," he said, "I'm doing night security."

"Oh." Her smile dropped. "Nice knowing you."

The air had cooled. "Sorry?"

"The new night guards never stay for long." She glanced around the area, and then leaned in so close he could see the sparkles in her eye shadow. "It's like this," she whispered. "Weird stuff happens at night."

"Weird stuff?" Daniel repeated, raising an eyebrow.

"Unexplained phenomena after hours."

"Like?"

Her eyes grew wide. "Strange noises, furniture being rearranged, displays messed up, lights going on and off for no reason."

NIGHT SHIFT

"Sweaters unfold themselves?" he said. "Sounds terrifying. I hope I survive."

Monique stepped away, unimpressed with his tepid reaction. "If you're like every other night guard we've had, you won't be laughing tonight. They usually quit after a week or so."

Daniel was intrigued by her dramatic warning. He motioned across the aisle toward the security office. "What about Mr. Oliver?"

She waved her red fingernails in the air. "Are you kidding? That old fart came with the place. Half the time I think he's one of the resident ghosts."

Someone cleared their throat. "Are you helping this customer, Monique?" A well-groomed woman wearing a blue vest and golden tie smiled at Daniel, and then gave Monique a scathing look.

He noticed the sparkling diamond display he was lazily leaning over. "Sorry…just looking," he said, backing away, embarrassed by the interruption.

"That's so sweet for asking, Lois." Monique beamed at the clerk. "But my break is almost due. I totally love your gold studs, by the way. Did they just go on sale?"

Lois produced a small white cloth and wiped Daniel's smudges off the glass.

Monique walked with him up the aisle. "I'm usually up on the first floor in Ladies' Fashions," she said brightly, unaware of the older clerk's disapproving glances. "Come find me tomorrow and I'll show you around. The Matinee Room on the top floor has the best cheesecake! Odds are we'll only have a few weeks together before the ghosts scare you away." She ended the invitation with a wink, and then disappeared down the corridor, her high heels clicking on the tile.

Daniel made his way to the foyer, relishing the lingering memory of her laugh. The toe of his loafers reached the end of the black granite tile where is edged the whited marbled pattern

13

of the main entrance.

He looked up at the banner over the gift shop. *Willard's—It's Just What You Need.* He pulled out the Magic 8 Ball keychain and smiled at its reply.

*Without a doubt.*

# CHAPTER TWO

D aniel arrived at Willard's an hour before his shift. He paused for a moment on the white marble tile of the circular foyer. A gold-coloured tree wrapped in twinkling lights stretched high and wide, forming a ceiling of stars over his head. The gift shop to his right was bursting with shoppers trying to find the perfect souvenir before the store closed.

Unlike most department stores with their wide-open areas and high ceilings, Willard's was composed of smaller sections connected by archways and curving corridors. A shopper could discover new sections by going up a small spiral staircase, or down a few steps into a sunken room.

Housewares had lavish dining room displays set with crystal glasses and polished silverware. An intimate seating arrangement in Home Furnishings was propped with a cashmere lap blanket and a bookmarked paperback, giving the impression the reader had just left the room.

Every display in every department was a vignette of luxury illuminated by some intangible quality—little pretend worlds to play in, if only for the day. Willard's wasn't selling merchandise, Daniel guessed; it was selling dreams.

He walked around clusters of well-dressed women sauntering along the jewelry counters and headed straight for the security office. Daniel gripped the doorknob, but then he paused, wondering if he should knock first—Mr. Oliver didn't strike him as the chatty type.

An eruption of raised voices came through the keyhole.

Daniel backed up, not keen on interrupting an argument his first shift. He waited in the middle of the aisle, but after a few minutes the voices were still going strong. Daniel looked at his watch and decided he had time to wander a bit, and hopefully to bump into Monique.

The elevator was the old-fashioned kind with a steel pull gate. He stepped inside and was greeted by a gentleman wearing a navy blue jacket and hat with a golden *W* on the front.

"Which floor?" the attendant smiled.

"First, please," Daniel said, silently giving thanks the security guards didn't have to wear hats.

With a white-gloved hand, the attendant pushed a button. "Ladies' Fashion and Housewares," he said with a bravado that seemed ridiculous. The old machine rattled and began to rise. The walls were painted gold and covered in a perfectly spaced pattern of tiny blue *W*'s. Daniel squinted, wondering how the attendant didn't go cross-eyed looking at this view all day.

Above the gate, a blue half circle was marked with the floor indicators from G, for ground floor, up to the number four, where Daniel guessed the restaurant, the Matinee Room, was located. He watched the golden arrow, now pointing at the G, slowly move up. It stopped at the one, and a gentle bell dinged.

Daniel unbuttoned his pea coat, feeling foolish roving through all the fancy dresses. Circular racks of endless outfits dotted the large floor space. Rows of countertops displaying purses and belts created tiny glass mazes. He turned a few times, trying to orient himself. He checked his watch again, and then shoved his hands in his jean pockets, suspicious Monique had set him up.

"May I be of service?" The voice was sultry and just behind his shoulder.

A smile automatically curled the edge of Daniel's mouth. Relief mixed with jittery anxiety as he turned. She was once again in her blue vest and gold tie, just like all the clerks at Willard's, but Daniel noticed Monique had a knack for standing out.

She looked quite satisfied that he'd come to her area. "You

NIGHT SHIFT

showed up for night shift after all," she teased. "I guess ghosts don't bother you."

He laughed and shook his head. "I don't scare that easily."

She rolled her eyes at this and Daniel theorized she heard guys lie to impress her all the time. "I was asking around," she began, "and Helen, one of my friends at the cosmetic counter, says they're always looking for waiters upstairs. But you could check out the Home Entertainment department…you like movies, right?" She tapped a fingernail on the display case. "I'm not sure about the Confectionery, though; the chocolate samples are great, but you'd have to wear a blue and white striped apron." She said this while staring across the department as if talking to herself.

Daniel tried to ignore the sudden heaviness on his shoulders. His earlier anticipation began to warp into disappointment.

Boxes tumbled down from a nearby display, followed by a stumbling clerk. Monique nudged him in the ribs. "Stacey," she said with an obvious air, as if the name explained everything. They walked over to the clumsily sprawled girl.

"Are you okay?" he asked, taking her elbow to help her stand. She was pale and slim with pixie-style hair.

"Thanks," Stacey said, dusting off her blue vest and skirt. "I was rushing and lost my footing."

He glanced up at the raised platform, where three mannequins were dressed in colourful rain gear with umbrellas.

"What's the big panic?" Monique asked her. "The display looks fine to me."

Stacey straightened her crooked vest. "Not everyone has the luxury of socializing during work hours."

Monique's face reddened. "Come on," she said, touching Daniel's arm. "I'll show you the rest of the floor."

They walked several feet before Monique started talking. "She's so jealous," she huffed. "Just because I have more friends than her, she's labelled me a gossip who hangs out in the makeup aisle and takes all the samples. I can't help it if I'm popular." She didn't wait for Daniel to answer. "And she's

17

always lurking around Ladies' Fashions, like she's trying to catch me doing my nails or something. It's creepy, actually."

"It sounds like you don't trust her," he said.

"I don't. Today she's supposed to be in Toys. She thinks she's some important fashion designer, but she's only a freshman in college. One day she came wearing a sweatshirt and flip-flops!"

Daniel tugged at his coat, trying to hide his black sweatshirt underneath. He stayed quiet, unsure how to comment.

"This is my after-school job," Monique continued, "and I look way more professional than her." She straightened her leg, showing off her foot. "See? At least I'm wearing stilettos."

"Very nice," he said.

"I go to Eleanor Roosevelt High," she said. "I graduate this year. What about you? Oh, never mind, that's stupid of me to ask. You wouldn't be working night shift if you went to high school." Daniel sensed she was hoping he'd offer his own history, but he remained silent.

She led him down a sweeping grand staircase to the ground floor. A sweet aroma made Daniel's mouth water; he looked to his right and saw a colourful archway leading to the Confectionery. He caught a glimpse of glass jars with glistening candy before Monique pulled on his arm, making him continue through the Beauty department.

She stopped by the makeup counters. Daniel found her quietness a bit unnerving—that and being surrounded by cosmetics. If his old hockey team saw him now, he'd never hear the end of it.

A stone dropped in his stomach. That life was over. The Daniel who scored goals and got high fives in the hallways was gone.

Monique began to inspect the lipsticks. "I sound like a bitch, don't I?" she asked.

He was surprised by her frankness. "No," he said. She selected a colour, and then drew a line across the back of her hand. She repeated the process with various shades until there was a rainbow of reds and pinks. Daniel glanced at his watch,

NIGHT SHIFT

wondering if the security office was open yet.

Monique suddenly pressed against his side. He couldn't remember the last time a girl had come that close to him on purpose. He was acutely aware of her softness, and the faint smell of her shampoo. "I need your help," she murmured.

"What? Oh...okay." He pointed to one of the red lines. "Um, that one, I guess."

She answered with a harsh whisper. "Not the lipstick. I mean Stacey. She's a thief, but I don't have any proof. You're security, right? Please say you'll help."

Daniel slouched. He was the last person she should ask for help—he was nobody's hero. "If she stole something, you should tell Mr. Oliver."

Monique dropped her gaze. "It wasn't anything from the store. It was something from me."

He could tell from her voice that she was trying not to cry. He pictured her standing in front of Mr. Oliver asking for help. The guard would probably grunt and then fire her on the spot.

"What did she take?" he asked.

"Never mind," Monique said, nodding across the counter. A stylish clerk behind the lipstick display interrupted them. She and Monique began to make plans for after work. Daniel looked back and forth a few times, feeling invisible, and decided this was his cue to leave.

"Wait." Monique turned and gave him a quick hug. "Thanks for listening," she said, letting her hand trace down his arm. "I have a feeling you'll last at least a few weeks on nights. Maybe they'll let you switch to another department. It's way more fun with me on day shift."

"Um, yeah," he said, feeling a blush creep up his neck. Everything moved fast in this city, he was discovering—even the girls.

The next time Daniel checked, the security office was open. A clerk from human resources was holding an armload of papers. "You'll need to fill these out," he said, passing over the stack of forms. "There is a fire safety manual with a quiz at the

19

end, and a health insurance form. We'll also need your social security number, and a copy of your driver's license." He continued for another minute, then finished with a curt goodbye.

Daniel looked around the empty office, tall potted ferns flanked a narrow arch, leading to a short hallway. He craned his neck and saw the walls were covered with framed photographs. One of the papers in his grip fell to the floor. Silently groaning at the amount of documents he had to fill out, Daniel chose a pen from a cup on the desk and started for the chair.

"Hey, are you the new night guy?" Two young men entered, dressed similarly in dark blue pants and light blue shirts.

"Yeah, I guess I am." Daniel shifted the papers, anticipating a handshake. "Are you working tonight, too?"

"No way," the first one said. He had short black hair, and judging by the tightness of the sleeve around his upper arm, Daniel guessed he worked out—a lot. "We only do day security."

"Oh," Daniel said, letting his hand fall to the side. Introductions were informal, apparently.

"You must be replacing the guy from last month," the second guard said. He took a small piece of paper from the desk drawer, scribbled a few words, and then tossed it into a large glass bowl sitting on top of a row of filing cabinets.

"And he was the one who replaced the other guy," the black-haired guard continued. He studied Daniel, and then, like his partner, he added another piece of paper to the bowl.

"Is that how you put in your hours?" Daniel asked. The guy with the papers forgot to mention payroll.

"It's a pool. Ten bucks to play."

Daniel smiled. "You mean for hockey playoffs?" he asked.

"No." The guards shared a smirk. "It's how long before you quit."

"Of course," Daniel said. "I forgot, the store is haunted."

"Don't take it personally. We do it for every new night guy."

Daniel's pulse quickened. "Really?" he said, staring at the

NIGHT SHIFT

black-haired guard. "How long did you put down?"

"One shift."

He looked at the second guard. "And your bet?"

"Six hours," he shrugged.

"Interesting," Daniel said. "One of the clerks said I'd last at least a few weeks."

"Which clerk?"

"Monique."

The black-haired one clenched his jaw, but the second guard replied first. "Monique gets off on flirting with the newbies," he said. "That's her style. She knows you won't be here long."

Daniel fought the urge to walk out of the office and never come back. But he couldn't do that, not after everything he'd been through to get here. He focused on the glass bowl, already half full of people betting on him to lose.

The second guard followed his gaze. "It's not our fault they always put the fresh meat on nights."

This was getting old. Daniel stood straighter and said, "Maybe that's because the guards on day shift have no balls."

"Daniel Gale." A raspy voice called out, making all three young men jump. Mr. Oliver stood in the doorway. "You're early. Good."

"Evening, Mr. Oliver," the two guards replied, suddenly docile. They wasted no time slipping out of the office.

Just before the door closed, the black-haired guy caught Daniel's eye and nodded toward the glass bowl. "Good luck," he grinned.

# CHAPTER THREE

"**M**orons," Mr. Oliver mumbled under his breath. He walked behind the desk and stood in front of the wall of monitors. Daniel held his papers, waiting for him to say something, but the old man's eyes remained fixed on the black and white images of the various departments systematically closing down for the night.

The small room was hot and stuffy. Daniel took off his pea coat and sat on the leather couch against the wall. He was halfway through the fire safety quiz when he heard clicking. One by one, Mr. Oliver was turning off each monitor until the only image was the main entrance. The last group of employees was gathered in the foyer.

"Come on," Mr. Oliver ordered. Daniel picked up his stack of papers and followed him down the aisle. "I don't care how good you are at video games or computer hacking," Mr. Oliver began. "That useless techno garbage is for the Electronics department. Your responsibility is to keep watch. Willard's is old fashioned. It doesn't need any fancy gadgets, laser beams, or motion detectors." They entered the foyer dominated by the golden tree.

"Uh-huh," Daniel said, noticing the twinkling lights wrapped around every branch. He stopped at the edge of the black granite tile while Mr. Oliver continued across the white marble pattern to the main entrance. He politely nodded to the last few clerks as they scurried by, and then locked the front doors behind them.

"It's simple," Mr. Oliver said. "The store only needs two things to be safe—me and a key." He joined Daniel, and then

started walking back down the aisle. "Your job is to do hourly rounds and make sure everything is in order. Anything out of place might need to be investigated. If there's something that looks suspicious, come get me."

The soft, glowing display cases in the Jewelry section sparkled with diamonds and precious stones. Daniel stared at Mr. Oliver's bent, arthritic back and suspected that if this old guy and a key were the only things keeping someone from robbing the store, ghosts were the least of his worries. Getting through the first week without being bludgeoned to death by a burglar was probably what the pool was really about.

"For tonight," Mr. Oliver said, standing in front of the elevator, "I want you to become familiar with the store and the espresso machine."

Daniel halted mid-stride. "Espresso machine?"

"It's in the kitchen, off the restaurant on the fourth floor." His tone indicated he'd made this speech a hundred times. "You work nights. You'll need coffee." Mr. Oliver pulled back the gate and waved Daniel inside.

"Wait," he said, holding up the half-filled-in forms. "What about this paperwork?"

Mr. Oliver took the stack. "I'll wait and see if you need to complete the long-term information."

Daniel couldn't ignore the obvious lack of faith in Mr. Oliver's voice. "Is that why I don't have a uniform yet either?" he asked straight out.

"No, I just forgot." Mr. Oliver handed him a flashlight. "You'll need this. The lights are dimmed at night."

Daniel motioned to the darkened main floor behind Mr. Oliver's shoulder. "I can see that."

Mr. Oliver stared at him, unflinching. "Sometimes the lights go on and off by themselves." He pulled the gate shut, enclosing Daniel in the antique elevator.

Ladies' Fashions was dead quiet. Daniel's footsteps echoed through the empty department. He ignored the dresses and coats, and took out the little black notebook from his back pocket. Tucking the flashlight under his arm, he opened to the

front page. His drawing of a cursive V made him smile. He flipped to the back, where instead of being crossed out, the address for Willard's was circled.

He ducked behind a cashier's counter, looking for a pen. Without warning, the hair on the back of his neck stood up. Daniel did a sweep of the department with the flashlight, but nothing was moving, or as Mr. Oliver would say, "seemed out of place."

The light reflected off the display with the two mannequins dressed in bright raincoats, and Daniel replayed the scene from earlier. Monique's flirting reminded him of what it felt like to be a regular guy. He'd been alone for so long that his social skills were practically non-existent, and so was his confidence. Her eagerness was a bit intimidating, but the attention made him feel good, and it made him want more.

Like a sudden clap of thunder, tires screeched down the aisle, ripping through the silence. Daniel dropped the black notebook and looked around wildly, but his field of vision was blocked by racks of clothing. An engine revved. What the hell? How could a car get into the department store? It sounded so *real.*

Daniel raced across the floor, feeling hangers whack him in the shoulders. He emerged from the clothing, standing in the aisle across from a shoe display. The engine revved again, but this time it was closer. A large flash of red streaked around the far corner.

Daniel doubted there was actually a ghost, but he couldn't ignore something as weird as this. If he didn't investigate, Mr. Oliver would fire him before his first shift was over. He pictured the glass bowl of paper bets and knew he had no choice.

He heard the distinctive catch of the steel gate being closed, but when Daniel reached the elevator, the shaft was an empty black void except for the dangling greasy cables. He watched the golden arrow slowly move up and then stop at the number three.

"Gotcha," he said. Daniel sprinted up the spiral steps of the grand staircase with one hand grabbing the brass handrail and

NIGHT SHIFT

the other holding the flashlight. He reached the landing on the third floor and crossed the threshold into the Toy department.

Zigzagging through pyramids of stuffed teddy bears, he finally reached the elevator, but the gate was pulled back, and the compartment was empty. He stepped inside and hit the G button. Mr. Oliver had asked him to report anything strange, and this definitely qualified.

"What is it?" Mr. Oliver asked, not even looking up from his crossword puzzle.

Daniel stood in the doorway of the security office, still red faced from his exercise, at once feeling very stupid. How could he describe what had just happened without sounding like a scared idiot? "I heard a noise," he said.

"Mm-hmm." Mr. Oliver made slow, deliberate motions with the pen.

"It sounded like..." his eyes fell on the glass bowl full of paper bets—he had to make it to six hours.

"It sounded like what?"

"Like...nothing," he hung his head. "It was probably nothing."

"Daniel," Mr. Oliver sighed, putting down the pen. "I need to ask you something important."

"Okay."

"What's the capital of Uzbekistan?"

"Huh?"

"It's the last clue I need," he said, pointing at the paper.

Daniel looked around the office, still wondering if there was a hidden camera. Mr. Oliver was the strangest old guy he's ever met. "How am I supposed to know that?"

"High school dropout," Mr. Oliver grumbled, already studying the puzzle again. "Willard's is old," he lectured. "Lots of things make noises at night. But there is one thing that works perfectly—the espresso machine. Next time you give me a report, bring me a cup."

Daniel fought the urge to give him a mock salute. He trudged back to the elevator, punched the four button, and then peeled off his sweatshirt, letting it drop to the floor of the elevator. He had no desire to carry around his stinky sweatshirt.

25

It's not like anyone else is in the store to steal it, he reasoned. His white T-shirt stuck to his sweaty back. "Willard's is very old," he mimicked. "Just like you, you old fart."

The bell dinged and Daniel pulled open the steel gate. Golden letters along the top of the archway spelled out *The Matinee Room*. He felt along the wall and flicked on a switch. Dozens of chandeliers glowed, bringing the art deco–inspired restaurant to life. A black-tiled floor contrasted with the crystal-embedded ceiling, while circular booths with blue velvet cushions took up the vast floor space.

Along one wall, a blue curtain fringed with golden tassels covered the floor-to-ceiling window, reminding Daniel of a theatre. Framed posters of vintage movies completed the look.

Daniel played with the dimmer switch before noticing a piano at the back of the room. Forgetting about the espresso machine, he walked between the round booths, eyeballing the instrument. He wasn't sure if it was real or just a display. He easily imagined some of the smaller booths in the middle pushed to the side, making room for a dance floor. The restaurant certainly had a cocktail hour kind of vibe.

Above the piano, a movie poster caught his eye: *One Touch of Venus,* starring Ava Gardner. Daniel ran his fingers along the top of the keys. He hadn't played for years. After his mother died, the songs sounded bitter, and his father would walk out of the room, stifling a sob. Daniel learned that letting go of the music was easier than hearing his father break down behind the bedroom door.

He closed his eyes and imagined his mother's lilting voice, making a request. Daniel placed the flashlight on the piano and tried a few bars of her favourite jazz piece. It sounded horrible; he was way out of practice.

Balling his hands into fists, he turned toward the elevator— the empty elevator. A breath caught in his throat: the sweatshirt he'd thrown in the corner earlier was gone.

He cut a path around the booths and pushed through the swinging kitchen door. The industrial-sized appliances and long stainless counters were clean and uncluttered, but the orderly room did nothing to ease his panic. He paced back and forth,

NIGHT SHIFT

and then reached into his pocket for the keychain. "Are there ghosts inside Willard's?" he whispered.

*Very doubtful.*

Daniel's breathing slowed down. He twirled the keychain around his finger a few times, trying to think clearly. It must be those day-shift jerks, he reasoned. He looked at his digital watch—they only had four hours left to scare him into quitting. Daniel cracked his knuckles and summoned some of his bravado from his hockey days. Bring it on, he challenged.

Strutting back to the piano, he grabbed the flashlight, trying to guess what their next trick would be. He was halfway to the elevator when the lights went out. He worked the flashlight switch, and then jiggled it up and down, but it didn't work. "Shit," he whispered.

Without warning, loud piano music cut through the silence and filled the empty room. Daniel's heart threatened to explode. Someone or some*thing* was playing his mother's favourite song—the piece he'd tried to play. He tossed the useless flashlight and ran to the elevator straight ahead.

Daniel's outstretched hands made contact with the iron mesh. His fingers grabbed the edge of the gate as he swung into the blackness. But his feet never landed on the elevator floor. His legs just brushed against the greasy cables where the elevator should have been.

# CHAPTER FOUR

Daniel ran through the air, frantically scissoring his legs, trying to get a foothold. In the pitch black his knuckles were being crushed by the folds of the gate. Finger by finger, his hands were becoming numb. *This is it*, he thought, blindly dangling by one hand, *after everything I've gone through, I'm going to die here, all alone*. His consciousness began to ebb, and his breathing slowed down. Soon, everything relaxed—even his grip.

"Hold on!" a girl screamed. Fingers wrapped around his wrist. Daniel jerked back to life from her touch and started flailing his legs again. "Give me your other hand," she demanded. Invisible fingers guided his hand to a bar. He grabbed hold and was able to bring his other hand over. "Move your foot to the left…yes, there. Now a little higher."

Daniel did as he was instructed, finding tiny ledges in the blackness. Her breath washed over his face as wisps of her hair brushed his cheeks.

"Damn it!" she said. Something bounced painfully off Daniel's forehead. Seconds later, it hit the bottom of the elevator shaft; his stomach lurched at the calculations. Her grip loosened and tightened a few times, and then she let go of him completely.

"Wait," he panicked. "Don't leave me!"

He heard her run away. There was a pause, then light from the chandeliers washed down the elevator shaft. Daniel saw how far the drop was. "Oh shit," he said, pressing his cheek against the cold steel, unable to move his head enough to find

NIGHT SHIFT

the next foothold.

The sound of rushed footsteps grew louder as she returned. "Look down, just a bit," she said in a shaky voice. "Use the ledge to the left."

Daniel kept his gaze focused and stretched his leg out to the side. They struggled together for every inch. Pale fingers grabbed him by the shoulders and gave one final pull. They spilled onto the floor, tangled together with the smell of grease around them.

Daniel stared at the crystal-embedded ceiling, waiting for his heart to stop smashing against his chest. She rolled away from his side, but stayed close enough that he could hear her short breaths.

He pushed himself up on his elbows and took a better look at his rescuer. She was sitting now against the wall, hugging her knees, staring back at him. Her hair fell around her shoulders in long dark waves.

Daniel got to his feet. "Um, thanks. You've got great timing," he laughed nervously, and took a few steps closer. She slid away from him, staying crouched on the floor. Daniel looked down and realized he was covered in grease. "Sorry," he said, backing up. "I'll wash some of this stuff off." Her silent stare was starting to freak him out. He gave her one last glance, then went into the kitchen and straight to the sink.

He kept his hands under the stream of water. Angry red ridges from the iron mesh marked his fingers. When his hands and arms were finally clean, he turned around. She was standing at the doorway, watching him.

He jumped a bit, startled by her sudden appearance. "Hey, are you okay?" he asked, hoping he sounded calm and in control. This time she nodded. "If you hadn't come along…" He paused and shifted his weight. "I mean, I thought it was only me and Mr. Oliver here tonight, and there was no way—"

"You're new."

Her interruption stumped him. Daniel noticed her white T-shirt was smudged on the shoulders where he must have clung to her. Over top she wore a tight black tuxedo vest. His eyes trailed down her skinny jeans until they disappeared into pink

29

high tops. He was immediately aware of how scuffed his dad's loafers were, and how greasy he felt. He took a step back and crossed his arms in front of his chest. "It's my first night," he finally said.

"Where's your uniform?"

Daniel was confused by her matter-of-fact tone. Maybe she pulled night guards out of the elevator shaft all the time. "Mr. Oliver forgot," he answered.

Her stare made the hair on the back of his neck stand up, although not in an unpleasant way. She stepped closer. "You look pretty scared for someone who's supposed to be a guard."

*Talk about a quick recovery*, he thought. Daniel wasn't sure how to answer. She fixed him with a poker face, like she was trying to read his mind. Her gaze was so intense he felt everything get warm.

He took a chance. "You're staring," he flirted, annoyed at how his voice shook a bit.

She looked him up and down and said, "It's not every day I meet a new boy."

"Boy!" He was a little insulted. "I'm almost nineteen."

"Congratulations."

He leaned back, putting more space between them. "Well, where's *your* uniform?"

"I do after-hours inventory," she said. "I don't need one."

Daniel lifted his eyebrows in surprise. "You work night shift too?"

"Obviously."

He took in her outfit again. "How old are you?"

She began to play with one of the buttons on her vest. They locked eyes and Daniel felt like he'd fallen down the elevator shaft after all.

"Is your head sore?" she asked, snapping him out of his daze. Clearly he was the only one swooning.

He gave his head a slight shake. "Everything is kind of sore right now," he said. She was so confusing, shy and scared one second, and then shooting him down the next.

She moved around the kitchen, opening drawers and cupboards. He watched her lay a clean dish towel on the

NIGHT SHIFT

counter, then add a small pile of ice from one of the refrigerated units. She pulled up the corners and gave it a quick twirl. "Here," she offered, pushing the ice pack down the counter. "You've got a bump over your eye."

He pressed the cool compress to his forehead. "Er...thanks."

"It's sort of my fault," she admitted. "The night-vision goggles slipped off when I was leaning over."

"Is that what hit me on the head?" he asked, peeking out from under the ice pack.

"Talk about a slice of bad luck. That pair is the display model from the Toy department," she explained. "The strap is pretty stretched."

Daniel began to laugh. "Since you were pulling me back from my death, I guess that's okay." He waited for her to relax, but she didn't even give him a smile. "Hold on," he said. "Why were you wearing night-vision goggles?"

"Why do you think, dummy?" she said. "So I could see in the dark."

*Dummy?*

Never mind the bump on the head—this conversation was giving him an even bigger headache. "How did you know you'd need them?" he asked. She opened her mouth, but he put up a hand, interrupting her. "And don't say it's because the store is haunted."

She practically yawned at his newsflash. He felt stupid for even bringing it up. "The electrical wiring at Willard's is a bit outdated," she said. "Didn't Mr. Oliver tell you that?"

"Yeah, he mentioned something...although he forgot to tell me the piano played itself."

She tilted her head, causing a wave of dark hair to partially fall over one eye. "I was trying to scare you," she reasoned. "I thought you were a burglar."

He looked at her incredulously. "I almost died!"

"Because you ran into an empty elevator shaft, dummy."

Daniel bit the inside of his cheek. Her uppity attitude was more annoying than the bowl full of paper bets. He had to think of a good comeback—he couldn't let her have the last word.

31

She studied the toe of her pink high top, her voice becoming softer. "Sometimes things seem more threatening than they are," she said. "Besides, I wasn't sure of the tune, your playing is off."

"Pardon me," he said. "I didn't know there was an audience."

"You just need practice."

Her advice was hardly encouraging. Daniel took another peek from the corner of his eye and caught her sneaking a glance at the kitchen door. "Waiting for your next victim?" he taunted.

She turned back to him, unscathed by his remark. "Is Mr. Oliver going to have to come up and make his own coffee?" she asked, nodding to a large machine on the counter. "He gets cranky if the guards take too long."

Daniel hated to admit she was right, but the last thing he needed was Mr. Oliver to find him covered in grease with an ice pack on his head, slacking off with a girl. He tossed the soggy towel into the sink and eyed the espresso machine with all its knobs and buttons. He stood in front of the stainless steel monster, feeling the point of her stare burrow into his back.

Her fingers began to drum on the counter. His neck grew hot and prickly, picturing the mad blush he felt rising up from behind the collar of his T-shirt. Finally, she let out an exaggerated sigh. "Give it up, buttercup," she said, motioning for him to step aside. "Watch me."

*Buttercup?*

She turned the dials with efficient speed. Daniel tried to memorize her instructions, but he kept staring at the little crease of concentration between her eyebrows. She held the mug steady and poured a thick, white dollop onto the surface of the caramel-coloured shot. With a small tool, she made quick motions, and a perfect cursive *W* appeared. She slid the mug toward Daniel, then stood back and waited for his reaction.

Compared to all the coffees he'd been drinking out of Styrofoam cups over the last few months, this was the best coffee in the world. "Wow," he said, taking a second sip.

"It's all in the tamping," she shrugged. "Now, your turn."

NIGHT SHIFT

The counter was soon sprinkled with coffee grounds and milk rings from Daniel's attempts. "It just takes practice," she said, dumping his latest failure.

"That seems to be frequent advice from you," he mumbled, discouraged at his lack of finesse with the machine—and with his flirting skills. He couldn't get her to smile, not even a tiny one. Her cold demeanour was downright spooky.

"It's true," she said, wiping the counter. "Repetition improves technique."

"Hmm." He stretched his arms over his head. "How long have you been practicing *your* technique?"

"Awhile." She glanced at the clock on the wall. "One more try, okay?"

Daniel made another coffee and held it out for inspection. She crinkled her nose and said, "Not bad."

He smiled, but then tried to shrug it off, wishing her simple compliment hadn't made him feel so pleased. She held out the small tool and gave him an encouraging look. He attempted a few wisps, trying to imitate her style.

"An amoeba," she said. "Original."

Daniel could almost hear a smile in her voice. He decided to try one last time and held out his hand. "By the way," he said, "I'm Daniel, the new night guard, not a burglar." He paused, and then gave her a sincere smile. "Or a ghost."

She reached out, only touching him for a second. "Nice to meet you…Daniel." She stepped backward, rubbing her arms. "This has been a real scream," she stammered. "But I've got to get back to work." She bumped into the counter, then turned and stumbled out of the kitchen.

He stared at the swinging door for a couple of beats, and then jogged after her. She quickly weaved a path through the booths. He picked up his flashlight, still lying on the floor, and joined her at the elevator. Her rushed exit made him nervous. He groped for any topic. "So, you do after-hours inventory, huh?" he asked.

"And rescue boys from untimely deaths." She pushed the button, calling the elevator from the ground floor. She wrung her hands, and then pressed the button again.

"I'm almost nine—"

"*Almost* nineteen," she finished. "I remember, Danny Boy."

He chose to ignore the nickname. "Mr. Oliver didn't mention anyone else would be working."

"Willard's is huge. Of course there's more than you and Mr. Oliver working at night. Day shift can't do everything."

As soon as she said this, his question seemed ridiculous to him. "How many others are there? I mean, I don't want to surprise anyone else in the dark, right?" *Or get the crap scared out of me again*, he thought to himself.

"The others?" Her cheeks brightened. "Oh, you'll probably meet them later, but we're all so busy, we mostly keep to ourselves."

When the elevator arrived, she hopped on without hesitating. "Coming?" she asked, holding the gate back.

Daniel made himself follow her. She swung the gate closed and pressed one of the buttons. He flexed his fingers—they still felt stiff. She cleared her throat, and tucked a wave of dark hair behind her ear. "Eighteen," she finally said.

"What?"

"I'm eighteen years old."

"Oh," he said. She didn't talk and act like most girls his age. He wondered what Monique would've done if she had found him covered in grease. Then another thought occurred to him. "What about school?" he asked, secretly hoping he wasn't the only one not enrolled in some kind of classes—at least they might have that in common.

"I'm homeschooled," she said.

"Homeschooled?"

"I'm very smart, ask me anything," she said.

Daniel had been a voracious reader, easily getting through every classic novel for English assignments. But once he'd started travelling, it didn't take long to grow sick of airport paperbacks. Eventually he'd given up books altogether.

He stood in the creaky elevator, trying to remember a question from his last exam. She tapped her foot impatiently, but he was determined to ask her something she'd have no clue about. He gave her a smug look. "Okay," he said. "What's the

34

NIGHT SHIFT

capital of Uzbekistan?"

Her forehead bunched up as she twirled a strand of hair around her finger. He was so intent on watching her, he didn't realize the elevator had stopped.

"Tashkent," she answered.

*"Gesundheit."*

"No," she said. "The capital of Uzbekistan—it's Tashkent."

He had no idea if that was the right answer, but she seemed so sure. He stared at the tiny blue *W*'s on the wall. "Yeah, of course. Good job," he mumbled.

She pulled back the gate and stepped out onto the first floor. "This is me," she said.

The elevator immediately felt empty and cold. Daniel moved forward and held back the gate. "So, will I see you again tonight?"

"Nope," she said. "I'll be too busy."

"Oh." An uncomfortable heaviness settled in his chest, and he wondered if he'd pulled a muscle. "Well, are you working tomorrow night?"

She pressed her lips together in a way that gave Daniel the feeling she was fighting a grin. "Let's just say, I'll keep an eye out for you," she answered.

Daniel guessed he wouldn't get more of an answer than that. Reluctantly, he latched the gate and pushed the G button. With a lurch, the elevator started to descend. "I guess this is goodnight, then?" he called out.

She linked her fingers through the gate. "Say goodnight, Danny Boy."

"Goodnight, Danny Boy," he echoed back.

Her face lit up and she laughed, smiling down at him through the diamond patterns. Daniel could only stare back, drinking up the image, watching until she disappeared from sight.

# CHAPTER FIVE

The crowd pressed in close. Daniel pushed ahead, squirming a path through legs and long coats. When he reached the glass, his small, three-year-old reflection blinked back at him. Then his eyes adjusted to the lights and the magnificent diorama came into focus.

His breath fogged the window as he greedily took in the whole display; he'd never seen a train set so elaborate. The ache to touch it was overwhelming. His fingers pressed against the cold glass, leaving prints.

She squeezed his hand, letting him know it was time to move on, and then crouched down, putting her face close to his. "We can't go inside," she said, her blue eyes sad and red-rimmed.

He stomped his foot and pulled away. All he wanted was to touch the train and watch steam come out of its tiny engine. The door was so close. His splayed fingers reached for the curly "V" on the shiny handle. Shoppers pushed their way outside, making him stumble back. She called his name, but he ignored her, and ran into the store.

Suddenly, he was in a flurry of strangers. He looked up at the faces rushing past, but she was not there, he was all alone. He took off his mitten, and started to suck the tip of his thumb. She screamed his name from the sidewalk, just outside the store. She looked as terrified as he felt.

He ran back outside and into her arms as she bent down and hugged him closer. He nestled his face into her hair, breathing in her perfume. She ran her fingers through his hair, calming

NIGHT SHIFT

him. He told her they should see the train together, but she shook her head.

"Not today, pet," she soothed. He started to fuss, but she held up a finger. "You must always remember, Daniel, even when things seem unfair and very sad, the world is full of magic and beautiful things. But how you see the world depends on which side of the glass you're looking from."

Daniel wanted to ask her a thousand questions, but he couldn't make his mouth work. The memory faded into a haze, leaving him alone on the sidewalk, now wearing his pea coat and scuffed up loafers.

"Danny Boy!"

He ran back inside and stopped by the twinkling golden tree. She was at the base of the grand staircase, near the back of the store. Her dark wavy hair swirled as she turned and began to run up the steps.

"Hey," he called out. When he reached the bottom, she had already rounded the corner to the first landing. Daniel began to sprint, running in an unending upward spiral. Without warning the steps disappeared, and then he fell through the darkness, arms and legs flailing.

He clutched the bed sheets and sucked in a huge gulp of air as if he'd been holding his breath. He looked at the alarm clock on the hotel's bedside table—it was three in the afternoon. He'd been asleep since he'd left work that morning.

Swinging his legs over the side of the bed, he bent forward, resting his head in his hands. He'd dreamt about his mother before, but never so vividly. He breathed deeply, convinced he could still smell her perfume.

His backpack lay in a heap at the end of the bed. He pulled it over and rummaged down to the compartment close to the bottom. Carefully folded and dry in a plastic bag were several white handkerchiefs. His father had always carried one.

"If it weren't for handkerchiefs," his father once told him, "I wouldn't have met your mom."

Daniel sat on the hotel bed wishing for that moment back. Instead of brushing off his dad, he would have asked to hear the story about how his parents met. Years later, after the accident,

37

Daniel would lie awake at night, making a list of all the things he never knew about his mother—even trivial things that never occurred to him. What was her favourite movie? Favourite colour? Favourite food? Did she like milk or sugar in her coffee? And what *was* the name of her favourite perfume?

He never asked his father these questions—it was too painful and the words felt clumsy in his mouth. As the routines of school and work gave a semblance of normality, Daniel quietly filed each one away, waiting for when his dad was ready to talk. But that time never came.

Daniel picked up a handkerchief and ran a finger over his father's embroidered initial. It was something tangible that reminded him he had once belonged to a family.

With the dream still fresh in his mind, he crossed the room and picked up the pair of jeans thrown over the wing-back chair—he wanted to write down everything. His fingers slipped into the back pocket, but the little black notebook wasn't there. He patted all the pockets and even searched his backpack, but the notebook was gone.

He groaned, remembering he'd left it on the cashier's counter last night when he chased after the phantom car. Panic started to rise in his chest, but there was nothing he could do until he got to work. Everything important he'd thought or wondered about the last few months was written inside that notebook. He prayed it was tucked under the counter and hadn't been read by a bored clerk. The only comfort was that his name wasn't inside.

He unplugged his iPhone from the charger and checked for messages. There was a text from Alice.

?RU

Alice was like her messages: short and to the point. Daniel had never seen her in court, but he imagined the advantage she had, at least until the other lawyer figured out that the petite woman sitting at the other desk was really a bulldog in disguise. More than once he'd witnessed her tear apart an intern for misfiling a document that she'd spent half the morning looking for.

As a frequent guest at his parents' table for Sunday dinners,

NIGHT SHIFT

she had loved to debate any topic. Daniel's father usually surrendered, good-natured but exhausted, by the bottom of the second bottle of wine. Alice was his parents' close friend first, and their lawyer second.

He hadn't seen her for months, but they kept in touch as he zigzagged across the map. After his dad's funeral, Alice's den had become his bedroom. He knew it wouldn't last long, though. When Alice had finalized Daniel's inheritance, he left high school and bought his first plane ticket.

She didn't protest too much. Alice reasoned he knew how to avoid trouble, and that he was entitled to grieve in his own way. For Daniel, however, it wasn't about grieving—it was about a quest. He'd spent the last few months searching the country, but he hadn't anticipated the loneliness. Travelling, he'd learned, loses its novelty, especially when you're by yourself, and there's no home waiting for your return.

He texted a short reply telling Alice where he was, and that he'd found a job. He cringed, knowing she would remind him again about finishing school, but that was on the bottom of his list. He opened the drapes and stood in his boxers, looking in the direction of Willard's. Buildings blocked it from view, but he knew it was there, waiting for his shift tonight. Hopefully his notebook would be too.

After a shower and shave, he changed into jeans and rolled up the sleeves of his fitted plaid shirt, keeping it untucked. He gave himself a critical look in the mirror. He could probably do with a haircut. Alice would certainly agree.

*Straight up. No kidding, kid.*

He checked his watch, wanting to be early for his shift, then he grabbed his pea coat and backpack.

The route to Willard's was dotted with street vendors. Washing down his bagel and cream cheese with a second cup of coffee, Daniel rounded the last corner, but then stopped short. A crowd huddled on the sidewalk in front of the store, stamping their feet to keep warm. There was a TV crew with a reporter. Feeling anxious, Daniel picked up his pace.

"This is Nancy Garner for Channel 3 News," the young woman began, her breath coming out like puffs of steam. "I'm

live from the front of Willard's, one of the oldest department stores in the city. This historic building nestled among the more contemporary businesses of the West Side is lovingly described as a true gem of Manhattan. The new spring window display was revealed earlier today, and it's everything we've come to expect from this retail treasure renowned for its opulent displays and luxurious styles. This year, in honour of Hans Christian Andersen's birthday, April 2nd, the depictions are from some of his most beloved stories."

Daniel couldn't believe a news crew was here for a window display. A few shoppers were taking pictures, and someone even had a camera set up on a tripod. He half listened to the reporter as he craned his neck to see over the crowd.

*The Little Mermaid* was on a blanket of sand and pebbles, looking down at the nearly drowned prince. The silver hair cascaded down her back, adorned with starfish and shells, while her iridescent tail curled elegantly on the beach.

In the next window, a large sparrow was suspended in midair by invisible twine, and upon its back, riding sidesaddle like a queen, was a beautiful girl.

"Thumbelina," Daniel whispered.

He felt a nudge and watched as a little kid wiggled by, pushing his face up to the glass. The last window depicted a child's playroom. A full sized tin soldier brightly painted in red and blue, stood on his one leg—his gaze pointed directly to an elaborate paper ballerina placed in the middle of the toy shelf. She wore a dress of clear muslin with a narrow blue ribbon decorated with a tinsel rose. A special light danced on the dress making her seem real.

Daniel noticed the little boy was very quiet.

"It's *The Steadfast Tin Soldier*, sweetheart," his mother said, studying his concerned expression. "Look, he's in love with the ballerina."

Out of the corner of his eye, he saw the young mother take her son by the hand, promising a visit to the Confectionery, and then if he was good, a trip to the Toy department. Daniel blinked a few times, feeling his chest tighten.

Clutching his coat, he made his way to the front entrance,

NIGHT SHIFT

where warm, soft light from the store spilled out onto the sidewalk. He walked by the reporter, finally wrapping up her segment. The running commentary didn't interest him, but her last words stuck inside his head, and echoed there for the rest of the night.

"These displays represent everything the store strives to achieve in its commitment to offering a unique and theatrical shopping experience." She gave the camera a big toothy smile. "Ask anyone and they'll tell you, Willard's is a special place full of magic and beautiful things."

# CHAPTER SIX

Daniel straightened the royal blue tie and studied his image, taking in the dark blue pants paired with a light blue shirt. He looked like some kind of junior achiever ready to accept an award for most promising young entrepreneur—definitely not his kind of award. The dress shoes, the only stylish part of the outfit, he'd bought in Menswear.

He mostly spent money on travel fare, hotels, and meals. Besides, living out of his backpack meant never wearing anything that had to be ironed. As he looked down, admiring his black Tom Ford lace ups, Daniel had a feeling that might change. After slipping one of the handkerchiefs into his pocket, he shoved his backpack and coat into his assigned locker.

Earlier, he'd rushed to Ladies' Fashions trying to locate the cashier's station where he was sure he'd left his notebook. He was met by a stern looking clerk, who wore her glasses on the end of her nose.

"No," she'd said, slightly turning her profile to him. "I haven't seen any notebook by that description in this work area." Then she gave him a quick dismissal, putting her attention on a customer waiting for a fitting room.

Now in his uniform, Daniel had to simply wait until the staff left for the day before giving the first floor a thorough search. He left the locker room with an uneasy anxiety settling between his shoulder blades.

The staff lounge had a kitchen and a large common area with leather seating. A large-screen TV was flanked by bookshelves. Daniel walked through, getting a few polite nods,

NIGHT SHIFT

mostly from the female staff. He recognized a pixie hairstyle and saw that Stacey was by herself, busy with her cell phone.

The security office door was closed, but Daniel walked in anyway. His shift was due to start, and he was in uniform now, not just a kid hoping to get hired. Two faces looked abruptly in his direction, making him wish he'd waited outside.

Mr. Oliver scowled at Daniel, and then turned his attention back to a portly man in a suit. "You know my opinion, Mr. Hadley," he said.

"Look at Harrods—" the man began, red-faced and talking quickly.

"This store is *not* Harrods," Mr. Oliver interrupted. "Harrods is nearly four times the size of Willard's. My system has been working for years. Nothing needs to be changed because nothing is broken."

"Your system is archaic," Mr. Hadley said. "The insurance company is particularly interested, and as store manager, I'm telling you, we need the proper technology. I've been talking with the shareholders and they all agree—"

"Not *all* of them," Mr. Oliver interrupted. "And as head of security, with over forty years of experience, *I'm* telling *you*, Willard's has all the protection it needs." Mr. Oliver patted his key ring for emphasis.

Mr. Hadley puffed out his chest. He smoothed a hand over his protruding jacket, and then tried, unsuccessfully, to fasten the bottom button. "We'll discuss this later," he said, out of breath as he stomped out of the office. Daniel could tell the store manager was beaten—for now.

Mr. Oliver waited until the door was closed again. "Don't mind him," he said to Daniel, easing himself into the chair behind the desk.

"What happened?"

"Nothing for you to be concerned about." He produced a newspaper from the desk drawer and began to flip through the sections.

Daniel considered Monique's suspicions about Stacey being a thief. "Was something stolen?" he asked.

Mr. Oliver gave Daniel a curious look over the paper.

43

B.R. Myers

"What are you talking about?"

"Well, uh…nothing." His cheeks grew warm. "I guess I just assumed." He felt stupid for blurting out that useless question. He looked away, pretending to be interested in the potted ferns that flanked the small hallway leading off the security office.

Mr. Oliver put down his pen and stood up. "As long as you're here," he said, "I should go over the general circuits with you." He led Daniel past the plants to a door at the end of the hallway. "This little room is the powerhouse of the store. Everything from the lights and the phones right down to the smoke detectors is controlled from here."

But Daniel was no longer listening—he'd stopped halfway down the hall, staring at a wall of historical pictures of Willard's through the decades. The largest was a black-and-white photograph of the store's famous colossal front. An intricate frame of scrolling designs made it push out a few inches from the wall. Daniel read the brass plate on the bottom.

*Willard's Grand Opening, April 1920.*

Mr. Oliver stood beside him. "Do you like history?"

Daniel continued to study the picture. "English was my best subject," he said, squinting closer at all the faces.

"Willard's has a lot of stories to tell," Mr. Oliver said.

"I thought it had a lot of ghosts."

"Who told you that?" His voice was sharp, making Daniel flinch.

"No one," he said. "It's just all the talk about it being haunted." Daniel considered mentioning the bizarre sounds from last night, but one look at his boss's fierce expression made him stay tightlipped.

"Ghosts." Mr. Oliver snorted. "You told me you don't believe in ghosts."

"I don't."

"What *do* you believe in?"

Daniel said the only thing he thought would make Mr. Oliver back off: "Keeping the store safe."

"It's the most important thing," Mr. Oliver said, his eyes growing wider, making him look like wizened elf. "Can I count

44

NIGHT SHIFT

on you?"

Daniel nodded, a little wary of his supervisor's behaviour.

"If you want to keep the store safe," Mr. Oliver continued, pointing to the large picture, "you've got to know all about her." A bony finger circled the large crowd of smartly dressed people in the front. "Now, that fella right there," he said, zeroing in on a handsome man in the middle wearing a bowler hat, "that's James D. Willard himself. He was only in his early twenties, and had inherited a shipping business and huge fortune from his father." Mr. Oliver put a finger to his chin. "I guess the lad got tired of travelling to all those exotic locations, so he bought the building, and after two years of renovations, turned it into a department store."

"It wasn't always a store?" Daniel asked, studying the image of the young entrepreneur.

"No," Mr. Oliver said. "It used to be a theatre. Not the movie kind," he clarified, reading Daniel's expression. "It was live theatre. Ever hear of vaudeville?"

"Like clowns and sword swallowers?" he said, still staring at the faces in the picture.

"Close enough," Mr. Oliver sighed. "There was usually one regular act, the big crowd pleaser that would guarantee high attendance, and other, smaller acts," he said, giving Daniel a rare grin. "Like clowns and sword swallowers, to warm up the audience."

"What was the big act?"

"It varied over the years, but the last one, before Mr. Willard came along, was a magician."

Daniel felt everything slow down—even time. "A magician," he repeated.

"Not a very good one, though."

"No?" He peeled his eyes away from the picture and looked at Mr. Oliver.

"A terrible accident happened on stage one night and the theatre closed down. The bank was foreclosing on the building." He paused and touched the golden *W* on his tie clip. "Who knows what would be here now? A parking garage? An office building full of those stupid half-walled cubicles? Depressing,"

45

he grumbled. "But, at the last moment, Mr. Willard made the bank an offer. And the rest, as they say—"

"Is history," Daniel finished.

Mr. Oliver dropped his chin, satisfied the lesson was over. Forgetting about the electrical room, he returned to the desk, where the newspaper was waiting for him.

When Daniel brushed by the potted ferns again, Mr. Oliver had already begun the crossword. The monitors were quiet; each one had been turned off except for the main doors. Daniel watched as several clerks buttoned up their coats. "Here." Mr. Oliver pushed a silver key across the desk. "The staff are eager to end their shift."

Daniel left the office and walked toward the main foyer. As he neared the group, each head turned his way. One familiar face pushed to the front.

"Well, well, well," Monique sang. "Look who survived the first night." She smiled, tossing her hair.

"Barely," he said. Daniel was hyper-conscious of the giggles and stares. He walked across the white marble tile to the front entrance, his new squeaky shoes filling the greedy silence. He held the door open as the clerks brushed by in twos and threes.

Monique waited near the back. "Guess I'm the last," she said, joining him at the door. Before Daniel could be flattered by her undivided attention, the real reason for her lagging behind was soon apparent.

There was a slight pout, then she batted her eyes at him. "I'm sorry about dumping all that stuff about Stacey yesterday. You just started, and the last thing you need to worry about is helping me. Maybe I should bring it up with Mr. Oliver." She hesitated and looked down the aisle as if the head of security would materialize for her. This was followed by a long sigh. "Who am I kidding?" she mumbled. "Stacey didn't steal from the store, she stole from me—security wouldn't care about that. Mr. Oliver doesn't even know who I am, even though I've worked here part-time since I was sixteen."

Daniel asked, "What did she steal?"

Monique dropped her gaze and fussed with a scarf around

NIGHT SHIFT

her neck as if reconsidering her choice in asking him for assistance. "It was a pretty gold medallion," she said. "A family heirloom. It went missing last week while we were both working in Ladies' Footwear. I never take it off! But at the end of the day when I was closing the cash register, I realized it was gone. I searched everywhere, but all I found was the chain on the floor behind the cashier's desk. Only Stacey and I were working behind the counter that day." She let the pause grow, and then added, "Interesting, don't you think?"

Daniel couldn't imagine where to start searching. He tried to picture the petite and clumsy Stacey stealing something from right under Monique's nose, but it seemed so far-fetched.

Monique studied him for a moment, then the corner of her mouth curled up. "Do you like my new lipstick?"

He cleared his throat. "Who wouldn't?"

"You're the one who picked it out," she laughed. "Don't you remember? It's called *Red-E-Or-Not.* Wouldn't that be a great job? Coming up with names for lipsticks all day! But this gig is pretty sweet too. There are the chocolate samples, the exclusive makeup lines…"

Daniel nodded as the monologue continued. He shifted his weight a few times, waiting for a break or at least for her to take a breath. He glanced outside. A few clerks were waiting in a huddle. One turned and waved at Monique to hurry up.

"I gotta go," she said. "Look, I don't think there's anything you can do to help me; it's her word against mine. You seem really nice, and you shouldn't get mixed up in something that isn't even your problem."

He could feel her helplessness. "I can at least look around tonight," he offered.

"Yeah?" Monique smiled. "Handsome *and* sweet, aren't you the total package." She stared up at him through thickly mascaraed eyelashes. He recognized that look; it was the one every girl gave him in school after he'd scored the overtime goal in the state championships. But he hadn't played hockey for over a year, and since then, the only looks he'd gotten were full of pity.

She asked, "I'll see you tomorrow morning, then?"

47

Daniel gave her a quizzical look. "I thought you said this was your after-school job."

"Tomorrow's Saturday, silly." She stood on tiptoe and kissed him on the cheek. "Have a good shift."

He watched Monique and her friends hurry through the cool night to the subway station. *Red-E-Or-Not*, he thought, feeling completely out of his league.

# CHAPTER SEVEN

By the time he passed the key back to Mr. Oliver, Daniel had cleared his head somewhat. Monique was proving to be a constant source of ego inflation for him.

Mr. Oliver grumbled something and handed over the flashlight. "Be back in an hour," he ordered.

Daniel ran up the steps to Ladies' Fashions. After several rounds of searching under the counters of every cashier's station, he was convinced the notebook was gone for good. Dragging his feet up the grand staircase to the second-floor landing, he crossed into Home Furnishings, and began searching all the cashier stations on this floor. He was momentarily distracted by a massive TV and leather recliners set up as a home theatre. A remote control was balanced on the armrest of an overstuffed couch, and he wondered how many channels the store got.

With a sulk, he looked at the remote longingly, then crouched down to look for his notebook behind the counter.

Muted conversation floated toward him. Daniel realized he'd forgotten to ask Mr. Oliver how many other night-shift workers there were besides the girl he'd met last night. Wondering if it was her, he suddenly felt self-conscious of his scruffy hair and nerdy uniform.

Daniel stayed hidden and peeked over the counter. The girl was pretty with blond curly hair. She was walking up the aisle and reading a book at the same time. A guy in jeans and a T-shirt was keeping in step with her. Definitely his age, Daniel thought, or maybe a year or two older. They came closer and

entered the home theatre.

"I can't believe Oscar agreed to meet this Daniel person," the girl said, her attention still on the book in her hands.

The guy rolled his eyes. "Oscar's humouring her. She's so desperate she's invented this Romeo to come save her. You heard her last night. You'd think friggin' Prince Charming dropped in for a visit."

"Worried about a little competition?" she teased.

He flopped on the leather couch and folded his hands behind his head. "Hardly," he said, flashing a confident smile. "Besides, he doesn't exist, so what does it matter?"

Daniel ducked back down. *Were they talking about the girl who rescued him last night?* He guessed they must be the other inventory staff she'd mentioned. But why the hell would they think he didn't exist? And who was Oscar?

He peeked over the counter again and saw the girl move the remote to the leather ottoman, just out of the guy's reach. "It would be exciting, though," she said, almost hesitant.

"Exciting is not the word I'd use," he said. There was something in his voice that put Daniel on edge. The girl opened the book again, but Daniel could tell she was only staring blankly, pretending to read.

The silence stretched like an elastic band, growing taut, straining the air between them. Daniel was trapped, certain even the slightest movement in his new squeaky shoes would give him away. He looked to his left and calculated whether it was possible to sneak behind the overstuffed chair, and then eventually escape to the aisle.

He'd need one hell of a distraction.

The girl plopped down beside the guy, her lips making a tight, straight line. Daniel squirmed in the shadows, sensing an argument.

The guy leaned forward with a playful look upon his face, "All right," he said in a gruff accent. "You're gonna need a bigger boat."

She replied by turning a page.

The guy tried again. "If you're good at something, never do it for free."

NIGHT SHIFT

Daniel frowned. He'd seen *The Dark Knight* four times, but quoting movie lines was the last thing he'd do to impress a girl. Then he wondered, *When do they do any work?*

The girl snapped the book shut so quickly it made both Daniel and the guy jump at the same time. "Don't you get it?" she accused. "This might be what we've been waiting for, and all you can do is joke and talk about stupid movies."

The guy held his palms up as if surrendering. "Babe, I wish it was true."

"Sometimes I think you'd rather everything stay the way it's always been."

The guy was quiet, his Adam's apple moving up and down a few times. "And you wouldn't?" he asked, sounding hurt.

Daniel's stomach flipped. He was stuck in his extra-squeaky shoes, crouched behind a counter, wishing he'd stood up when they first came over.

The couple slouched into the leather furniture, both looking defeated. She was the one who broke the silence. "What *do* you want?" she asked.

He reached for her and she drew close, tucking into his chest. His fingers played with a golden curl. The guy closed his eyes and Daniel could tell he was fighting the answer. "I want whatever you want," he said.

She looked up at him, beaming with hope. "*Jaws,*" she smiled, "and *The Dark Knight.*"

He laughed weakly, and then leaned down and kissed her.

Daniel was unable to turn away. *No way,* he thought as the making out intensified, and a T-shirt got pulled off. *There's no way they're really going to...actually.*

The voyeuristic curiosity was overriding the guilt. They didn't break apart, and the promise of a home theatre with a million movie channels became a distant idea as Daniel realized the real show was about to start right in front of him.

He looked down at the toe of his new Tom Fords. *Hello, pervert,* they shone back up.

There was a muffled giggle followed by a moan. Daniel looked to his left; if he needed a distraction, this was his best opportunity. He crawled forward, wincing with every squeak of

his shoe, expecting the boyfriend to pick him up by the back of the hair, ready to beat the crap out of him.

With the ninja-like ability of someone desperate to stay hidden, Daniel managed to navigate the home theatre by using the extra-large furniture as cover. Safely out of earshot of the lovers, he ran into the elevator. His heart was pounding like a bass drum. He punched the three button, and wiped a hand over his face. He caught his breath as he closed the gate and replayed the scene with new bitterness.

At one time he'd been on his way to becoming the most popular guy in school. Now he was homeless and getting his thrills from watching a couple of strangers go at it. A familiar detached emptiness came over him; he was going into zombie-mode. No wonder he was perfect for night shift at Willard's, he thought dully; he was a ghost most of the time anyway.

The golden arrow pointed at the three. Daniel walked into the dimly lit Toy department. His hand automatically touched the flashlight dangling from his belt. Brightly coloured kites hung from the sky-blue ceiling, painted with clouds. There was even a whole area devoted to board games, with the floor painted like Scrabble.

A permanent, electric race car track weaved throughout the department. Daniel felt like a kid again, and he wondered if there was a train set on display. He closed his eyes and heard his mother's voice from his dream. "The world is full of magic and beautiful things," he whispered.

He turned the corner, and came to a complete stop. At the other end of the room, beside a *Star Wars* Lego display, was a child-sized, candy-apple-red convertible. A prickly sensation ran down his spine. He pulled out the Magic 8 Ball keychain. "Are there ghosts inside Willard's?"

*Don't count on it.*

Daniel pressed his palm on the hood—it was warm. In a heartbeat the whole department went black. He reached down, but his fingers only felt an empty loop where the flashlight had been.

# CHAPTER EIGHT

Ice water poured into Daniel's veins. He imagined ghoulish fingers inches away, ready to drag him to the elevator shaft, intent on finishing him off for good this time. The faces from the black-and-white picture flashed in his mind, distorted and threatening. The ghost of James D. Willard was roaming the aisles, looking for peeping perverts.

Without warning, he was hit from behind and fell to his knees. Something bounced away. He tried to stand, but not before another blow ricocheted off his head. Daniel put down a hand for balance and touched one of the projectiles. *I'm being assaulted by basketballs,* he thought incredulously. The air rushed by his ear as another ball narrowly missed his head. He turned and lobbed one of the basketballs at his invisible attacker.

"Ow!" a voice called out.

Daniel ran and braced for impact, but he was suddenly airborne. Marbles rolled noisily around him. His elbow whacked down on the tile, but he had also tackled the ghost. Wrestling blindly, he grabbed at a bit of fabric.

"Let me go!" a boy screamed.

Daniel felt him thrash around like a swordfish caught on a line. The lights came on and he stared into the red, scrunched up face of a kid. "Quit it," Daniel said, trying to contain the little offender.

"Get off me!"

"Petey!" A familiar voice shouted. The pair stopped fighting and turned her way.

"You," Daniel said.

She stood in a denim miniskirt, glaring down at them disapprovingly. Her black sweatshirt was off the shoulder. Daniel saw a hint of lace on the white tank top underneath. She tapped her cowboy boot on the floor. "What's going on?" Her tone made them both spring to attention.

Daniel brushed off his pants, trying to fix himself up.

Her gaze fell to the boy. "Petey! I told you to be more careful. Is this your mess?"

"He attacked me!" the boy said, pointing at Daniel.

"He turned off the lights and started throwing basketballs at my head," Daniel said, pleading his case.

"Don't forget about the marbles," the boy added.

Daniel rubbed his elbow and said, "I won't."

"Is that true?" she asked the boy.

"He was touching my car," he said. "He could have broken it!"

She pointed her finger. "First of all, it's not *your* car; it belongs to the store. Second, you can't attack someone in the dark, especially the new night guard. Now clean this up."

He nodded timidly and began to crawl along the floor, gathering up the marbles.

She took a few steps toward Daniel. "You're not going to tell Mr. Oliver, are you?" she asked quietly. "I mean, about Petey being here."

"Oh," Daniel said. He was still recovering from his attack and hadn't thought about how weird it was to find a boy in the Toy department after hours. "So…why *is* he here?"

"His mom lives in my apartment building and works nights. He's only eleven. Sometimes her sitter is sick, so I bring him here with me." She looked up at Daniel hopefully. "He's usually pretty good."

"Uh-huh." He watched Petey walk over to the car then use his T-shirt to shine the hood, wiping off any fingerprints Daniel had left behind. "I guess he likes the car."

"Will you keep our secret?"

"Hmm." Daniel concentrated on smoothing out his tie, stalling, pretending he might turn them in. He liked that she was

NIGHT SHIFT

waiting on him, and that she needed his help. He pursed his lips, then said, "Sure."

She let out a breath and gave him a smile. Daniel's heart sputtered. "Thanks," she said. "And trust me, he won't be any trouble."

"On one condition, though," he said. "Tell me your name."

"Don't tell him, Mary," Petey called out.

She shot Petey a look.

"Mary?" Daniel said. He liked the way it felt on his lips. He said it over and over in his mind.

"Are you all right?" Petey asked him. "You look kind of red and splotchy."

Daniel snapped back, "Probably a concussion from your little marble experiment."

"You shouldn't run in the dark," Petey replied. "It's dangerous."

Mary said, "I'd think a drop down the elevator shaft would make you more cautious." The sarcasm was hard to miss.

"I had my flashlight," Daniel said, touching the empty loop on his belt as if to confirm his story. "But I must have lost it."

Mary stared accusingly at Petey. "Come on, give it up."

Petey's shoulders drooped, then he reached behind his back and handed over the flashlight. "Sorry," he mumbled.

"You picked it from my belt? Impressive technique," Daniel said. "I didn't feel you at all."

Petey and Mary shared a glance. "He has to be extra sneaky," she said. "You know, trying to stay hidden from Mr. Oliver and everything."

"Don't worry," Daniel reassured her. "I'll keep your secret, but what about the others? There was a couple on the second floor tonight. She had curly blond hair, and the guy was tall."

"That's Ruth Ann and Jonathan," Petey said. "They're cool with me."

"You met them?" Mary asked, her face suddenly pale.

His heart started to race again, replaying the image of the two lovers. "Not exactly," he said, avoiding eye contact, taking extra time to put the flashlight back in its holder.

"Did they see you?" she asked.

55

"God, I hope not," he said. "I mean, I'm pretty sure they didn't…um, know I was there. They were across the floor—like, way across."

She looked relieved, and then she gave Daniel a half-smile. "I guess I should warn you," she said, "Ruth Ann is a chronic bookworm."

"With a photographic memory," Petey added, rolling his eyes.

"She likes to quote stuff," Mary explained. "A lot."

"And this is bad?" Daniel asked.

Mary said, "It gets a bit tedious. She loves to read, and feels it's her duty to 'broaden our minds.'" She made air quotes.

Petey grinned. "Jonathan drives her crazy when he plays dumb."

"Only he's not usually *playing* dumb," Mary said, huffing at the end for effect.

Daniel nodded, even more confused than before about the conversation he'd overheard. There was a quiet gap, each of them unsure of what to do next. Daniel wondered if Petey was going to be hanging out with Mary all evening. He surprised himself by coming up with a plan on the spot. "How about a trip to the kitchen?" he suggested to her. "I could use a few more lessons with the espresso machine."

"Excellent," Petey said. "I'm starving. I'll grab my sweater."

"The three of us…great," Daniel said hollowly as Petey disappeared around a display of action figures.

Mary said, "I was going to heat up some leftover spaghetti. You can join us, if you want."

Daniel wanted that very much. His disappointment at having to help babysit was suddenly lifted by her invitation.

They jostled inside the elevator, with Petey staying near the edge, clumsily pulling a sweater over his head with one hand. Daniel sensed he was still sore about the car, and was purposely giving Daniel more than enough room, either out of spite or suspicion. He turned his attention to Mary, admiring the black sweatshirt again. "Hey," he squinted. "Is that mine?"

"I found it in the elevator last night," she said. "Crumpled

NIGHT SHIFT

up in the corner."

"Because I threw it there!"

"No wonder, it was filthy." Mary was unapologetic. "I had to wash it twice."

He pointed to her bare shoulder. "And cut the neck out?" he asked.

The muscles in her jaw clenched. "Here, then," she said, pulling it over her head, and flinging it at him. "You can have it back."

He stood, clutching the sweatshirt to his chest, staring back at her. "Well," he said, "you're also wearing my tank top. Can I have that back now too?" As soon as the words were out, he regretted them. Mary looked ready to spit nails. Daniel felt stupid for even trying to flirt with her; he bet Monique would have laughed if he'd tried the joke on her.

Petey rolled his eyes. "Can we get going already?" he asked. "I'm starving." He pulled the gate with one hand, but it didn't move. He tugged a few more times, grunting with the effort.

"Let me help," Daniel offered. Draping the sweatshirt over his shoulder, he gave the gate a strong pull. It wasn't stuck like he assumed and it whipped across, latching loudly.

Petey screamed as blood spurted from his arm. On the other side of the gate, his hand hung limply. Daniel frantically yanked on the handle, but it was locked tight.

Petey continued to scream as tears streamed down his face. Daniel pressed the sweatshirt against the meaty wrist wound, but Petey continued to struggle. He watched in horror as Petey jerked out of his grasp and landed on the elevator floor—holding a bloody stump where his hand used to be.

# CHAPTER NINE

An arc of red splatters peppered the pattern of blue *W*'s on the elevator wall. Petey was pale and unmoving. Daniel let out a garbled scream. "Call 911," he said to Mary, tossing her his cell phone. He then dropped to his knees, trying to press the sweatshirt against the pulpy mess. Mary folded her arms across her chest and let out a long sigh.

"Call 911!" he repeated. Then Daniel looked closely at the stump, red liquid trickled out of tiny plastic tubes.

"Dismemberment?" Mary moaned. "That's the third time this month. I'm getting so sick of your practical jokes."

"Practical joke?" Daniel said. He swallowed a few times, trying to coax his stomach back down.

Petey opened his eyes, realizing the joke was done. "I can't help it," he said. "Ruth Ann screams every time, it only encourages me." He pulled out the fake stump and pushed his real arm out the sleeve.

Mary reached through the gate and dislodged the rubber hand. "I can't believe Willard's actually sells these gross things," she said, hitting the four button.

"Are you kidding?" Petey said. "These sold out in just a week! A new shipment came in yesterday." Mary looked like she was about to give him a lecture. "Relax," he explained. "It's just the display model."

Daniel regarded Petey suspiciously, then said, "You seem to know a lot about the inventory of the Toy department."

Mary jumped in before Petey could answer. "Wait until Oscar hears about this," she scolded him.

NIGHT SHIFT

"Who exactly is Oscar?" Daniel asked, still not sure if he might be sick.

"He's *our* supervisor," Mary explained.

"And he's really strict," Petey whispered. "Plus, he can sniff out a lie by looking at you."

Daniel pretended to cough into his fist, convinced his earlier Peeping Tom act was written all over his face. He caught Mary's eye. "He knows about your babysitting situation, I take it?" he asked.

"Who're you calling a baby?" Petey grumbled, clearly insulted.

The elevator came to a stop on the fourth floor. "Anyway," Mary reconciled, "I'm sure he's no worse than Mr. Oliver."

Daniel took little comfort in that information. From Jonathan and Ruth Ann's conversation and what Mary was telling him, Daniel figured Oscar was the head guy who ran the store at night. But if that was true, why hadn't Mr. Oliver mentioned him?

They left the splattered elevator and stepped into The Matinee Room. Mary went ahead with Petey into the kitchen, giving him cleaning instructions.

From the kitchen, a deep voice mingled with Mary's while dishes clinked in the background. Daniel pictured a more crotchety version of Mr. Oliver, growling around the counters and appliances.

The kitchen door swung open. A man stood in the doorway with a plate of steaming spaghetti and meatballs in one hand, and a basket of bread in the other. He was tall and dark, with an athletic build and wearing a dress shirt and slacks, his smooth ebony skin and stylish demeanour the exact opposite of Mr. Oliver. He reminded Daniel of a sophisticated detective on TV—the kind who got paired with a sloppy and crass partner.

Daniel swallowed dryly. Mary and Petey weren't kidding. Oscar's stare was enough to make him sweat. He was sure *PERVERT* was blazed across his forehead in neon letters.

"Why, you're just a kid," Oscar said in a deep, steady voice, sounding more shocked than condescending. He only had time to slightly lift an eyebrow before he got pushed to the side.

59

A woman wearing a red cocktail dress and black stilettos strutted out of the kitchen.

She stood in front of Daniel, sipping a pink martini, her wrist wrapped in strands of pearls. "Look at you," she purred. Her blond hair fell in perfect waves over one shoulder. She walked around him like a lion circling a nervous circus trainer. Daniel imagined dark blue sweat stains spreading under his arms.

"Mary told us there was a new boy working in the store," she said. "But I think Monique and the other silly gossips described you more accurately. You certainly look like you could be the doorman for *Abercrombie & Fitch*."

It sounded like a compliment, but there was an edge to her voice that matched her cold stare. Daniel wished a hole would swallow him up.

But her look had the opposite effect on Mary. She sighed tiredly and motioned her hand in a grand gesture that oozed of cynicism, "This is Blanche," Mary said. "She's in charge of Ladies' Fashions."

Blanche's expression softened. "Don't be silly, doll," she said. "I'm in charge of *everybody's* fashion." She gave Mary a critical up and down, paying particular attention to the boots. "Oh, my nerves! Are you working the rodeo lounge tonight? At least you're wearing a skirt. I can't remember the last time you dressed like a girl."

"Not everyone wants to play dress-up," Mary said. "Besides, it's spaghetti, not caviar and cocktails."

"Baloney," Blanche said. "Armani works for any occasion."

Daniel stood in a fog, trying to recover from the icy introduction. The others rushed around him, getting plates from the kitchen, preparing one of the booths with napkins and cutlery.

Mary slid into the booth and motioned for him to join her. He noticed her bare arms were covered in goose bumps. The guilt prompted him to apologize. "I'm sorry about the tank top joke," he said. The black sweatshirt was lumped under the table, now soggy from Petey's joke. "I'll wash this and give it

NIGHT SHIFT

back...it looks better on you anyway."

Petey was watching them. He laughed and reached for a glass of wine. "It's about time something interesting happened around here."

"Nice try," Oscar said, sweeping the glass away.

Daniel noticed the other wine glasses. "Isn't drinking against the rules or something?"

The clatter of forks and knives stopped, and all heads turned toward Oscar. "Daniel," he said, patting his thin mustache with a linen napkin, "how long have you worked here?"

"This is my second night." His voice went high at the end like he was asking a question.

"Mm-hmm." Oscar nodded. "Well, I've been here longer than two nights." He picked up the bottle and topped off his drink.

Daniel concentrated on taking small bites of dinner. His stomach was in knots. Either Mr. Oliver had concocted an elaborate test to see how easily he would shrug off his duties, or Daniel was surrounded by weirdos. He was beginning to suspect the reason the night guards left was because of the creepy after-hours workers.

"Tell me, Daniel," Blanche said from across the table. "What do you think of the new spring collection in Ladies' Fashions?"

He waited, trying to decide if she was serious; she was the last one he wanted to piss off. "Um...I really don't—"

"You haven't a clue, have you?" Blanche interrupted. "My Maureen would know, she had wonderful taste in clothes and could spot a trend faster than any of the Dumb Doras working here."

"Maureen used to work in Ladies' Fashions," Mary explained. "But she retired a few years ago."

"She may come back!" Blanche said. "Someone that talented doesn't disappear!" She rolled a meatball around her plate, and her voice became melancholy. "We made such a great team, our displays always got attention." She took another sip of her martini. "Now I'm forced to stick it out in Sleepwear

surrounded by flannel pajamas with bunny patterns. I'll never understand why grown women want to sleep in something with a cartoon character on it."

Mary cleared her throat. "What kind of mood is Mr. Oliver in tonight?"

Daniel was grateful for her attempt to change the focus of the conversation. "Actually," he started, "he and Mr. Hadley were talking about a new security system."

"What kind of new system?" Oscar asked, his brow lined.

"I'm not sure, but he mentioned something about the insurance company."

"Why now?" Mary asked. "Is there a special event coming up?"

Oscar sat back and took a sip of wine. "I trust Mr. Oliver's instincts. Whatever the situation, he'll act appropriately."

Everyone began eating again as if Oscar's word was good enough to consider the matter resolved. Daniel took a piece of garlic bread, while sneaking glances around the table. *Willard's?* he thought. *More like Wackos*. He had a hard time imagining Mr. Oliver complimenting Oscar in a similar fashion.

Mary noticed his practically untouched plate. "Aren't you hungry?" she asked.

He smiled at the sincerity in her voice, but the unexpected company was making him uneasy.

"Where's Jonathan and Ruth Ann?" Petey asked, still pouting a bit from being denied the glass of wine. "I want to show them my severed hand trick."

Mary took a chunk of garlic bread and dipped it in her sauce. "I think Ruth Ann mentioned something about a huge shipment of new movies Jonathan had to catalogue for Home Entertainment. They should be here soon."

Daniel nervously glanced at the elevator as if the mere mention of their names would summon them directly. He decided it was time to escape—again. The last thing he needed was to run into a jealous boyfriend who may or may not have seen him creeping out from behind the counter.

He glanced at his watch, pretending he was late, and then pushed out of the booth. "I should go. Mr. Oliver is probably

NIGHT SHIFT

wondering where I am." He wanted to make it clear, in case this was a test, that he was no slacker. Then he added for good measure, "Besides, there's a missing necklace I promised I'd look for tonight. And thanks for the food," he said, looking more at his new shoes than the faces around the table. "It's been a long time since I sat down with anyone for a real dinner."

"See ya later, Mac," Blanche said, not even glancing from her plate.

Daniel grabbed his sweatshirt and made his way down the grand staircase. They were definitely weird, but he was the odd man out. He'd completely forgotten what it was like to eat with other people. He pushed open the staff door harder than necessary, making it slam against the wall.

He looked around the break room and found a small stackable washer and dryer in the kitchen area. He threw the sweatshirt in the washer, wishing he'd kept his mouth shut. Since he'd begun travelling, his mealtimes had been a rotating blur of diners and airport lounges—and always at a table for one.

Daniel guessed that was probably his first and last invitation to their exclusive dinner meetings. He pictured himself perched on the end of the leather couch in the security office, drinking cold coffee while Mr. Oliver barked out crossword clues.

The washing machine chugged along, and he thought of Mary, cold with her bare arms. Maybe that was the only sweater she had to wear tonight. He went to the change room and pulled his plaid shirt from the locker. He gave it a quick sniff test— yup, still good.

He passed the security office and realized he'd forgotten to bring Mr. Oliver his coffee. He opened the door, but the desk chair was empty.

Daniel looked at the blank monitor labeled "The Matinee Room" and weighed the consequences. It couldn't it hurt to check on her, he reasoned. He reached up and clicked on the live video. A black-and-white view of the restaurant came into focus. Mary and the others were still sitting at the booth.

Daniel got the creeps imagining Mr. Oliver standing in the

63

same spot, spying on him. He shook off the shivers and searched for a dial, but there was no audio. Mary stood up and crossed her arms in front of her chest. Oscar dropped his chin, then put his napkin down on the table.

Daniel's insides squirmed when Jonathan and Ruth Ann entered; Jonathan looked much stronger standing up. A few more words were exchanged, and then they noticed Daniel's leftover spaghetti. Ruth Ann put a hand to her mouth, but Jonathan looked totally pissed. He talked quickly while making agitated gestures. The source of the conflict was obvious. Daniel's heart picked up, thumping out an SOS in Morris code.

Jonathan pointed a finger and took a step closer to Mary.

There was a rush inside Daniel, a mixture of anger and adrenaline that propelled him out of the security office.

He ran up the spiral staircase with one hand already in a fist. He'd only been in one fight, and that was during a hockey game—it lasted for two punches before the refs called it.

Daniel may have been wrong to spy on Jonathan and Ruth Ann, but there was no excuse for this douche bag of a guy to feel so insecure that he was dead set against Mary inviting Daniel to dinner.

He rounded the last step to Ladies' Fashions just as Mary slid down the handrail on her hip. They exchanged fleeting looks of terror and surprise. Unable to stop her forward momentum, Mary slammed into Daniel. He lost his footing and fell back. His head smacked the tile and everything went black.

NIGHT SHIFT

# CHAPTER TEN

Daniel had to blink a few times before Mary's face came into focus. Their noses were practically touching. "Oh no," she panicked, pushing off his chest. "Are you okay?"

He touched the back of his head. "You know," he winced, "we've got to stop meeting like this."

Mary watched him get up. "Sorry," she said. "It's usually the safest way to travel around here."

Daniel gulped at the steep incline of the stairs. "Seriously? Why would you even try to do that?"

"It's how I polish the brass handrail," she shrugged, rubbing her bare arms.

"I thought you only did inventory."

"I take pride in keeping Willard's pristine," she said. There was an underlying playfulness to her tone.

Daniel tentatively touched the back of his head, a small bump was already forming. "How long did it take you to learn that?" he asked. "I mean, one little slip and—"

"It takes practice," she interrupted. "Repetition means better technique."

"Uh-huh," he said, certain he'd have to suffer multiple concussion to practice riding the handrail. There was a silent gap. Daniel wondered if he should mention the argument he'd witnessed on the monitor, considering he was on his way to intervene on her behalf—but she didn't look upset, and questioning her about Jonathan would force him to confess that he'd been watching her on the monitor. What the hell was with him and spying on people tonight?

65

She rubbed her bare arms again.

"Um...here," he said, holding out his shirt. "The sweatshirt is in the washer. I didn't want you to be cold, so I thought, if you didn't have anything else to put on..." he left the sentence hanging.

"Is this yours too?" she asked.

"Well, yeah."

Mary pulled it on and ran her fingers up the sleeve. "It's soft." Her expression lightened. "Blanche would faint if she saw me in this," she said.

"No way, on you it works."

Mary looked like she was trying to decide if he was joking or not. "Actually," she started, "I came looking for you. I was wondering if you wanted some help."

He smiled, relieved he wasn't the only one lying tonight. "Oh, sure. Wait...help me with what?"

"You mentioned Monique's missing necklace."

Daniel paused, trying to remember if he even gave Monique's name. Gossip at Willard's, he reasoned, reaches night shift employees as well. Still, he questioned how much he should divulge. "The thing is," he said, "she thinks another clerk stole it." He explained what Monique had told him, leaving out Stacey's name—he had no proof, after all.

Mary twirled a strand of hair around her finger, then motioned for Daniel to follow her to Ladies' Footwear. Cutting a path between the stiletto displays to the cashier's desk, she crouched down to study the shelves under the counter. Her hand lightly touched the various spines until she got to the binder labelled "Log Record of Packages Received." She opened the dark blue folder and traced her finger down the last page.

"And there it is," she said with an air of satisfaction. "Monique signed for a shipment of hiking boots that day."

"So?"

"Look around," she explained. "It's only high heels and dress shoes here. Hiking boots belong in Sporting Goods."

"Which is on the second floor," he added.

"Very good," she smiled.

His chest filled up, making him stand a little taller. They

NIGHT SHIFT

continued down the aisle and stopped in front of the display where Daniel first met Stacey. Two mannequins were dressed in brightly coloured raincoats. Mary picked up a pair of abandoned rain boots covered with daisies.

"Are we going outside?" he asked.

"You'll see." Without any further clues as to what she had planned, he followed her into the elevator. "Since Monique signed for the hiking boots," she began, "I'm guessing she carried them up herself—Saturday is the busiest shopping day of the week."

The golden arrow moved up and stopped at the two. Daniel held back the gate for Mary. "The store always needs tidying up after hours," she said. "You'd be surprised the things people try to hide in the displays. Gum wrappers, paper clips, used tissue. It's like we're one big trash can."

"One big trash can," Daniel repeated. They walked through the various showcases of plush seating arrangements in Home Furnishings.

Mary said, "Imagine Monique's necklace got caught and broke off when she put down the package. If the area was full of shoppers, she may not have noticed." They meandered around a few displays until the area opened onto a pretend camp site.

Daniel was surrounded by birch trees and tents while a real fishpond gurgled in the middle. "Cool," he said. "I haven't been here yet."

Mary put down the rain boots and said, "I have to ask you something."

"Okay."

"If you saw a shiny coin lying on the floor in this area, what would you do?" She looked like she already knew the answer.

"A coin?"

"Yes."

"In this area?"

"Uh-huh."

Daniel didn't want to get this wrong, but all he saw were tents, trees, and the fish. He crossed his fingers behind his back. "Throw it in the pond, and make a wish?" he guessed.

67

Mary went over to the wall by the cashier's desk and flicked a switch, making the fountain stop. She changed into the rubber boots and returned to Daniel's side. His flashlight shone a beam into the water.

"Hold on," she said, rolling up the shirt sleeves. "I think I see it." She walked through the shallow pond, scattering the gold koi.

"Are you totally sure about this?" he asked.

Mary's eyes twinkled back at him as she reached into the water. There was a swift exclamation of excitement, then she lifted her dripping fist and shuffled back to Daniel. He reached over to help, but she moved so effortlessly, she was out of the pond without needing his assistance.

She opened her hand to reveal the gold medallion. "I give you one missing necklace," she announced.

"Nice!" Daniel was truly impressed.

"You helped too."

"Of course," he said. "Turning on the flashlight was the turning point of the investigation."

She smiled at his joke, and then handed over the piece. "When you give this to Monique, try to ease her paranoia about Stacey—it's a bit unfair of her."

Daniel slipped the medallion in his pocket. "How did you know it was Stacey she suspected?" he asked. "I made sure not to mention her name."

Her smiled slipped, just barely. Then Mary said, "It's no secret Monique doesn't like Stacey. Of course she'd blame the person she wants to see fired."

"Fired? That seems a bit extreme. Monique didn't strike me as the vengeful type. But then again, I've just started working here. You've know her longer than me."

"I've never met Monique," she said, pulling off the wet boots. "I only work night shift, remember?"

Daniel couldn't place what was wrong. An idea was lurking below the surface, teasingly close; it was like waking up in the middle of a dream.

Mary dried her hand on the denim skirt, and then sat down by the pond, stretching her feet out. "If you don't mind," she

NIGHT SHIFT

said, patting the spot beside her, "I need some help with a mystery I'm working on."

Daniel took in her long, bare legs. "Mystery?" he asked, sitting down.

"Mm-hmm," she said. "How did you get here?"

He made a joke to distract her. "We took the elevator, remember?"

Her expression stayed serious. "I mean, working the night shift at Willard's. I heard you arrived in the city only a few days ago."

"Why so curious?" he asked.

"I'm not sure." Mary studied him, and then added, "I can't help it, I find you so..."

"Charming? Desirable? Tempting?"

She reached over and flicked his arm.

"Ow," he laughed, rubbing the area.

"So," she began again. "What brought you to Willard's?"

Daniel thought of the missing black notebook. He bought a few seconds of time, then reached into his pocket for the keychain.

She waited for more of an explanation, then asked in a slow, deliberate manner, "A mini Magic 8 Ball?"

Daniel let it roll around in his palm. "It's the reason I'm in New York," he said. His stomach flip-flopped—it always did when he lied. "I mean, that's how I decide all of my trips. I pick two cities on the map, and then I see what answer comes up."

"You're kidding."

Daniel let out a nervous laugh. "I'm dead serious. It's never steered me wrong. It even told me to apply for a job here." Okay, that was only half a lie, he told himself.

She tilted her head. "And you always take the first answer it gives you?"

"Well..."

"See?" Mary waved a hand toward the keychain. "There's nothing magic about it, you keep asking until it gives you the answer you want or you play the odds." She took the keychain from his hand. "There are twenty different replies, right? Ten outcomes are positive, five are undecided, and the other five are

69

negative."

"Oh…yeah, everybody knows that." *Is there nothing she doesn't know?* he thought.

"So you tailor the question in a way that will most likely give you the response you want. For instance." She held the Magic 8 Ball between her fingers and asked, "Will Mr. Oliver fall asleep in the office tonight?"

*It is certain.*

Daniel felt his stomach unclench, relieved the conversation had taken this turn. "Give it a real test," he challenged. "Pick something that you hope is a negative answer."

Mary gave him a sly grin, and then asked in a spooky voice, "Will Daniel be the next night guard to run out of the store terrified?"

*Without a doubt.*

# CHAPTER ELEVEN

Mary shook the keychain again.
*Most likely.*
And again.
*You may rely on it.*
Then...*My reply is no.*

"Ah, well," Daniel said, snatching up the keychain. "That proves the future is always changing, impossible to predict."

"Sure. It's only a toy, right?" Mary kept her eyes on him. When she spoke again her voice was soft. "Earlier, at dinner, you said you hadn't sat down for a meal with anyone for a while."

"I've been on my own." He rubbed a smudge off his new shoe with his thumb. "I didn't think it showed."

"You're lucky," she said. "I never get any privacy."

"Trust me, the novelty wears off fast. I wouldn't choose it to be this way." He took in the fake landscape with the perfectly straight tents. He didn't realize how long he'd been quiet until he noticed she was staring at him. Her concerned expression melted into a shy smile.

"Penny for your thoughts," she said.

Daniel let go of the gloominess. She had this sweet kind of nostalgia that was sort of nerdy but completely endearing at the same time. He'd never figure her out, but he knew he wanted to keep trying. *Talk about a mystery,* he thought. "Um...the tents and outdoor stuff," he said, "remind me I haven't been camping for years."

"Really? What's it like?" she asked.

B.R. Myers

Daniel looked at her, unbelieving. "You've never been camping?"

"I'm a city girl," she said. "So, what's it like?"

"It's great." He smiled a bit. "Cooking over the fire, hearing all the soft animal noises at night, the stars, the ghost stories…"

"I thought you didn't believe in ghosts," she teased.

"You do when you're camping!"

"All right," she said, lying on her side with her head propped up in her hand. "So it's great. Anything you *don't* like about camping?"

"Burning food over the fire, hearing animal noises at night, and ghost stories."

She laughed. "But the stars are still good?"

"The night sky in the country is amazing. As a city girl you're really missing out."

She picked at the fake grass. "Tell me about it."

"I'm kidding! You live in the most incredible city on the planet." He turned toward her. Their toes were almost touching.

"I don't get out much. I'm homeschooled." She began to make a list with her fingers. "I work night shifts, and the boy I spend most of my time with is an eleven-year-old prankster." She took a quick breath. He thought she was going to speak again, but instead she sat up and hugged her knees.

Daniel had a feeling she was holding back. Maybe he wasn't the only one with a secret. He waited for her to continue, but she turned away and sniffed.

"Are you crying?" he asked.

"No." She sniffed again.

He reached into his back pocket. "Here," he said, passing her the white handkerchief.

"Sorry, I'm not usually this pathetic," she said, patting her eyes. "I feel like I've been doing the same thing forever, you know?"

"Yeah," Daniel said, flipping through his memories of airport lounges. "I know the feeling."

She ran her thumb over the blue initial embroidered on the corner. The handkerchief remained perfectly white. Mary didn't

72

NIGHT SHIFT

wear makeup.

"It was my dad's," he told her. "His name was Will. Anyway, he always told me to carry a handkerchief, in case I saw a pretty girl crying. I've had that one since I was five."

She laughed and said, "You're very good."

"Not really. Any idiot would give you something when you start to cry."

"No," she said. "We're supposed to be talking about you, and here I am spilling my secrets."

"Secrets?" he repeated provocatively. "I don't remember hearing any secrets."

She slid his handkerchief into her back pocket, then pulled on her cowboy boots and stood up. "Never mind," she said. "It's stupid anyway." She started to walk away.

"Whoa," Daniel said, running after her. "You didn't even give me a chance. One hint. Come on."

"It's embarrassing."

"Of course it is," he said. "That's why it's a secret."

"It's not really that interesting. The more we talk about it, the more disappointed you'll be when you hear the truth."

He stepped in front of her to make her stop. "So tell me now, and we can get on with life." He looked at his digital watch. "Mr. Oliver is expecting me."

"Okay," she waved. "See you later."

He let out an exasperated sigh. "Mary!"

"Daniel!"

They stared at each other, but neither one made a move. "Mine is worse than yours," he said.

"Try me."

Daniel took a deep breath. "I've been travelling for months by myself." He paused, and then the rest of the words tumbled out. "I have no family. I have no real home. I own four shirts, and you're wearing one of them. All of my coworkers placed bets on when I'm going to quit, and my boss is a cranky old fart who makes me feel stupid and guilty at the same time."

Mary's mouth fell open. "You win."

He slipped his hands into his pants pockets and touched the keychain, but its usual comfort wasn't there. They walked

73

together toward the grand staircase. She stayed quiet, proving that he shouldn't have told her the truth. People acted different once they found out. They treated him with awkward pity or avoided him altogether.

When they reached the second-floor landing, he said, "Look, I'm sorry I told you all that stuff. I don't want you to feel like you have to—"

"I've never been on a date," she interrupted.

It took Daniel several seconds to respond. "Nice try," he snorted. "But the whole 'beautiful but lonely girl' thing is way too cliché for someone as smart as you." He read her expression and his sarcastic grin faded. "Seriously?!"

Mary looked at the ceiling and groaned.

He blinked a few times and asked, "Is that something you wish to rectify?" Oh, shit! Did he just say *rectify*? "I mean, would you like to go on a date?"

She pushed her shoulders back. "Is that a rhetorical question?"

Daniel ran a hand through his hair in a desperate attempt to tidy it and mustered his best dimple. "Would you like to go on a date with *me*?"

Her eyes grew wide. "How?"

"However you want," he answered, a bit confused by the question.

"When?"

"Tomorrow night?"

"I'm working," she said.

"Me too."

"But…"

"We'll hang out again," he said, thinking up a plan on the spot. Then he added, "But without the rain boots."

"You want to take me on a date," she asked slowly, "inside the store?"

"Sure," he said. "And if you want, a show next time, or a museum, or anything else…"

Mary stared back at him and the passing time made her answer unpleasantly obvious.

The smile on Daniel's face started to harden into a moronic

NIGHT SHIFT

grin. "Do I have to ask a third time?" he dared.

"No."

"No, I don't have to ask you a third time, or no, you don't want to go on an amazing, fun, fabulously entertaining date with me, since I've given you, literally, the shirt off my back, and my late father's handkerchief, and—"

"Hold on." She eyed him carefully, and then reached into her back pocket. Daniel thought she was going to return the handkerchief, but instead she held out his little black notebook. He moved forward, but she pulled it out of his reach.

"How did you get that?" he asked. Then he tried to look confused. "I mean, what does some random notebook have to do with me?"

"Give it up, buttercup," she said. "I know it's yours. I found it last night on the cashier's counter."

They regarded each other, unsure who should make the next move. "It's mine," he finally said, holding out his hand. "Give it back, please."

A flash of emotion, maybe pity, crossed her face. She gripped the notebook, then placed it in his hands. "Sorry, I can't help it. I'm curious. I was going to slip it into your locker later, anyway."

He ran his thumb over the soft cover. There was an elastic around it now, with a small pen tucked inside—her additions, he assumed. "Thanks," he said, placing the notebook under his arm. He met her eyes again, but the pity was no longer there. "Aren't you going to ask me anything?" he demanded.

Mary studied him. "I think you've shared enough. Maybe someday you'll tell me why there's a list of department stores all over the country, crossed off, but Willard's is the only one circled."

"Yeah, maybe." He stepped forward and she instinctively moved back. A smile tugged at the corners of his mouth. "Do I make you nervous?" he asked.

"No." She sounded insulted. "You were in my personal space."

"Personal space? I thought you were curious about me?" Making her flustered gave him so much enjoyment. He took

75

another step closer.

"Daniel," she stammered.

He held the black notebook up. "How much did you read?"

She decided to inspect the toe of her cowboy boots. "All of it," she admitted.

All of it! Daniel felt his heart race. "Well, there must be some questions you're dying to ask? Aren't you even a little…curious?" He saw a flash of excitement in her eyes: Mary had a weakness. "I might spill some secrets if you watch a movie with me in the home theatre tomorrow night."

She stepped backward. "All right," she agreed.

"Really?" his voice went up. He wasn't expecting that answer.

"But it has to be secret. We're supposed to be working."

Talk about a one-eighty. He talked fast before she could change her mind. "Of course," he assured her. "Mr. Oliver and Oscar won't suspect a thing."

Mary nodded as if they'd sealed a business transaction. She motioned behind him. "Mr. Oliver is expecting you. Say goodnight, Danny Boy," she ordered.

He gave her a salute, then turned on the spot, and headed toward the ground floor. "Goodnight, Danny Boy," he called over his shoulder. He whistled down the grand staircase, hearing his new shoes tap on the marble steps.

When he reached the golden tree in the main foyer, he slipped his hand into his pocket and heard the Magic 8 Ball clink against the gold medallion. A chill raced through his veins.

Daniel replayed everything he'd said to Mary tonight. How is it possible that Mary knows so much about Monique without ever meeting her? And how was she so sure the notebook belonged to him?

# CHAPTER TWELVE

"No way!" Monique squealed and plucked the tiny medallion from Daniel's palm.

He gave her a tired grin, his eyelids working to stay open. "You might want to clean it, considering it's been sitting at the bottom of the fishpond for a week."

"Yeah," she said distractedly, still staring at the gold piece. They stood in the staff break area, just outside the locker rooms. Blue-vested clerks brushed past them in a nonstop parade on Willard's busiest day of the week. Daniel glanced at his watch—his shift was officially over an hour ago. He doubted he'd be able to stay awake for the walk back to the hotel.

"Um, so," he began, fighting a yawn. "I guess Stacey is off the hook."

Monique stopped smiling. "Don't blame me for accusing her. A girl has to follow her instincts. And there's something about her that's...I don't know. Shifty, I guess."

"Shifty?" Daniel wasn't sure if he should laugh.

She shook her head. "Never mind, guys don't understand. But thank you so much for this." She went on tiptoes and hugged him. "I knew I could count on you," she said.

When he opened the door to his hotel room, Daniel could hardly focus. He threw his backpack on the bed and started to undress. Then realized he had nothing clean to wear to work tonight, or for his date. Monique was certainly making her intentions clear, but it was Mary he couldn't stop thinking about. There was a mystery about her that he found unsettling yet incredibly alluring—like Willard's itself.

The plastic laundry bag hanging in the closet held most of his clothes. After he called the concierge, Daniel fell into bed, and was asleep before his head hit the pillow.

The evening wind bit through his coat, and whipped around his newly cut hair, freezing his ears. He would have preferred a barber shop over the hotel spa any day, but after his shower, Daniel had taken one look in the bathroom mirror and put in another call to the concierge. What was the point of showing up in clean clothes if his hair looked like a freaking tumbleweed?

He saw the familiar royal blue banner up ahead. A small collection of people were gathered on the sidewalk admiring the Little Mermaid display. She commanded the attention of all the faces on the other side of the glass with her jewelled hair and luminous features. *It's only natural,* he reasoned, *to be drawn to something so beautiful.* Daniel thought about the phrase from his dream, now copied in the back of his little black notebook, "*...how you see the world depends on which side of the glass you're on.*"

Running the last few yards, he pushed through the main doors, eager to leave the cold gray world outside. There was a comfortable order to Willard's as shoppers browsed, and then moved on. The flow of foot traffic around the display cases and aisles was constant and smooth—like blood vessels travelling through veins. Daniel stood on the white marble tile of the main foyer and took a deep breath, feeling the energy of the store.

He changed into his freshly pressed blue shirt and pants, and went directly to the security office, but the door was closed once again. He didn't want to risk interrupting another meeting, so he backed away without knocking.

Monique was perched on the edge of the rainwear display. She slipped her foot out of her heels, and flexed her toes a few times.

She turned and saw Daniel. "Check you out, Mr. GQ! I like the new hair."

He touched one side, self-consciously. "It's not so much shorter," he said.

"No," she grinned. "It still has that tousled thing going, but

NIGHT SHIFT

now it's more sexy than shaggy."

Daniel had no idea what to say. Being around Monique was like being in a sauna; he got sweaty, he couldn't breathe, and his cheeks were constantly flushed.

"Anyway," she continued, wiggling back into her stilettos, "I'm glad you dropped by."

"How's that?" he asked, leaning against the cashier's counter.

She took a tube from her blue vest pocket and applied a fresh layer of lip gloss. "I get off in an hour."

"I start work in an hour."

"Then we'll have to make the most of what little time we share," she laughed. "Today was awesome, I made so many sales, and I'm so happy you found my necklace."

"And Stacey?" he asked carefully.

"That's the best part," she said. "Shifty Stacey wasn't in today. So I didn't have to see her shifty eyes or her shifty face at all." Then she reminded him, "A girl's intuition trumps all else."

*Even logic,* he thought.

"But enough about me," she said. "Is it getting too creepy, working at night with Mr. Oliver?"

"No," he smiled. "The store's actually pretty cool at night."

She moved in closer. "I guess you haven't met the Bloody Assistant yet?"

The ghost stories were getting old, but he decided to indulge her. "Okay," he sighed. "I'll bite."

"Don't be like that," Monique pouted. "I had to do a paper for my history class. All the facts are in the newspapers in the library archives. I didn't get an A, though; my teacher called it 'a lot of glamorous gossip.' She said the crime section wasn't exactly renowned for its authenticity. But I can tell you this." She lowered her voice. "In the early nineteen hundreds, this building used to be a theatre."

"I know," Daniel said. "A lousy magician couldn't afford the rent, so the bank sold it to Mr. Willard."

"Not quite," she said. "The magician made a horrible mistake onstage, and the volunteer from the audience ended up

79

dead. He disappeared that night, disgraced."

"What does that have to do with the assistant?" he asked.

"She was murdered days before the horrific finale. But here's the catch: they never found her body, only a huge pool of blood in her dressing room backstage." Her eyes grew wider with each gruesome detail. "The police recorded her death as an unsolved homicide. I've seen the original blueprints of the theatre. Guess where her dressing room used to be."

"Wait a minute," Daniel said, letting the panic come through his voice. "I was doing a round in Menswear last night, and there's one change room door that always stays locked."

"Oh my God!" Monique put a hand over her heart.

"I had my master key ready to open the door, but then I thought of all those night guards who quit and maybe," Daniel paused and swallowed loudly, "…maybe whatever was inside the locked change room is the reason why they leave."

"What did you do?" she whispered.

"I had no choice," he said. "I opened the door."

"And?!"

"A woman was covered in blood, talking about revenge. Do you think that was the Bloody Assistant?"

Monique let out a disgusted huff. "Wait and see," she said, poking him in the chest with a red fingernail. "I bet you'll be crying tears of terror on my shoulder soon enough."

"Haven't you heard?" he said, picturing the glass bowl in the security office. "Anyone who bets against me loses." Feeling superior with that awesome comeback, he gave her a wink and started down the aisle.

"Interesting, though," she called out, making him turn around. "How did you know Menswear was the original backstage area?"

Daniel's smile faded. "I didn't," he said.

"Have a nice night," she smirked, happy to have the last word.

# CHAPTER THIRTEEN

The door to the security office was ajar. Daniel walked in and noticed Mr. Oliver had begun shutting off the monitors.

"You're late," he snarled, clicking the screens off row by row.

"I was here earlier," Daniel said. "But the door was closed. I thought you might be having a meeting."

"Is your hand broken?"

"No."

"Ever heard of knocking?" Mr. Oliver turned around. "Mr. Hadley was here with a representative from the insurance company. He's considering recommendations about new electronic security measures. You might not have to worry about showing up for work when you're replaced by a laser beam." Mr. Oliver brushed past Daniel. "I'll see the clerks out tonight," he said gruffly.

Daniel stood alone, staring at the glass bowl full of paper predictions for his last day. It occurred to him that instead of quitting, he might get fired.

He began night rounds, trying to look somewhat responsible. He found Mary on the first floor, leaning against one of the cashier's counters with her back to him. Despite his mood, he couldn't help but smile. Her jean cutoffs were layered with black leggings and a tight black T-shirt. Her usual pink high tops were replaced with silver ballet flats. She reached up and twirled a strand of hair.

She turned around as if she had felt the weight of his stare.

"Daniel," she said, sounding panicked. "I didn't think I'd see you this early."

His mouth went dry—she wasn't alone. Jonathan and Ruth Ann were behind the counter, huddled in front of the computer screen with a cellophane bag full of candy open in front of them.

Jonathan jerked to attention, partially blocking Ruth Ann. He glared at Daniel.

Whether it was the previous unwarranted criticism by Mr. Oliver or the fact that Daniel was used to guys like this on opposing hockey teams, he refused to be intimidated. He stepped up to the counter, eager to show them he wasn't afraid of jerks with big muscles. "You must be Jonathan," he said.

Jonathan lifted his chin. "How do you know my name?" he asked. Daniel was caught off guard by the quiver in his voice. What reason would Jonathan have for being scared?

Mary let out a breath, and then added with an impatient tone, "How do you think, moron? We talked about you and Ruth Ann at supper last night."

Jonathan's nostrils flared like a racehorse in the starter's gate. Ruth Ann's blond curly head peeked around his shoulder. Mary watched her friends closely, her face turning a deeper shade of red. Daniel was pressed to guess if she was angry or embarrassed.

"Um," she said, motioning toward the computer monitor. "Ruth Ann was checking out the new window displays. It's fairy tales this season…she loves fairy tales." Mary nodded encouragingly to Ruth Ann.

"Why didn't you look at them on your way into the store?" Daniel asked.

Ruth Ann's mouth opened slightly but no sound came out.

"The sidewalk was too crowded with onlookers," Mary said quickly. "We couldn't get a decent view. This is much better." She motioned toward the monitor.

On the screen was an image of the first exhibit. The nearly drowned prince was lying across the sand with his eyes closed. Above him, looking down at his face with reverence, was the Little Mermaid.

NIGHT SHIFT

Jonathan stared at his silent girlfriend. "Babe?" he said anxiously.

Ruth Ann closed her eyes. When she spoke her voice was barely above a whisper. "'But to her he sent no smile, he knew not that she had saved him,'" she recited perfectly.

Mary and Jonathan relaxed their shoulders in unison. Ruth Ann gave Daniel a shy smile, and then held out the bag of sweets under his nose as an offering.

"Oh, thanks," he said, taking a chocolate-covered jujube and popping it into his mouth. She smiled more widely this time, and Daniel felt a thin layer of apprehension peel away.

"Yeah," Jonathan said, "but her love for the prince killed her in the end." He clicked the mouse and brought up images of the Thumbelina display. "Giant bird saves freak," he mumbled.

Ruth Ann swatted his shoulder. "The sparrow rescues Thumbelina," she said, more confidently this time. "But when they reach his nest, the fairy king is waiting, and she agrees to marry him. So the poor sparrow flies away, brokenhearted." She closed her eyes again. "'We can fly away, over mountains, into warmer countries, where the sun shines more brightly than here; where it is always summer, and the flowers bloom in greater beauty.'" She nodded at the end, satisfied, and then took a peppermint from the treat bag.

"Here's a special one," Jonathan continued in his sarcastic drawl, now looking at the last window.

Ruth Ann brightened and spoke in her same dreamy tone, "'Only the tin soldier and the dancer remained in their places. She stood on tiptoe, with her legs stretched out, as firmly as he did on one leg. He never took his eyes off her for even a moment.'" Then she frowned, "Unfortunately, they both ended up in the stove, burnt together."

"Interesting themes," Jonathan said, looking pointedly at Daniel. Jonathan managed to flex a muscle while waving a hand at the monitor. "The whole 'doomed lovers from different worlds' thing Hans had going on."

"They're only stories." Mary glared across the counter. Daniel's eyes flicked back and forth between them, sensing a showdown.

83

Jonathan grabbed the treat bag, and then reached for Ruth Ann. "This is so stupid," he said. "We're out of here." She threw him a scowl and made him stand alone in the aisle. "Oscar said he wanted to see us about vacation. Remember?" he said, emphasizing the last word.

Ruth Ann started to say something, but then changed her mind. She gave Mary an apologetic shrug, then followed Jonathan down the aisle. His grumbling echoed back until they turned the corner.

"What an ass," Daniel said out loud. He glanced at Mary and quickly changed his tone. "Sorry."

She lifted a shoulder. "Don't worry. He's a completely harmless moron."

He swallowed, thinking about the waves of hatred coming off those "completely harmless" biceps.

Mary walked around the counter. "Ruth Ann forgot to log off," she said, typing on the computer. After a few clicks, she met his gaze. "Hi," she said.

Daniel had been planning for this moment since he woke up, but now that she was standing in front of him, he had nothing but a mouth full of cotton, and a brain that had decided to shut down.

She began to meticulously peel a tiny piece of tape off the counter. "I have an hour to spare," she said. "Instead of a movie, we could get some putters from Sporting Goods and do a quick round of mini golf through the store? Ruth Ann and I do it all the time, it's actually pretty fun."

Daniel pictured Mr. Oliver watching them on the monitors. "I'm not sure," he said.

"You changed your mind," she said. "I wondered why you didn't tell Monique you had a date tonight."

He frowned at this comment.

"She talks," Mary explained. "A lot. A word of caution, though; if you take *her* out, no detail is too small for her to regurgitate."

"Whoa." He laughed and held up his hands. "Where did that come from?" He tried to read her expression, but she only wanted to study the floor. "Look," he pleaded. "Mr. Oliver gave

NIGHT SHIFT

me a warning. And I'm pretty sure whacking a golf ball around the glass display cases would be the fastest way to get fired."

There were a couple of beats of silence, then she said, "Oscar wouldn't like it either."

"I'm sorry."

"It's okay," she shrugged. "It's not like I got dressed up or anything."

"Actually," he began, ready to bury her in compliments.

"All right, Mary," Blanche's voice interrupted him. "Time to strip off." She emerged from across the aisle with clothes draped over her outstretched arms.

"Not *now*, Blanche," Mary said.

Blanche plopped the pile of outfits down on the counter. "You promised to finally wear girl clothes tonight," she sulked. Blanche flipped through the hangers and held up a short black dress, gathered at the bottom. "Now, this is precious," she said, pressing it up against Mary. "And you've got the perfect legs."

"I don't like it," Mary said. "The bottom is weird."

"Doll," she rolled her eyes. "It's a bubble dress by Vera Wang." Blanche chose another hanger and pursed her lips, studying the gray silk shirtdress. Daniel watched, while Mary's eyes darted around the room, never meeting his gaze.

"Blanche, please," she said, squirming on the spot.

"Anna Sui is very much your style," Blanche said, "if you had any." She spun around and looked at Daniel. "What do you think, Mac?"

The heat rose underneath the collar of his shirt. Daniel had the feeling he was standing on thin ice. He wanted to make up for cancelling their date, but he didn't know what to say, and it seemed like he was making everything worse. Finally, he just went with the truth. "I think that Mary would look good in anything," he said.

"Yes," Blanche agreed with a tired sigh. "An idea she challenges every day."

Mary took the silk outfit and added it to the pile on the counter. "Thanks, Blanche," she said. "But I can't play dress-up tonight. There's inventory to sort through." She finally looked at Daniel. "Don't worry about Mr. Oliver," she said, serious and

85

businesslike. "He's worried about some other things right now. You won't be fired." Then she turned and walked away.

Blanche reached in her pocket and ran after Mary. She flung a long strand of pearls around her neck, like a lasso.

"Blanche!" Mary choked.

"You promised," she said, pointing a finger.

"You know I hate jewelry."

"Long pearls are a classic." She looped one more strand. "There," she said, standing back to study her efforts. "You almost look like a girl."

"Whatever," Mary grumbled, continuing down the aisle.

"Wait," Daniel called out. "Do you want to go on a round with me later? If you finish inventory and have a spare half hour or so...? Maybe?"

"No thanks, Mac," Blanche said. "You're not my type."

"He meant me," Mary said. She looked down at her pearls then back to Daniel. "It's probably for the best we just do our jobs tonight," she said.

Daniel stood there, watching her go, wishing the moment hadn't gone sour.

Blanche returned to the counter and gathered the clothes in her arms. "These won't hang themselves back up."

"Do you need help?"

"No," she said, lifting her nose in the air. She stared critically at his uniform. "Nice shoes."

He was surprised by the compliment. "Thanks, they're Tom Ford."

"I know. And mark my words," she said, looking him up and down again, "I'll have you in Armani by the end of the month." She ignored his baffled look, and disappeared around the corner toward Formal Attire.

Daniel roamed the dimly lit Menswear with his hands in his pockets. Every suit, sweater, and shirt were meticulously showcased. He paused by a small table displaying handkerchiefs. An image of his parents crept up from his memories. "Willard's is full of magic and beautiful things," he murmured, lost in thought.

NIGHT SHIFT

A noise from across the department snapped him out of his stupor. Daniel brushed by the suits and stopped near the change rooms.

Someone was crying.

He turned the corner and looked down the long cream coloured hallway, lined with doors. Plush leather chairs were situated at the end by a three-way mirror. Daniel listened to the intermittent sobs, silently cursing Monique and her stupid ghost stories about murdered magician's assistants. He tried to swallow his heart back down his throat. "Anyone there?" he called out.

There was a sniff.

The change room doors had a one foot gap at the bottom. Daniel knelt down, resting his cheek against the carpet. He let out a relived breath, then pushed himself up and tapped on the door.

"Mary?" he gently prompted. "I can see your silver shoes." Daniel waited for a reply, but she only sniffed back. "I'm sorry about tonight," he continued. "I can't risk losing this job." There was nothing but silence. He stared at the door, wishing he knew what to say. "The truth is, I really like you…okay? And I want to tell you about the notebook. I think that maybe you can help me." He paused, but she made no noise. "Please open the door. I feel like an ass. I don't want you to cry."

Daniel shifted his weight and then let out a frustrated sigh. He gripped the handle—it was sticky. He let go and stared at his blood-covered palm. Without warning, the change room door flung open.

87

# CHAPTER FOURTEEN

The long dark hair was matted and tangled. Her face was an unrecognizable pulpy mess. Daniel's back slammed into the wall as bloodied hands clawed at his sleeves, leaving splotches of red on his shirt. He gritted his teeth, smelling a foul odour…garlic?

As he remembered the spaghetti sauce from last night's dinner, the scene took on a whole new meaning.

"Petey," he growled, pushing the hairy mess away.

Explosive laughter echoed down the hallway. Jonathan was bent over, holding his stomach. "Holy crap! You should see your face."

"There's something wrong with you guys," Daniel said, wondering if Monique had told him the story of the bloody assistant on purpose. Were all the staff ganging up on him tonight?

Petey pulled off the sloppy wig. "You're right," he laughed, stepping out of the silver shoes. "I've got to start using water. These gags with fake blood take too long to clean up."

Daniel's top was ruined. He pushed past Jonathan and went directly to the locker room. He changed back into his faded Henley shirt, then dropped his uniform in the clothes washer. Mr. Oliver was sure to fire him tonight. How was it that he could get yelled at for not arriving early enough to meet with the insurance company, but it was perfectly fine for Jonathan and Petey to keep pulling these stupid gags?

Daniel rubbed his face, still nervous from the scare. He pictured Mr. Oliver with his nose in the paper and his back to

NIGHT SHIFT

the monitors—the monitors he always shut off. He thought about the window displays and how Jonathan was determined to make him look stupid in front of the girls.

"Screw that," Daniel told the washer. He jogged up the grand staircase and headed for the second floor—Sporting Goods, to be exact. The golfing section.

He found Mary tidying up in the Leisure section. A narrow path flanked by high bookcases opened into a cozy reading area with overstuffed loveseats and an electric fireplace. It took some convincing on his part to drag her away from cataloging a new shipment of hardcovers, but she finally agreed to spare him an hour.

Mary suggested they start by teeing off at the top of the grand staircase. It was soon obvious that she had played this game more than once. Her ball never rolled under displays or got lost under racks of clothing. In fact, she hit the perfect shot nearly every time. Daniel's stroke count was almost three times her score once they had reached the ground floor.

"Another hole in one," he moaned. "How is that possible?"

"I've had a lot of practice," she said. "Repetition improves technique."

They were in the gift shop, surrounded by merchandise adorned with an image of the colossal storefront. One entire wall displayed teddy bears wearing the famous blue-and-white-striped aprons.

Mary retrieved her golf ball out of a coffee mug decorated with a blue *W*. "It's not my fault I got a perfect bounce off the makeup counter."

"Which could have easily smashed," he said. "You hit the ball too hard from the landing."

"Said the sore loser."

They walked out of the gift shop and stood in the main foyer. "One more?" she suggested. "We're aiming for the Confectionery."

Daniel lined up his ball on the black granite tile. "So how long have you been practicing?" he asked.

"Awhile."

His ball rolled down the main aisle before it gently bumped

against the wall and came to a rest. Mary's shot sailed through the air and pinged off an archway, barely missing a glass display case. It bounced out of sight, far beyond his ball.

Daniel's earlier cavalier attitude was slowly ebbing, being replaced with visions of Mr. Oliver throwing open the security door and scowling at them. They exchanged worried looks, but the door stayed shut. Daniel let out a relieved sigh, then gave her a wink and walked up the aisle, resting the club on his shoulder.

"I mean, how long have you worked here?" he whispered as they passed the security office.

She pulled him farther into the shadows. "Why?" Her voice sounded guarded.

"How come none of the night guards last longer than a few weeks? Other than almost falling to my death, and Petey's stupid stunts, nothing else has happened to make me want to run out the main doors screaming. Have you ever been spooked by anything at night?"

Mary made a snorting kind of noise from the back of her throat. "Believe me, I've *never* run out of Willard's."

"Right," he sighed. Mary seemed to enjoy giving him ambiguous answers. They reached his ball first. His next shot bounced a few times and rolled past the elevator. "But why is Mr. Oliver the only night guard to stay? It doesn't make any sense."

Mary picked at the rubber grip of her club. "'Just because we don't understand, doesn't mean that the explanation doesn't exist.'" Her cheeks flushed. "It's a quote from *A Wrinkle In Time*. Ruth Ann has a lot of favourites."

The change in her demeanour was obvious. Why was he hassling her about stupid ghosts? Not only was he a total loser who couldn't hit a golf ball, but he had managed to somehow insult her. He decided to drop the creepy talk, and reminded himself he was on a date—sort of.

"Um...penny for your thoughts," he said. He mentally did a facepalm. Great, now she thought he was making fun of her. "I mean..." He cleared his throat. "Do you have a favourite book, too?"

NIGHT SHIFT

"I don't know," she said. "Anything by Jules Verne or Edgar Rice Burroughs, I guess."

Daniel wasn't expecting that. "A sci-fi fan, huh?"

"I like H.G. Wells, too."

They navigated their shots through the maze of jewelry counters, and then under an archway into the Confectionery. Shelves as high as the ceiling housed glass containers glistening with candy. There were white peppermints stamped with the blue *W*, sugared fruit, licorice strings, jelly beans by the thousands, rich, creamy caramels, large rainbow suckers the size of his head, and bricks of sponge toffee. Daniel half expected Willy Wonka to come strutting around the corner.

The soft light from the long chocolate display case cast shadows in the corners. Mary put the coffee mug at the end of the room, and returned to her shot.

"What's the best thing about travelling?" she asked. Her ball curved toward the cup and found its target with a soft clink.

"It's a good thing I didn't make any bets on this game," he said, taking a few practice swings.

"I thought anyone who bets against you, loses."

He missed his shot. "How did you...?" His ball disappeared into the darkness, forgotten.

Mary's fingers played with her pearl necklace. "I envy you," she blurted out. "You've been to so many different places."

Daniel wondered if she was hinting at the notebook. He decided to keep her in suspense. "What's stopping you?" he teased. "Grab a backpack from Sporting Goods, and we'll head out tomorrow. You don't even have to pack a lot. We can share my shirts."

She laughed softly.

The corners of Daniel's mouth curled up. When he made her laugh he felt like a genius. "I'll take you anywhere you want to go," he added, half serious. "We're both eighteen—hell, I'm almost nineteen. We can do whatever we want."

She gazed across the room, into the shadows. "I've never been to the beach," she said.

"You're kidding."

91

"I'm a city girl, remember?" She said it lightheartedly, but Daniel could hear the sadness underneath. "Is it true the horizon looks perfectly straight where the sky meets the ocean?"

Daniel dropped his voice. "I never thought about it before, but yeah, I guess it does."

"I can't picture it. But if I saw it with my own eyes, it would make sense." She paused. "I'd really like that."

"The beach it is then—I promise." They stared at each other, letting the moment linger. Mary looked away first, breaking the spell. He propped his putter against the wall. "Travelling isn't all that great, though," he reconciled. "Even the nicest hotels are still hotels. Nothing can replace home."

"Home," she repeated. The slight edge to her voice caught his attention.

"What about you?" he asked. "What's your family like?"

Mary picked up the mug, still containing her golf ball, and gently put it down on the glass counter. "Everyone I care about is close by," she simply said.

"You're lucky."

A look of disbelief crossed her face, but was quickly replaced by the know-it-all-stare he was more familiar with. She started to twirl her hair.

Daniel recognized the gesture. "It's killing you, isn't it? I'm surprised you lasted this long. You must have at least one question about the notebook."

"I only get one question?" She sounded indignant. Then she took a deep breath and began. "In the last six months, you've visited major cities all over the country. In each, there was a store or business with one thing in common: every company began with the letter *V*." She paused and looked at him.

Daniel nodded for her to proceed.

"Then, around three months into your travels, you expanded your trips to include every major shopping centre, no matter what the name. Soon, afterwards, smaller department stores began to get crossed off your list. It looks like you were concentrating on toy stores."

She continued. "I found out that thirty percent of those stores were going out of business, and that half of those stores

NIGHT SHIFT

had been bought out in the last year by a larger corporation."

Daniel couldn't hide his shocked expression. "How do you know all this?"

"I like research," she admitted. "Google has made my life so much easier."

"Uh-huh. Go on."

Mary began to pace, tapping her lower lip with her finger. "I can only conclude that you've been looking for something in all these places, but only one store isn't crossed off—Willard's."

Daniel's heart was racing. "Impressive," he said.

She squirmed on the spot, clearly impatient. "That's all you're going to say? You're supposed to spill!"

He held up a finger. "One question."

She gave him a judgmental look. "What I can't figure out is why a fancy cursive capital *V* led you to Willard's."

Daniel glanced at the mug. "Are you serious?" he laughed. "For someone who works here all the time, that's the one obvious clue. I guess you're not as smart as you think. Admit it, you don't know the store as well as I do."

He waited for the witty comeback. Instead, she hit him with a stare that sent a trickle of goose bumps down his arms. She stepped closer, the toes of her silver flats almost touching his Tom Fords.

Daniel swallowed. A few seconds ago he had had all the power. How had she managed to twist the situation? Mary leaned closer into *his* personal space. "That sounds like a challenge," she said.

He watched her stroll along the wall, letting her fingers brush against the glass candy containers. She unwrapped a sweet and popped it into her mouth. "Can you guess which candy is the most popular?" she asked, dropping the wrapper on the counter in front of him.

Daniel pushed the long sleeves of his shirt up his forearms, preparing to tolerate her quiz. "No idea," he said.

"It's the caramel-filled chocolate *W*." She slipped behind the counter. "Do you know why?"

"Because anything with a *W* is a big seller around here?"

93

She ignored his sarcasm. "No," she said. "It's because the chocolate and caramel taste better together than on their own." Mary offered him a *W* from one of the silver trays. She came out from behind the counter. "Well?" she asked.

He finished in two bites. "This one is solid chocolate," he said, wondering why she gave him the wrong flavour. He looked at the empty wrapper on the counter. "What candy did you choose?"

She tipped her face upwards. Her voice was soft. "A caramel."

*Holy shit.*

Daniel's pulse raced for a totally new reason. His eyes trailed over her face, stopping at her mouth. The light from the counter played off her delicate features. He was suddenly breathless. "Mary," he said, "you're perfect."

The effect was instantaneous. "Um…what time is it?" she stammered. "I think we took too long. I'll take the putters back to Sporting Goods."

"Wait," he said, reaching for her.

"I'm sorry." She brushed past with their clubs. "I have to get back to inventory. Oscar's reheating lunch leftovers in an hour if you want to join us." And she left without waiting for an answer.

Daniel listened to her footsteps fade up the grand staircase. The tray of chocolate *W*'s stared back at him. He'd never felt so unsure about anything in his life.

# CHAPTER FIFTEEN

In the Matinee Room, the same booth as before was set with a platter of sliced glazed ham, coleslaw, rhubarb chutney, and steamed asparagus with hollandaise sauce.

Daniel watched the others set the table. Wine glasses, silverware, a basket of rolls—their jobs were well rehearsed, and he felt an unexpected twinge of pity for Mr. Oliver, sitting in his office all alone. He wondered if Oscar and Mr. Oliver were territorial enemies, with neither one stepping on the other's boundaries. Mr. Oliver was definitely old school, and Oscar was having gourmet meals with his staff. Hardly a cozy coworker relationship.

Without asking, Jonathan poured Daniel a glass of wine.

"But I'm working," Daniel said.

"So am I," he said, his tone a little more conciliatory than earlier. "You know, I had my doubts, but pulling pranks on you is more entertaining than any movie I've seen in a while."

Daniel took a sip. "Whatever," he said, disappointed by the bitter taste. Blanche sat with her arms folded, regarding him with a pout. Mary took the seat at the end of the booth. She hadn't spoken to him yet, and he wondered what he'd said that upset her so much.

He'd planned to avoid any further awkward encounters, but after staring at her empty caramel wrapper for a while, he pulled himself together, mustered some confidence, and came to seek her out. He'd let her down, he now realized. Her first date, and he assumed her first attempt at a kiss as well, was a total disappointment. Could he convince her to give him a second

chance?

"All right," Oscar snapped. "Which one of you gave Petey wine?" Daniel almost dropped his glass at the sudden outburst.

"Just a little," Petey pleaded. "I read that kids in France drink wine every day. And their cancer and obesity rates are way lower than ours."

Oscar smoothed out his mustache and said, "Sip, not guzzle."

"Keep her lit, Petey!" Jonathan said, clinking their glasses.

Ruth Ann reached for the rhubarb chutney. "So, Daniel," she smiled, "what do you think of the store? Do you like working here? The Confectionery is my favourite! Everything going well tonight?" Her eyes flicked to Mary.

Daniel was struck by Ruth Ann's exuberant reaction. "It's been—"

"Bloody fantastic," Jonathan interrupted. Petey laughed, spraying the table with a mouthful of wine.

"Oh, my nerves!" Blanche jumped up to blot the mess. "Think of the linen!"

Oscar slapped down his napkin. "For once," he scolded, "could you fools behave at the table?"

Mary glared across the table at Jonathan. "Making fun of a murdered girl? Grow up, moron. I'm so sick of hearing about ghosts."

Jonathan swallowed his food and gave her a smirk. "Petey and I were just going ape. You should have seen Daniel's face. Even the bug stuck up your arse would've laughed."

"I don't know why people fixate on the morbid stories," Ruth Ann said thoughtfully. "No one ever talks about the day the power went out and twins were safely born in the elevator, or all the wedding proposals that have happened in this room." She paused for a moment, then smiled. "Remember the Christmas parties Mr. Willard hosted each year for all those orphans?"

"Exactly," Mary agreed. She turned to Daniel, barely making eye contact. "Willard's is full of gossiping clerks—not ghosts. There's nothing inside this store that can hurt you. And if you don't believe me, ask your Magic 8 Ball." She stabbed a

NIGHT SHIFT

few pieces of ham with her fork.

"By the way, Mary," Jonathan said, "Daniel feels horrible about making you cry."

"It wasn't me, idiot. It was you and Petey."

"Hey, regardless." Jonathan patted his chest and nodded toward Daniel. "It hit me right here, dude. Ouch!" He looked accusingly in Ruth Ann's direction.

Mary stared at her plate. It seemed to Daniel that Jonathan was getting more enjoyment from hiding his insults with jokes. The room was filled with the sounds of clinking cutlery as everyone resumed their meal. Daniel silently prayed for a change in topic.

"So, Mac," Blanche said, sipping a blue martini. "Mary tells us you're a homeless orphan."

"Blanche!" Mary rebuked.

"Is that true?" Petey whispered, his eyes widening. The others stopped eating.

"Yeah," Daniel said, "it's true." He waited for someone to squirm and cough, but everyone kept staring, waiting for him to continue. "It's not a big secret," he said. "My mom was in a car accident when I was eleven, and my dad died last year." Six pairs of eyes blinked back at him. "He, um…he had cancer." He recognized the uncomfortable silence. People never knew what to say, so they said nothing at all.

Ruth Ann choked out a muffled sob and blew her nose in her napkin. "This is just like *Oliver Twist*."

Jonathan finished his wine. "More like *Superman*," he said, dismissively.

"Don't be ridiculous," Ruth Ann said, putting the napkin down. "His parents put him in an escape pod just before their planet was destroyed. Oliver Twist was an orphan, who eventually found his true family."

"But his parents didn't die tragically," Jonathan argued.

"The mother died giving birth to him!"

"So? Superman lost his parents *and* his home at the same time."

Ruth Ann scowled at her boyfriend. "Let Daniel decide," she said.

97

He watched their conversation like a bizarre tennis match. No one had ever argued over the story of his parents' deaths before. "Are you serious?" he asked.

Ruth Ann's expression was shocked. "I'm always serious about literature," she replied.

The others snickered softly. Daniel felt a gentle nudge against his elbow. Mary mouthed "sorry." He gave her half a smile.

"What are your plans for the future, Daniel?" Oscar asked.

"I'm not sure," he said. "Travelling is something my mom insisted upon ever since I was a kid. We took a lot of trips when I was younger. She believed firsthand experience was a better than any book in a classroom."

"Hmm." Ruth Ann frowned.

"After my dad died," he continued, "our lawyer helped me sell the house, and I put what I wanted to keep into storage. Then I grabbed my backpack, and bought the first of many plane tickets." Daniel was surprised how easily the words came out. "My mom always said, destiny was something you had to go out and find."

"So you've been on a quest?" Jonathan asked. "Like the Holy Grail."

He studied Jonathan, pretty sure he was visualizing the *Monty Python* version. "I've only been travelling," he said, uneasy another book versus movie argument would break out. Mary stayed quiet; apparently she wasn't ready to mention his notebook either.

"And now you're with us," Petey smiled.

Petey's countenance was so genuine, Daniel automatically smiled back. He realized Petey was the same age he was when his mom died. "That's right," he said. "I guess I am."

When most of the plates were empty, Ruth Ann looked over at Mary and said, "Maybe you and Daniel can pick out something for dessert from the Confectionery," she prompted.

"We were already there," she said, under her breath.

"Oh!" Ruth Ann grinned, then she read Mary's expression. "Oh."

Daniel pretended to take in the details of the restaurant,

NIGHT SHIFT

hoping Jonathan wouldn't pick up on the obvious awkwardness in the air. He focused on an antique clock on the wall that resembled an oversized pocket watch, but instead of a number twelve at the top, there was a golden *W*. Daniel squinted at the time, and then checked his watch—the old clock was off by ten minutes.

He excused himself to make a plate for Mr. Oliver. He figured a little extra effort toward his boss may help smooth things over. Mary followed him to the kitchen and stood in the doorway, watching him. "That's nice of you," she said. "No one has ever done that, he'll appreciate it."

Daniel wondered why Mr. Oliver was never invited to their 'night shift' suppers in the Matinee Room. He guessed his earlier assumption about Mr. Oliver not approving of how Oscar runs his inventory staff might be true after all, or maybe he just didn't enjoy their company.

Later, Daniel sat on the couch, listening to Mr. Oliver. Whether it was the food or the fact he had probably had a nap, Daniel's boss was in a much better mood.

"How long have you worked here?" Daniel asked.

"Almost my whole life," Mr. Oliver said.

"There's a lot of gossip about the store, I wonder how much is true."

Mr. Oliver used his napkin and placed it over the empty plate. A careful smile slipped into place. "You should study the history of the area," he said. "Around the time Mr. Willard bought this building, the state was on the verge of voting for Prohibition, the First World War was dragging its feet, and the Spanish Influenza was about to wipe out thousands of lives."

He folded his hands over his chest. "I was eighteen when I first came to work here. I know it's hard to imagine an old guy like me being young and full of life like yourself. Truth is, I walked in one day looking for a job—any job, really; it didn't matter. And do you know who interviewed me?"

"No."

"Mr. Willard." He paused and squinted at the ceiling. "That was almost forty years ago."

99

B.R. Myers

"Really?" Daniel did the math in his head. Ruth Ann must have heard about the Christmas parties from someone else.

"Mr. Willard was around seventy, and very distinguished looking. He dressed in a suit and tie every day. He had a gold pocket watch that he always carried with him, hanging on a chain from his vest. It was an exact replica of the antique clock in the Matinee Room. He was fastidious about winding it every morning to make sure it kept the exact same time as his watch. He was a bit eccentric that way."

Mr. Oliver's finger tapped the *W* on his tie clip. "He did card tricks for all the children, and always had a bag of *W* peppermints to hand out. Everyone liked him. He was like Mr. Hadley, only smart, not such a silly ass."

Daniel stayed silent. He considered the description of the present store manager somewhat biased. Mr. Oliver continued to reminisce about the glory days with Mr. Willard. Every detail began to weigh Daniel down, making him sink farther into the leather couch. He imagined himself, decades from now, sitting on Mr. Oliver's side of the desk, still wearing the blue security uniform, mumbling about pranks and ghosts. The air left his lungs—he suddenly felt seventy years old.

"I've spent my life taking care of Willard's," Mr. Oliver said, unaware of Daniel's pale face. "I've been worried about who would replace me when I retire." He opened the top drawer, took out a shiny key, and pushed it across the desk.

"Am I taking your place?" Daniel asked. A bubble of panic started to expand in his chest.

Mr. Oliver let out a tired groan. "You seem smart at times, and then you open your mouth. It means you can unlock the front door without having to use my key."

"Oh." Daniel's shoulders relaxed. "I guess this means you don't think I'll get scared off by ghosts."

"No," Mr. Oliver said. "Not yet."

100

# CHAPTER SIXTEEN

The golden arrow stopped at the number four. The chandeliers were turned down low. The stillness of the room gave Daniel an uneasy feeling. He took Mr. Oliver's plate to the kitchen and placed it in the sink. Everything was clean and tidy—like the others had never been there.

The song was so soft that Daniel wasn't sure if he was hearing anything. He peeked through the kitchen door and saw Mary playing the piano near the back of the restaurant. He carefully walked around the booths, watching her hands move effortlessly over the keys, never missing a note.

She looked up, surprised to see him. "Oh," she said, her hands frozen in midair.

"Hey, don't stop," he said.

She held his stare for a few beats, then wiped her palms on her cutoffs before she started the song again.

"What's it called?" Daniel asked, standing against the piano.

"'Gymnopedie No.1.'"

He was disappointed his presence did nothing to interfere with her performance. She was playing perfectly. It was a stark contrast to his own nervous pulse. "I wonder if you're better than me at everything?" he teased, trying to get her attention.

She considered his comment for a moment, then said, "You just have to practice. Have you been to the Music Room, yet? The Steinway is gorgeous to play on. You should try it."

"Maybe a duet sometime?"

"Ask your Magic 8 Ball."

"I don't have it with me."

Mary stopped playing. "Liar," she said, sliding down the bench to make a space for him. Daniel took his place beside her, aware of how close she allowed him. Their thighs brushed together. She showed him the chords for the left hand while she played the melody.

"Not bad," she praised after a few minutes.

"It's simple, but really pretty," he said, concentrating on the keys. "Unlike the title, 'Jim No Pees.' Is it about some old guy who can't go to the bathroom?"

"'Gymnopedie,'" she laughed. "I think it means, dance."

"Like you don't know for sure," he said. When they finished, he pulled the keychain out of his pocket.

She looked triumphant at catching him in a lie. "I'm worried about your unhealthy dependency," she said. "When was the last time you made a decision without using that thing?"

Daniel let it roll in his palm; it felt comfortable there. "I've had it for seven years," he told her, "but I only really started using it when I began travelling."

"Seven years!" Mary gently took it from him. "How much did it cost?"

"Um, fifty cents, I think. It came from one of those treat machines in the grocery store. I was hoping for the Rubik's Cube."

"I'm really good at Rubik's Cube."

"Of course you are."

She inspected it closely. "Why didn't you keeping trying for the Rubik's Cube? Fifty cents isn't much."

Daniel's stomach dropped. His hands gripped the edge of the piano bench. "My mom didn't have any more change in her purse. And we...and I never went back. It didn't seem important." He took the keychain from her and placed it on the piano. "It was the last thing she ever gave me."

NIGHT SHIFT

There was a gap of silence.

"Earlier," Mary began, "when we were talking about the notebook—"

"That's right," he interrupted. "I owe you an answer." Daniel steadied himself, then began his story. "When I was a little kid, like maybe three or four, my mom and I took a trip to a big city. I remember walking down the sidewalk, amazed by how fast everything moved, and how the tall buildings went on forever. We stopped in front of a toy store that had the most amazing train set I'd ever seen."

"A toy store that started with a *V*?" she guessed.

"Or so I thought." He paused and smiled at her curious expression. "She wouldn't let me go inside. I did sneak in for a few seconds. But she didn't follow me, she looked terrified. I ran back to her, and we never returned."

Mary said, "I don't understand. All this time you've been looking for that toy store?"

Daniel tapped the Magic 8 Ball. "You know how you build something up in your mind, until it's all you can think about? And you're convinced that if you get that one thing, you'll be happy, but when you finally find it, you're still unhappy?"

"You're unhappy here?"

Daniel let his shoulders fall in a silent sigh. "No. Maybe. I don't know. This memory is a connection to my mom, but I never knew the whole story." He began to list off the questions that had kept him awake all these months. "Why didn't she come in with me? Why didn't we ever come back? I totally forgot about it until after she died. Then I couldn't stop obsessing. I'm not sure what I hoped I'd find. I never thought past walking through the main doors."

Mary studied his face. She reached up and twirled her hair. "But why Willard's?"

He held up his palm and spread his thumb away from his fingers. "There was a cursive *V* engraved on the door handle. I was little, so it lined up perfectly with my eyes." Then he held up his other hand in an identical *V*. "But I was wrong," he said.

103

"It was only part of a letter." He touched both thumbs together, joining the *V's*. "When both doors close, the two *V's* form—"

"A *W*!" she finished. "How could I have been so stupid?"

"I guess when you come through the front doors every day, you miss the obvious."

Mary stared over his shoulder into space. "The *front* of the doors," she repeated. "Of course. That's why."

Daniel waited for her to continue, but she stayed silent. He wondered if she was disappointed to have the riddle solved so unspectacularly. He looked to the Magic 8 Ball for an answer, but it just stared back at him. "After my mom died," he said, "I used to think she was talking to me through the keychain. Stupid, huh?"

"No," Mary soothed, looking into his eyes, no longer daydreaming. "I'm sorry about the ghost talk at dinner. I didn't realize."

A little bit of weight lifted off Daniel's chest. It felt good to share his story with someone. He said, "The truth is, I've been travelling for so long by myself, I'm starting to feel like a ghost—like everything is a dream, and I'll wake up in my bedroom, hearing my parents' voices in the house." He turned to her. "Does that sound totally crazy?"

"Reality is subjective. Everyone has their own unique perception of life." She placed her hand next to his on the bench, their fingers almost touching. "But, yeah, I get it. You want something real."

"I *need* something real."

She gave him a sad smile, "Me too."

Daniel didn't sense pity; she was sharing his grief, taking some of the sadness from him. He suddenly wanted to share everything. He turned his whole body toward her, but then he stopped and focused on something over her shoulder. The time on the antique clock on the wall hadn't changed since before dinner.

Mary followed his gaze. "That clock hasn't worked in over twenty years," she said.

NIGHT SHIFT

"Mr. Oliver told me it was a replica of Mr. Willard's pocket watch. How come it isn't fixed? I thought everything in the store had to be perfect."

Mary tucked a stray wave behind her ear. "It's not broken," she said. "Mr. Willard was the only one allowed to wind it up. After he died, his pocket watch went missing. The staff let the antique clock run down naturally. Out of respect, the hands remain in place, untouched by time."

"How did he die?"

"He was over ninety years old," she explained. "He went for a walk in the park one morning. They found him sitting up with his eyes closed and a smile on his face. The store put a brass plaque on the bench." She turned her back on the clock, and, Daniel assumed, the subject as well.

He looked at a framed movie poster on the wall behind the piano. "'One Touch Of Venus,'" he read out loud.

Mary cringed. "It's so bad. Jonathan only gave it one star. But it's Ava Gardner, so he had to watch the whole thing."

"If it's so bad, why is it on the wall?"

"Mr. Willard was rumored to have escorted Ava Gardner to the premiere in 1948."

"Seriously?" he said. The former store owner was becoming more legendary by the hour. "What's it about?"

She picked a piece of lint from her black leggings. "A lonely department store clerk kisses the statue of Venus on display, and brings her to life."

Daniel pulled a face. "Isn't that necro-sicko or something?"

"I think you mean necrophilia—and let's not go there." She cleared her throat. "The proper theme is about true love and the power of a first kiss."

Daniel took in the image of Ava Gardner wrapped in a toga. "He falls in love with a statue, but she's a beautiful woman at the same time?" he asked. Mary didn't answer him. He started to reach for the keychain when he noticed, at the very end of the piano, a small pile of caramel candy wrappers.

"I'm sorry about earlier, with the chocolates," she said,

105

smoothing out the frayed edges of her cutoffs. "It's not exactly my style. I'm much better with books and computers—but meeting new people and going on fake dates?" She waited for a second, then answered her own question. "Not so much."

This shy and vulnerable version was so different from Mary's usual demeanour. It made Daniel feel protective of her. "Right now," he said, "there's nowhere else that I want to be." As soon as he said it, he knew it was true. Everything he'd been worried about vanished; the *V* on the door handles, Mr. Oliver's stories about Willard's—even ghosts. Nothing was as important as being with Mary on this old piano bench.

She held his stare. His pulse sputtered, then began to pound. He reached up and gently held her chin between his thumb and finger.

"Daniel, I've never—"

"Shh." His lips brushed against hers, stealing a chaste kiss. Then he kissed her again, longer this time. He felt her smile under his touch. She responded timidly at first, then more sure as the moment grew.

Daniel was shivering and on fire at the same time. It was like fireworks were going off inside his chest. He breathed her in, slowly moving his mouth with hers, the sensation of warm caramel filled him up.

Their lips touched once more, then she leaned back and asked, "Real enough?"

Daniel cupped her face in his hands. "Yes," he said. "Definitely real."

# CHAPTER SEVENTEEN

Daniel stood with his back to the Confectionery as Mary came flying down on the brass handrail. He held his breath when she got a perfect liftoff at the end. She was airborne for a second before he caught her in his arms. They walked along the illuminated makeup counters, enjoying the quiet closeness.

"Let's do this again, for *real*," he said, squeezing her hand. "When's your next night off?"

"Are you working tonight?" she asked.

"Yes."

She smiled. "Me too."

He reached for his cell phone. "At least give me your number," he said. "I'll bring in some takeout."

Mary slipped behind one of the counters. "Give me yours," she said, holding a pen, ready to write on her hand. Daniel smoothed his thumb over the back of her hand and gently wrote his number, then he included his initials. "There. D.G.," he said. "When you wake up, you'll know which guy to call."

She licked her thumb, then rubbed out the G and replaced it with a B. "For Danny Boy," she teased back.

He rested his elbows on the counter, memorizing the contour of her smile. "I know you're insanely curious. Now that you've discovered my big secret, am I less interesting?"

Her voice dropped to a devilish whisper. "I'm not even

close to figuring you out," she said.

Daniel looped her long strand of pearls over his head, encircling them both. Her lips were warm and still tasted like caramel. Mary sighed, kissing him back. Every sound he elicited from her sent his pulse throbbing.

"What time is it?" she asked, breathless.

He chuckled. "Time for you to get a watch." He reluctantly freed himself from the necklace and undid his watch. "Borrow mine," he said, fastening the strap around her thin wrist. "Now," he explained, pressing a few buttons. "I've set the alarm to remind you to call me—DB. What do you like? Chinese, pizza, Greek, Mexican?"

"I've always wanted to have McDonald's."

"You've never had McDonald's?"

"I know, it's not very sophisticated. Never mind, Chinese sounds great." She looked down at the watch. He stayed at the counter, grinning at her stupidly.

"Say goodnight, Danny Boy."

"Goodnight, Danny Boy," he said. "And remember, if you have any complaints, my skills improve with practice."

Mary combed her fingers through his hair and pulled his mouth to hers. "Repetition does improve technique," she said, starting the kiss all over again.

It seemed like Daniel had only closed his eyes for a second before the afternoon sun sliced across the room across his hotel bed. His hand reached out, patting the bedside table, looking for the watch that wasn't there. *Oh, right.* He smiled. He sat up and scratched his blond bedhead, trying to focus.

He started the coffeemaker and unplugged his phone from the charger. He frowned. Mary hadn't called yet, but he did have a text from Alice.

**U got a job!! Going 2B in court all day. LMM**

Daniel left a message at Alice's home number. When he'd decided to leave high school in the middle of his last year to travel, one condition she insisted upon was that he speak to her

NIGHT SHIFT

at least every couple of weeks. This was the first time she'd had
to remind him to call.

On the subway he received stares for whistling. He got a
painful shove in the back for daydreaming in line for coffee and
not moving up. Walking down the sidewalk, he smiled into the
bitter wind. By the time he arrived at Willard's for his shift that
evening, Daniel was overcome with a desire to buy presents.

He started at the gift shop, arranging for an elaborate treat
basket to be mailed to Alice. Then he bought a souvenir T-shirt
for himself, and his favourite purchase: the very mug Mary had
used for their golf game.

He then wandered through the Jewelry section, looking at
watches for Mary. She didn't seem to like anything too sparkly,
so he passed on the elegant styles for something more
appropriate from Sporting Goods. He chose a runner's watch
with a water resistant feature—in case she had to search the
fishpond again.

Along the shelves of the Leisure section, Daniel was drawn
to a coffee table book about exotic beach locations, but he
finally decided on a backpackers' guide to Western Europe. He
stuffed the last shopping bag into his locker and checked his
phone again. Yup, lots of battery life and the ringer was loud
enough—but there was still no call from Mary.

Daniel meandered around the outermost perimeter of
Ladies' Fashions. He paused at a counter and noticed the long
strand of pearls Blanche had put on Mary. He pressed his hand
on top of the glass.

"May I be of service?" a voice came from behind him.

He faced Monique's rival, feeling the blood rush to his
cheeks. "Hey, Stacey, right?" he said, hoping he didn't look
guilty. He removed his hand from the glass surface. "Sorry
about the fingerprints."

"We have to clean them twice a day anyway," she said. "It
could be worse, though; the Confectionery has to do it every
hour. Nose prints from the little kids pressing up against the
chocolate case and all that."

109

Daniel thought of Mary. "It's one of my favourite spots, too."

"Oh!" Stacey looked over his shoulder. He turned and recognized the portly Mr. Hadley. Daniel was impressed that he'd managed to fasten the bottom button of his vest today. He was accompanied by a man with thick horn-rimmed glasses and a fedora. Mr. Hadley was smiling and gesturing with wide arms while the other gentleman nodded.

Stacey did a quick primp as the men drew near. "Good evening, Mr. Hadley," she smiled, practically curtseying.

"Yes, good indeed," Mr. Hadley said. "Saturday is the busiest and the best at Willard's. Make sure to keep busy, Stephanie. We want those spring coats flying off the hangers!"

Stacey forced a smile. "Of course," she said.

The other gentleman gave her a polite nod and then turned to Daniel. Mr. Hadley waved a hand. "Mr. Travis," he said. "This is one of the new night guards, he works with Mr. Oliver."

Mr. Travis said. "Pleased to meet you…?"

"Daniel," he said.

There was a pause, then the man smiled, his eyes crinkling behind the thick glasses. "May I ask, Daniel," Mr. Travis started, "how long have you worked nights?"

"This is my first week."

"Must be overwhelming," he sympathized. "There's so much to become familiar with. I understand the store has a reputation for quick turnovers in the nighttime security department." Mr. Hadley nodded as confirmation.

"I guess," Daniel answered, a little confused.

"Tell me," Mr. Travis asked, "how often does Mr. Oliver check the fire alarm systems?"

"Um, I'm not sure."

He tilted his chin up slightly. "Are you familiar with the safety procedures in case of a power failure?"

"Not exactly." Daniel shifted his weight. "But I know where the electrical room is, and I did a quiz on fire safety." His

NIGHT SHIFT

voice faded off, knowing the more he spoke the worse it sounded.

Mr. Travis and Mr. Hadley exchanged glances. "What's it like working with Mr. Oliver? I understand he's been with the store for many years."

"He mostly keeps to himself in the office. I think he's anxious to retire." His words hung in the air and he wished he'd phrased them differently. "What I mean—" He tried to back pedal.

Mr. Travis pulled out a Blackberry and started thumbing buttons.

"Thank you," Mr. Hadley said. "I think that's enough for today." He continued down the aisle with Mr. Travis by his side.

Daniel and Stacey watched the pair continue down the aisle. "What's that all about?" he asked. Stacey ignored him and walked toward Sleepwear with slouched shoulders. Daniel decided to leave the area before Mr. Travis thought of any more questions he wouldn't have a sweet clue how to answer.

He moved along the aisle and pulled out his phone, but there was still no message from Mary. Maybe she'd had a shower and lost his number because the ink got all blurry?

"Hey, you!" Monique was standing at her usual cashier's counter, in front of the rainwear display.

"I just got cornered by Mr. Hadley," he told her.

Her eyes grew wide, greedy for gossip. "What happened?"

"He didn't say much, but some guy he was with asked a bunch of questions."

"Was he short with glasses? And looked like he walked out of an insurance commercial?"

"Sort of."

Monique nodded and said, "He's been lurking around the last few days. There's a rumour the store is planning something big to boost Spring sales." She flipped her hair over her shoulder. "I'm meeting some friends later," she said. "I'd ask you to come along, but you must be working tonight."

111

"Actually," he said, "I have a date."

Monique's mouth formed a perfect red lipstick O. "Oh, really," she said.

"I'm meeting her later. She works here," he added. "You might know her."

She leaned to one side, sticking out a hip. "What's her name?"

"Mary."

"Mary?" Her face screwed up. "You mean from the gift shop?"

"No."

She laughed and put a hand to her heart. "Thank God. She has grandchildren."

"My Mary does after-hours inventory."

"After hours?"

"Yeah, she does night shift here, too." He checked his phone again, but there was nothing new. His disappointment was warping into fear. What if she'd been hit by a car? What if she was in Emergency somewhere with a horrible stomach flu? He blamed himself for not getting her number in return.

"Daniel," Monique said, her voice weirdly quiet, "you and Mr. Oliver are the only ones who work nights."

His watch alarm beeped. Daniel pulled up his sleeve to hit the reset button, but of course, his arm was bare. Monique's head swivelled around, trying to locate the source of the annoying sound. She stepped up on the platform with three raincoat-clad mannequins.

"Mary told me people hide all sorts of stuff in the displays," Daniel said, watching her walk over to the third model.

"Is this some kind of joke?" Monique pulled back the raincoat's sleeve, revealing his watch. She began pressing buttons, but the beeping continued. Daniel was quickly by her side, and silenced the alarm.

"Why would Mary put—" he started, then he paused. All the blood in Daniel's body dropped to his feet. There, on the

mannequin's hand, in his own writing, were his phone number and initials.

# CHAPTER EIGHTEEN

Daniel staggered backward, falling to the floor.
"Are you okay?" Monique crouched beside him, taking his elbow.

He stared at the third mannequin, wearing the daisy patterened rain boots. His gaze travelled up to her face.

Those eyes.

That hair.

Sweet Jesus, those lips.

"Are you going to be sick?" Monique's voice broke through his building panic. She tugged his arm.

Daniel managed to get his legs under him, and he stood up. "It can't be real," he whispered.

"You look like you just saw the Bloody Assistant," Monique joked nervously, as if she was worried he might be sick all over her new stilettos.

"That's it," he said, letting out a ragged breath. "Petey and Jonathan must have been spying on us. This is just another one of their jokes."

"Petey and Jonathan? Who are you talking about?"

Daniel waited for them to jump out from behind a clothing rack, choking with laughter. But after a minute, it was still only Monique beside him.

"Look," she said, nodding toward the counter. "It's getting late, and I've got to close up the register. Maybe you should go lie down on the couch in the security office or something."

"Uh-huh." He examined the mannequin's hand again. Even the smudge beside the B was the same. "For Danny Boy," her voice echoed in his mind.

Ignoring the curious looks from shoppers, he rushed toward Sleepwear, almost running into Stacey. "Are you all right?" she asked. He gawked at the mannequin behind her, dressed in bunny flannel pajamas—Blanche.

He stumbled through the store, finding all of them: Ruth Ann wearing a Willard's blue-and-white-striped apron in Kitchenware, Oscar in Business Attire, Jonathan wearing a souvenir T-shirt in the gift shop, and finally Petey, posed in Children's Wear, staring longingly at the entrance to the Toy department.

He made it down the grand staircase without tripping or falling into anyone. He passed through the Confectionery and along the glass display cases of diamonds. He stood outside the security office, pressing a hand against his chest, afraid that his heart would explode. What the hell would he say to Mr. Oliver? His brain was sending too many signals. Run. Freeze. Scream. Throw up.

Daniel cupped a hand over his mouth and sprinted to the main entrance. He lurched across the white marble foyer and pushed out the glass doors into the cold, bitter night.

He wandered for over an hour with his hands shoved in his jean pockets. Daniel didn't bother to return for his jacket. Besides his phone, all he had was his wallet. His mind was in damage control. Breathe. Walk. Breathe. Walk.

When he finally realized someone was calling his name, she was also pulling on his elbow. Monique squinted through the drizzle, holding his arm, looking up at him, worried.

"You look like shit," she said. "Are you okay?"

"No."

"Where's your date?" she asked, looking down the street. "Did she stand you up?"

"Not exactly."

"Come on," she said. "You need to warm up." She led him

by the hand into a brick building.

The floor vibrated with techno music. Monique cut a quick path to a table in the corner, under a low-hanging light. She peeled off her coat, then disappeared into the crowd. Daniel's pocket started to vibrate. Too scared to check the caller ID, he put his phone face down on the table, praying it would stop.

Monique returned with two drinks. "You look like you need something stronger, but it's mostly Cokes and Red Bull here." She pushed a tall glass toward him and took a sip of her own drink. "There's no booze allowed." She motioned to the dance floor, where bodies were jumping and slamming into each other. "Naturally, most of the jerks here are drunk."

She scanned the crowd, then turned to back Daniel. He could feel her staring. Finally, she said, "Is this about the nerdy insurance guy?"

"No."

"Did Mr. Hadley fire you or something?"

Daniel shook his head. "No, I didn't get fired."

"Oh crap! Please don't tell me you quit."

He hugged his stomach and rocked forward, feeling the nausea creep back.

She put down her drink. "Listen to me," she said. "Willard's isn't haunted, okay? Sure, lost stuff always shows up within a week. And yeah, there's always food and wine missing from the kitchen. But really, do ghosts eat? I'll admit it's kind of weird when Home Furnishings looks like someone's had a party." She grabbed Daniel's arm. "Once there was a tray with dirty martini glasses and half-eaten canapés on it!" Her laughter petered out when she saw his pained expression.

"I didn't quit." *Not officially, anyway,* he thought.

"Thank God." She put a hand to her chest. "I bet three weeks. Promise me you'll hang on until at least the end of the month. Hey! Don't look at me like that. I didn't even know you when I added my guess to the glass bowl." Monique crossed her legs, making one foot bob up and down to the music. "You're freaking me out. Did you discover some really good dirt on

NIGHT SHIFT

Stacey, but it was so disturbing that it blew your mind?"

"No."

"Too bad, I was kind of hoping for that."

Daniel put his head back and closed his eyes. The throbbing music was a nice distraction. He let it fill his ears, concentrating on the lyrics, trying to get lost in the darkness.

Monique leaned close and squeezed his shoulder. "Your phone is ringing," she said, pressing the phone to his ear, looking worried.

He had no choice but to answer. "Hello?" he said.

"I'm waiting in the staff room," Mary told him. "Your uniform was still in the washer from last night, so I put it in the dryer."

Daniel put a shaking hand over Monique's, and slipped the phone out from her grip.

"Where are you?" Mary's voice came through again.

He put a finger to his other ear and sniffed. "I'm having a few drinks with Monique," he said. "Since you'd been on your feet all day, I thought you'd want the night off."

There was a pause. A very long, terrifying pause.

Daniel bent forward, cradling the phone. "Please tell me it's a joke. Tell me Petey and Jonathan thought it would be funny if they wrote my number on a mannequin that looks exactly like you." He closed his eyes.

"Come back," she begged. Her tone scared the hell out of him. "Just…come back to me."

"That's it? That's all you can say?!" His voice broke up. There was a muffled sob before the line went dead. He pushed the phone far across the table.

"Okay," Monique said. "Let me guess. Was that your date?" She rose out of her chair for another quick scan around the room, and then sat back down, this time closer to Daniel. "I can't believe somebody stood you up," she said.

He shook his head. "It's complicated."

She batted her mascara eyelashes. "There's nothing wrong with enjoying the company of the person you're with," she

reasoned. "Maybe I'm just what you need right now."

He stared down at her hand on his thigh. She was real. She was normal. She never messed with his head, and he always knew what she wanted.

Monique tilted up her face and quickly kissed him on the lips. Daniel hardly had time to react. She leaned back and smiled at him, but he could only stare back dumbly.

*This was all wrong*, he thought.

Kissing Monique felt fake. He let the loud music fill him up. The pulse of the base pounded from the floor all the way to his scrambled brain.

"Let's get out of here," she said, dragging him to the door. There was a crush of bodies by the door as a pair of bouncers pulled a drunk guy outside.

A bouncer with black hair gave them a strange look. Daniel recognized him as one of the day guards who'd placed a bet in the glass bowl his first night.

"Hey, Sean," Monique pleasantly chirped, taking hold of Daniel's waist. "Working hard?" she asked.

Sean's dark eyebrows came together. "As usual," he said. His jacket sleeves stretched tightly over his biceps. Daniel was tempted to make a scene just to get the snot kicked out of him. Unconsciousness sounded pretty good to him right now. Monique pulled Daniel to the curb, and into a waiting taxi. She probed through her purse and pulled out her phone.

The cab driver raised his voice over the radio. "Where to?"

Monique was busy texting. "Where to?" Daniel repeated. He didn't recognize his own voice. The driver frowned at him in the rear-view mirror. "Gramercy Park Hotel," he said.

Monique gave him a playful grin. "Whoa, fancy. You don't mind if I get dropped off first, do you? I'm already late and I might miss the best gossip. My friends are so funny. We all work after school, and with—"

His phone vibrated, and he automatically answered.

"It's Ruth Ann." Her voice ripped through him like barbed wire. "I thought you should know, Monique was treated for

NIGHT SHIFT

herpes last year." Then she hung up.

Daniel held the phone to his forehead and groaned. Monique tucked in close to his side. "Are you all right?" she asked, her face lined with concern. "Hey, I'm sorry. Don't go back to your hotel. Come meet my friends, okay? Are you in the mood to party?" she asked.

"No," he said. "I'm in the mood to forget."

She reached up and touched his cheek. "Yeah," she said. "I know the feeling." He braced himself for another kiss, but she only leaned her head on his shoulder. They rocked back and forth as the taxi moved through the night traffic. He closed his eyes, trying to erase the image of Mary on the pedestal.

Mary.

She had ignited a spark inside, making him believe he might have a chance at being happy again.

Monique's cell phone rang. She made a surprised giggle and reached for her purse.

The cab stopped at a red light. Daniel pressed his forehead against the window, watching his breath fog up the glass. He reached up and wiped it clear. Across the street, the Willard's royal blue banner whipped back and forth in the rain. Daniel pictured Mary using his father's handkerchief to wipe her tears.

The moment had seemed sincere, but now everything she'd ever said was coloured with suspicion. Nothing made sense to him. She acted so embarrassed about never being on a date. *Was that a lie?*

His shock started to warp into panic as his mind wandered to unfounded assumptions. *She's probably made out with every night guard that's walked through the main doors.* And when they found out the truth, they got freaked out and left—just like he did.

She must be laughing with the others, celebrating her latest success of ridding the store of another lovesick night guard. He'd been entertainment for them. Daniel pictured the glass bowl of bets. If he was going to quit, it would be his choice and on his terms, not because he got scared and ran away.

The light turned green and the cab rolled forward. "Stop!"
Daniel yelled. The driver slammed on the brakes. Monique
swore as her phone bounced out of her hands. "Sorry," he said,
jumping out. "This is my stop." He ran across the street,
dodging another cab as it blared its horn.

Daniel stood alone, panting in front of the main doors. His
angry reflection glared back. Reaching into his back pocket, he
pulled out the cold steel key and jabbed it into the lock.

# CHAPTER NINETEEN

Daniel whacked a golden branch, sending a few twinkling lights across the main foyer. He marched down the aisle toward the grand staircase, calling out her name, hearing it echo through the empty department.

He stopped at the base of the stairs—Blanche glared at him with one hand on her hip. She was wearing a pink silk robe and long pearls. "So, you decided to show up after all. I didn't think you had the guts," she gloated. "Well, don't just stand there looking all balled up. Get a wiggle on, the boys are waiting." Her heels clicked up the marble steps, disappearing into the shadows.

"I came back for some answers," he called out.

"Good luck, Mac."

He followed her up the staircase, taking the steps by twos. When they reached the Matinee Room, Jonathan and Oscar were already waiting. He stole a sideways glance at Blanche, suddenly feeling very vulnerable. He wondered if Jonathan was thinking of scenes from *The Godfather*. Daniel realized too late that he should have stayed in the cab with Monique.

At their usual booth, a half-eaten chocolate cake rested on a glass stand. Nothing made any sense; it was like being lost in a maze of disjointed dreams. His body went hot and then cold. His fists clenched at his sides. "Isn't this nice," he said. "Celebrating the loss of my sanity with a little dessert."

Oscar stood up like a gunfighter preparing to challenge the

town drunk. "Before you start hurling accusations," he warned, "you need to hear the whole story."

"Oscar may have about twenty years on us," Jonathan said, full of cheek, "but he *is* the reigning Wii boxing champ."

The anger that had driven him to charge into the store for answers gave way to hurt confusion. "Mary used me," he said, his voice sounded wounded. "You all did."

"She uses the term boy-toy, actually," Jonathan said, relishing in Daniel's discomfort. "She was going to take you to see *Phantom* next week."

Blanche snorted as if he'd messed up the punchline to an awful joke. "He's lying," she said to Daniel. "None of us have left the store." She paused and let that information sink in before she dropped the next bomb. "Not for the last forty years."

"Forty years?" Daniel repeated. The blood pounded in his temples, making him lightheaded.

Jonathan licked chocolate icing off his thumb. "Actually," he said, "when Ruth Ann mentioned *Oliver Twist*, I was biting my tongue not to say *Lars and the Real Girl*. Which wouldn't have been funny at the time, but now of course is totally hilarious."

Daniel wanted to punch the smirk right off Jonathan's face. "Your stupid pranks are the reason all the guards quit, right?" he asked, fighting the bile burning his throat. "Since I was Mary's *boy-toy*, does that mean Ruth Ann gets the next guard?"

In two swift strides, Jonathan had grabbed the front of Daniel's shirt in his fist, and wrenched him closer until their noses were only inches apart.

"Stop it!" Blanche screeched. Angry tears dropped on her pink robe. "None of us wanted you here to begin with, only Mary—she saw you as an experiment."

Her words hit Daniel like a slap. "Why me?" he asked.

"Why *you* indeed?" Blanche choked out, then dropped her head and cried into her hands.

"That's enough," Oscar ordered. He motioned to Jonathan,

NIGHT SHIFT

who slowly let him go. They hurried him to the elevator, leaving a weeping Blanche behind. Oscar whipped the gate closed and slammed the G button. Daniel kept himself wedged in the corner.

When the fourth floor was out of sight, Oscar hit the control panel again, making the elevator stop. Jonathan put a hand on the wall to steady himself. Daniel's heart pulsed in his throat. Even the little blue $W$'s on the gold walls swirled into threatening patterns around him.

"You want answers?" Oscar said, pointing a finger in his face. Daniel could only nod; his ability to speak had left him. "Good. Then listen."

It may have taken only half an hour to explain their situation, but time had a way of slowing down inside Willard's, making Daniel feel like he'd been sitting on that elevator floor for years. He uncrossed his cramped legs. "So," he croaked, his forehead slick with sweat. "You're the only ones in the store who come to life at night?"

Oscar looked down at him, totally in control. "That's right," he said, absentmindedly picking a piece of lint from his blazer.

"And you've always...lived this way?"

Oscar crossed an ankle over one foot and leaned back. "We have to live by the rules; we can never leave the store, or be seen moving by anyone from the outside."

"Or we'll die," Jonathan spat out, "instantly."

"I don't understand," Daniel said, for what seemed like the thousandth time. "Mary saved me that night."

"She risked her life to save yours," Oscar said.

Daniel replayed their first meeting. "Her night-vision goggles fell off."

Oscar explained, "She knew she couldn't save you without turning on the lights, but that also meant—"

"—I could kill her by looking at her."

"After that first dinner together," Oscar said. "I told her

she had to make you leave. She argued that it was obviously safe to be with you, but I knew it wouldn't end well. I tried to convince her you didn't belong with us, and that it was wrong to lie to you. But Mary is stubborn, she wanted more time with you."

"She couldn't help it," Jonathan yawned. "You're such a hot stud." He drew lines between the blue *W*'s with his finger.

Daniel ignored the jibe. "I saw you arguing on the monitor," he said.

Oscar tilted his head to the side. "Mary didn't trick you. We've never had anyone else in our lives."

Daniel looked at him incredulously. "Why me?"

"She was hoping to find that out," Oscar said. He paused and regarded Daniel on the floor; crumpled, sweaty, and confused. "I know this is a horrible shock," he continued, "but you owe Mary an apology. Your behaviour is unacceptable. And when you do something hurtful to one of us, we all feel it."

"Is that another mannequin rule?" he chafed.

"No, it's because we're a family."

Their answers weren't bringing Daniel the satisfaction or comfort he wanted; instead, each detail clung to his heart, squeezing it tightly. "Does Mr. Oliver know?" he finally asked.

"We've never had any contact with him," Oscar said. "I believe he's aware of something, but he has no idea we exist. And if he does, it's the best-kept secret. He's worked here for almost as long as we've been alive."

"That's forty years!" Daniel said. "But Petey's a kid." He closed his eyes, certain his head was going to crack open.

"We don't age," Jonathan confirmed, sounding bored.

Daniel guessed he was probably let down there hadn't been a fight. "But you're actually people," he said. "I mean you eat, and you…and Ruth Ann are a real couple."

"Damn right," he said, still a little defensive.

"We're just like you," Oscar said, unfazed by the whole scenario. "But when we sleep or need to be safe—presto, statue."

"But Petey still acts and talks like a kid. How can he be living for forty years and not at least mentally mature somehow?"

"That's a very astute observation," Oscar said. Despite the situation, the praise in his voice buoyed Daniel's spirit. "My theory is that Petey's brain as well as his body is stuck at eleven years old." His expression became grave, then he said, "In a way, it's a blessing. Imagine being stuck in a kid's body, but with the intellectual capacity of a middle aged man. He'd go insane."

Daniel's fingers gripped the back of his neck. "I feel like I'm in the middle of a Tim Burton movie."

Jonathan unexpectedly lit up, "Oh man, he's the master. *Edward Scissorhands* was beyond epic."

Daniel stared at his Tom Fords, deciding to stay quiet. The elevator began to move. The golden arrow slowly descended, then pointed at the G.

Oscar held out his hand and helped Daniel stand. They walked through the jewelry displays and stopped across the aisle from the security office.

A new idea occurred to Daniel, one that almost took his breath away. "Were you always like this…or did you have lives outside the store?" And could it happen to me, he wondered, wishing again he'd stayed in the cab with Monique.

"This is the only life we've ever known," he replied gravely.

Daniel stared at the frosted glass of the closed security office door. "Now what?" he asked, exhausted.

"That's something only you can answer," Oscar said. He sighed and gave him a pat on the shoulder.

Daniel peeked inside the office, but Mr. Oliver wasn't there. An unfinished crossword lay on top of the desk. He pulled the Magic 8 Ball out of his pocket and something dropped to the floor. He stared down at his key.

Daniel grabbed the glass bowl full of bets and put it on the desk, covering the crossword. Then he threw his key on top. "I

quit," he said.

He ran down the aisle toward the archway of the main foyer. Mary was sitting under the twinkling golden tree with her arms wrapped around her knees and her shoes off to the side. Instead of her usual jeans, she was dressed up in a black mini dress. She studied him with red eyes.

Daniel considered making a run for the front door, but something in her expression made him pause. "Oscar ordered me to apologize," he said. "So…I'm sorry."

She stood up quickly and blocked his way. "Don't hate me because I couldn't tell you the whole truth," she said.

He fought to keep eye contact. "Save your breath," he said. "Oscar already told me everything."

"He doesn't know everything."

Her riddles were driving him crazy. "So you've got all the answers?" he asked. "Then why did you risk your life for a complete stranger? Of all the security guards, why me?"

She looked down at her stocking feet. "You're the only one who ran into an empty elevator shaft," she said.

He turned on his heel, heading for the entrance. "Great! That clears everything up."

"You don't understand. I had no choice."

Daniel kept his stare fixed on the main doors. "Blanche told me about being your little experiment," he accused.

"She's just angry and jealous." Mary touched his elbow. He withdrew from her so quickly, it embarrassed both of them. "I had no choice," she repeated. "When I first saw your face—"

"—it should have killed you."

"There's something else…something I didn't tell the others." She waited to make sure he wasn't going to walk away. "It was like I already knew you. And that I could trust you."

Daniel glared at her. "What do you want from me? You took me into your world. You made me happy again. And now—" His voice cracked and he swallowed back angry tears. "And now I have to give it all up. I have to leave."

She reached for his hands, linking their fingers together.

126

NIGHT SHIFT

"No," she whispered.

Her touch set off the usual rush of blood. He felt dizzy listening to her hurried breathing. Daniel pulled her closer and pressed his forehead to hers. His voice was frail, desperate. "I'm going to be alone again. Is that what you want?"

"I want you to stay."

"Please, I don't understand," he begged. "At least help me understand what's going on."

"You don't have to understand, just believe."

Daniel let go. "I can't," he said. He reached the end of the granite tile where it edged against the white marble pattern of the main entrance. His shoe seemed stuck at the line.

"You don't have to run away again," she said.

He spun around. "What?"

"You haven't been travelling all this time. You've been running after an old memory, living in the past. Never staying in one place long enough to—"

He cut her off. "Long enough to find a new family? Well, guess what. I stopped running, and look how it turned out. I told you last night, I needed something *real*." He pointed to the main doors, "And that's what I'm going to find out there."

"Don't leave," she pleaded, reaching for him again. "You don't even know where you're going. You don't even know what you want!"

Daniel brought his face close to hers. "I want my parents to be alive," he said. "And I want to go home." He twisted out of her grasp, and ran across the white marble tile. He stopped at the door for one last look.

The toe of Mary's stockings reached the edge of the black granite. Her splayed out fingers pressed against the air. "This is as far as I can go," she sobbed.

The image of her pushing against an invisible barrier was too much. "I'm sorry," he choked. "This is too fucking weird."

He ran out of Willard's into the cold, wet night.

127

# CHAPTER TWENTY

Daniel lifted his head, and then moaned as stars crashed behind his eyelids. He blinked, trying to focus. The bed was perfectly made. He'd slept, or rather passed out, on top of the hotel bedspread. His shirt was crumpled up beside him, but his jeans were still on.

Tiny bottles littered the bedside table. He glanced across the room and saw the mini-bar was wide open. With a grunt, Daniel swung his legs over the side of the bed. There was a crunching sound followed by a pop. Pain shot up through his foot.

"Shit. Shit. Shit," he said, hopping to the bathroom. He sat on the tiled floor with his foot resting on the edge of the tub, a shard of glass poking out of his heel. He swallowed a few times, fighting off the nausea. His tonsils felt like they were sticking together. He picked out the shard, then wrapped a towel around his foot and grabbed the counter, pulling himself up.

Daniel's insides sank. "Call me" was written in bright red lipstick across the mirror. His trembling fingers traced the letters. "Red-E-Or-Not," he sighed. Somehow, Monique had ended up in his hotel room. He didn't remember much of anything from last night—he didn't even recognize himself. His hair was messed up and eyes were red and swollen. "Who the hell are you?" he asked his reflection. He didn't even know if he was still a virgin.

Daniel wiped that embarrassing thought bubble away. He

NIGHT SHIFT

was in no shape to deal with all the complications. He filled one of the glasses with tap water and downed it in one swallow. He kept the tap running and drank several more glasses. It stayed in his stomach for only a minute before he kneeled over the toilet, throwing it back up.

When he was finished, he splashed cold water on his face until it was numb. He limped out of the bathroom and opened the top drawer of the dresser—it was empty. His brain was only able to focus on one thought: get to the airport.

Daniel had no luggage. The backpack and his jacket were in the locker at Willard's. The image of Mary begging him to stay made him stumble. He pinched the bridge of his nose. "Get to the airport," he murmured.

He opened all of the drawers, flinging what little clothing he had on the floor. Then he patted his jeans, but other than his Magic 8 Ball keychain, his pockets were empty. He slammed the minibar shut and knelt on the carpet, searching the floor.

"Shit," he whispered.

He sat on the edge of the bed, desperate to remember. Leaning back, he closed his eyes, thinking about the day before. He was sure he had his wallet when he left the store. It should be somewhere in the room, at least he hoped it was.

A buzzing made him jerk upwards. He grabbed his throbbing head, cursing the sudden movement. His phone was under one of the pillows. The caller ID sent a wave of relief over him. He cleared his throat. "Hello?"

"Hi, kid!"

"Alice," he said. He imagined her sitting behind her huge desk, covered in piles of paperwork.

"Sorry about yesterday," she said. "Work is crazy and I didn't make it home until past midnight. So I waited for a more decent hour. How are you, anyway? Your last message made it sound like things were pretty cool in the Big Apple."

Goose bumps peppered his arms. "Um, yeah," he said, pulling the edge of the spread over his bare shoulder. "Sorry, what did you say about yesterday?"

"Nice," she moaned. "Make me grovel. Okay, kid. Trust me, you don't want me to sing, but happy birthday all the same. Well, one day late, anyway."

Daniel's breath caught in his throat. He had totally forgotten his own birthday.

Alice misinterpreted his silence and said, "Look, I won't pretend everything is peachy. I know this was a hard one, being the first birthday without either of your parents, and maybe you wanted to let it pass this year."

Daniel realized Mary had been wearing a party dress. "There was a chocolate cake," he answered, heavily.

"Glad to hear it. But I have another reason for calling you today." She let the silence grow. Alice was all about the drama. "There's a second inheritance—not from your parents' estate, an anonymous one that was to be activated on your nineteenth birthday."

Daniel woke up a bit. "You're kidding."

"I don't kid, kid." Then she told him the amount. "A little over five million."

"That's a lot of zeros," he said, feeling the earth swoop.

"Too many for a nineteen-year-old," she said. "Now listen, I want you to promise me you'll finish school. I'm still your guardian, and technically I control your money until you're twenty-one. You don't have to move back and enroll in your old high school, but you do need to start some kind of course."

Alice's "firm but fair" voice was oddly comforting. Daniel had had a normal family life, firmly middle class, but never anything lavish. Now he was suddenly a millionaire. "Did my parents know?" he asked.

"No."

"Can you tell me anything about it? I mean, what if this person is crazy? Should I be worried? Is it legal?"

"It damn well better be legal. There's no name, but there's an address you can look up if you want to play Hardy Boys." There was a pause, then she said, "Talk about kismet."

"Kismet?"

NIGHT SHIFT

"It means fate. Geez kid, see what I mean about getting an education? Here, write this down."

Daniel had her repeat the address, but he didn't write it down—it was already circled in his black notebook.

# CHAPTER TWENTY-ONE

Daniel shifted his weight, making the wooden chair squeak. The silence was unbearable. It was like being interviewed all over again. Mr. Oliver's hands were pressed flat on the green blotter. When Daniel had sheepishly knocked on the door a few minutes earlier, Mr. Oliver only nodded to the chair. Since then, he'd been quiet, staring him down.

Daniel squirmed again.

*Squeak.*

"Um, look," Daniel began, unable to stand the passive interrogation. "I'm not sure how to ask you this, but—"

"No phone call," Mr. Oliver interjected. "No note. No message. Only a key left carelessly on top of my desk."

Daniel knew this wasn't going to be easy. "There was a...situation."

"The very key I personally gave to you," Mr. Oliver continued, his voice rising.

"It's just that—"

"I don't care if you're having girl trouble, or if your car got stolen or if your favourite TV show got cancelled. The most important thing is keeping the store safe. In all my years working at Willard's, I've never met a more incompetent guard than you."

Daniel's mouth fell open. He couldn't help but be insulted. "I may have left your precious key without a note, but I'm not

incompetent."

Mr. Oliver said, "You left the main doors unlocked! Everything in the store was at risk because of your carelessness. I should fire you on the spot."

Daniel had no desire to stay at Willard's, but he didn't want to see it harmed either. "I don't want my job back," he said.

"Hmm," Mr. Oliver said. "That's unexpected."

Daniel wasn't sure if he was being sarcastic or not. "It's not because of ghosts," he clarified. "Willard's isn't what I need right now, I guess. The reason I came back is because I need to ask you something."

"A letter of reference for your next unsuspecting employer?"

"No." He tried hard not to roll his eyes. "It's about an inheritance."

The door opened, and one of the day guards walked in, holding a clipboard. "Sorry, Mr. Oliver," he said. "I've gone down the list, and no one can work tonight."

Mr. Oliver snatched the clipboard. "Even this guy?" he said, pointing to the list of workers. "The narcoleptic?"

The day guard shook his head. Mr. Oliver turned to Daniel. "One more shift and I'll give a letter of reference," he offered.

"I don't need a letter of reference."

"You're the only one who doesn't believe in ghosts," Mr. Oliver said. "You're supposed to give me two weeks' notice, actually."

Daniel almost laughed at the absurdity. "You mean like the other guards, who left because they were scared?" he challenged. "I bet they didn't have to give you two weeks."

Mr. Oliver was unimpressed. "I never got a chance to ask them, because they never came back." He paused and lifted a white eyebrow. "Unlike you." There was a mysterious hint to his tone that made the hair on Daniel neck stand on end.

His eyes were drawn to the glass bowl of bets. He thought of Sean and his jerk friend from the first day. He'd promised himself he'd quit on his own terms. He reasoned it might be

easier to talk to Mr. Oliver about the inheritance after hours. Daniel knew that if he left the store, he'd never come back—this last shift was his only chance to get some answers, and he was certain Mr. Oliver knew something.

"All right," he agreed. "I'll work tonight."

The day guard slouched out of the room. Mr. Oliver nodded, then opened a desk drawer and handed over the silver key. "Don't be such an idiot this time," he said.

On his way to the staff room, Daniel passed two disgruntled clerks talking with the day guard who had just left the office.

"Crap," one complained. "I would have won."

Daniel gave them a sympathetic shrug, knowing that whoever bet tomorrow's date would be happy. As soon as he got some answers and found his wallet, he was heading straight to the airport.

Thoughts of a quick getaway, though, were dispelled when he opened his locker. Lying perfectly folded on top of the shopping bags and his backpack were his plaid shirt, his uniform, his father's handkerchief, and his watch. He held the handkerchief up to his face and inhaled—it smelled like Mary.

"Damn it," he whispered. He'd acted like such an ass. He cringed, remembering what he'd said about making out with other guards, when all along he was the only one she'd ever met. He had no idea what to say to her now.


Daniel stayed in the shadows, intent on doing his rounds as invisibly as possible. Each noise made him jump. His shoulders were aching from all the tension. When he reached the third floor, he walked down the aisle along Children's Wear and ended up at the entrance to the Music Room. Thankfully it was empty.

The walls were decorated with autographed pictures of famous musicians. Brass and stringed instruments were displayed in neat rows. A pristine grand piano, illuminated with low-hanging lights, dominated the middle of the room.

Daniel played a few chords. Even with his unpracticed hand, the tune on the fine instrument was sweet.

Ruth Ann clapped slowly from the doorway. "You've got some nerve, showing up," she said.

He swallowed his thumping heart, unable to think of any answer that would satisfy her. So he told her the truth. "I didn't get fired."

She threw daggers across the room with her eyes. "There was a rumour you'd quit. Some staff were already counting their winnings. Three nights would have been a new record."

He kept quiet about his arrangement with Mr. Oliver.

"I'm not a mean person," she said. "I'm protective of Mary. And…and I lied about Monique having herpes. Mary's my best friend and I'm on her team, you know." She pushed a blond curl off her forehead. "You really hurt her."

Daniel knew he should have looked for Mary right away, but he dreaded the confrontation and the image of her posing in her mannequin form still made his stomach twist. "I need some answers," he finally said, hating how his voice shook.

"You *need* to see something."

At the back of the room, on a raised platform, a mannequin stood holding a microphone. She was dark skinned and wore a sparkling evening dress with long sleeves and high heels.

Daniel studied the mannequin. "Is she real like you?" he asked.

"She was, until one night Clara never woke up. None of us know for sure, but I think she missed the music too much. There was another mannequin, her name was Virginia, and she was Clara's best friend. When she played jazz on the piano…" Ruth Ann sighed. "Clara's voice was on fire."

"What happened?"

"One night Virginia wasn't in her display. We looked all over the store, but the only thing we found was Petey, huddled on the floor, crying. Virginia was like a mother to him, their bond was very strong. He doesn't remember much, it was so long ago, but he still hates to talk about it."

135

She looked up at Clara. "We used to be here every night trying to wake her up, but it's too sad to see her this way. It's been months since I've come in."

"Can she hear you? I mean, when you're," he motioned toward the mannequin," you know, in pose…are you aware of what's happening around you?"

"If we concentrate. Mostly I find eavesdropping on the clerks too boring, so I usually end up sleeping the whole dayshift. But I think Clara has been asleep for so long she's unreachable."

"How long has she been asleep?" Daniel asked.

"Almost three years."

"Jesus," he whispered. This scared him more than he wanted to admit. He wished Ruth Ann hadn't told him this story; he didn't want to know any more about them. He only wanted to know about the inheritance, and then leave for good.

Ruth Ann continued. "I'm not sure what's worse, not knowing what happened to Virginia or having Clara still with us, but unresponsive." She turned to Daniel. "When you left, Mary was devastated. I stayed with her all night. Then I had to spend the whole day worrying I would find her like this."

"I'm sorry," he said, truthfully. He stayed quiet after that, unable to think of a way to bring up his inheritance, certainly not after hearing Clara's story.

He followed Ruth Ann out of the Music Room and along Children's Wear. She paused and straightened a few baby sleepers, gently smoothing out the tiny outfits. She stifled a sniff then quickened her pace.

Daniel was embarrassed to see this side of her. What the hell could he say? They had nothing in common. He wasn't even sure if he'd had sex and she was brooding over baby outfits. He chose an obvious topic. "So," he started. "How long have you and Jonathan been together?"

"From the very beginning," she answered without hesitating.

"You've been together for forty years?" he almost tripped.

NIGHT SHIFT

Forty years seemed like an eternity to him.

"I still remember the first time I saw him—the sparks were always there." She made a face. "Although he drives me crazy with all his movie talk."

"Yeah," he said, keeping tight-mouthed about her book quoting.

"It's so frustrating," Ruth Ann continued, clearly passionate about the topic. "Willard's has all the movie channels. Anytime Jonathan wants to see one of his top choices, he only has to pick up the remote. But the Leisure section can only carry so many titles. Most of my favourites have been off the shelves for years."

"I thought you had a photographic memory."

"I do."

"You can recall any passage you want, right? Isn't that like picking up the remote?"

She snorted. "It's not the same as holding a book in your hands. Nothing can replace the thrill of turning the page to read what happens next."

"What about the staff room? The bookcases are full of titles."

"Oh, please." She waved her hand in the air as if to dispel the very idea. "Drugstore paperbacks meant to pass the time."

Daniel couldn't fight the smile. "You're a book snob."

"Never mind," she huffed. "You don't understand. No one here does."

They walked a little farther, then he said, in his best storytelling voice, "'Do you know why swallows build in the eaves of houses?'"

She stopped and regarded him with a complete look of shock. "'It is to listen to the stories,'" she answered. "That's from *Peter Pan*! How did you know that?"

"*Peter Pan and Wendy*," he corrected, smugly. "It was my favourite as a kid. My mom read it to me almost every night." They shared an unexpected smile and continued walking.

"I'm sorry about your mom," she said gently. "And your

137

dad."

"Thanks. I've been thinking about them a lot lately."

When they reached the landing, Ruth Ann put her hand on the brass handrail and motioned toward the upper floor. "Come on," she sighed. "Everyone's getting ready to eat."

Daniel was torn; he wanted to escape further confrontations, but Mr. Oliver wasn't giving him any answers, and the others might know something about his inheritance. He followed Ruth Ann in silence.

# CHAPTER TWENTY-TWO

D aniel paused under the archway to the Matinee Room, content to stay hidden behind a collection of large potted ferns.

Ruth Ann said, "I don't hate you, but I'm not going to hold your hand." He watched her join Jonathan, who was putting a platter of bacon on the table. The smell of fried tomatoes and onions made his mouth water; he hadn't eaten anything since yesterday.

Daniel approached the booth tentatively and noticed with relief that Mary was missing.

Oscar spoke first. "Welcome back." He stood proud and dapper as usual. Tonight it was designer jeans and a silk crew neck sweater. "Trying to stick it out until the last bet in the glass bowl?"

Certain his voice would shake, Daniel shrugged in a kind of "no-comment" gesture. His desire for information slunk down the grand staircase like a guilty shadow.

"Come back to finish what we started last night?" Jonathan asked, his tone and the half-hidden fist by his side leaving little room for doubt as to his meaning.

Daniel glanced at Ruth Ann. Had Jonathan told her what Daniel had said? Petey huddled close to Oscar, staring at the floor. Shame burned across Daniel's cheeks. Mary wasn't the only one who deserved an apology. A clanging from the kitchen

made everyone jump.

Petey said, "Mary's a bit, um…"

"Pissed," Jonathan finished.

Daniel made a path toward the kitchen. He flattened his hand against the swinging door, silently counted to three, and then pushed through.

Mary stood by the sink, wearing a white T-shirt and ripped designer jeans. Her gaze flicked back and forth between her plate of steaming omelet and his face. He ducked as the plate whirled over his head, smashing into the wall, showering him with egg and tomato. The others quickly crowded the doorway.

"Are you crazy?!" he cried out, still crouching on the floor.

Mary pointed at Daniel. "You," she said, her voice trembling, "have no right to show up like nothing happened."

Daniel wobbled to his feet. "I had to come back," he said.

"Great, you came back. Now you can leave," she said, hatefully. "There's no invisible barrier for *you*."

"Are you that angry with me?" he asked. "Or did you never really like me that much to begin with?"

Mary didn't flinch. "Which answer makes more sense to you?"

Oscar put up his hands. "All right, fools, that's enough. Petey, go get Blanche." He shook his head at the messy kitchen. "I need another adult."

Mary started to sweep up bits of omelet.

Daniel watched for a couple of painful seconds, then he bent down, collecting the larger chunks of plate.

"I can do this without your help," she snapped.

"I had to come back."

"I heard you the first time," she said.

Oscar crossed his arms. "Actually, I'd be interested to know what changed your mind."

Daniel tried to gather his thoughts. "Once I believed what I was seeing," he said. "I crossed a line. Now, I need more answers."

A look of understanding crept across Oscar's face. "Fair

NIGHT SHIFT

enough," he conceded.

"'The eye only sees what the mind is prepared to comprehend,'" Ruth Ann quoted from the doorway. Then she added with an air of importance, "Robertson Davies."

Daniel placed the shards in the sink. He wiped his hands on his jeans, then repeated what Alice had told him.

"Sure," Jonathan said, not bothering to hide his sarcasm. "All this time there's been a huge pile of money waiting for you and the anonymous donor stipulated that you be told on your nineteenth birthday."

"Alice confirmed it."

"And the only information you were given was this address?" Oscar asked, smoothing out his moustache. "Do you have any idea who it might be?"

Daniel shrugged self-consciously. "Well, I was kind of wondering if it might be one of you."

Ruth Ann snorted. "We have no money."

"Besides," Jonathan said, we didn't even know you existed until Mary came blabbing all excited after she pulled you out of the elevator shaft."

"Yeah," Daniel said, remembering the night he eavesdropped behind the bookcases. "What about Mr. Oliver?"

Ruth Ann clasped her hands. "Holy smokes," she said. "This is just like Pip and Miss Havisham." She glanced at them expectantly, but no one replied. "Hello—*Great Expectations.*"

"Except it wasn't Miss Havisham who left him the money," Daniel said. "It was the convict from the graveyard in the first chapter."

"I know that!" she said. "I'm only making a comparison."

Jonathan put a consoling arm around Ruth Ann, then said, "So, if it isn't us, Mr. Oliver, Miss Havisham, or Colonel Mustard in the billiard room with the candlestick—who is it? Wait, why do I even care?"

Mary glared at the floor, content to let the others busy themselves with Daniel's problem.

Sneakers slapped on the tile. Petey sprinted toward them.

"It's Blanche," he said between breaths. "You gotta come, now!"

# CHAPTER TWENTY-THREE

Blanche's screams echoed up the grand staircase. Mary and Ruth Ann slid down the railing. Daniel watched helplessly as the others followed suit, leaving him scrambling to take the steps two at a time.

Ladies' Sleepwear was bathed in the soft glow of several chandeliers. Racks of pajamas and fluffy robes blocked Daniel's view. He followed them through a maze of lace-trimmed nightgowns and satin slippers till he saw Blanche. She was wearing a black evening gown, and twirling in a three-way mirror, squealing with delight. "I can't believe it! Isn't it gorgeous?" she exclaimed.

"Yes," Oscar said, shooting Petey a look. "The dress is beautiful."

"Not just beautiful," she said. "This is a replica of the dress Audrey Hepburn wore in *Breakfast at Tiffany's*!" She adjusted the diamond clip that held her hair in an elegant bun.

Daniel had never seen Blanche happier or more beautiful.

"Wow," Ruth Ann said. "Where did you find this dress?"

"I woke up like this! It's a miracle!"

"I guess the new Spring line is certainly to your liking," Jonathan joked. "You'll look great for movie night. Hey, maybe we should watch *Breakfast at Tiffany's*?"

"This isn't from the Spring line," Blanche said. "This dress is one of a kind. I remember it." She became quiet, running her

hand along the seam. "This dress was made by Maureen."

The others exchanged uneasy glances.

Daniel frowned. "But I thought Maureen was...um, gone?"

"She dressed Blanche as the showcase mannequin," Mary explained matter-of-factly. "She retired, I told you that."

Oscar let out a sigh. "Blanche, what does this mean?"

"It means my prayers have been answered! My Maureen has returned!"

"Are you sure?" Ruth Ann asked. "Maybe the dress was found in storage and someone decided to put it on you."

Blanche scowled at her. "Even if a truckload of vintage vogue was dropped off at the door, these Dumb Doras wouldn't know what to do with it."

She strutted over to Daniel, then turned her back to him. "Please look inside and read the tag, Mac."

*Please?*

Daniel flipped up a square black tag with his finger and read out loud, *"By Maureen."*

"See?" Blanche beamed. "I'm so happy I could dance." She grabbed Daniel and started to twirl. He spun around with her, clumsily navigating the racks of robes and nightgowns. Blanche squeezed his shoulders. "I think you've changed something about the store. This is the beginning of all our wishes coming true. Maybe Maureen can be with us now, too!"

He released her, feeling the blush warm his ears. Wishes coming true? What was he getting into?

Blanche linked arms with Petey on one side and Oscar on the other. "This calls for a round of martinis," she announced happily. The trio disappeared around the corner, with Blanche talking excitedly all the way to the elevator.

"I thought she hated me," Daniel said.

Mary joined Ruth Ann, putting more space between herself and Daniel. "Well, maybe Maureen is back," she suggested.

Ruth Ann chewed her lower lip. "After retiring five years ago? I'm not sure."

"This is a surprise, I take it?" Daniel said.

144

NIGHT SHIFT

"That's the understatement of the year," Jonathan said. He took one of the satin nightgowns and held it up to Ruth Ann.

She swatted it away. "Maureen simply stopped coming to work. Blanche thought she was sick or on vacation, but then a few clerks mentioned her retirement. The thing is," she said, dropping her voice dramatically, "there was no retirement party."

"And there's been no news about her?" he asked.

Jonathan smirked. "Only Blanche complaining about her outfits every day."

"Every day?"

"For five long years," Ruth Ann confirmed. "This dress is a big deal."

Daniel shifted his weight. "Maybe I can find out something. There must be past employee records in the store somewhere." *Whoa. What was he saying? He had a plane to catch!*

"I've already tried," Mary said, with an impatient edge. "Her employee file states she's a code 230—early retirement due to medical leave. The next of kin on file is a brother in the Midwest. I called one night, pretending I was with Human Resources, doing an address update. He was vague and cut me off, saying Maureen had retired and wouldn't be returning to Willard's."

Ruth Ann hugged her elbows. "We'd never say this to Blanche, but we think she died."

Daniel glanced at his watch—it was already midnight. Mary lightly touched her own wrist. She caught his eye for a moment, then looked away.

"Okay." Jonathan clapped his hands once. "As much as I love spending time surrounded by ladies' underwear, the movie network is showing *Raiders of the Lost Ark*." He reached for Ruth Ann. "If we hurry, we can catch the runaway boulder scene."

"Are you kidding?" she asked him.

"What? Indiana Jones is one of your favourite literary

145

characters."

"*Tom Jones*," she said, exasperatedly. "Besides, this is more important than one of your stupid movies! What are we going to do about Maureen?" The couple looked expectantly at Mary.

"Security office," she declared.

Jonathan and Ruth Ann joined Mary, while Daniel timidly followed.

They paused outside the office door. After Daniel made sure it was clear, Mary pushed by him and sat down at the desk in front of the computer. "We'll need to access the security videos from today," she said.

"Um," Daniel began. "I don't have a password."

"Uh-huh," Mary replied, already typing. "What a mess," she said, clicking the mouse. "Mr. Oliver has all kinds of files open, but nothing to do with security. It looks like he was online shopping."

"Anything kinky?" Jonathan asked, leaning over her shoulder.

"Don't be gross," she said. "It was only the Consumers Plus site."

Daniel had only been inside the national franchise a few times. It was typical marked-down, wholesale merchandise—nothing like Willard's. "Why would Mr. Oliver be shopping online when he works here?" he asked.

Mary logged in under Mr. Oliver's name. Soon, all of the security files were on the screen.

"You know his password?" Daniel asked, unable to hide the admiration in his voice.

Ruth Ann boasted, "Mary's a pro at opening locks and hacking into e-mails."

"It's called searching," she corrected. "For clues to help locate items on the Lost and Found list."

"You broke into *my* locker," Daniel reminded her. Jonathan shot him a look, then pulled Ruth Ann away to stand guard by the door. Daniel moved closer to Mary. "Did you look in any of

NIGHT SHIFT

the shopping bags?" he asked.

"I returned your things." She stared back, daring him to push his luck. "Why?"

Their foreheads were almost touching. A pulse of heat grew in his stomach, then slowly spiralled downward.

"How long is this going to take?" Jonathan whined from the doorway.

Mary stiffened, then moved away and began to type again. She didn't take her gaze off the screen. "The cameras in Ladies' Fashions switch views every few minutes. I have to keep skipping through until I get to Sleepwear. Wait...here!"

Daniel glanced at the wall of monitors. "Why aren't you checking the actual videos?"

"Once the monitor is turned off, all the footage gets erased," Mary explained. "That's why it's saved on the computer as backup." Mary concentrated as she scanned the black-and-white images. The angle didn't show Blanche's display, but it gave a full view of the cashier's desk and surrounding area. A salesgirl with short dark hair placed a large, flat box on the counter. Several other clerks gathered around.

"I wish they'd get out of the way," Ruth Ann complained. The scene switched to Footwear. Mary growled and skipped ahead. When the monitor showed Sleepwear again, the young clerk was holding up Maureen's *Breakfast at Tiffany's* dress. Mr. Hadley stood beside her, looking very pleased.

Mary twirled her hair and scanned the rest of the footage. "I don't understand," she said, more to herself than the others.

Jonathan pointed to the clerk holding the dress. "For someone who's supposed to be dead, Maureen looks great."

Mary rolled her eyes. "That's not Maureen, you moron."

"Who is it?" Jonathan grinned. "She's hot."

"Who cares if she's hot?" Ruth Ann said. "More importantly, why does she have Maureen's dress? And why does Mr. Hadley care?"

"I know her," Daniel said. "That's Shifty Stacey."

147

# CHAPTER TWENTY-FOUR

Mary spun around and stared at Daniel, waiting for an explanation.

"Stacey was trying to get Mr. Hadley's attention the other day," he said. "Monique thinks she's up to something." Daniel's chest grew tight—he still hadn't called her.

"Sounds like Monique has all the answers," Mary said. "You guys make a super great team."

Jonathan snickered. "Somebody's jealous."

Mary marched over to the long row of filing cabinets and pulled out one of the drawers. Her fingers ran over a thick rows of tabs, then she chose a thin yellow folder. "Stacey's employee file," she said, opening it on the desk.

Ruth Ann read over her shoulder. "Look at the education section," she said, pointing to the form. "She's enrolled in fashion design at Cazanovia College."

"That's no surprise," Daniel said. "Monique told me as much."

Ruth Ann gave him a critical look and said, "By the way, you should be working on your high school diploma. With all the online courses available, there's no excuse for neglecting your education."

"You looked at my file?"

"Of course," she answered. "That's how we knew about your birthday. Don't change the subject. You need to study. I could tutor you, I'm always up for a challenge."

NIGHT SHIFT

Daniel was all too aware of Jonathan's death stare, and getting his GED wasn't worth losing a limb.

Mary closed the file and tapped her finger on the cover. "There's nothing in here that connects her to Maureen."

Ruth Ann took the file and returned it to the cabinet. The sound of footsteps echoing down the jewelry aisle made everyone jump.

Before Daniel could blink, Jonathan grabbed Ruth Ann's hand and ran around the potted ferns down the hallway. He stared at Mary, not sure what to do.

She hesitated, then raced after the others. He followed her along the wall of black-and-white pictures and through a door at the end of the hallway. It was like he'd been dropped inside a computer; the electrical room was covered with wires and blinking lights. There must have been hundreds of little switches. He swallowed, remembering Mr. Hadley and Mr. Travis quizzing him about this place.

They stayed quiet, listening to Mr. Oliver move around the office. Once it was clear he'd settled, they began to whisper.

Jonathan struck a theatrical pose and said, "Well, here's another nice mess you've gotten me into!"

A smile curled up Ruth Ann's mouth. "*Sons of the Desert,*" she answered.

Mary began, "I've been thinking, since we're not sure why Stacey has Maureen's dress, we should keep it secret."

"Poor Blanche," Ruth Ann said. "She's convinced Maureen is back."

Daniel said, "I don't understand their connection." He paused, trying to figure out how to ask the next question. "I mean, she didn't know about your life, like I do...right?"

Mary shared a look with Jonathan and Ruth Ann, then her shoulders slumped like she was too tired to put on the charade any longer. "Blanche used to leave her signed notes," she told him. "When Maureen misplaced things, I'd help find them at night. It was Blanche's idea to leave a little message with the item. Then one day, while adjusting a new outfit on Blanche,

she called her by name."

Ruth Ann continued, "Eventually, it became normal for Maureen to talk to her."

"But you never met her?" Daniel asked. How could Blanche be in love with someone she'd never spoken with? It sounded so painfully desperate, yet self-indulgent at the same time. "If Maureen was so important to her," he said, "why didn't Blanche just risk it?"

Ruth Ann's face fell. "Are you serious? That would be suicide! It's like telling someone they might be able to fly, but the only way to know for sure is to jump off a building."

An unexpected shame made Daniel dip his chin, staring at the floor. He was only now beginning to appreciate how much Mary had risked the night she saved him—how quickly she'd made the choice. Did she regret saving him?

Jonathan stretched his arms over his head and yawned. "I'm bored. Anyone bring cards?"

Daniel's eyes wandered over the blinking circuits. His head started to throb; the only thing in his stomach was a coffee he'd bought off a vendor five hours ago.

Mary cleared her throat importantly. "As long as we're stuck here, you might as well learn something." She pointed to the various panels. "Each column of switches has a code at the top," she began, keeping her eyes on the wall, not even turning toward Daniel. "Every floor has a separate panel for the lights and power. Then there's the master switch…"

Daniel nodded, trying to concentrate. The small room was twice the temperature of the hallway. Mary took out a clip from her jeans pocket and piled her hair up. He unbuttoned the top of his shirt and loosened his tie.

"…and the phones as well," she said.

"Sorry?" Daniel wiped his brow.

"This area is the store's brain," Mary said, slightly perturbed. "Everything is run from here; the power, the phones, the fire alarm."

"What's that one do?" Jonathan said. He reached out to

NIGHT SHIFT

touch a red button at the top of the first panel.

Mary slapped his hand away. "That's the sprinklers, idiot."

Daniel was desperate to leave this sweltering room and their bickering. He checked on Mr. Oliver and found him asleep in the chair with his chin resting on his chest—this was probably their best chance to get past.

He headed back down the hallway for them, but then paused in front of the black-and-white picture of Willard's Grand Opening. The large, ornately carved frame stood out from the plainer ones. He studied the face of James D. Willard. Maybe if he stared at it long enough and hard enough, answers would start pouring out…but that was crazy. Pictures couldn't talk.

Mary emerged from the electrical room, red-faced. "Those switches aren't toys, jerk. Ever hear of a power surge?" she said. "You almost wiped out the electricity for the whole store."

"You mean like the explosive diarrhea after Oscar's chilli?" Jonathan asked. He stopped beside Daniel and squinted at the picture. "Just think," he said, his voice uncharacteristically flat. "All of those people are dead now."

Daniel concentrated so hard, a face emerged—his own reflection. He wasn't sure who he was anymore. All he used to care about was finding this store, but now that he'd found it, he felt more lost than ever. He was obviously meant to come here, the inheritance would have brought him to Willard's looking for his benefactor—but why? He wished he could be that little kid again, looking at the train set from the sidewalk. "The world depends on which side of the glass you're looking from," he recited.

"What did you just say?" Ruth Ann stared at him, uncertain.

Daniel was unnerved by her reaction. He explained the memory of his first trip to Willard's. He reached into his back pocket, pulled out his black notebook, and began to read. "'You must remember, even when things seem horrible and very sad, the world is full of magic and beautiful things. And how you

151

see the world—'"

"'—depends on which side of the glass you're looking from,'" Ruth Ann finished. Then she continued, "'I've travelled the globe searching for my heart's content. Then I looked inside myself and found home. I brought back beautiful things from my trips around the world to showcase in one great place. And you too shall surely feel it in your own hearts, because when you walk through the front doors, you will find that Willard's is just what you need.'"

Everyone was quiet. Ruth Ann pointed to the picture. "That's the speech Mr. Willard made the day he opened the store. The day this very picture was taken."

Daniel almost dropped his notebook. "That makes no sense."

"Mary and I have researched the store's history to death. Your mother somehow knew that phrase by heart."

Daniel gave her a weak smile. "Coincidence?"

"'Coincidence is God's way of remaining anonymous,'" Ruth Ann quoted. "Albert Einstein."

Jonathan said, "That's lovely, babe, but am I the only one getting a serious case of the shivers? This is weird—and we're used to some pretty weird shit."

Daniel silently agreed. He stared at the black-and-white picture, trying to coax the answer from the dead. He stepped back and his eyes grew wide. He walked to the end of the hallway and put his black notebook up against the wall of pictures. "The electrical room only comes out this far."

"Okay," Jonathan said, slowly.

Daniel pointed at the potted ferns. "And the office ends right at the corner." He looked at them with a huge smile on his face. "Don't you see?" He spread his arms in front of the wall covered with pictures. "This whole area of about twelve feet has nothing behind it."

Jonathan scratched his head, looking doubtful.

Mary's eyes flashed with excitement. "There must be something behind this wall. Maybe the picture is a clue?"

NIGHT SHIFT

"Or maybe," Daniel said, examining the elaborate scrolling pattern around the image, "the frame is."

Jonathan asked, "You think a dream about your dead mother is telling you there's a secret hidden behind the wall? Isn't that a little unbelievable?"

"Said the talking mannequin," Daniel rebutted. "And it wasn't a dream, it was a memory."

Mary squinted with her nose inches from the frame. "I don't see anything."

"How about an M?" Daniel asked, his voice rising. "Right here." He pointed to a raised cursive letter in the lower corner.

"Shouldn't it be a W?" Jonathan said, rolling his eyes.

"Exactly," Mary breathed. Moving swiftly, she reached down, and put her finger against the letter.

Ruth Ann made a desperate noise, "Stop! Maybe we should…uh, prepare ourselves. We don't know what's behind that wall. What if it's a trap? When Professor Van Helsing opened Lucy's tomb to prove she was a vampire, she sneaked up behind him, ready to attack."

"Oh please," Jonathan said. "This is just like that haunted house movie, *Rose Red.* I bet behind this picture is a staircase that leads to nowhere." He hummed a few tunes of spooky music.

"No. Wait!" Ruth Ann said. "It's 'The Tell-Tale Heart.' There was a body hidden under the floorboards. Think about the missing magician." She put a hand to her mouth. "We're about to solve a hundred-year-old mystery!"

"That's it," Jonathan lectured. "No more *Scooby-Doo* for you."

"It was Edgar Allen Poe!"

"Yeah, him too."

"Enough already," Daniel whispered harshly. "You're going to wake up Mr. Oliver. Jesus, you guys are exhausting."

"Welcome to my world," Mary said dully. She pressed down on the M, but nothing happened. "There's got to be a way," she frowned.

153

"Oh well," Ruth Ann said. "At least we tried. I say we go make treat bags. There was a shipment of new sour chews." She looked around, hoping for any takers, but the others were still staring at the wall.

"It's probably dead space," Jonathan said, enjoying the role of devil's advocate. "Full of wires and crap."

"Did you have to say 'dead'?" Ruth Ann whispered.

Mary turned to Daniel, her face full of hope. "What if it's a passage to the outside? Maybe this is why you're here!" Her words tumbled out excitedly. "It all fits—the memory of your mom, and why we're safe with you. The inheritance was set up so you'd come find us and help us leave. This is it, Daniel!"

Her unexpected praise made him feel like a superhero. Finding out what was behind this picture was as important to him as it was to Mary. His heart pounded with the possibility of helping her escape. She could live on the outside. She could be normal. She could be…*real*.

"Hold on, genius," Jonathan said. "Are you saying we're finally going to leave Willard's, and it's not because of all the research we've done over the years, but because Daniel showed up one day, looked at a picture we know by heart, and figured out the greatest secret in the store?"

Mary's expression fell. "When you say it like that," she mumbled.

Daniel's heart broke a little. He knelt beside her and took a closer look at the letter. A smile tugged the corner of his mouth. "'The eye sees only what the mind is ready to comprehend.'" He turned to her and asked, "What's the most popular chocolate in the store?"

She stiffened by his side and tilted her nose into the air, but the blush betrayed her. "The caramel-filled chocolate *W*," she answered.

"Exactly. Not the caramel-filled chocolate *M*." He pressed his finger into the frame and twisted his wrist. The small letter rotated one hundred and eighty degrees. There was a soft click, and the picture swung open.

# CHAPTER TWENTY-FIVE

"You found what?" Oscar asked. He and Blanche were settled on a leather sofa in the home theatre with Petey eating a bowl of popcorn between them.

Ruth Ann held a bag of sweets and said, "A secret room with *no* bodies."

Blanche put down her martini, a light purple one this time. "I call it a Mauve Maureen," she told them. "But really, you're not making any sense."

"Okay, it's like this," Jonathan started. "Daniel's mother's ghost told him—"

"It's a memory," Daniel interrupted. "Not a ghost story."

"And then he and Mary triggered a secret lever," Ruth Ann explained. "The whole picture swung open like a real door!" She popped a few chocolate-covered candies into her mouth.

Jonathan helped himself to a handful of Petey's popcorn and said, "Well, you have to step over the lip at the bottom."

"Like the Gryffindor common room," Ruth Ann added, cheerfully.

Oscar's gaze slid back and forth between Jonathan and Ruth Ann.

"But there's no bodies?" Petey asked, almost disappointed.

"It's only a bare room," Daniel said. Mary, he noticed, remained quiet, slumped in a chair by herself.

"Nothing?" Blanche pouted. "Not even a closet? Check

again, they keep extra merchandise all over this place. Maybe
there are some vintage dresses in there!"

"Sorry," Ruth Ann said. "There are just four walls, a
chandelier, and one huge, dusty rug. It's tacked down and
practically covers the whole floor." She wrinkled her nose. "It's
faded and old, though."

"And this is the shocking part," Jonathan said, wiping his
greasy hands on the back of his jeans. "It's dark blue with a
huge gold *W* in the middle…or an *M*, depending on where
you're standing."

"I've already checked," Ruth Ann told them, importantly.
"There are no messages in the design around the rug's border."
Everyone blinked at her, expressionless. "Well," she said,
letting her voice drop, "it was in a Nancy Drew book, once."
She stayed quiet and decided to concentrate on picking out a
sugar-covered almond.

"I don't think anyone has been in that room for decades,"
Daniel said.

"That's useless," Petey grumbled. "It sounds too small to
be any fun."

"Nah," Jonathan said. "But the doorway is wide enough for
a mattress," he grinned at Ruth Ann.

"I can't believe this," Oscar said. "Did it occur to any of
you that crawling through a hole in the wall might not be the
wisest idea? Ruth Ann, I'm surprised, you usually show more
common sense than this."

"Actually," Jonathan said, taking more popcorn, "we made
her go in. She was too scared."

Ruth Ann nodded, trying to look blameless.

"What if you had gotten trapped?" Oscar asked. "How
would we know where to look for you?"

The others suddenly become interested in their shoes.
Daniel felt like he was in the principal's office. "I have a
phone," he reasoned.

"You can't take chances like that," Oscar said. "Be smart. I
don't want you fools to disappear too." His words quivered at

NIGHT SHIFT

the end.

It was unsettling to see Oscar like this, his hopelessness palpable. Daniel remembered his father's similar expression, even years after his mother's car accident—Oscar, he realized, was mourning.

Blanche reached over the bowl of popcorn and put a hand on his shoulder. "They're perfectly safe."

"Yeah," Jonathan said. "Besides, how much more can happen this week? Come on."

Mary finally spoke, her voice kind, almost careful. "It's almost Easter. And soon, it'll be summer. And before you know it, the Halloween decorations will be up."

"Then Christmas," Blanche finished, squeezing Oscar's shoulder. "Maybe things will be different this year?"

Petey crunched into the popcorn, breaking the somber quiet.

"All right," Oscar said, back to his usual authority. "Does anyone have any clue why there is a secret room with apparently no use?"

Daniel noticed that everyone, including himself, instinctively turned to Mary. She picked at the frayed rip in the knee of her jeans. "Forget it," she said. "It's just another part of our cage." She stood and walked toward the elevator with her head hanging low.

"She's not realizing the obvious," Jonathan said, after she was clearly out of earshot. "The room may be small, but there's enough space for a hot tub in the corner."

Daniel checked his watch. He knew he couldn't stick around, he needed to talk with Mr. Oliver—this was his last night, after all. He arrived at the office with a coffee and croissant. Mr. Oliver accepted the offering with a cold glare.

*Old fart.*

Daniel shoved his hand in his pocket, and touched the keychain.

"Is there anything you have to report, Daniel Gale?"

The full name thing was getting to be a bit much. Even

with everything else that had happened to Daniel, Mr. Oliver's remarks still managed to get under his skin and burrow deep, but he'd come back to Willard's to get answers, not his approval. "Actually," Daniel said, "I found out something interesting yesterday."

Mr. Oliver bit into the croissant and reached for his crossword puzzle.

"I have a trust fund," he said. "A substantial trust fund."

Mr. Oliver stopped chewing. "Good for you," he said. "I have a substantial ulcer, a bunion, and arthritis."

*Useless, lazy dinosaur.*

Determined not to be put off by his bad temper, Daniel continued. "But it's anonymous, you see. I don't know who set it up, and I want to be able to thank that person. Interesting, don't you think?"

Mr. Oliver narrowed his eyes. "Yes. Interesting how some people have a trust fund and the rest of us have to work all of our lives. Speaking of work, why don't you do some?"

Daniel left the office and wandered the store in a clueless funk. His mission to get information was failing miserably. Time was moving too quickly, his last shift at Willard's would be over in a few hours.

Daniel stood across from the Toy department, on the third-floor landing. He had no answers about his inheritance and new questions were rising every hour. He paused—"Gymnopedie No. 1" floated down the aisle from the Music Room.

He hid in the shadow of the archway, watching Mary play. At the back of the room, Clara stood in her perpetual coma of depression. Could she hear Mary playing? he wondered. Were any notes making their way through her deep sleep? He shivered, imagining Mary up on a pedestal, unwilling to wake up.

The music stopped.

Daniel approached the piano. "Keep playing," he said. "It's the only nice thing I've heard all night." He could tell by the expression on her face that his candour wasn't appreciated.

NIGHT SHIFT

"Aren't you all manners and compliments," she said. Her hair was still up in the clip, with a few dark tendrils hanging to her shoulder.

Daniel was breathless, but not from the taking the stairs. No matter what she tried to do to make herself look plain, it was useless—she was too beautiful. He stayed beside the piano; she didn't make room on the bench for him this time.

He felt the weight of her silence.

"Tonight," he began, "after we told the others about the room, Oscar didn't seem so keen on finding a way out of Willard's."

Mary looked surprised by his observation, as if she expected such details to be lost on him. "If we ever did find a way out, Oscar would never leave the store—he has reasons, but it's his story to tell."

Daniel was secretly relieved; he could only take so many dramatic revelations.

Mary glanced at the stage area near the back of the room and said, "Ruth Ann told you Clara's story."

"Yes."

"At first I was so angry. I never understood how she could do that to us. But when I watched you walk out the main doors for the last time, I finally understood."

Daniel reddened. He would never be able to take those words back.

She pushed away from the piano and began to pace, keeping her eyes on the floor. "I shouldn't have asked you to stay. Willard's is my prison, not yours. I've been trying to escape for decades. I know it by heart and there's no way out for me." She stopped and met his gaze. "Don't waste your time here."

"Waste my time?" he asked. He wasn't expecting this speech. It pierced him to hear her sound so desperate.

"The store is luring you in with hints at something spectacular, an inheritance from a non-existent benefactor and a secret room that has no purpose."

159

"Are you kidding? Even Blanche thinks I'm a good luck charm, and she hates me. How can you ignore the fact that since I've arrived at Willard's all these new revelations have started? Number one," he started to count on his fingers, "I'm the first person you've met in forty years from the outside. Number two, we just found a secret room—"

"A room that has no purpose."

"—number three…" he paused.

"Yes? What's number three, Daniel?"

"You have no idea why you exist, and…I might be the only person who can help you find out."

Mary's eyes widened, hopeful, then her gaze slid to Clara. "But what if that's the reason we all ended up here," she said. "We have no memory other than waking up in the store. What if one night shift, you can't leave the store either, and then you wake up the next day in a display thinking you've always been here?" She leaned closer and he felt her intense gaze. "Are you willing to risk it?"

The closeness of her made his heart beat fast. "I was meant to find the store."

"Maybe it's a trap, though. That would explain why your inheritance is anonymous." Mary's voice took on an eerie quality.

"If you're trying to scare me, it won't work."

Her features softened. "There's nothing you can find out that I haven't already learned. You should leave—while you still can."

She started to walk away, but he reached out and took her by the elbow, then took a step closer. Their bodies were connected all the way down to their toes. He remembered how her kisses tasted like caramel. "If I leave it will be on my own terms," Daniel said. "And not because you have no use for me."

They held each other's stare for several heart beats. Then she said, "It's not worth the risk."

"Give me one good reason why," he breathed.

She stared at his mouth, then licked her lips. "Because,"

she said, her voice raw, "it *is* fucking weird." She pushed
against his chest and he stumbled back, bumping into the grand
piano. "Trust me," she said, "it's better for both of us this way."

# CHAPTER TWENTY-SIX

*Yes, definitely.*

Daniel shook the keychain again.

*Without a doubt.*

"Damn," he whispered.

*Signs point to yes.*

He closed his eyes, made a fist around the ball, and then repeated the same question. "Should I go to the airport?" He slowly uncurled each finger.

*My sources say no.*

"If you say so." The exercise was moot. Daniel had given Mr. Oliver his official resignation, agreeing to work two more weeks of night shifts. He reasoned there was too much unfinished business going on inside Willard's to leave immediately; besides, he still hadn't found his wallet.

He sat on the edge of the hotel bed. The tiny bottles were gone, the bathroom mirror had been wiped clean, and the soiled towels were replaced with pristine, perfectly folded ones. Everything about the other night had been erased—except one thing. His phone stared back at him from the charger.

He dialed Monique's number before he could chicken out.

"Oh my God!" she answered, sounding slightly clogged. "You're still alive!"

"Hey." Daniel cringed at his lame reply.

"I was sure you'd left for good, but then Sean told me you

worked last night. The guys were so pissed! Gavin would have won almost two grand if you'd quit." She paused to sneeze. "Sorry. Anyway, I'm glad you called. You really had me worried."

Is this how a girl talked to you after you'd slept with her? He was totally clueless about how to respond. The only thing that kept him from hanging up was that she didn't sound upset. He chose to focus on her last words. "You were worried?" he asked.

"You came out of the store all slobbering and stuff. I was ready to take you to the hospital, but you kept talking about getting back to your hotel. So—"

"—so you made sure I got up to my room." He closed his eyes, seeing bits of his memory resurface, playing out like a movie. He remembered snippets now—Monique didn't leave in the cab, she had the driver pull over to the curb and wait.

"Your eyes were darting all over the place," she continued. "You were completely paranoid. I thought you and Mr. Oliver were doing drugs in the security office or something. I even said that to snap you out of your creepy coma, but you didn't think it was very funny. I opened one of those little rum drinks, hoping you'd calm down."

Daniel heard her blow her nose in the background.

"Anyway," she said, "you were in no shape to go anywhere, let alone the airport. You know what happens to suspicious-looking guys at the airport, right? I totally saved you from a gross body search. So, I hid your wallet while you kept yourself busy practically drinking half the minibar."

Daniel tensed up. "I don't remember very much."

"I'm not surprised," she said. "You're a cheap drunk. Most of the booze spilled down your shirt." She lowered her voice to a playful whisper. "I had to help undress you."

A knot tightened in his chest. "Um…I don't—" he stammered. "I mean, that night's still pretty much a blank for me." He prayed she would figure out what he was hinting.

"Hey, when I left your pants were still on. If anything else

happened, I wasn't a part of it!" She laughed, triggering a coughing fit.

Daniel looked at the ceiling and silently thanked God. In his old life, he would have been thrilled to have a girlfriend like Monique. But things were so complicated now…plus, he wanted to remember his first time. "I definitely owe you," he said when she came back on the line.

"You can make it up to me on our next date, but it'll have to wait." She sneezed. "I'm sick."

"Sorry."

"About me being sick or having to wait for the next date?"

Daniel opened his mouth and then paused. "Both," he finally decided.

"Good. Look, I gotta go, I'm supposed to have my phone off if I'm too sick to go to school."

"Yeah, sure. Get better. Oh, hold on!" he said. "Where *is* my wallet?"

Monique laughed when she realized it was still missing. "I wedged it behind the mirror."

Daniel said goodbye, then walked over to the mirror and pulled out the bottom corner. His wallet slid down the wall into his waiting hand. He placed it inside the top dresser drawer, then, as a second thought, he tossed in the keychain as well. "You guys fight it out," he yawned. "I'm too tired."

The next few days were a constant disappointment. Mr. Oliver was more cantankerous than ever. Stacey managed to slip out the main doors unnoticed each night. And Monique, usually his best source of information, continued to fight the flu.

She texted him, promising to look for her school report about Willard's. They made a date to see each other as soon as she recovered. Since Mary was throwing attitude or completely ignoring him altogether, Monique's positive attention was his only reprieve from loneliness.

Just past midnight, Daniel trudged up the grand staircase, exhausted from all the dead ends. He reached the second-floor

NIGHT SHIFT

landing, only having a second to react. "Whoa!" he said, catching a small orange ball before it hit his face.

Jonathan came around the corner on Rollerblades, carrying a hockey stick. "Just the sucker I'm looking for," he smirked. Daniel was used to Jonathan's petty threats, but he recognized the small ball, and his anticipation nullified any foreboding.

The aisles had been expanded by shoving the furniture off to the side. After a quick trip to Sporting Goods, Daniel was gliding on Rollerblades. It wasn't exactly like skating, but the sensation was enough to make him realize how much he missed it.

After his mother's car accident, the one thing that kept Daniel and his father from drowning in depression was the hockey rink. His teammates welcomed him back without any of the clumsiness the adults seemed to be struggling with. The familiar toilet humour in the locker room was comforting. He didn't have to talk about it. He didn't have to explain himself to anyone, he only had to play. The routine of early weekend practices and road games gradually shaped a life for them again, moving forward, giving them hope for the future.

Daniel cross-cut around a corner, feeling his muscles respond to the familiar workout.

"Hey," Jonathan said, surprised. "You're good."

Daniel caught his breath. "I used to play a lot."

"Okay, you're on my team."

The sudden camaraderie made Daniel anxious. "I'm going to do one more lap," he said, already skating away. With a hockey stick in his hand, he raced faster around the store. He looked down, wishing he'd taken the ball to practice stickhandling. A sharp blow to his ribs sent him flying into a leather couch. Jonathan's laughter echoed across the floor.

"You should always keep your head up." Mary towered over him, holding a hockey stick. "Since I missed with the plate, I thought I was entitled to one good hit."

Daniel struggled to stand. "I'd say you got it that time," he winced, holding his side.

Jonathan took Daniel aside. "Team huddle." Petey ran over excitedly, dragging his own hockey stick.

"Hey, Daniel," he grinned. "You skate awesome!"

"All right." Jonathan put his arms over their shoulders. "It's like this, Ruth Ann and Oscar are the other team with Mary in goal."

"What about Blanche?" Daniel asked. Jonathan motioned with his head to the side. She was lounging on a leather settee with a pink martini.

"I call it a Blushing Blanche," she said.

"You don't play?" he asked.

She pointed to her red-soled stiletto. "Mac, are you headless? I'm wearing Louboutins!"

Jonathan assigned Petey as goalie, and then said to Daniel, "I should probably tell you—"

"Let me guess, the girls play rough."

Jonathan took the face-off against Oscar. "And remember," he said to everyone, "it's Daniel's first time playing hockey, so let's go easy on him."

Daniel spent the first half of the game suffering the wrath of Ruth Ann. He was more bruised and battered than any game he'd ever played.

"Ruth Ann!" Blanche sang. "Dirty play, doll. Mac gets a penalty shot."

"I'm not going to shoot at Mary," Daniel said, cradling his elbow. "Let Petey take my place." But Petey stayed in goal, looking at the floor. Daniel skated back to him. "How come you're not in Rollerblades?" he asked.

"I can't really play," Petey told him. "None of the Rollerblades are small enough for me."

He crouched down. "Are you sure?"

Oscar joined them. "Nothing suitable in Children's Wear, either."

"Sometimes it sucks being the smallest," Petey mumbled.

Daniel studied him closely. "When I was eleven my friends and I played street hockey all the time, but we never had

anything like these fancy Rollerblades." He gave Petey a nudge. "So do you know what we did?"

"No."

"We ran with our sneakers on."

"And it was still fun?"

"It was the best. In fact, I haven't worn Rollerblades in a few years," Daniel explained. "I'm probably getting a blister. I'm going to have to change into my sneakers," he shrugged, trying to be casual. "Are you still in?"

"Yeah, my sneakers will work," he replied.

Oscar gave Daniel a small nod of approval as Petey ran down to take his penalty shot. He let out a whoop when he scored and the game continued with everyone in sneakers.

Mary disappeared as soon as the hockey sticks were put away, but Daniel wasn't disappointed. The exercise had given him hope, and he decided to take some overdue advice.

The Music Room was dark and quiet. He turned up the lights over the piano. After a few nervous adjustments of the bench, he started to play his mother's favourite jazz piece. Just like with the hockey, the muscle memory was still there, imprinted on his brain and in his fingers.

He could almost hear Ella Fitzgerald singing along. His confidence grew, and the notes flowed nicely. The singer inside his head was much clearer and louder than before. He slowed down his playing, but she kept singing.

A chill ran down his spine. The voice wasn't in his head. It was in the room—with him. Daniel's hands froze above the keys. She emerged from the shadows, hitting the last note with such ostentation, it reverberated off the walls. The lights above the piano hit the black sequins of her dress, sending mini rainbows across Daniel's chest.

"Honey, you play that piano like it's on fire!" she squealed. She frowned, and then snapped her fingers in front of his face. Daniel gasped. "Are you all right?" she asked.

"Clara?"

"That's right," she said. "Where are you from?"

"Huh?"

"Are you a transfer from Bloomingdales? Blanche and I always wonder if that's going to happen someday. It's crazy to think we're the only ones who exist. Mary always rolls her eyes at us. But look at you," she laughed, "you're living proof. I can't wait to show you off to everyone. How long have you been here?" she asked.

"Um...a few weeks."

Clara chuckled. "You're going to love Willard's," she said, putting her hand on her hip. "What's your name, honey?"

"Daniel," he choked.

"Well, it's nice to meet you, Daniel. Now keep playing that song, it's one of my favourites, and I feel like I haven't sung it in years."

He began to play *Blue Skies* again. Clara closed her eyes and started to hum. She picked up the tune effortlessly. He added new chords, and soon a stream of song floated down the aisles and around the grand staircase, filling Willard's with Clara's voice once again.

# CHAPTER TWENTY-SEVEN

The table was heaped with maple-basted turkey breast, roasted asparagus, slivered almonds, sweet potato puree, caramelized Brussels sprouts topped with red onions, and brown-sugar-glazed carrots.

Oscar held up his wine glass. "Spring is a celebration of the rebirth of hope, and a reminder of the promise of life everlasting. I can't think of a better time to hear our Clara sing again." The others raised their glasses and said, "To Clara."

Earlier, the reunion had filled the Matinee Room with screams of disbelief. Clara had her own moment of stupefaction when she found out how long she'd been asleep and the truth about Daniel.

Jonathan had filled her in. "Mary threw a plate at his head last week."

Clara laughed, looking at Daniel. "Is that what the girls have to do to get your attention?"

"That's nothing," Jonathan grinned. "Wait a bit, they love to fight in front of everyone."

Daniel stayed quiet. He couldn't help but feel Jonathan was taking advantage of the situation, making sure each comment was both embarrassing to Mary and insulting to himself.

During the meal, the others took turns telling Clara everything she'd missed in the last three years. She sat beside Daniel, slapping his shoulder whenever the news shocked her. Her enthusiasm was infectious and he liked her immediately.

When the laughter petered out, Clara became serious. "No one has hollered or stomped their feet. I wish you would get mad at me, because the fact is, I left you all." Her eyes welled up. "I was hurting so much, I didn't want to go on another day. I gave up all the love, and all the fun, and all the living so I wouldn't feel the misery anymore. I had no idea I was gone for so long. I can never make it up to you, but I promise, it will never, ever happen again."

"Oh, Clara," sobbed Blanche. "My makeup is running."

Oscar stood up and put a hand on her shoulder. "It was lucky enough to come back before too much time passed. No one is mad at you. We're so full of happiness, there's no room for hate."

"I'll drink to that," Jonathan cheered, lifting his glass.

Oscar looked unimpressed, but he refrained from any scolding and instead shook his head, then sat down. A thunderous flatulence erupted from his seat. He grumbled and tossed the Whoopee cushion like a Frisbee across the room.

Petey clutched his stomach, laughing. "Aw, man," he choked. "That was classic!"

Clara laughed with the others and said, "I forgot how beautiful this is."

Daniel suspected she wasn't talking about the chandeliers or the crystal-embedded ceiling. He understood completely, Clara was talking about Willard's itself—the world within the store.

The meal was topped off with a raspberry-filled, triple-layer vanilla cake. Petey saved the meringue frosting for last, scraping the plate repeatedly until Oscar gave him a look. He put down his fork and tried to hide a yawn.

"Let's get you back to your display, precious," Clara said. She and Blanche stood up, reaching for Petey. Clara turned to Daniel. "And thank you, gorgeous," she said.

"For what?"

"For playing that music! I think that's the reason I woke up," she said. "I heard that jazz song and I thought Virginia was

NIGHT SHIFT

playing. It's the only thing that could bring me back to my family."

"My pleasure," he smiled.

She ruffled his hair playfully. "Oh, I just love you!"

Oscar cleared away the dishes as Jonathan and Ruth Ann helped take everything else into the kitchen, leaving Mary and Daniel sitting across from one another.

He was used to Mary ignoring him, but this time she held his stare with the strangest expression. "What is it?" he asked.

"Your eyes," she said. Then she shook her head as if to erase what she'd just said. "Nothing." She motioned to the grand staircase. "Walk me back?"

They descended to the first-floor landing in silence. Curious, he sneaked glances out of the corner of his eye. She was rigid and staring straight ahead. Clearly, she was pissed that he was still around.

He wondered if telling her about his resignation would ease some of the hostility. There was an unexpected punch to his heart. He should leave, forget about them and start a new life…a real life. But then he remembered how amazing it felt when she smiled at him.

All he wanted was to make her happy. All he wanted was to see her smile one last time, then he could leave the store for good.

"Mary, I—" he started.

"I need your help," she interrupted. "I haven't told Blanche about Stacey yet…obviously, but I can't keep lying to her. I have this feeling time is running out, and the longer we wait, the more dangerous it will be."

Daniel was relieved her focus was on Blanche. "I'll make sure to speak with her the next time she's working," he promised. "Once we find out how she got the dresses, we'll find Maureen."

She shivered and rubbed her arms. "I'm almost afraid to know the truth," she said. "It doesn't feel like there's going to be a happy ending."

They continued through Ladies' Fashions in silence and then stopped in front of Mary's display. Daniel looked up at the platform she shared with the other two mannequins. One bright raincoat was left abandoned beside the daisy patterned boots.

He blurted out his question without thinking. "Can I watch you change?" he asked. "I mean see how you turn…you know, into—" he pointed at the other mannequins, unable to finish the sentence.

"Why?" she asked.

He desperately tried to think of the right thing to say. "It will make more sense to me," he said. "Please, I'm not making fun."

The familiar little crease formed between her eyes. God, he loved that little crease.

She surprised him by agreeing. "Okay," she said. "But you have to stay in place."

Daniel stomped both his feet. "Rooted to the spot," he said.

Mary relaxed both hands by her sides as she slowly exhaled. Her eyes glazed over, and she became very still. Daniel squinted, unsure at first, it happened so smoothly.

He circled her, trying not to make a sound. It was Mary, and yet it wasn't. Beautiful—but cold, and hard. He studied her hand, now in perfect pose by her side. His fingers lightly touched the tips of hers, but he felt nothing. No warm rush to make his skin tingle and send his heart racing.

He peered closer and stared at her mouth. She looked so real! Suddenly she blinked. He stumbled back, biting his cheek not to scream. Screaming right now would be bad. Very, very bad.

Her mouth was a hard line. "I told you not to move," she said.

"I needed a closer look," he explained, trying to catch his breath. "I had no idea you could do it so fast."

She studied him for a couple of breaths. "It's weird, isn't it?"

"No," he said softly. "It's magical…it's beautiful."

NIGHT SHIFT

"Beautiful?" She rolled her eyes. "Now that the demonstration is over, do you have any questions?"

Daniel knew he had to tread carefully here. "Well, how do you do it?"

Mary assumed her matter-of-fact tone. "All I have to do is concentrate and it happens," she told him. "It's the safest form for us."

"But you seem so…" He paused, searching for the right word. "Vulnerable."

"We haven't broken yet."

Daniel shuddered, imagining horrible scenarios. "How did it start?" he asked. "Oscar said you've been alive for forty years. Do you remember the beginning?"

Mary sat down on the platform. "The first time I opened my eyes, I was standing down the aisle." She motioned with her hand. "I knew my name and that the store was my home. I began to explore, and I soon found the others. Each of us had the exact same experience—and we all knew the rules without ever hearing them."

"You mean about being seen moving and leaving the store?"

She nodded. "We can only go as far as the black granite tile. It's like there's an invisible barrier pushing us back. And when we get tired and fall asleep, it happens then too."

Daniel tried to read her expression. She sounded like she was teaching a class, but he could sense the hopelessness underneath.

"One time Blanche froze while sitting down and she ended up behind a drum display in the Music Room." She smiled slightly and a laugh almost escaped. Daniel smiled too, imagining Blanche part of a rock band.

"We can still hear the sounds around us, though," she said. Mary paused, and her smile fell into a solemn expression. "If we concentrate."

He remembered how Ruth Ann found the clerks gossip boring. He wondered why hearing the staff during the day made

173

Mary sad. "Is that all you know?" he asked.

"We only have the computer to work with. You already know everything Ruth Ann and I have researched." Mary let out a sigh, "Mostly, I've been trying to find a way out."

"I thought leaving the store would kill you."

She stared across the department, her voice cold. "Sometimes," she said, "I've been willing to risk it."

# CHAPTER TWENTY-EIGHT

The cool, rainy spring finally broke one sultry day, giving a sample of the hazy summer to come. Daniel walked through the store noticing the inside was also changing.

One section of the Confectionery was dominated by various sizes of chocolate Easter Bunnies. Hundreds of pastel coloured eggs decorated the twinkling branches of the golden tree in the main foyer. Gift bags stuffed with tulips were scattered at the base. The slogan in glossy white letters on the side of each tote read, "*See What's Coming up this spring at Willard's.*"

Daniel also felt a change in his mood. He still carried his keychain, but had stopped checking with the Magic 8 Ball about the airport. Even though he only had a week left, he wanted the business regarding Maureen to be settled first.

Clara's awakening had brought a whole new energy to the store at night. She asked him to play for her every shift, coaxing him with compliments on how much he'd improved with all the practice. When she found out about his mother's extensive jazz collection, she was adamant that he bring records into work.

He had contacted Alice asking for certain boxes from storage, and to send them express. He remembered labelling all the important things. "Send anything with 'jazz' or 'Mom' written on the box," he'd told her.

Monique was finally back to work and had arranged to meet Daniel before her shift ended. He was still unsure about including her in his quest for information, but he'd already

taken the initial step, and it was too late to turn back. A jumpy kind of nervousness came over him; he wondered if this was how a skydiver felt before they stepped out of the plane.

He found her at the makeup counter laughing with another clerk. "There you are!" she said. "I didn't recognize you with your shirt on."

The clerk and Monique did nothing to smother their giggles. He felt slightly betrayed and worried what else she'd told her friends about his antics that night. "You look like you're feeling better," he said, shyly.

Monique's attention was on the little blue bag with a gold *W* being passed over the counter by the clerk. She slipped beside Daniel and they walked toward the grand staircase. "The new summer line finally came in," she grinned. "Helen is so cool, she always keeps a few samples for me."

"Can we go somewhere and talk?"

"Talk?" she flirted.

Daniel's pulse sped up. The direction of the conversation was getting sticky. He ignored her hint and focused on Blanche's mystery. "I need some information," he said. Then, deciding a little flattery couldn't hurt, he added, "And there's no one at Willard's who knows more than you do."

She paused at the base of the stairs. "What kind of information?"

"It's about…" Daniel glanced around. "Stacey," he whispered.

"I knew it!" Her eyes lit up.

He led her up the stairs. "It's really important, but we can't talk about it here. Do you have time left on your break to have a coffee or something in the restaurant?"

"I'm not on break."

He stopped for a second. "Oh."

Reluctantly, he followed her to her cashier's station in Ladies' Fashions. Mary, now dressed in a pink pencil skirt, matching silk blouse, and high heels, was on her usual platform. Goosebumps covered his arms. It was bizarre to know that

NIGHT SHIFT

behind the vacant stare and unblinking eyes, Mary existed somehow. He peeked up at her from the corner of his eye, wondering if she knew he was near. Daniel waited for the flick of an eyelash or the blush of her cheek.

Monique stowed her bag of samples under the counter. "Okay," she said, leaning on her elbows, anticipating a delicious tidbit of gossip. "Spill it!"

Daniel stopped a few feet from the platform, still staring at Mary. *Was she listening right now?* "Um, spill what?" he asked.

She rolled her eyes, impatient with his lack of finesse in delivering gossip. "You said you had information on Stacey."

He tore his eyes away from Mary. "No, I said I *need* information on Stacey."

"Yeah," she grinned, prompting him. "But why? Something to do with security, right?"

"It's something to do with the dress she brought in."

Monique's posture instantly deflated. "It's just a dress," she scowled. "All that attention," she began, "for one clerk who, by my calculations, has never made a sale. Can you guess which clerk gets the least amount of attention, yet has the best sales record in Ladies' Fashions?" She gave him a pointed stare. "Hmm?"

"You?" he guessed.

Monique didn't even bother confirming his answer and continued her tirade. "Today she struts in with a long box under her arm, and everyone goes crazy. You'd think no one ever saw a dress before. The popularity must be a real change for her. She's usually off by herself. "

"Today?" Daniel frowned. "I'm talking about the black one. The *Breakfast at Tiffany's* knockoff."

Monique eyed him suspiciously, "Okay, how did you know that?"

"I'm a bit of a vintage movie buff," he stammered.

"Weird, that's what Stacey said." She crinkled her nose and held his stare for a couple of seconds. "Anyway, that one's gone. She brought in a new one today." Her pinched-up look

177

dissolved, and she gave him a wink. "It's over in Sleepwear if you like looking at lingerie."

Daniel stretched his neck, trying to see over the racks of clothing to where Blanche was on display. "Where is she getting them?"

"She's a design student, remember?" Monique put her hand to her stomach. "She's so fake she gives me cramps."

"What makes you think she's fake?"

"Every time her cell phone rings, she slinks off, whispering. When she comes back, she's all blotchy and twitchy. I don't call her Shifty Stacey for nothing."

Daniel said, "It sounds like she's guilty."

"Exactly," Monique said, poking him in the chest with her finger. "She's shifty *and* guilty—she's shilty!"

"I think you're full of shilty."

She looked smugly at Daniel, and then repeated her mantra: "Don't underestimate a girl's intuition." Her gaze shifted and focused on something in the distance.

"About that school report," he began. "Do you still have the blueprints to the theatre?"

She turned her attention back to him. "Why is that so important to you, anyway?"

He shrugged, "I'm interested in old magic."

Monique surprised him by reaching across the counter. "Putting a love spell on someone?" She grabbed his collar and gave him a clumsy kiss. Then she patted his chest and laughed loudly. "Call me later. Okay?"

His eyes flicked guiltily toward Mary. "Okay," he said. Monique zoned in on a group of shoppers looking at blazers down the aisle. The rate at which she changed gears was dizzying.

Sean strutted along the display counters. As they passed each other Daniel gave him a nod, but Sean frowned back. "Not your colour, numb nuts," he said.

Daniel ignored the stupid remark, but stopped in front of the next full-length mirror. "Shit," he whispered, wiping

NIGHT SHIFT

Monique's lipstick off with the back of his hand.

He made his way toward Sleepwear, feeling like a fool, but slightly grateful. Sean might be a dickhead, but at least he'd told him about the lipstick instead of laughing behind his back.

"I thought you worked nights?" a familiar voice asked. Stacey was standing beside a display of lace bras and matching underwear. It was all Daniel could do to keep his eyes focused on the slight clerk.

"I'm Stacey," she said, misinterpreting his expression for confusion. "We met a few times before." Daniel guessed Mr. Hadley wasn't the only one who forgot her name on a regular basis. He felt a little stab of pity for her.

"Of course," he said. "The display with the umbrellas." That day seemed like a hundred years ago. "Um...I wonder if I might be able to ask you something."

"Sure," she answered.

"There was a black dress on one of the mannequins—the *Breakfast at Tiffany's* one?"

"And?" she sounded guarded.

"Well..." He paused, knowing there was no other way than to just ask. "Where did it come from?"

"I didn't think security guards were interested in fashion." It didn't sound like an offhand remark. She was already suspicious.

Daniel was drowning fast—his interrogation skills sucked. He tried to imagine what Oscar would say. "I'm kind of a movie buff," he said, hoping it sounded legitimate.

Excitement flashed across her eyes. "Then I'll see if you can guess which movie inspired me to make this dress." Stacey led him to a platform nearby. He was frantically flipping through all the dresses in every movie he'd ever seen. All he could picture was Julie Andrews twirling around the hillside in *The Sound Of Music*.

"So?" Stacey asked, waving her hand toward the display.

*Please be a nun*, he prayed. Daniel looked at Blanche in the strapless dress and only one word came to mind. "Wow," he

179

said. It was a jaw-dropping floor-length chiffon gown, adorned with iridescent sequins. The low-cut bodice sparkled with gems all along the top seam.

"Okay," she laughed. "With that reaction, you're off the hook."

"You made this?" he asked, wondering if it would fit Mary. He was lost in an image of her gliding toward him with her arms out stretched, smiling…waiting.

Stacey's voice interrupted his daydream. "I'm a design student," she said. "You were never lovelier."

"Excuse me?" he asked, uneasily.

She laughed again. "The movie! Rita Hayworth and Fred Astaire?" She looked at him expectantly.

"Oh." He let out a relieved sigh. "I've never heard of it."

"I thought you said you were a movie buff."

He fumbled his words, "What I mean is that I'm a real movie buff for movies that just came out. Yeah."

Her cell phone rang. Daniel took a step back, grateful for the interruption. Stacey's brow furrowed, and her ears turn bright red. She pressed the phone to her chest, and said, "I have to take this." She rushed to the back of the room by the fitting area.

As he watched her go, a sinking feeling came over Daniel. Monique's intuition he worried, was spot on.

# CHAPTER TWENTY-NINE

The hotel room was dark. Daniel rested his hand on the empty space in bed beside him. He pictured Mary's hair splayed across the pillow and groaned softly. What the hell was he doing? She wasn't even human! Besides, she could barely tolerate being in the same room with him.

The alarm clock beeped. "Oh, shit!" He whipped back the covers and ran to the shower.

Combing his fingers through his wet hair, he pulled on a pair of jeans and a white T-shirt, then grabbed his backpack and raced out to his first errand.

Daniel walked into the security office and stopped short, startled by the person standing in front of the wall of monitors. He stared at the man wearing the fedora and trench coat. "Can I help you?"

The man pulled his attention away from the video screens. He chuckled, then said, "I'm Mr. Travis." He smiled behind the horn-rimmed glasses and extended his hand. "Daniel, right? I met you while Mr. Hadley was giving me a tour."

Daniel shook his hand. "Right, sorry."

"Quite impressive video coverage," Mr. Travis said. "It's like eyes are watching the store all the time."

*More like ears are listening*, Daniel thought. He rubbed the back of his neck, not sure what to do next. The silence was starting to make him uncomfortable, but leaving the office felt

wrong. "Um, Mr. Travis, what are you doing in the security office?" he asked.

"I'm waiting to see Mr. Hadley," he said, patting a brown leather satchel lying sideways on the desk. "I have no official capacity. But the safety of the store is of great interest to me and the people I work for."

Daniel remembered what Mr. Oliver said about the insurance company planning on replacing the security officers with more technological equipment. He said, "It's the usual basic setup every store has, right?"

Mr. Travis produced a white cloth from his pocket. He took off his glasses and began to polish them. "Almost too basic. Tell me, how old you are?"

"Eight—nineteen," he stammered. "Why?"

"Part of my market research deals with anticipating trends. Particularly a consumer of your age demographic."

"Market research? I thought you were from the insurance company."

Mr. Travis put his glasses back on. He pulled out a business card and offered it to Daniel.

Daniel's mouth fell open. "You work for Consumers Plus," he said. "What does a big-box chain want with Willard's?"

Mr. Travis straightened some papers escaping from the bulging briefcase. "I'm only doing some preliminary consulting."

"About what exactly?" Daniel visualized the one-storey warehouse with fluorescent lighting bouncing off every crammed surface. An uncomfortable sensation came over him, imagining processed cheese slices and car tires on display in place of the Confectionery.

"I believe in doing my research," Mr. Travis explained, patting the brown satchel again. "In fact, the history of Willard's is very intriguing. You may be interested to know the store used to be a vaudeville—"

"—theatre," Daniel finished. "Everyone knows that." He couldn't explain why he was acting so defensive.

NIGHT SHIFT

"Yes, but the story of Willard's goes back farther."

"Really?" Daniel let the silence linger. He thought of Mary's mysterious existence. "How so?" he asked.

Mr. Travis smiled. "The store's founder, James Willard, was the son of a wealthy shipping merchant, George Willard. Every account of the business tycoon paints him as a self-made millionaire, but he was also blue blooded—family home on the Upper East Side."

Daniel knew nothing about blue bloods and the upper class. He listened intently wondering if any information, no matter how random, could shed light on Mary's mysterious existence.

Mr. Travis reached into his briefcase and pulled out a map of Manhattan. He spread it over the green blotter, covering Mr. Oliver's desk, and pointed to an area close to where 14th Street and Park Avenue meet.

"It was families like George Willard's that would travel to Union Square for entertainment. When Fifth Avenue began to develop into the exclusive 'Ladies; Shopping Mile,' the highbrow audiences pulled the theatres closer to their homes." Daniel followed Mr. Travis's finger as it moved over the map. "And a whole new strip of upper-class theatres opened, stretching up to 23rd."

"You mean Broadway?"

Mr. Travis chuckled, "Yes, but back then it was called the Rialto. And Willard's was one of those original theatres. The location was unique in that it was close enough to Broadway to be appealing to the upper class, but was in an industrialized part of the neighbourhood, making its audience an interesting mix of aristocrats and immigrant families. That's the great thing about this city—it's dynamic, always changing. And change is part of survival."

Daniel looked up from the map. "Willard's is doing more than surviving," he said. "Look around—everything is perfect."

Mr. Travis adjusted his glasses. "Including the cracked ceiling in the Matinee Room?"

"I've never noticed."

183

"And the elevator? Apparently it's so unpredictable the store has to employ an operator to ensure everyone's safety."

"You might have a point," he mumbled.

Mr. Travis tilted his head and gave him a small smile. "With its history and architecture, Willard's is an extraordinary time capsule from more elegant days. You could say it's a real…treasure." He paused and then lowered his voice. "But there are certain security issues that need to be addressed."

Daniel felt a chill. "What do you mean?" he asked.

Mr. Travis touched his chin, and seemed to question whether he should go on. "Don't take this as reflection on your work ethic, but the night shift system Mr. Oliver has established and continues to defend is not only archaic, but it is completely unsafe as well."

Daniel looked at the wall of monitors—the monitors Mr. Oliver turned off every night. "You'll never find anyone more loyal to the store," he said.

"Mr. Hadley can't understand his reluctance about my proposed improvements. Let me be blunt: one day a tragedy may occur if the proper precautions aren't put in place. I'm hoping Mr. Oliver will see that I'm only here to help."

Daniel turned the business card over and over in his hand. There didn't seem to be an easy answer for what Mr. Travis was worried about.

"Daniel," he said. "I hope I can count on you."

Loud voices came from the electrical room down the hallway. "Read the fine print on my contract, Hadley!" Mr. Oliver said. He appeared from around the corner, batting one of the potted ferns out of the way.

Mr. Hadley followed closely. "You're not listening to reason," he said. His face was an alarming shade of red. He took a deep breath, straining the threads of his vest buttons.

Daniel was sure he was going to have a heart attack on the spot. Mr. Oliver stopped in his tracks, almost causing Mr. Hadley to run into his back. His eyes flicked back and forth between Daniel and Mr. Travis.

Mr. Travis cleared his throat. "Daniel and I were discussing the interesting history of the Willard's family."

"Is that so?" Mr. Oliver said, his voice hard. He looked at the map spread out on the desk. "Since I'm the only one in this room who ever met James Willard, I can tell you he's rolling in his grave right now."

Mr. Hadley sighed and ran a hand over his balding head.

"Daniel," Mr. Oliver barked. "Go change into uniform."

Eager to leave the anxiety-charged room, he left and continued to avoid the office. After Daniel let out the last clerk and locked the main doors, he reluctantly checked in with Mr. Oliver. He found him sitting at his desk squinting at the computer screen. Daniel recognized the logo for Consumers Plus, and was hit by a wave of guilt. He could have defended Mr. Oliver, or at least defended the store and its old-fashioned business model. He wished he knew who to trust.

Daniel knocked on the door frame. "I'm going to do a quick round," he said, "and then I need to leave the store for a bit to do an errand. Is that okay?"

"How long is a bit?"

"Maybe a half hour."

Mr. Oliver turned back to the computer and waved him off. Daniel hesitated. "While I'm out, do you want anything?"

"Yeah," he grumbled, "to be thirty years younger."

It took Daniel fifteen minutes to return to the store. Fumbling with an armload of paper bags, he paused in the foyer and looked through the archway toward the security office, but the door didn't open.

He went to the second floor and found the others in Home Furnishings, lounging on a leather sectional. He could hear Mary and Jonathan arguing about the secret room.

Petey ran up to him, wearing a soccer jersey and shorts. "What'd you bring?" he asked, sniffing the air. "Is it food from the outside?"

"Good guess," Daniel said, handing him a paper bag. He

watched as Petey pulled back the folded edge.

Mary was sitting on the arm of plush leather chair. No longer in the skirt and blouse combo from her display, she smoothed out her black T-shirt. "You seem like a Quarter Pounder with Cheese kind of girl to me," he said.

"You brought us McDonald's?" A small smile played on her lips, then the expression eased away. She took the food with a quiet thank you.

Jonathan slapped a hand on his shoulder. "Hey," he said. "You're like our very own delivery boy."

"Man," Daniel shot back. "Delivery Man."

Petey tried to drink the milkshake. "I'm getting a headache," he said, pumping the straw a few times.

"Yeah," Daniel said, trying to catch Mary's eye again. "That's normal."

Jonathan picked up a handful of fries. "Mary's under the impression we can't fit a hot tub in the corner of the secret room. Something about plumbing and electricity," he said.

"Hot tub," Oscar mumbled. He accepted a Big Mac combo from Daniel with a polite nod.

Jonathan grinned. "Mary's been pretty eager to get the bachelor pad all fixed up."

"Shut up." She threw him a look. "It's useless to let a perfectly good space go to waste."

Clicking heels interrupted dinner as Blanche and Clara arrived.

"Hello, monkeys," Blanche said, twirling on the spot.

Daniel took in her outfit. "Wow," he said. "What are you wearing?"

"Versace." She posed in her tight leather pants and jacket. "But the Louis Vuitton boots are what really pulls it all together." She stretched out her leg, showing off the knee-high footwear.

"It's dinner, Blanche," Ruth Ann groaned. "Not a Lady Gaga concert!"

"Just because you and Mary insist on dressing like a couple

NIGHT SHIFT

of Casual Friday drop-outs, it doesn't mean the rest of us have to slum around in jeans every day. Besides," Blanche continued, "why bother showing up, if you're not going to stand out?"

Jonathan smiled. "I thought you stood out quite nicely in the Rita Hayworth dress."

"Didn't I!" she beamed. "But I have to be careful, that fabric is so delicate."

Clara sat down beside Petey and gave him a one-armed hug, her wrist coated in diamond bangles. "Girl! I can't wait to see what you'll wake up in tomorrow night."

Blanche nibbled on a French fry, dreamily staring across the room. "I remember the ice blue chiffon one that Grace Kelly wore in *To Catch a Thief*."

Ruth Ann dug a ketchup packet out of the bottom of her paper bag. "That movie was actually based on a novel called *The Cat*."

The mention of the book reminded Daniel of his other surprise. "I've got one more thing for Ruth Ann." He put a small card on the coffee table, and pushed it toward her.

She picked it up and frowned, then her eyes grew wide. "I don't believe it!" she said, through a mouth full of hamburger.

Jonathan read over her shoulder, and then hit Daniel with a steely-eyed stare. "Why does it have *your* name on it?" he asked.

"It's a library card," Ruth Ann said. She closed her eyes and pressed it to her chest.

"You can go online and reserve any title you want," Daniel explained, enjoying her reaction. "And then I can pick it up for you. They have movies, too," he added, nodding to Jonathan. "So you guys can have theme nights or whatever."

Ruth Ann studied the card again. "I never realized this before," she said. "You have the same last name as Dorothy in *The Wonderful Wizard of Oz*!"

"Well, go reserve it," Daniel said.

"Like right now?" She waited three seconds before jumping off the couch and running with a handful of fries to the nearest

187

cashier's computer.

Daniel felt a hand on his shoulder. "Thank you," Oscar said. "When you do something nice for one of us, we all feel it."

He stared at his feet, unsure what to say. He knew he was leaving, but he wanted to do this for her, plus he wished it would make Mary like him again. Maybe he could buy Ruth Ann an e-reader and set up an account so she could download books.

"Yeah, that's great," Jonathan said under his breath. "Another thing I could never give her."

Daniel refused to meet Jonathan's angry gaze, determined to ignore his pissy attitude.

"Hey," Petey said, already moving on to his chocolate sundae. "What kind of burger did you get Mr. Oliver? Do they make a soft one for denture wearers?"

Daniel was grateful for the shift in conversation. "Actually," he said, "I don't think he was in the mood for a Happy Meal." He related the earlier episode in the security office with Mr. Hadley. "Did those two ever get along?" he asked. "Mr. Oliver's attitude is driving him crazy. Plus, that guy from Consumers Plus is always looming close by."

Mary's forehead bunched up. "Consumers Plus?"

"Yeah, Mr. Travis," Daniel said. "He's here as a consultant or something to look at the safety issues."

Oscar used his napkin. "This isn't the first time one of the managers tried to change something about Willard's. Don't worry, each time Mr. Oliver has always had the last say."

The others started chatting again, but Daniel was unconvinced. He reached into his pocket for the Magic 8 Ball. He needed to talk to Mr. Oliver. He excused himself from the group and walked to the elevator.

Mary caught up with him just as he was pulling the gate, and said, "I have to talk to you. Meet me in the kitchen after you see Mr. Oliver." She held both their bags of food. "I'll reheat this for us."

Daniel could feel his pulse start to hum through him. What

NIGHT SHIFT

did Mary want to talk about? He thought of different scenarios as he walked down to the security office. He tapped softly, then entered when there was no response. The desk chair was empty. The wall of monitors was blank except for the lone video image of the main doors. Mr. Oliver was asleep on the leather couch. Obviously, the stress of Consumers Plus and Mr. Travis wasn't taxing enough to keep him from napping. Smiling, Daniel backed out of the office.

He ran his hands through his hair a few times, and rocked back on his heels in the elevator, wishing the golden arrow would move faster. At first, Mr. Travis's words had scared the crap out of him, but now they made him laugh. "If proper precautions aren't in place a tragedy will occur," Daniel repeated in an exaggerated voice. "Like jewel thieves storming through the glass doors?" he snorted.

Then a voice inside his head whispered, *And what if they did? What's to stop them?*

A sleeping Mr. Oliver and a pair of glass doors were the only things standing between Mary and the outside world.

"Oh, shit," he whispered. Mr. Travis was right.

The golden arrow pointed at the four. The elevator stopped and a gentle bell dinged. Mary was on the other side of the gate, red-faced and staring at him hard.

"We've got a problem," she said.

# CHAPTER THIRTY

He followed Mary into the kitchen. She was wearing a bomber jacket with the price tag hanging from the sleeve. "What?" she defended. "It's not like it's leaving the store. Besides, it's on sale."

"Must be nice, getting to wear whatever you want."

"Nice?" She regarded him with an expression of indifference. "I've always been surrounded by luxury, but I've never had anything to call my own."

He stayed quiet, wondering if she'd ever get tired of chastising him. He watched her open the oven, checking on two plates laden with fast food. The smell of French fries made his stomach rumble.

"Tonight, before you arrived," she said, using a folded dishtowel to pull out the hot plates, "I finally hacked into the class lists for Cazanovia College. Stacey isn't in any of the fashion courses—she's a business major."

Daniel switched gears from worrying about Mr. Travis. "Really? Why is she pretending? And how does she have Maureen's dresses?"

Mary's lips stretched into a grim line. She packed the paper bags with the reheated food, her movements stiff. "I don't know," she said, clearly frustrated. "Maybe Maureen donated them to the school."

"Donated?" he casually considered the possibility, then a horrible realization occurred to him. "You mean as in after she

NIGHT SHIFT

died? Does Blanche know this?"

Mary stared down at the salt packet she was absentmindedly poking with her finger. "No," she said. "She's convinced Stacey has Maureen's permission, and that Maureen will show up as a surprise."

"A part of her must realize that's probably not going to happen."

Mary barely raised her eyes. "It's what she needs to believe in. You're the only one who knows…not even Ruth Ann."

Daniel's pulse skipped a few beats. Despite the morbid conversation, feeling included by her made him happy. "What should we do?" he asked, making sure he emphasized the "we."

She let out a ragged breath, then said, "I don't know, but maybe some fresh air will help." She skirted around and reached into one of the low cupboards. "Petey picked this from Mr. Oliver years ago." She retrieved a key, hidden at the back of the shelf on a hook. "It was almost as good as escaping," she explained, nodding to a blue steel door at the end of the kitchen.

Loaded down with their warm food and a few brownies from the fridge, Mary led Daniel through the locked door. He followed her up a flight of cement stairs to another door, and out onto the rooftop of Willard's. He stopped at the threshold, feeling the cool wind against his face. The flat, pebbled surface seemed to reach out across the skyline.

Mary used a piece of wood to keep the door ajar. She pocketed the key and walked over to a tent set up against the brick wall that shared the doorway. She disappeared inside, then a couple of seconds later, a light turned on, making the tent look like a huge glowing pumpkin. Two enormous plush cushions were suddenly pushed out, and Mary followed, holding a lantern.

Daniel's mouth twitched. "And you said you'd never been camping."

She threw a plaid blanket at his chest. "Don't even go there," she warned.

They sat in the squashy seats within the small circle of light

from the lantern and ate their supper together.

"Wowzers," Mary said, chewing her burger. "I had no idea it was this good. What is this again?"

"Quarter Pounder with Cheese," he laughed. "That's nothing—dip your French fry into your chocolate shake."

Mary did as he instructed. "Mmm." She closed her eyes. "No wonder people get addicted to this stuff."

Daniel smiled and adjusted the blanket over his shoulders. He glanced around the rooftop. "I don't understand," he said. "I thought you couldn't leave the store. Why isn't there an invisible barrier on this door?" He licked a dollop of ketchup off his thumb, then motioned to the propped open entrance.

Mary looked up, concentrating on the stars. "The barrier is at the roofline," she said.

"Really?" He was fascinated. "How do you know for sure?"

She ignored his question and pointed to a faint line barely recognizable in the darkness. "Do you see the border I painted over the pebbles?" she asked. "I did that after we first came up here. The store is surrounded by taller buildings, but there's a blind spot where we're blocked from view. It's only safe if we're on this side of the line. Although, I'm usually up here by myself—the novelty wore off long ago for the others."

Daniel's eyes trailed over the little vignette that Mary had created. The tent was lined with sleeping bags and more cushions—she'd even strung up tiny battery-operated Christmas lights. The whole scene gripped his heart.

"Do you like to stargaze? I've taught myself all the constellations," she said, now leaning back all the way on her cushion. "Do you know any?"

Daniel took a few bites of his burger and chewed thoughtfully. "I have a feeling you know more than I do."

"Sometimes I like to make up my own."

"Show me."

Mary nodded, accepting the challenge. "Start at the North Star at the tip of the Big Dipper," she said, pointing to the sky

with a fry. "Then move down diagonally to the little one. Go up to the cluster then back down to the lower star. And finish at the bluish one. Can you see it?" she asked playfully.

"The letter *W*?"

"Yes! I can't believe you got that."

"There are *W*'s all over the sky. Wait, never mind, that's just two *V*'s together."

She laughed and reached for another handful of fries. Daniel smiled. He rested back on his own cushion, silently practicing the phrase in his head a few times. "Stars are beautiful," he recited carefully, "but they may not take an active part in anything, they must just look on forever."

Mary turned to him. "Very apropos, Danny Boy."

"It's from *Peter Pan and Wendy*," he told her. "My mom read it to me all the time."

"I know," she said, softly. "Ruth Ann told me."

This didn't surprise Daniel. "You guys share everything, huh?"

"She's my best friend," she explained. Mary licked the salt from her fingertips, then let out a long sigh. "I don't know what I'd do if Ruth Ann disappeared one day. Poor Clara, she still misses Virginia." She waited a few beats before elaborating. "I think Petey saw or heard something that day, but he's blocked it from memory. It's been such a long time. I haven't thought about her for a while, but since Clara woke up…" She let the thought wander off.

They stayed quiet, content to lazily stare at the sky. Flashing lights of an airplane crossed through one of Mary's constellations. "It's hard to believe people are all the way up there," she said, dreamily.

Daniel scoffed at her remark. "Airplanes," he grumbled. He pictured himself stuck in a chair in the sky while Mary gazed up, watching him from the rooftop, as he flew farther away from her. His chest constricted, making it painful to take a deep breath.

Mary turned to him. "Will this be your first Easter without

your dad?"

"What?" Daniel's mind was still on a plane surrounded with strangers. "Um, yeah it is."

"I'm sorry," she said.

He stayed quiet, pretending to be interested in the stars.

Mary tried again. "What was your mom's name?"

"Everyone called her Gigi," he said.

Her brow furrowed. "You mean like the movie?"

"I guess so."

She grew quiet, then offered him a brownie.

"It has a *W* on the top," he said, noticing the store's iconic symbol.

"They stamp it from a thin layer of peanut butter fudge."

"Seriously?" He peeled off the smooth, thick *W* and let it melt on his tongue. Daniel was full and satisfied, and his chest didn't feel so tight anymore.

Mary reached for her second brownie and started asking him about his childhood.

Daniel was so relaxed he didn't hesitate to share his memories.

"Then one time," he told her, "we were driving and my mom pointed out a rainbow. I was only five or six and I asked dad to drive faster so we could catch up to it—I was convinced we would reach the end."

"Looking for a pot of gold?" she teased.

"I didn't even think about that, I just wanted to see the end with my own eyes. I wanted to hold it in my hand. Dad started to explain the theory of light refraction, but Mom turned around from the front seat and told me to keep chasing the rainbows."

They sat cross-legged in front of each other and finished the last of the brownies, letting the sounds of the traffic from the avenue below echo around them.

"Did you ever read *A Princess of Mars*?" Mary asked.

"No. Is that H.G. Wells?"

She shook her head. "Edgar Rice Burroughs. Anyway, at the beginning of the story the main character, John Carter, is left

to die in a remote desert cave after narrowly escaping an attack by an Apache tribe. But he has an out-of-body experience and walks away from his corpse. Standing in the Arizona night, he looks up at the stars. His eyes go to the brightest star—Mars. He imagines how amazing it would be to go there, and suddenly he's flying through space. And poof, just like that, he's on Mars."

"Just like that?"

"Yeah," she said with a little laugh. "It's my favourite part. Imagine, being able to make a wish on a star and escape to your own utopia…just like that."

A battle waged inside Daniel. He was drawn to her, but was repelled by his own desire. It was unnatural—freakish even. But he longed to trace that little line between her eyebrows whenever she frowned at him. He wanted to wrap her long waves of hair in his fingers. He wanted to breathe her in, taste her, fill up his senses with her.

"Mary," he said, and her name on his lips sent a hum down his spine. "You're so beautiful."

Her expression hardened.

It felt like someone had emptied a barrel of ice over Daniel's head. "What's wrong? I'm only trying to compliment you."

"It's not a compliment for me, it's an insult. Being perfect and beautiful means I'm inhuman, fake. I'm forced to be on display…except for me, there's no price tag." She took a few breaths, trying to calm down.

"I'm sorry…I didn't mean it that way." Daniel ached to reach out and hug her.

Mary brushed a hair away from her face. "In all the years I've been trying to discover who I am, and why I'm here," she said. "I've always been struck by the same thought—this confined life was never my choice. Willard's is my prison, no matter how beautiful and perfect it is." Her voice was small and sounded far away. "And when everyone else is busy and I'm alone, I can't shake the feeling that I'm nothing more than some

kind of prized possession."

He could read the hurt in her eyes. "You're not something to be bought or sold," he said. "No one owns you, Mary."

A quiet look passed between them, and her expression relaxed, almost curious. "Sometimes," she said, "when you say certain things or look at me a certain way, it feels…familiar."

The wind picked up, but neither of them mentioned going back inside. Mary stood and gathered the food wrappers that had blown around. When she sat back down, her leg brushed up against Daniel's, but instead of inching away, she kept it there, pressing against his thigh.

He froze, not daring to move, pretending to be interested in picking out the last few fries. He was acutely aware of the exact spot where she was touching him. The heat began to spread over him, like ripples from a pebble thrown in a lake.

"I always wondered what would be worse," she said. "Never leaving the store, or having a taste of something wonderful only to lose it and be left with the memory."

"Is this about Mars?"

"Sort of." She looked at him in a way that made his pulse race.

"Maybe all you have to do is make a wish, and it will happen, just like that."

She leaned toward him, so close he could make out a tiny salt crystal on her lower lip. "Just like that?" she whispered.

He was sure she could hear his heart pound. He wet his lips, imagining her kiss would taste like salt and chocolate.

His phone rang, making them both jump. Daniel cleared his throat, then answered the call. "Mr. Oliver," he started. "I was just in the office, but…oh. Sorry. Hey, Monique."

Mary stood up and backed away. "I'll give you two some privacy," she said.

Daniel watched her leave as Monique's voice squealed into his ear about the latest *Vampire Diaries* episode. He picked up a fry, and then tossed it back down—it was stone cold.

# CHAPTER THIRTY-ONE

Daniel paced the floor of his hotel room, rubbing the back of his neck raw. There was no way to contact them, no way to know if they were all right, no way to know if they needed him for anything.

He'd been off the last few shifts. None of the guards, not even Mr. Oliver, worked every night. Still, when he didn't see his name on the schedule, his anxiety had been building. If he called the store, whoever was working security that night would answer, but what would Daniel ask them about?

*"Say, any screaming coming from Ladies' Fashions?"*

*"By any chance was there a mannequin lying broken in a tangled heap at the bottom of the grand staircase?"*

His sleep was sporadic, filled with nightmares of Mary hanging from the rooftop by her fingertips or being caught moving by one of the guards, freezing her in mid-scream...forever. Each time he woke up sweaty and twisted in the sheets.

Then there were the other dreams about Mary. He ignored every instinct that told him what he wanted was impossible. It was unnatural, he tried to convince himself, it was bizarre, and it scared the hell out of him. He even tried to replace her face and body with Monique's, but it was useless.

If he was this worried being apart from them for only two days, how would it feel when he left for good?

Daniel arrived earlier than usual for his next shift. He

opened his locker and stared at the crumpled blue gift bags with the golden *W*. *It would be a waste*, he reasoned, *and they are friends, in a weird sort of way. Friends can give other friends gifts, right?*

He took out the Willard's shopping bags, and then shoved his backpack inside. In the middle of the staff room, a group of clerks were chatting excitedly around the information board. Clipped from the morning paper was a picture of a smiling Mr. Hadley in front of the store.

## Willard's Announces Fashionable Contest

**Mr. Hadley, manager of the luxurious department store, announced Willard's will host a prestigious contest for a select group of fashion design students. The front window displays, famous for lavish depictions, will be given over to the young designers to show off their best creations. The winner of this influential event will have their design showcased at the Waldorf-Astoria in September as part of Couture Fashion Week, and be awarded a summer fellowship with the illustrious design firm Giorgio Armani.**

A familiar face appeared by Daniel's side, pulling him away from the group. "So," Monique asked, with an edge to her voice, "guess who managed to squeeze into the contest even though she just started design school?"

Daniel didn't have to think too hard about this one— Monique's tone and rigid posture gave it away. "Shifty Stacey?" he guessed. Monique clicked her tongue in a satisfied way, as if to say, "told ya."

"By the way," she said, her thinly shaped brows knitted together. "Are you coming down with something? You were all distant and weird on the phone the other night."

Daniel coughed into his fist a few times. "No, not really," he said. Their phone conversation hadn't lasted long, and he couldn't remember much of what she'd said.

NIGHT SHIFT

She looked at him with apprehensive eyes. "It's happening again, isn't it? Night shift is creeping you out. Maybe you can switch to day shift," she suggested. "Then we'll get to see each other more often! We can have breaks together in the Matinee Room! I love the cappuccino with the *W* in the foam. And after work we can catch the train…"

"Uh-huh," Daniel said. He kept nodding, but her voice wasn't reaching his ears. Across the room, Sean entered from the lockers, dressed in jeans and a windbreaker. He caught Daniel staring, and started to walk toward them. Monique squeezed his arm, trying to get his attention.

"Sorry, what?" he asked, missing her last question.

Monique noticed the bag under his arm. She cocked her head to the side, then flashed him a coquettish grin. "You've been spending money?" she asked mischievously.

"A few things for a friend."

"Oh, a *friend*, huh?" her voice lifted at the end, like she was unsure, but Daniel could hear the underlying confidence. "Can I see?"

He handed over the large blue bag and watched as she carefully kept the gold coloured tissue intact. She pulled out the watch and her smile of anticipation fell. "Oh," she said, followed by a long pause. "A waterproof watch." She gave Daniel a confused look, then unwrapped the second item. "And a book…about camping?"

Daniel pulled a tight-lipped smile. "My friend really likes the outdoors," he explained.

"Good for them," she said brightly, but the emotion didn't reach her eyes.

Daniel glanced away, feeling like an idiot. No matter what he did, he always ended up disappointing someone. Monique expertly rewrapped the items and to his surprise, she started giggling. Daniel wondered if she was trying to picture herself camping.

Sean came up beside them. "I thought you should know," he said to Daniel, keeping his body turned away from Monique.

"Mr. Oliver is in a shitty mood. He and Mr. Hadley had a huge fight in the security office. That fathead came out so red-faced I thought we were going to have to call 911." He stopped to chuckle at his own joke. "Anyway, heads up to keep your distance tonight."

"Er, thanks," Daniel said. Sean gave him a quick nod and turned on his heel, heading to the door to the main floor. "You know," Daniel said, with a hint of quiet astonishment as he watched Sean leave, "he's not that bad for a jerk."

Monique didn't reply.

He checked his watch—he needed to hurry before the store closed and Mary woke up. "I have to get changed into my uniform," Daniel said, motioning to the locker rooms.

Monique came out of her daydream and snapped her head in his direction. "What are your plans this weekend?" she asked, all smiles again. "We still haven't had that date yet. Are you going home or staying in the city?"

"I'll be working," he said, automatically.

She gave him a funny look. "Are you kidding? Tomorrow is Easter Sunday."

Daniel was speechless. He missed Good Friday? He held his breath, picturing himself pacing his hotel room, completely oblivious to the outside world, totally focused on Willard's.

"So," Monique continued, "if you're not working, maybe we can meet up?"

Daniel couldn't compete with her tenacity. All he wanted was to lock the main doors and start night shift, but she was looking up at him, still waiting for an answer. "I've got plans" was all he could come up with.

"Oh," Monique said. "Sure, right, me too. My mom is making me help her do an egg hunt for my little cousins." She paused and made a face, trying to lighten the clumsy conversation. "And I'll make sure to look for that history report this weekend. You know, if you're still interested."

The hidden meaning in her last sentence wasn't lost on him. "Yeah," he said. "I'm still interested." His stomach

NIGHT SHIFT

flipped. *Why is every decision so complicated?* Daniel picked up the shopping bag and tucked it under his arm. He wondered if she was waiting for him to kiss her goodbye. "Um, happy Easter," he said, a little too cheerfully.

Monique stifled a yawn, then said, "Right. You too." She gave him a tired smile and dragged her high heels to the ladies' change room.

Daniel went straight to Mary's display. He scanned the last few groups of shoppers and waited until no one was watching, then he placed the Willard's bag at her feet. From his pocket, he pulled out a note he'd written earlier. He folded it several times until it was small enough to slip into her mannequin hand.

*Easter*, he thought, smiling to himself as he took the grand staircase to the ground floor. The store would be closed for two whole days. He wondered if it was possible to convince Mr. Oliver that he could do night shift on his own, just this once. Then he could stay with Mary and the others all weekend. There would be no interruptions, and no one to hide from. Remembering Sean's warning, he steadied his courage before entering the office.

Mr. Oliver was already turning off the first row of monitors. He barely made eye contact with Daniel as he grunted out an order—nothing unusual there. Whatever argument had occurred earlier had no effect on his boss. With his back still turned to Daniel, he mumbled a few more words.

Mr. Oliver pointed across the office to a box covered in thick brown packaging paper. "Came for you today," he said. "Someone from day shift signed for it."

Daniel read the return address and smiled. It was from Alice.

Mr. Oliver said, "Any particular reason you used this address?"

Daniel picked up the box—it was heavy. He smiled again. "I didn't want to have to lug it from the hotel," he reasoned. "I guess I should look for an apartment." Apartment? That came out a little too fast.

*Click…click…click.*

Mr. Oliver shut off a few more monitors. "I assumed with your final shift coming up in a few days, you'd be moving on."

"A few days!" His voice cracked. "That soon?"

Mr. Oliver nodded at the clipboard on his desk. "I still need someone until the end of April. Interested?"

Daniel didn't even reach for his Magic 8 Ball. "Pencil me in," he said. Then he added quickly, "Do you really need two night guards working over the holiday weekend?"

"Why?" There was an unmistakable bark of irritation to Mr. Oliver's tone. "You want it off? I'll have a hard time getting a replacement at such short notice…not many volunteer for night shift, you know that."

"No," Daniel said. "I was wondering if you'd want the holiday off and I would stay here, um…by myself."

Mr. Oliver's white eyebrows slowly came together in a suspicious grimace that reminded Daniel of Clint Eastwood facing down an enemy in one of those old Westerns. He took in a long breath through his nose, still staring at Daniel. Then finally he said, "I'll think about it."

With his spirits running high, Daniel made his way to the elevator. Balancing the package on one hip, he pulled across the gate and punched the number one. A few days left? Time had a way of speeding up inside Willard's, while outside it dragged on, empty and lonely.

Daniel was still thinking about time when he ran into Mary. It had been two days since he saw her. The air left his chest all at once as he drank up her image. She'd changed into her ripped jeans. He noticed that she was wearing his black sweatshirt— and the waterproof watch. Her hair was piled on top of her head with a clip, exposing the soft skin of her neck. A smiled played on his lips, his looming resignation long forgotten.

She pulled his note from her jean pocket and read it out loud. "Thought it was TIME you had something to call your own." She met his gaze and touched the watch on her wrist. "Thank you," she said.

NIGHT SHIFT

"You're welcome," he said, certain that everything in the world was perfect.

She motioned to the package. "More takeout?"

He told her about his request for things from storage. "It's mostly music for Clara," he said. Mary insisted they open the box right there on the floor. She disappeared around the corner, then returned with a pair of scissors.

She read the postmarks. "How far is your home from here?" she asked, slicing into the tape.

"Like a two-and-a-half-hour flight."

They pulled back the cardboard tabs, and dug into the box. Daniel found a stack of CDs and lined them up on the floor. "There's a stereo in the Music Room, right?" he asked, flipping over a case, reading the songs on the back.

Mary didn't answer. She had a book in her hands.

"Oh man," he sighed. "I haven't seen that in years."

"*Peter Pan and Wendy*," she said, handing it to him.

"Dad must have packed it away right after the funeral." Daniel read the inside cover, "To Sissy, Love Mama, Christmas 1911." He grinned at Mary's confused expression. "My mom loved old bookstores." He passed it back to her. "Ruth Ann might want to look at it."

"You think!"

Daniel reached into the box again and pulled out a few more balls of paper, revealing the lone item at the bottom. He placed it on his lap, staring at the front.

Mary's voice broke through his daze. "You can't show this to Ruth Ann, she'll go ballistic!"

"Huh?" He tore his eyes away from his lap.

She pointed to the pen marks over the type. "Did you do this?"

Daniel squinted at the markings. "Oh yeah," he said. "That's the way she read it, so I wanted it to match."

"What do you mean?"

"My mom always said Petey Pan instead of Peter Pan. So I wrote a *y* over all the *r*s, and—" he stopped and locked eyes

203

with Mary. "Huh, another coincidence," he said, thinking of his mother and the speech Mr. Willard gave on opening day. *How you see the world depends on which side of the glass you're looking from.*

Mary put the book down and slid beside him, letting their knees touch. "What's that?" she asked, looking at what he was holding.

Daniel stared at the bare skin through the frayed rips of her jeans. "Um, a photo album."

She ran her hand over the cover. "Show me," she said.

A swell of heat filled up his chest. "Only if you show me yours first," he sputtered, hoping to pull off a casual laugh. Mary stared back, her gaze steady and unflinching. Daniel tensed, feeling a nervous tingle travel over his skin. He reached forward, holding his breath as his fingertips barely grazed her cheek.

"Will you show me your pictures?" she asked, as if he was eating a sandwich and not leaning in to kiss her.

He dropped his hand, feeling his heart crumple in on itself, and passed her the book.

Mary hungrily turned through the first few pages. "Is this you?" she asked, pointing to a baby on a blanket.

"Yup." Even though her latest rejection stung, he couldn't leave her side.

"Is there a picture of your parents in here?"

Daniel conceded to her curiosity and flipped to a page that showed several pictures of a Christmas morning.

She pointed to a handsome man holding a little boy on his knee, and asked. "Is this your father?"

The photo brought back vivid childhood emotions for Daniel, and despite her latest snub, he couldn't help but grin. "I must have been around five or six," he said.

Mary made a small choking sound. "And is this your mother?" she asked, pointing to the pretty blond woman kneeling in front of the Christmas tree. Her arms were wrapped around a young Daniel, holding a train.

NIGHT SHIFT

"Yeah," he said. They were quiet for a moment. "I totally forgot about that train," he said, breathlessly. "It had a special key that made it go. No one else had one like it. Mom told me it was made special just for me." He smiled, lost in the memory.

When he finally looked over, tears were running down Mary's cheeks, her lips quivering. "Daniel," she said, still pointing to the blond woman. "This is Virginia."

# CHAPTER THIRTY-TWO

"What?" he asked, leaning forward, certain he misheard her through her tears.

"I don't know how," she choked. "But this is Virginia."

"No," he said gently, as if delivering bad news to a child. "That's impossible. She only looks like her." He reached for the handkerchief in his back pocket.

Mary wiped a hand across her face, ignoring his gesture. "I saw her every day for twenty years! This is Virginia," she said pleadingly, tapping the photograph again. "It explains everything."

"Explains everything?" he repeated. "It explains nothing." He laughed nervously then took the album from her. "What you're saying is impossible, Mary. And I think you'd agree, I've got a deep capacity for believing in the impossible." The joke fell flat. He turned away and started placing items back in the box, his hands had started shaking.

"It's the truth," she said.

Daniel gritted his teeth. A dull ache began to grow inside his chest, making it hard to breathe. "Why are you saying this?" his voice faltered. He reached for the last of the CDs. Her fingers gripped his wrist. "Don't," he whispered, but he did nothing to move away, he couldn't resist her touch.

"Daniel." Her voice was soft but urgent.

He slowly turned his head and looked at her. Uneven

NIGHT SHIFT

blotches covered her face and neck, and tears still clung to her eyelashes. "Was this Petey's idea?" he asked, almost pleading. "It's another one of his practical jokes, right?"

"It's no joke," she said. "I swear."

The ache in his chest began to move up his throat, he tried to swallow it back down. Daniel wished he would wake up in the hotel room and start the evening all over again.

His silence encouraged Mary's resolve. "Your mother is Virginia," she began. "She lived with us in the store."

"Stop it," he pulled out of her grasp. "Why are you throwing out these weird stories about my dead mother?" A mix of bile and fear churned in his stomach.

Mary nervously wet her lips. "You play the piano just like her, you look just like her—the same eyes, the same hair, the same smile. I can't believe I didn't see it earlier."

Her words echoed in his head, distorted like they were underwater. He focused on a spot over her shoulder, taking sharp breaths through his nose. The adrenaline was building, making his words tremble. "Do the others know?" he finally asked.

Mary shook her head. "No." Her voice was weak. "I was suspicious about why you seemed familiar. I hadn't really thought it was possible for Virginia to be your mother, but when you arrived tonight with your family album, I had to see the picture first to be sure."

"And now you're sure?"

She nodded.

Daniel took one more deep breath, then grabbed the box and jumped to his feet.

"What are you doing?"

"I'm going to ask the others," he called out, racing to the elevator.

Mary was quick and managed to run in behind him before he slammed the elevator gate closed. He thumped his palm against the number three button. "Let's see what's going down in the Music Room, hmm?" he said, mockingly.

207

"You don't understand. It's not just the pictures."

"Really? Enlighten me!" He snapped. His shock was distorting his fear into anger. Daniel felt like he was trapped in a speeding car, headed for a cliff.

"Your father's handkerchiefs came from the store. It's the same blue initial!"

He speared her with a damning glare. "Do you have any idea how many tourists visit the store every week? All that proves is that the handkerchiefs were bought here."

Mary continued as the golden arrow moved toward the number three. "You told me everyone called her GiGi. I thought it was her name, like the movie. But it was her initials, wasn't it? G.G. for Ginnie Gale? What if Virginia shortened her name after she left Willard's?"

He waited five seconds before answering her. "Coincidence," he said, staring straight ahead. "It's only another stupid, freaky coincidence." The gentle bell dinged, interrupting the argument. He swung open the gate and marched through the Toy department.

"Please stop!" Mary ran alongside, tugging on his elbow, trying to slow him down. "Listen to me. The only reason Clara woke up is because she heard you playing the piano. She actually thought you were your mother! All those songs you play by heart from your mother's record collection are the same songs she played for Clara."

He broke free and ran across the Scrabble board floor, then down the aisle toward the Music Room. Clara's laughter floated down the aisle. He rounded the corner and stood at the entrance to the Music Room. The box was suddenly snatched from his hands.

Mary took a few steps backward, holding the box. "You can't tell them about Virginia like this, at least not until you've calmed down. Please, just wait and listen to me. This will break Petey's heart."

"What about breaking my heart?" he spat. Then he grabbed her arm with one hand and the box with the other.

NIGHT SHIFT

"Daniel and Mary!" Oscar stood fuming at them. The others filtered out, watching with shocked expressions.

Daniel lifted his hand and stepped away from Mary. She put the box down, then gave it a shove with her foot, pushing it even farther away from him.

Oscar looked back and forth between the two of them. "Would somebody mind telling me what is going on?"

Jonathan gave Clara a little nudge. "Told you," he said, his voice full of anticipation. "They love to fight."

Daniel had no more patience, his reasoning was frayed and barely intact. "Mary has a theory," he said.

Mary clutched the photo album to her chest. She whispered a few words, but only a creaking sob came out.

"Go on, then," Daniel goaded her. "Show them the evidence." Mary ignored him, refusing to budge. Daniel tried to wrench the album from her grip, but she held on tightly. They continued to wrestle until Oscar pushed them apart, breaking up the struggle.

Jonathan's face broke into a grin. "Ruth Ann, go get the popcorn!"

"Oh, my nerves!" Blanche said, her glamorous face contorted with disgust. "What is wrong with you two?"

Oscar took the album. "That's enough," he said, straightening out his sweater. "Damn fools, fighting over a book."

"It's mine," Daniel said. "Give it to me."

Oscar ignored his request. He opened the album to the first page. An amused expression played over his face. He looked at Daniel and said, "You were a fat baby." He turned the next page and suddenly his smile dropped.

Clara frowned at him. "Oscar?" she asked, unnerved by his reaction. She moved to his side and looked at the album, now shaking in his hands.

Daniel helplessly watched as the disastrous scene unfolded. His eyes jumped from face to face, hoping to find a snicker or a half-hidden smile to let him know this was all a joke, a horrible,

209

misguided joke. But no one was laughing; even Jonathan had turned pale.

Clara's hand flew to her mouth.

"Impossible," whispered Ruth Ann. She reached out for Jonathan to keep from falling.

Clara closed the album and held it to her chest. Blanche steadied her as she began sobbing.

The sound of a skateboard made everyone look down the aisle. Petey was holding a bag of assorted candy. He stopped beside the discarded cardboard box and picked up the worn, hardcover *Peter Pan and Wendy*.

"Hold on." Petey frowned, flipping through the pages. "Is this a joke?" He glanced at the others for an answer, and then started at Clara's teary face. "W-what's wrong?" he asked, sounding small.

Clara cleared her throat and tried to speak, but her words were too thick to make any sense.

Daniel rubbed a hand over his blotchy face. He walked over to Petey and crouched beside him. "My mom," he began, "read this book to me almost every night. It's still one of my favourites."

"Yeah," Petey said. "But my name—?"

"I know," he interrupted. "My mom would always say Petey Pan instead of Peter. That's the way she read it, and that's the way I learned to love it. So, I wrote a *y* over every *r*."

Some of Petey's worry melted away. "Whoa," he laughed. "Was she mad?"

"No," he said, "she actually got a little sad."

Petey put a thin arm around Daniel's shoulder and gave him a hug. "I bet you miss her," he said, innocently.

"Of course," Daniel said, touched by the gesture. He ran his fingers down the page. "It's yours now."

Petey stared at the worn book. "From you?" he asked.

"No," he said, "from her."

"I don't understand," Petey's eyebrows crinkled together.

Clara walked over and stood beside him. "Precious," she

NIGHT SHIFT

said, touching his shoulder. "We found out something. It's going to hurt, but you need to know."

"You're scaring me," he said, instinctively stepping closer to Daniel.

"Come over with me," Clara encouraged, reaching for his hand.

"I want to stay here," Petey said. Daniel gave a slight nod to Clara. She passed him the album and he opened to a random page. Petey's face lit up. "You're in full hockey gear! How old were you?" he asked excitedly.

"Um...ten. I think."

Petey laughed. "It's weird to see you my size." He turned the next page of the album, and stared unblinking, staying quiet. The next page was turned more quickly, then another, and another, until he was flipping through, not even pausing to look at the photos anymore.

He dropped the album and backed away from everyone. "No, no, no." His voice rose with each word, gulping for air in between.

Clara put her arms around him, holding him tight until his sobs slowed down to a whimper. "I know," she soothed, brushing his hair back with her hand. "Let it out, you'll feel better."

Petey eventually calmed down enough to speak. "How?" he asked, his words muffled by Clara's chest.

"We don't know," she told him.

He looked down at the album lying open, showing a picture of a picnic with a young Daniel hugging Virginia on a blanket strewn with food. "For years," Petey began, "I've had nightmares, thinking she was locked up somewhere in the store, unable to get out, or smashed to pieces and lying rotting in a dump somewhere."

He sniffed, then lifted his face, and hit Daniel with a dark look. "But all along, she was having picnics with you. Reading to you. Watching you play hockey. You, you, you!" he screamed. "Why not me? Why wasn't I enough to keep her

211

here?" Tears began to stream down his face again. "Why?"

Daniel could only shake his head.

Petey grunted, then lunged at Daniel's chest. "I hate you," he growled, landing blows on Daniel's chest.

"Stop…listen," he begged, struggling to hold on to Petey's flailing fists.

"If she hadn't left, she'd still be alive! I HATE YOU!"

Clara grabbed Petey from behind and pulled him into a hug. He collapsed into her embrace, still sobbing.

Daniel dropped his arms, gave the box one last glance, then turned his back on all of them and ran away.

# CHAPTER THIRTY-THREE

D aniel sat on the floor of the change room and leaned against his locker, going over everything in his memory. The day his mother brought him to the store was more warped than before. Why did she bring him here if she didn't want him to go in? She was terrified when he ran into the store. Maybe it was a warning. Maybe he should leave now. He put his head between his knees to stave off the continuous threat of blackouts.

He was determined not run away into the night like last time—at least not until he got some *real* answers. Questioning Mary and the others tonight was unthinkable, but there was one other person who had been at Willard's just as long.

Daniel knocked on the security office door and walked in without waiting for an answer. Mr. Oliver's usual frown changed into an expression of surprise. "What happened?" he asked, a rare tone of concern under the question.

Daniel sat down on the leather couch and focused on keeping his voice steady, afraid he'd break down. How the hell was he going to ask about his mother? "Willard's isn't like other stores," he said, "is it, Mr. Oliver?"

There was a sniff, then he replied, "Hearing noises again?"

"No."

"Change your mind about wanting to work the holiday night shift by yourself?"

A weight pulled on Daniel's heart. Only a few hours ago he was full of hope, anticipating uninterrupted time with Mary and

the others. He ignored Mr. Oliver's question, but replied with his own. "Why have you worked here for forty years when so many others have quit?"

He blinked once then said, "Because I don't believe in ghosts."

"That's the only reason?"

"Why?"

"It just makes me wonder." Daniel swallowed, unsure how to ask about Mary and the others without sounding like he needed to be taken to the psych ward. *Hey, you know some of the mannequins come to life at night, right?*

Mr. Oliver leaned over the green blotter. "And I might wonder why a nineteen year old who just inherited a large sum of money would keep working the night shift instead of traveling around the world."

"I gave my resignation," he said. "Remember?"

Mr. Oliver considered Daniel's answer for a moment. Then he smoothed out his tie, letting his finger tap the *W* on the golden tie clip. "Is this about Mr. Travis?" he finally asked.

It took Daniel a moment to digest the question; Mr. Travis was the last person on his mind.

Mr. Oliver's eyes brightened. "What was he saying the other day when Mr. Hadley and I interrupted you?"

"I don't really remember," Daniel said, trying to rearrange the mess that his brain had become. "Something about upgrading safety, I think. He seemed to know a lot about Mr. Willard and his father."

"Hmm." Mr. Oliver sat back in his chair. "Told you all about George Willard, did he? Did he mention the gold bars?"

Daniel was totally lost as to where this line of questioning was leading. "No, only that his family was rich and that he was very successful."

Mr. Oliver breathed in slowly. "He's not the first treasure hunter to come sniffing around."

"Treasure? I thought he worked for Consumers Plus?"

Mr. Oliver winced at the mention of the big-box franchise.

NIGHT SHIFT

"He does, but his interest in this store goes back farther than any contract he agreed to work on. George Willard was a miser and turned all his fortune into gold bars. After the death of a sibling, James became the sole heir to the family fortune. When he bought this building, he took the gold bars out of the bank and began renovating." He paused and waited for a reaction.

Daniel kept still, trying to erase the memory of Petey screaming with tears running down his cheeks. Mr. Oliver smacked his lips, and then let out a low grumble from the back of his throat.

"The part Mr. Travis finds interesting," Mr. Oliver continued, "is that the gold bars were removed from the bank, but never converted to cash."

Daniel's head was twice its weight—his neck was sure to snap under the pressure. "Please," he begged, his voice nothing more than a hoarse whisper. "Tell me what you want me to do. I can't stand these riddles anymore."

Mr. Oliver slammed a palm on the antique desk, making the computer monitor wobble. "Don't be fooled by his knowledge and so-called research," he warned. "He wants to turn Willard's upside down on a fool's errand—no matter what or who he destroys." Mr. Oliver stared at Daniel. "You said keeping the store safe was the most important thing." One white bushy eyebrow lifted. "Can I still count on you?"

Daniel had a staring contest with the glass bowl. What if Mr. Oliver knew nothing and he fired him on the spot for insanity? He'd never get the answers he was looking for, and he'd never see Mary again. At that moment Daniel simply couldn't—and didn't want to take that chance. "I'll work the rest of my shifts," he said, flatly.

For the rest of the evening, he kept to the ground floor, afraid to venture any higher. No one was on his side. He paused under the golden tree in the main foyer. He twirled the keychain on his finger a few times, then caught it in his palm.

*Ask again later.*

His heart shriveled; even the Magic 8 Ball was letting him

215

down. He slumped against the tree and looked up at the twinkling branches above him, pretending they were stars.

When he checked on Mr. Oliver again, it was four in the morning. The head of security was asleep in the chair with his chin resting on his chest. Daniel wasn't sure which version was real—the useless, non-threatening one, or the ranting one with paranoid tendencies. Everything inside Willard's was one big damn illusion, he realized.

He gently shook Mr. Oliver's shoulder and convinced him to go home early, promising to stay on for the holiday as the lone security guard. He stood at the main door, watching Mr. Oliver shuffle in the rain to the cab. A rush of fresh air blew across Daniel's face. He took a deep breath of the real world, then stepped back and locked the doors.

Daniel was numb inside, but he still craved a sign of encouragement, one or two kind words meant just for him, one answer to prove everything he'd had to go through wasn't pointless. He reached inside his pocket, pulled out the keychain again, and stared down at his open palm.

*Better not tell you now.*

Daniel closed his fist around the Magic 8 Ball. The volcano of fear and rage boiled in his gut, threatening to explode. He ran up the grand staircase straight to the top. He didn't stop for an umbrella or a jacket.

Go directly to the roof, do not pass go, do not collect two hundred dollars.

The rain soaked his shirt as he stared at the roofline. His knuckles were white from clutching the keychain. He brought his fist to mouth and whispered, "Are you really with me?" A rivulet of water traced a path down his back as he slowly straightened each stiff finger. The rain bounced off the inky window.

Daniel read the answer, then launched the Magic 8 Ball into the air, sending it in a high arc over the edge, and down five storeys to the concrete below. He fell to his knees, and stayed frozen like a forgotten statue. Eventually, the rain

NIGHT SHIFT

petered out to a mist.

Behind him, he heard the squeak of hinges. Footsteps crunched on the pebbled surface, but he didn't turn around. He insensibly wondered if Petey was strong enough to send him over the edge, too.

"Do you want to be alone?" she asked, matter-of-fact.

Her tone didn't surprise him; they were beyond any awkwardness now.

*Alone? Been there, done that,* he thought. Daniel shook his head. "No, Mary," he said. "I don't want to be alone."

She crouched next to him, not touching, but he could feel her presence, her warmth. "I'm sorry," she said. She gently tugged on his elbow, leading him to her tent.

He followed her inside and sat down on one of the cushions—it reminded him of a genie's lamp. She turned on the tiny lights strung along the ceiling. A small, short table had a plate of nachos covered in melted cheese, olives, and onions, with a bowl of salsa on the side.

Mary reached into the far corner, and pulled out two bottles. Daniel raised an eyebrow when she passed him a beer. He held the cold drink, listening to the last of the rain drip off the tent. Then he took a long swig, almost finishing half. Mary had a sip from her own bottle, then pulled away a clump of chips and cheese, and dipped a few into the salsa.

Daniel did the same and was surprised how hungry he was. He swallowed a few more mouthfuls, then chased it with the beer.

Mary watched him carefully.

"How?" he asked.

"I don't know." She waited a few beats, then said, "But I finally know why we're safe with you. And she must have been the one to set up the inheritance." Mary's cheeks flushed. "And all those times when your mannerisms seemed so familiar to me, like I was reliving another moment with you..." She hesitated. "I guess I know the real reason now. You're so much like her."

217

Daniel rolled an olive between his fingers. "I don't understand. How could she keep that a secret for all those years?"

A pained expression flashed across Mary's face. "Maybe she was going to tell you, but never got the chance."

"The car accident," he sighed. Daniel popped the olive in his mouth and finished his beer. "I used to lay awake at night making lists of all the things I never knew about her. Simple stuff like how she drank her coffee. What her favourite colour was. Everyday things, not something like this." He paused and took another handful of chips. "I wonder if my dad knew."

Mary gave him a tired shrug, then opened another beer for him. She grew quiet as Daniel nursed his second drink. "I think that would have been a deal breaker," she reasoned. "No matter how much he loved her. I'm guessing she'd want to keep her past a secret, afraid he'd leave."

"Yeah," Daniel said. The beer was making him comfortably numb. "It's weird enough to think of your parents that way, let alone when one of them used to be—"

"—I get it," she interrupted.

"I didn't mean—"

"—no, you're right. How else should you feel?" Mary ate a few more nachos and tipped back her beer.

He'd hurt her feelings and it bothered him more than he wanted to admit. Here he was, sharing beers in a tent full of pillows with the girl who made his blood rush every time he looked at her. But he wouldn't let himself go to her, he just couldn't. He must have been staring, because she gave him an odd look over the table.

He took another sip. "Petey hates me."

"It won't last," she said. "He likes you too much. Besides, you have other fans," she added. "What about Monique?"

He almost laughed at the absurdity of what his life had become. "I don't know," he admitted. Nothing was simple anymore.

Mary picked at the label on her bottle. "It's none of my

business, but if you like her you should know—she's not exactly everything she seems to be."

"Great, another girl with a secret." He took a long drink and plunked down his beer, spilling a bit. He wiped his mouth with the back of his hand and burped. "Sorry, secrets give me gas."

Mary looked unimpressed. She took a drink, then sat up and let out an enormous belch. "Beat that," she challenged.

"Jesus," he said, waving a hand in the air. "That was disgusting. But unfortunately for you, I have plenty of ammo, I was holding back."

They shared another beer and were both pleasantly buzzed by the time Daniel admitted Mary was the champion. "You're even perfect at burping," he said.

When their giggles petered out, he lay back, staring at the little Christmas lights. "I wish I knew why this was happening. How could she be one of you, then somehow leave one day, and be real after that?" He moaned and ran a hand over his face. "I think my head is going to explode."

"I know what this is," Mary said, seriously.

"What?"

"It's fucking weird."

He stared back at her, then they both burst out laughing again.

Daniel picked at the last few bits of cheese globs hardened on the plate. "Do you remember the very first thing you ever said to me?"

Mary crinkled her nose. "Something snotty about you looking too scared to be a guard?"

"No," he said. "Before that, in the dark, when I was about to drop from the elevator gate—you told me to hang on. I feel like I'm back in that shaft again, dangling above the abyss of insanity."

"*Dangling above the abyss of insanity*," she repeated importantly. "Sounds better than leaping from psychopathy."

Daniel studied her, the earlier giddiness suddenly gone.

"You mean the roof?" he asked unbelieving.

Mary glanced out the open flap toward the city skyline. The clouds were clearing away, hinting at the bright morning to come. "That's how I know the barrier exits," she admitted. "I tried to jump—but it pushed me back." She turned to him, her lower lids filling up. "Please don't tell the others. I kept it a secret...even from Ruth Ann."

"That first night," he said. "I'd decided to let go, just before you called out. I was going to let myself fall down the shaft, but you came and told me to hold on." He gave her a small smile. "So I did."

She blinked and two fat tears rolled down her cheeks. Daniel offered her his father's handkerchief. Silently she blotted her face, then sniffed. "Black," she said. "Virginia—I mean your mom, she drank her coffee black."

Daniel leaned forward. "And?"

"And her favourite movie was *Wings of Desire*."

He scooted even closer, hungry for any detail. They talked for another half an hour until a beeping noise interrupted them. Mary pushed a button on her new watch and gave him an anxious smile. "Come with me," she said.

She led him to the Matinee Room and positioned him on a spot in the middle of the floor. "Stay here," she commanded. She zigzagged through the booths to the far edge of the room by the floor-length window, pulled back the long, royal blue drape, revealing the view of the city, then returned to his side.

"What are we waiting for?"

Mary checked her watch again. "You'll see in fifty-four seconds."

Over the next minute, the sun dawned. Streaks of sunlight hit the crystal chandeliers, creating a speckled room of a thousand rainbows. She looked up at him, "I thought I'd help you catch the rainbow."

Daniel watched a tiny coloured spectrum move over his palm. He opened and closed his fist a few times, mesmerized.

"It only happens with the sunrise," she explained. "The

NIGHT SHIFT

windows face the east."

Daniel stared at the dots of colour as they moved across his skin. "It's beautiful," he whispered. "Thank you."

"What are you going to do?" she asked. "Are you going to leave again?"

He smiled at the rainbows on his hand. "Not right away," he decided. "And until I do…I'm going to hold on."

"Me too."

# CHAPTER THIRTY-FOUR

He chased her through an archway into one of the more luxurious living room displays. "What do you want from me?" he asked. "You're driving me crazy."

"Me?!" she said. "You're the one who can't decide which girl he wants."

Daniel stepped closer. "That's not true. I know who I want to be with...it's just..." He stopped himself from finishing the sentence. "What do *you* want?"

Mary took a deep breath, then wrapped her hands behind his neck and pulled his mouth down to hers. "I want this."

Her tongue slipped into his mouth, hesitant but seeking. Daniel answered hungrily, speeding up the kiss. Elbows bumped together as their hands tugged at each other's clothing, sending buttons bouncing along the floor.

She pulled him down with her onto the leather couch. Daniel slid his hand down her side, pausing to slip his fingers under the edge of her T-shirt. She held her breath, frozen under his touch. He squeezed his eyes shut, afraid to see what was under him. Then she spoke. He relaxed—she was still human. "I love you," she whispered.

He squinted in the darkness and reached out. Instead of the hotel alarm clock, he felt a bag of chocolate-covered jujubes. Daniel turned on the bedside lamp, illuminating the newly cleaned and furnished secret room.

NIGHT SHIFT

The longest wall was lined with bookcases. In the corner, there were two wingback chairs and a small table in between. His backpack was in a heap on the floor, beside the twin bed. He swung his legs over the edge and sat up.

A loud tapping on the door got his attention. He called out and watched as part of the wall swung back. Mary's head peeked around the opening. "Hey," she smiled. "I brought you a cappuccino."

Daniel tucked the duvet around his waist and patted the bed for her to sit beside him. "Thanks," he said, taking the steaming mug.

Mary's gaze lingered on his bare chest. "How did you sleep? Is the bed comfortable enough?"

"Yeah," he answered. "The room definitely has that Willard's touch. And you?" He took a drink, watching her over the brim of his mug.

She nodded and began to study the room, looking at everything except Daniel. He was grateful for her unexpected shyness. He stared at her hands, remembering how they'd been undressing him in his dream a minute ago.

"Since we have the store to ourselves," she said, "there are a few things I'd like to try with you."

Daniel choked on his cappuccino.

"I have a few theories," she said, ignoring his reaction. "But I need your help."

"Help to do what exactly?"

"Get dressed. I'll wait for you outside."

Daniel pulled on a pair of jeans and rolled up the sleeves of his fitted plaid shirt. Mary stood against Mr. Oliver's desk with a huge basket of chocolate treats. "Happy Easter," she said, tossing him a foiled-wrapped egg.

He grinned. "What time is it, anyway?"

"It's almost four in the afternoon."

He grabbed a few more eggs and followed her to the main foyer. Mary positioned him on the patterned marble in front of the main doors. He swallowed the last of his chocolates, and

223

gave her a confused look. The toes of their sneakers were almost touching.

She raised her hand and placed it flat against the invisible barrier. He was standing on the white side of the tile—the side she has never been on. "Pull me," she said.

Daniel wet his lips. He entwined his fingers with hers, and then very slowly, he started to pull.

Nothing happened. It was like trying to move a huge boulder.

Mary placed her other palm toward him, fingers fanned open. "Try again," she begged.

Holding both of her hands, he took a small step backward, toward the main doors. "Pull harder," she urged, her voice shaking. Their knuckles turned white. He held his breath, putting all his strength into the task. When he looked up, Mary's face was contorted and purple. He let go and she stumbled back, taking huge gulps of air.

He crouched on the floor, helping her sit up. "Oh my God, are you okay? Can you breathe?"

She nodded. "I always wondered about that," she said, "being pulled through instead of pushing. But there's never been anyone who I could test the theory with." She smiled weakly. "Until you of course."

"What did it feel like?"

She winced. "Like I was being wrung out."

"It looked like you were choking," he said. "Don't ever ask me to do that again. I thought we agreed last night—no more death wishes."

"This wasn't a death wish, it was an experiment. Besides, I had no idea that was going to happen."

Daniel studied her. The desperation in her expression scared him. "It almost killed you."

"*Almost* being the operative word," she said, dismissively. "I can't help it, I'm a very curious person." She motioned toward the grand staircase. "I'm also a very impatient person. No point in hanging around this useless spot all afternoon.

Besides, Oscar's expecting us in the kitchen."

She pulled him down the aisle, chatting like nothing had happened. Daniel glanced back at the foyer, and the image of Mary gasping in his arms sent a chill down his spine.

The meal that night was lavish. Boneless leg of lamb with roasted vegetables, carrot pudding soufflés, hot buttered rolls in the shape of bunnies, and a glazed lemon cheesecake with raspberries. Daniel couldn't help but notice Blanche was uncharacteristically withdrawn. Petey was still evasive, doing his best to ignore everyone. He ate quickly, and then slunk off to the Toy department with Blanche clicking in her heels behind him.

The conversation began to revolve around Virginia. Daniel spent most of the time listening. He pushed the last bite of lamb around the plate.

Mary was luminous in the candlelight. *She thinks she's so close to getting what she wants,* he worried. "I'm sure Petey knows more about what happened that night," she said.

"That makes no sense," Jonathan said, doubtfully. He loaded up his fork and took another sip of wine. "Why would he be lying to us all these years?" He said this to no one in particular, but he stared at Daniel as if he were withholding information.

"I don't think he's doing it on purpose," Mary explained. "He's repressed it subconsciously. It's common with a traumatic event."

"Oh!" Ruth Ann exclaimed. "This is just like *Sally Lockhart and the Ruby in the Smoke.*" Daniel joined the rest of the table in giving her a confused look. "Am I the only one who reads?" she said, exasperated. "Sally is a young girl with a mysterious past. While investigating her father's death she goes into an opium den. When she walks into the smoke-filled room, she's transported to an early memory of when she was a very young child. What she sees in the vision proves to be true, and helps her solve the mystery."

Ruth Ann looked at them hopefully, waiting for someone to

figure it out. "Don't you see? We need to jumpstart Petey's memory."

Clara howled with laughter. "We can't make Petey smoke opium!"

Ruth Ann looked indignant. "Of course not! But lots of things that appeal to our senses can trigger a memory. We have to come up with something that was particular about Virginia and then introduce it to Petey in a way that will help him remember."

"Like the power of suggestion," Mary smiled, relishing the possibility. "One signal prompting another until it produces a result."

"Like hypnotizing?" Jonathan said, trying to keep up with the girls. Daniel noticed his usual bravado was somewhat diminished.

Oscar leaned back in his chair and smoothed out his mustache. Everyone paused over their plates, waiting for his verdict. "I'm not entirely sure this is safe," he said. "There are considerations you need to address, one of them being Petey's willingness to participate, the other figuring out what to use as a trigger." He gave Mary a small nod of approval. "But I suppose it's worth a try."

"A song?" Clara suggested. "Virginia used to play a lullaby for Petey on the piano."

Everyone turned to Daniel. He clutched his hand closed, feeling his nails dig into his palm. "Sorry," he answered. "But I never heard her play." He was embarrassed to admit that his mother's great talent was never shared with him.

Clara touched his shoulder and said, "If I sang the notes, do you think you could learn to play it?"

Daniel glanced at Mary's hopeful expression. He was terrified, but how could he deny her this chance? "Yeah, okay," he agreed. "We can practice tomorrow."

Well past midnight, Ruth Ann and Jonathan joined Mary and Daniel in the secret room, gorging on leftover Easter candy.

NIGHT SHIFT

"I thought we were going to play Twister," Jonathan said, slumped in one of the wingback chairs. "The clothing optional version, of course."

Ruth Ann peeked over the cover of her latest pick from the Leisure department and threw an egg at his head.

"It's the game that keeps you in knots," Daniel said. He was sitting on the floor with his head leaning against the bed, lazily chewing on jelly beans. He was much more relaxed now that talk of hypnosis had finished. Jonathan, he noticed, was also inclined to let the conversation stay safe, and he was grateful for that little miracle.

Ruth Ann put down her book with a pout, then stared pointedly at Daniel. "I wish I had something new to read," she said.

"I'll go by the library this week," he promised. "But, um…what about an e-reader? Then you wouldn't have to depend on me to pick them up for you." He wasn't sure how to bring up his resignation. He'd kept it a secret so long, telling them now would feel like he was admitting to something devious.

Ruth Ann lifted a shoulder, partially ignoring his suggestion. She stared across the room at Jonathan, watching his fingers drum a beat on the thigh of his jeans, totally oblivious.

Mary sat cross-legged on the bed. She tapped Daniel on top of the head. "When are you going to practice with Clara?" she prompted. "You could start tonight, it's still early."

"Oh, for Christ's sake," Jonathan sighed, suddenly animated. "Not this again."

"Don't you care about the truth?" Mary asked him. "Don't you care about getting out?"

"Not if we have to traumatize Petey," Jonathan said. "Besides, have you asked Daniel how he feels about this? Maybe he'd like a week or two to get used to the latest weirdness."

His last word hung in the air.

227

"Besides," Jonathan added, "we haven't made a decision about naked Twister yet."

"Oh, damn it!" Ruth Ann said. "You don't care about Petey or Daniel. Everything is always a joke to you!"

Her uncharacteristic outburst made Jonathan's face lose all its colour. "Babe, it's not safe," he stammered.

"How can you say that with Daniel sitting right in front of us?" Ruth Ann's voice rose an octave. "He's proof Virginia was able to leave the store—"

"—at what cost, though?"

"—and have a life, and a family."

"Things are fine. We shouldn't mess up what we've got. I like things the way they are."

"Not me!" Ruth Ann was breathing heavily, trying to keep her anger in check. Daniel wanted to shrink inside himself. Mary looked shocked to hear her best friend unleash like this.

Jonathan reached for her, but she pulled away. "You don't know what it's like," she said, her voice thick from fighting tears. "I spend the whole day listening to babies cry in their strollers. All I want to do is lean over and pick them up, but I can't because we're stuck inside these useless bodies! We're useless! Our lives are useless! How can you be happy?"

Jonathan swallowed, "Babe, please don't…"

Her eyes hungrily searched his face for a clue. "You don't even want a family, do you?" she accused. Before he could answer, she ran into the hallway, leaving them staring at the open door in the wall.

Jonathan turned to Daniel. "Everything was okay until you showed up," he said, sounding more tired than angry. With his head hung low, he followed Ruth Ann into the hallway, letting the door shut quietly after him.

Mary hugged her knees. "Sorry," she said. "I keep forgetting how weird this is for you." There was a long, quiet pause, then she added, "Let's not make tomorrow all about Petey—we can do whatever you want."

Daniel pushed himself up on the bed and sat beside her.

NIGHT SHIFT

The hurtful echoes from Ruth Ann's words suddenly dissipated. He smiled and gave her a nudge. "How about a lesson on sliding down the bannister? Or a mini golf tournament."

"Or a pie eating contest," she teased.

"I love pie!"

Mary laughed and a warm wave rolled through him. They traded smiles a few times, then the silence lingered, becoming obvious. He leaned back on his elbows, his eyes wandering down to the little band of skin showing between her shirt and her jeans.

*Sweet Jesus.*

This was better than the dream. She was here, inches from him, on the same bed.

"Maybe we can play together?" she said.

"Huh?" Daniel straightened up, pulling at the bottom of his shirt.

"Our duet, remember? I'd like to play on the Steinway with you. The piano in the restaurant is so clunky."

"Right. Yeah, of course." His mind rewound back to their first kiss in the Matinee Room. Their conversation that night had a new meaning now, of course. In particular, he remembered her remark about the Ava Gardner poster. "That movie, the one about Venus," he asked. "How did it end?"

Mary hesitated, then said, "Even though the clerk loves her, she realizes they can never share the same life. She goes back to the pedestal and returns to stone. When the lonely clerk starts work the next day, a new employee shows up looking just like Venus."

"So, she came back after all?"

"No, Venus remains frozen in pose." Mary stared at the royal blue rug with the golden *W*. "It's a happy Hollywood ending for the clerk, though."

Daniel didn't know what else to say. "No wonder Jonathan only gave it one star."

"Yeah." She yawned into her hand and slid off the bed. "I'll meet you in the Music Room in six hours or so?"

Daniel considered reaching for her, willing to bet that she'd stay a little longer. "You're leaving already?"

She stopped at the door, then her eyes slid over the bed. "Trust me," she said. "You don't want me to fall asleep in your arms." She walked into the hallway. "Say goodnight, Danny Boy," she called over her shoulder.

The door closed completely, shutting him inside, all alone. "Goodnight, Danny Boy," he said.

# CHAPTER THIRTY-FIVE

Daniel sat at the piano in the Music Room, listening to Clara hum a few bars of melody. She stopped and gave him a nod, prompting him to experiment with several chords.

"I think you almost have it, gorgeous," she said.

He was surprised at how quickly he was learning the song. "I wonder," he said, "if she might have played this for me when I was really young, like when I was a baby?" There was a hopeful lilt to his question.

"She must have; you play like it's familiar to you." She studied him for a moment, then slid down on the bench. "Virginia was so talented, and full of music, you obviously get that from her. But that wasn't her greatest attribute. She was one of the most loving and nurturing souls. I can see a lot of that in you, too. It's only natural that she was the one to care of Petey. We rely on each other, but she was the main influence in his life."

Daniel felt a little stab of jealousy at the mention of Petey's name. "Did she teach him to play?"

"She tried," Clara laughed. "But he squirmed too much. Never could sit still long enough to learn the notes properly. Musical ability isn't one of his attributes."

There was a comfortable connection with Clara, not only because of the music, but because she had been his mother's

confidant for so many years. He asked, "If she loved you all so much, how could she leave without a word? And why didn't she come back for the rest of you?"

Clara grew quiet and folded her hands on her lap. "I've thought about that a long time. I believe that whatever took her away from us was beyond her control. I'm not sure if we'll ever find out all the answers. But at least we know she was having a wonderful life, and that makes me happy." She patted his cheek. "And if she hadn't left, we wouldn't have you, gorgeous!"

Daniel smiled at her touch. "Did she ever say anything about my dad?"

"No. Did you ever ask how they met?"

"Growing up I never cared about it, really. After the car accident I wanted to know everything, but my dad was completely shut off from those memories. It hurt to talk about, so I stopped asking. I thought that once enough time went by I could ask again."

"But now he's gone too," Clara said, softly. "Don't worry, with all of us working toward the same thing, we're bound to come up with an answer. The right inspiration will come along." They both looked up, hearing footsteps. "Speaking of inspiration," she smiled.

Mary came over to the piano. "How's the lullaby?"

"He already knows it," Clara praised.

Mary beamed down at him. "Can I hear it?"

Daniel's heart skipped a few beats. "Sure," he nodded. He wiped his palms on his jeans a few times, then began to play the sweet melody. Clara left the bench and put an arm around Mary's shoulder.

Mary looked thrilled. "It even sounds familiar to me," she said. "I'm sure it will make Petey remember." She turned to Clara. "Can we get him right now?"

"Easy, girl," Clara warned. "Petey's not going to be tricked into anything. You know he's slier than a fox. He has to agree to it first."

"We've been waiting for twenty years to find out what

NIGHT SHIFT

happened!"

Clara moved her head to the side. "What's wrong, Mary, everyone not working hard enough on your latest escape plan?" Then she sauntered out of the room, already singing by the time she passed under the archway.

"You got in trouble," Daniel teased.

Mary gave an impatient snort. "Maybe it's because she just woke up, that the time doesn't seem to drag along for her like it does me," she grumbled.

"I think it depends on the company you keep," he said. "For me, the time inside Willard's always goes faster than the outside. I can't believe the weekend is almost over. I hardly got a chance to break in my bachelor pad. "

Mary ignored the suggestive tone of his voice. "How about a sliding lesson?" she suggested instead. He followed her down the grand staircase to the ground floor, listening to her tips on riding the brass handrail. "We'll start practicing here," she said.

"Did you expect me to fall down all four flights?"

"No," she said, pointing to the Confectionery, "my reason is purely about satisfaction. Let's sugar up before we start."

They sat on the bottom step, sharing red licorice ropes and a handful of candy-covered chocolates. Daniel secretly smiled, noticing how Mary left the blue-coloured ones until last. He made a surprised sound then pulled his phone out. "I completely forgot about Alice," he said, starting to type an Easter message.

"Will she be mad?"

Daniel grinned and kept texting. "She's probably stuck behind a huge pile of files. Alice always takes work home."

"That's kind of sad," Mary said.

"I guess, but she loves her job. Plus a lot of people depend on her to win in the courtroom." He tucked the phone away, and stole another licorice from Mary's fist.

"You learned the song so quickly," she said, between chews. "I wonder if we should also think about the other senses, like sight, touch, and smell. We could use one of the pictures from your album." She turned to Daniel. "What's wrong? You

233

look pale."

"Maybe I ate too many sweets." He stood and began to walk down the aisle.

"Okay." She wavered, then fell into step beside him. "I think you're right about the sugar, but the good news is that Oscar's making curried lamb on rice for dinner. Hopefully you'll feel better after that."

"Uh-huh." He wondered if she was happy to keep him around only to test her various escape theories. *It's not like she's hiding the fact she's desperate to leave Willard's.* The thought was so obvious, he thought it must be true.

His footsteps were dull thuds against the tile. This Easter weekend was nothing like he'd hoped. Mary, he noticed, was content to stroll along, probably hoping to rush the front doors again.

They continued walking through the various departments until he led her to the secret room. Mary stood alone at the threshold, "Um…" she started. Daniel's phone chimed. He reached into his back pocket, expecting to see a reply from Alice. "Wow, is she always that fast?" Mary asked.

He looked up from the screen. "No," he said. "It's from Monique. She found that history report, but she's not working until next weekend."

"Oh."

"But she can meet me tonight if I want."

"Oh," she said again. "So…what do you want?"

Daniel put on his coat and grabbed his backpack. "I guess I'll go get that report." He walked through the security office and down the elegant corridor toward the main doors. Mary's sneakers slapped the tile behind him as she ran to keep up. He walked a few extra feet beyond the black granite, purposely leaving her behind.

She glanced at her waterproof watch. "I guess we'll have that lesson on the banister later tonight?"

"There won't be enough time." Daniel paused at the door, "This is what you want, right? Getting clues about the store and

## NIGHT SHIFT

finding a way out is the most important thing to you, isn't it?"

Mary chewed on her lower lip, then simply nodded.

Daniel gave her one last look, but she didn't say anything. He tugged on the backpack, stepped outside, and then locked the main doors behind him.

# CHAPTER THIRTY-SIX

The next evening was comfortably mild. Daniel only wore his gray zip-up hoodie and jeans as he walked down West 23rd Street. Monique's report was in his backpack. He stopped outside a three-storey limestone building. Its long windows and arched entrance reminded him of Willard's. He pushed against the door and walked into the Muhlenberg Branch Public Library.

He approached the modern-looking circulation desk and inquired about books on hold under his name. The librarian told him they had ten items ready to be picked up, and another thirty on reserve. She looked over the top of her glasses at him. "Catching up?"

"Insomnia."

While she began to stack Ruth Ann's favourites on the counter, he studied the area. The library appeared to be around the same vintage as Willard's, but the inside was totally tech savvy. "How old is this building?" he asked her.

"Over one hundred years," she smiled, scanning the barcodes. "We had a major renovation over ten years ago, though."

"Oh?"

"Mm-hmm. What an amazing transformation; the windows were lengthened to bring in more light, the outside stonework was cleaned and restored, the whole building was fitted with new wiring, new heating and air conditioning units." She took a

NIGHT SHIFT

breath and added with a smile, "And a wonderful community space was added to the third floor. The elevators were updated as well."

"So, it all worked out," he said, trying to imagine Willard's with a facelift.

"Of course." She handed him back his card. "It revitalized the library for another hundred years."

Daniel thanked her and stuffed the books into his backpack. Monique's folder was flattened between *To Kill A Mockingbird* and *Shane*.

He arrived for his shift with an aching shoulder. After changing into uniform, he stood by the main doors for the last of the clerks. He lugged the backpack through Ladies' Fashions, taking a route that took him by Mary's display, but judging from the folded skirt and high heels left on the platform, she had already left.

Yesterday, there was a definite moment by the main entrance when he could have spilled out his heart to her. Instead, like a jerk, he tested to see if she'd let him go to Monique…and she had.

Daniel pulled on the backpack again. He hurried up the aisle toward the grand staircase, but then he paused in front of Sleepwear. He stood eyeballing the lilac-scented room. Something was off. In all the weeks Daniel had been at Willard's, he'd never seen anything out of order; every dress, jacket, shirt, and shoe was always in place.

But here, racks of robes were bunched too close together, and long scuff marks lined the carpet. He searched the area, but other than the slightly messy state, there was nothing to report to Mr. Oliver.

He made his way to the second floor and walked along the tall row of bookcases that led to the cozy reading area by the electric fireplace. Ruth Ann was hidden behind the cover of her latest read, while Clara and Mary were talking on one of the loveseats.

Daniel opened his backpack and poured out the entire

contents around Ruth Ann's feet. She squealed and jumped up, giving him a big hug. He glanced around the room, grateful Jonathan wasn't present.

"What's that?" Mary asked, pointing to the Monique's binder mixed in with the library books.

Daniel picked it up. "Anyone interested in a little glamorous gossip?"

Twenty minutes later, Mary was going over the whole thing for a second time. Her hair was tightly twirled around her finger. "This tells us nothing that we didn't know already," she scoffed.

Clara grinned. "What were you expecting, a few lines about a forgotten secret passageway?"

"I wish Monique still had the blueprints, though." Mary dropped her voice and glanced at Daniel. "Maybe she left them at your hotel room last night?"

Ruth Ann looked shocked, then her eyes darted to Daniel, waiting for his answer.

"She thinks the blueprints got thrown out," he said, purposely dodging her hidden meaning about the date. "She doesn't remember anything remarkable about them. I even asked about the secret room."

"You told her about the secret room?" Mary sounded insulted.

"No," he said. "I only mentioned the large amount of dead space around the security office."

"Dead space is right," Clara teased. "It doesn't even have a hot tub!" She laughed loudly at her own joke, then pushed herself off the loveseat, smoothing out her latest black party dress. "I'm going to check on Blanche. Maybe she needs help picking out shoes."

"Where are Petey and Oscar?" Daniel asked.

Ruth Ann answered without taking her nose out of her stack of books, "Oscar took him to play Wii boxing to try and work off some of that anger."

"Great," Daniel said, "now he'll be able to punch me

238

NIGHT SHIFT

harder."

Mary made room for him on the loveseat. "It seems last night was a waste of time," she said, watching him carefully.

"It wasn't," he simply said. Mary was intrigued and he couldn't deny himself the satisfaction of having her full attention. He smiled and said, "In fact, I found the original columns in the crime section very entertaining." He brushed close to her shoulder and read out loud.

**April 11, 1918**

### Great Disaster for Great Magnifico

**Famous illusionist and hypnotist, The Great Magnifico, was disgraced from the stage after an act went terribly awry. Members of the audience gave testimony describing the volunteer that night as "going up in smoke" after a horrendous explosion on the stage during the Time Travel illusion.**

**The new addition to the famous stage show was a much-needed boost to the Magician's repertoire that included mind reading, psychic phenomena, and the phantasmagorical "Lady in the Box." Wide speculation hints the Magician was hasty to try this new trick, trying to compete with Houdini's vanishing elephant act, presently playing to sold-out crowds in the Hippodrome.**

**However, the Great Magnifico has saved the best trick for last and has disappeared into thin air, leaving the theatre and all the props behind. State authorities are contacting adjacent detachments, preparing for a nationwide manhunt. The building and all items have been taken over by the bank. At the time of this printing, no one has stepped forward to offer the identity of the missing volunteer.**

Ruth Ann shuddered. "It's so creepy. No wonder the clerks think Willard's is haunted."

"Maybe the Great Magnifico is stuffed in the walls somewhere," Mary said, sounding annoyed. "I bet Mr. Willard caught him and did a little vigilante justice. A wrecking ball will find his skeleton someday."

"Mary! Don't be so morbid," Ruth Ann moved up on the chair and tucked her feet under her.

Talking of Mr. Willard reminded Daniel of Mr. Oliver's rant the other evening. "Have you ever heard of gold bars being hidden in the store?" he asked them.

Ruth Ann's eyes stayed on the page. "Yes," she mumbled. "But that story has been retold and recycled so many times no one bothers with it anymore. If that much gold was hidden in the store, we would know about it. You're more likely to come across the Great Magnifico than find treasure."

Daniel slumped back. He was beginning to understand some of Mary's frustration. None of the clues seemed to lead anywhere. It was one huge maze of fairytales—like Willard's itself.

He glanced at Mary, lingering on the little line of concentration between her eyebrows. "So, the Time Travel illusion," he prompted. "Any thoughts?"

"What do you mean?" she asked.

He waved a hand at the article. "A magician with a time-travel act gone wrong in the very building you woke up in forty years ago? Don't you think there's a connection?"

"Time travel?" Ruth Ann peeked over her book and made a face. "Do you know how dangerous and tricky that would be? Even the possibility of it can lead to disastrous results."

"Yeah, but—" Daniel began.

"No, seriously," Ruth Ann interrupted, a determined expression on her face. "I've watched enough movies with Jonathan to know, Hollywood has been trying to teach mankind the same thing for decades; if you mess with the time space

NIGHT SHIFT

continuum, the time-space continuum will mess with you."

She let her chin drop, suddenly interested in the books on her lap. Daniel noticed her eyes were slightly reddened and puffy. Mary made a generic comment about her library selections, to which Ruth Ann could only nod. Wordlessly, she gathered up her titles, then disappeared around the bookcases.

A few minutes passed in silence. It seemed Ruth Ann had once again left an awkward charge to the air.

Daniel studied the cozy room, noticing it wasn't much different from the setting of his dream. His body became tense. It was so quiet, every creak on the loveseat sounded embarrassing.

"What would you do?" Mary asked. "If you could travel through time, what would you do?"

He was surprised by her question, but he wasn't unprepared to answer. "This isn't the first time I've thought about it," he confessed. He picked at the fabric on the loveseat. "I used to fantasize about going back to keep my mom from getting in the car that afternoon, or to make my dad see the doctor before the tumour grew too big."

"I'd never doubt your heroics," she said.

Daniel half laughed, the idea of him being heroic ridiculous. "What would you do?" he asked.

"Go back to the night your mom left the store. I'd spy on her from the shadows to see how she did it."

"Why not go to the night you woke up? I can't imagine you and the others spontaneously came to life at the same time for no reason."

"Me neither!" She scooted closer and pointed to the article. "See, right here," she said. "It says all the props in the theatre became property of the bank. If Mr. Willard bought the store, he would also own all the props, including everything on stage that last night."

"Including a time machine?" he guessed.

Her eyes were sparkling. "Do you know what the oldest thing in the store is?"

241

"Mr. Oliver."

Mary laughed and he couldn't help but smile. "No." She tucked a wave of hair behind her ear. "It's the antique clock in the Matinee Room. I think it might have been original to the building, and maybe somehow connected to the magician."

Daniel gave her a mischievous grin. "What do you think would happen if we wound up that clock?"

Mary touched her bottom lip with the tip of her finger, then she shook her head and said, "Nothing, probably; besides, it's not supposed to be touched."

Seeing her so hopeful only to be disappointed again played with his heartstrings. He couldn't help but want to make her happy. "What harm could come from winding up an old clock?" he suggested. Daniel put his arm on the back of the loveseat. "Aren't you even curious?" he teased. "I bet it's driving you crazy."

Mary tossed the report to the side. Her gaze trailed up his chest until she was staring into his eyes. "I'm curious about a lot of things," she said.

Daniel could feel the heat from her body. Every cell was screaming for him to kiss her. A small groan escaped from the back of his throat.

"But, no," she said. "I don't want to touch the clock. If you went back in time to save your parents, then you'd still be in high school. And you'd never come to New York to work night shift at Willard's. And we…we would never meet. You see?" Then she laughed as if she'd made a joke and no one got the punchline.

Daniel's heart pounded against his ribs. The thought of returning to a life where Mary didn't exist scared the hell out of him. "I'd still find you," he said.

Clara barged into the area out of breath. Mary and Daniel jumped away from each other as if shocked.

"Blanche is missing!" she said. "I've checked all her favourite spots; the evening gowns, the shoes, I even went back to her display twice!"

NIGHT SHIFT

Mary stood and put an arm around Clara, trying to calm her down.

Daniel said, "Sleepwear looked messed up when I came on shift tonight."

"Today I eavesdropped on one of Stacey's cell phone conversations," Mary said, turning pale. "There was mention of not having enough money, and that time was running out. She sounded scared."

"But I didn't see her go through the main doors when all the clerks left." Daniel and Mary locked eyes. "Oh shit," he said. "I didn't see her because—"

"—she didn't leave at the end of her shift," Mary finished.

Clara's mouth fell open. "She's still in the store?!"

Mary made a plan to check the security monitors. Huddled outside the office, they listened to Mr. Oliver snoring. "Any other ideas?" Daniel asked her.

Mary reached up and twirled her hair. "Clara, did you check the window display?"

Clara shook her head, too upset to talk. Daniel followed Mary down the corridor. They stopped by a door painted to blend in with the wall. "Use your key," she instructed.

He unlocked the door and stepped up into the window display, in plain view of anyone coming down the sidewalk for a midnight stroll. Daniel tiptoed around the *Little Mermaid*, *Thumbelina*, and *The Steadfast Tin Soldier* displays feeling like a stagehand that got caught when the curtain went up.

"Sometimes they replace the mannequins," Mary explained from behind the safety of the door.

But Blanche wasn't in the window display either. Clara began wringing her hands, whimpering at the deluge of horrible possibilities. Had she been taken to the refuse room? Was she trapped in another secret compartment of the store? Or worse, did she leave without a trace, just like Virginia?

Daniel walked beside Clara, unsure how to comfort her. They followed Mary down the aisle. "Where is the best place to hide in the store?" she asked no one in particular.

They entered the main foyer and found Jonathan slumped at the edge of the granite tile. His face was pale and tired. When he saw them, he stepped back and ran a hand over his face.

Mary explained the situation to him. He nodded while inserting a scathing glance at Daniel once every few words. When she mentioned secret hiding places, his face brightened.

"Follow me," he said. He took them through the archway into the Beauty department and went beyond the counters to the side wall. There was a door hidden from view behind a tall display case. Jonathan reached up and took a key from the door trim. Daniel gave him a suspicious look. "What?" he said, defensively. "So Ruth Ann and I have a few of our own hiding spots—not everyone has their own bachelor pad." He added under his breath, "Not that it's been getting any use lately."

With the others hiding off to the side and out of sight, Daniel slowly opened the door. "Stacey?"

She sat on the floor of the supply room with her face in her hands. In the corner, perfectly posed in her mannequin form, wearing a modest trench coat, was Blanche. Stacey lifted her face. "Please," she sobbed. "I don't know what to do."

He crouched beside her. "What's going on?" he asked.

"I had no idea she was so heavy. And I don't even have a car to take her!"

*Her!*

"I don't understand."

Stacey took a few breaths, then gave him a defiant stare. "I'm trying to take her to see my aunt."

"What?"

"My Aunt Maureen, she used to work here as Head of Ladies' Fashions."

"The dresses," he sighed.

"She was such a talented seamstress and loved old movies. There are chests full of dresses she's made over the years of her favourite actresses." She stopped talking and blew her nose. "Are you going to call the police?"

Daniel didn't feel like putting in a 911 call for a clerk

NIGHT SHIFT

locked in a storage room with a mannequin. He wondered if she was crazy. "Um…Stacey," he asked. "Why are you taking Blanche to see your aunt?"

Stacey narrowed her eyes. "How did you know her name is Blanche?"

# CHAPTER THIRTY-SEVEN

His eyes widened, certain that Stacey would press him further. Instead, she turned her attention back to Blanche. Daniel let out a long sigh. "I can help you," he said. "But you need to tell me everything."

Stacey was exhausted and out of options. "When I was seventeen," she began, "my dad let me fly to New York by myself so I could stay with Aunt Maureen for a few weeks. She was always sending me fashion magazines and newspaper clippings about movie stars—I loved getting mail from her. I grew up in the country, and her letters were my escape." She fidgeted with a tissue, folding and unfolding it on her lap.

"When she brought me to Willard's, I was in awe. As soon as I walked through the main doors it was like I was stepping into the best dream I had as a child." She frowned at Daniel. "Does that make any sense?"

"More than you know."

Stacey barely acknowledged his reply. Her gaze was unfocused and Daniel imagined her memory was playing on the wall, like a movie. "She talked about her friend, Blanche, and I assumed they worked together. My aunt had a lifestyle that my father didn't exactly understand or talk about, so I knew this friend was probably someone very special, a lover even. I was so nervous," she continued. "I wanted to make a good impression. She bought me a package of chocolates, and we took the grand staircase up to the first floor. She introduced me to several young clerks, then finally I remember asking about

Blanche. Her eyes lit up and she took me over to a display."

Daniel winced, guessing what was coming next. Flashbacks of the night he discovered the truth about Mary, replayed in his mind.

"The beautiful mannequin was wearing one of Aunt Maureen's favourites, the Tiffany Dress. She wasn't joking! She even started talking to her while I was standing there. A few of the salesgirls were whispering and laughing. I was mortified. I ran out of the store and called my father right away."

She paused like she was waiting for him to interrupt. Daniel could see dark circles under her eyes. Soon, the tears began to flow again.

"I was so stupid," she confessed. "My father took the next flight out and had my aunt examined. He put her in a facility soon after. The store was very professional when they found out and ended her employment with a simple retirement letter. It was basic, only giving the date of her last day of work—the same day I came to the store and met Blanche."

Daniel never thought of calling Alice the night he found out about his mother. She would have put him in a *facility* too. Daniel was trying to deal with the hardest thing in his life, and he had no one to help him. And neither did Stacey, he realized. "I'm sorry," he said.

She rested her head against the wall of shelves. "After four long years, I forced myself to come back and visit Aunt Maureen. I was shocked when I saw her. I had no idea her mind could deteriorate her body and soul as well. I couldn't leave her again, so I transferred my college credits."

"And got a job working at Willard's," Daniel guessed. "But why bring in the dresses?"

Stacey used her tissue again. "I needed to convince Mr. Hadley to let me enter the contest. I was trying to win so I could take the mannequin out of the store when the display got moved to the Waldorf-Astoria. But Fashion Week isn't until September, and my aunt doesn't have that long."

"She's dying?" His voice rose in panic; he couldn't help but glance at Blanche.

"She keeps trying to leave the hospital and come to the store; she's afraid she's late for her shift. A few times she's fallen. She needs constant supervision. I've been getting calls from the hospital administrator at work. I've argued so many times about the care she's getting. They tell me to hire a private nurse and take her home."

Stacey gave him a desperate look. "I can't afford that! She seems so miserable, but then I'll mention the store and she perks up, talking about Blanche and the dresses. Once I told her Blanche would be by, since then she's always asked for her."

"If money is the only thing standing between your Aunt seeing Blanche again, I think I can help," Daniel offered. "With enough private care, she could come to the store…even after hours. I'll arrange it."

Stacey let out a small laugh. "I wish it was that simple. She can't be moved, Daniel. The doctor says that she's finally dying. That's how they told me, *finally dying,* like I was hoping for it."

She sniffed then stuck out her chin and sat up straight. "I have to make up for my mistake. When my aunt sees Blanche again, at least she'll have a little happiness before she dies. I'm taking this mannequin out tonight, and there's nothing you can do to stop me."

Daniel thought of how his mother was able to leave the store and live a normal life. "You don't have to steal her," he said. "There may be another way."

Once he convinced Stacey that she wouldn't be in trouble, and that he'd take care of the mannequin, they finally left the tiny supply room and walked to the main doors. "Don't worry," he reassured her. "You don't have to do this alone."

"We'll talk tomorrow?"

"I'll be waiting at the end of your shift." *Hopefully with a plan*, he thought.

Her eyes filled up again. "My aunt doesn't have much

NIGHT SHIFT

time." She stepped out the main doors and ran to the waiting cab.

Daniel made his way through the shadows of the Beauty department. He could hear their voices, one sobbing and two calmly taking turns saying soothing words. They were on the bottom step of the grand staircase. Blanche, still in the trench coat, was crying into her hands. Clara had an arm around her shoulder while Mary held a box of Kleenex.

"It's my fault," Blanche cried into a wad of tissue. "They made her retire because of me."

"No," Mary explained softy. "Maureen has a terrible disease."

"But she talked to me about all of her favourite movies, and her life outside the store. Stacey's wrong. The doctors are wrong. Maureen isn't sick. They put her in the hospital because she thought I was real. Well, she's right. I am real, we all are!"

She stumbled over and gripped Daniel by the shoulders. "You need to explain to them that Maureen isn't crazy. Maybe she's like you—able to live with us. You have to tell them, Mac! My Maureen has been wasting away in a hospital, lonely and neglected, while I've spent every day since she left complaining about clothes! My stupid, stupid clothes!"

Daniel caught her as she folded to the floor, letting out great rolling sobs.

Once Blanche had exhausted herself, they took her to the Matinee Room. Clara stayed with her in their booth while Mary and Daniel went into the kitchen.

Mary plugged in the kettle and took down a teapot from the cupboard. "I can't believe that Blanche has been waiting all these years for Maureen to return to work, while Maureen has been waiting for Blanche to visit her."

Daniel watched her move around the kitchen. "Do you think Maureen really knows what Blanche is?"

Mary ran her finger along the white cup trimmed with a blue *W*. "I think Blanche was real enough to her. The disease turned it into something…bizarre."

249

He caught her gaze and she turned away. The subject matter was a little too close for comfort. They stayed quiet while Mary finished up. She took the tea tray out to the table with Daniel following, unsure what to say.

Blanche took the tea from Mary and wrapped her perfectly manicured fingers around the cup. "Oh, doll," she sighed. "I've been remembering Maureen during her last months at the store. I can pick out moments when she would show up sounding a little scattered, unable to remember the date or forgetting the names of salesgirls. And there were all those misplaced items. The other girls started talking about how they would always have to double check her work. Finally, the day came when she wasn't allowed to work cash anymore. By then, even her discussions with me had become confusing."

"It's terrible," Clara said, taking a sip of tea.

The meal that night was a quiet one; hardly anyone touched their lasagna. At last Mary broke the silence. "What are we going to do? Stacey wants to take Blanche to the hospital."

Daniel sensed an unavoidable confrontation. "I told Stacey there may be a way," he said, staring at Petey, "but only one person knows the answer to that."

"What?" Petey said, barely making eye contact. "You mean the day Virginia left *me*?"

"Please, pet," Blanche pleaded. She tried to touch his hair, but he pulled away.

"Look," Petey said. "She went missing. We didn't know anything until Daniel showed up with his precious pictures. Ask him, he knows more about her than I do."

"How can you say that?" Daniel said. "I lost her when I was eleven. I hadn't even begun to know her, but you had her for twenty years!" Petey pushed away from the table and ran to the grand staircase. "Sorry, Oscar," Daniel mumbled to his plate.

Oscar nodded and finished his mouthful of food. "It's good for him to hear that," he supported. "I'm sure another

NIGHT SHIFT

opportunity will come around."

Blanche twisted the napkin in her lap. "But Maureen is getting worse," she worried.

"Maybe it's time for the lullaby," Clara said. "I'll sit on him if I have to."

"We could hypnotize him," suggested Jonathan. He sat stiffly beside Ruth Ann. Daniel noticed they hadn't even brushed elbows the whole meal.

Clara looked doubtful. "You can hypnotize people?"

"Me? No, of course not," he said. "But it works in the movies all the time. Hey, The Great Magnifico would come in handy right about now, huh?" But his joke was wasted—no one was in the mood to laugh.

Daniel looked at Blanche's pleading face. "My mom always wore the same perfume," he said. "I can't remember the name, but it's something else to try, right?"

"That's right," Clara said. "She did! But it's been so long I can't recall it either. And to be honest, it's her music I remember most, not which perfume she wore."

Mary asked Daniel, "If you smelled it again would you recognize it?"

"Probably. It's been years, though."

Blanche reached over and squeezed his hand. "Thanks, Mac."

Daniel left his meal untouched and lied about needing to do a quick round. So many things depended on finding out the truth about his mother. He wasn't sure he wanted to know what really happened. Did his mother leave everyone behind on purpose, or was she forced? Neither choice gave him any comfort.

When he arrived at the Beauty department, Ruth Ann and Clara had everything set up. Along the glass counter, tiny strips of paper were placed in front of perfume bottles. Ruth Ann stood behind the display, smiling through a tense expression.

"Thanks for setting this up," he said. "It looks like it took a lot of work."

251

"Don't worry," she said. "You don't have to smell everything, I narrowed it down to the perfumes that were around when Virginia, I mean your mom, was alive. Holy smokes!" she winced. "I mean when she would have worn it. Sorry…er, let's get started, okay?"

He picked up the first piece of paper and slowly inhaled. "Nope." Ruth Ann threw that slip away and put the bottle back on its shelf.

Soon the garbage can was full of discarded paper samples. He was almost finished smelling half the perfumes when Mary arrived, holding several bottles of water. "Any luck?" she asked.

Clara gave her a little hug. "Nothing yet, honey."

Daniel moved down the counter and said no fifteen more times. He pinched the bridge of his nose with his thumb and finger. "I think I'm getting a perfume headache."

A bowl of coffee beans was thrust under his nose. "It's to clear the scent," Ruth Ann explained.

Clara put a hand on his shoulder. "Do you need a break, gorgeous?"

He shook his head. "No, we're almost there. How much do you want to bet it's the last one?" They all laughed nervously. *But what if it's none of them?* he thought. *Then what?*

Blanche arrived in a black button-up sweater with pearls and a flared skirt. She looked at the garbage bag full of paper slips, and the last two bottles of perfume left on the counter. "Paper slips!" she gasped. "Perfume needs to be smelled when it's on the skin."

Ruth Ann said, "No way. Look at him! He's exhausted and his eyes are red. He can't smell all the perfumes again. Besides, who would wear them?"

Blanche set her jaw, then took Mary by the shoulders and plunked her down on the stool. Blocking Daniel's view, she dabbed the perfume on one side of Mary's neck. "All right, Mac," she ordered, "smell her."

Painfully aware of everyone watching, he moved in close,

letting his cheek brush against hers. His lips were almost touching her skin. The memory of kissing her made his face grow hot.

"Well?" Blanche asked, slightly amused.

He pulled back and shook his head. "It's lovely, but that's not it."

Clara spoke up. "Try again, Romeo."

Mary squirmed on the stool and pointed to her opposite ear. "Blanche put the perfume on the other side."

Daniel wished his ears would stop burning. He bent forward again, careful to not touch her this time, and inhaled deeply. He hesitated, then took hold of Mary's shoulders, and moved in for a longer test.

Suddenly there was a connection. His brain filled up with episodes, long forgotten but stored in that part of the mind that locked away little tidbits of life. The memory was real, and so was his racing heart. His mother was humming in front of the mirror, brushing her hair, then she reached for the bottle of perfume.

Daniel opened his eyes. "This is it."

"Are you sure?" Blanche said, excitedly.

"I'm positive!"

Ruth Ann looked at the bottle. "Chanel No. 5, a classic."

Daniel examined the bottle and brought it to his nose. "I remember now, she always kept it beside her jewelry box." He closed his eyes again. His heart remembered, too; how encompassing her hugs felt, how her toast was the only thing he could eat when he was sick, and how she made him feel like he was the most important thing in the whole world.

"Let's get Petey," Clara said. "Oscar can reason with him." All the girls nodded.

Mary studied Daniel for a moment. "Come whenever you're ready," she said. He heard the softness in her voice and wondered if she could guess what he was feeling.

The girls climbed the grand staircase, their comments echoing back to him through the dimmed department. He stood

against the glass counter, holding the perfume, and then he buried his face in his father's handkerchief.

# CHAPTER THIRTY-EIGHT

Daniel held back and watched from the entrance to the Music Room. Everyone was already there. Petey sat on the piano bench with his arms folded in front of his chest. *You and me both, Petey,* he thought.

Mary came up to him, but stopped when she saw his blotchy face and red eyes. "What's wrong?"

Daniel almost laughed. He pressed his mouth into a line and looked down. She took him into the aisle, away from the others. "You can do this," she coaxed. "Clara said you've got the song down perfectly."

"That's not it."

"Then what?"

"What if Petey *does* remember? What am I going to find out about my mom? That she didn't care about hurting you guys, or that she was threatened to leave? I know how Petey feels," he confessed. "She left me and my dad without saying goodbye too." His hand slipped inside his pocket, searching for the keychain that wasn't there. "I'm scared," he admitted.

Mary linked her fingers through his. "Hold on, Daniel," she whispered.

He squeezed her hand and asked, "Can I do this?"

"All signs point to yes."

They walked back into the room, still holding hands. Jonathan leaned against the wall with his arms crossed in front of his chest, partially hidden in the shadows. Petey was kicking

255

up fuss, with Oscar standing over him.

"Petey," Oscar began, "we all admire your tenacity, but you should know your jealousy is having the opposite effect that you desire."

"What does that mean?" he grumbled.

"It means your behaviour is distancing you from the people who love and care for you instead of bringing them closer."

"I don't care."

Oscar smoothed out his mustache—a classic Oscar manoeuvre that meant, "Fine, I'll pretend you're in charge."

"I already told you," Petey spat out. "I don't remember anything. When I woke up that night she was gone!"

Oscar continued, "Sometimes, a particular smell or a song can trigger a memory. Everyone has worked very hard trying to help you remember Virginia. Why do you think we've worked so hard for this?"

"Because Blanche needs to see Maureen," he said.

"Yes. And why would we do this for Blanche?" Oscar asked.

Petey waited a few beats, then sniffed. "Because we love her."

"Exactly." Oscar sighed. "Will you at least *try* to remember? That's all we're asking."

Petey looked at Blanche. Her hands were clenched together in a white-knuckled grip. "If you leave the store," he said, "are you going to ever come back?"

"I don't know how it works, pigeon," Blanche told him honestly.

"Will you come back for us if you can?"

"You bet a pile of rubes I will."

"All right," he murmured.

Mary sat down beside Petey so he could smell the perfume. Daniel took his place at the high end of the bench. His hands were shaking so badly the first few chords made him cringe. Petey frowned at the keys until the song was over.

"Again," Petey asked. His voice had lost its earlier spite.

Everyone watched, not daring to speak. Daniel complied, and this time the song was almost perfect. Petey looked up and gave Daniel a tiny smile. "You play like her."

"Do you remember anything?" Blanche asked.

Petey bunched up his forehead like he was really concentrating, but after a few moments he said, "Nothing new."

Ruth Ann spoke up. "Even if you don't remember anything right now it doesn't mean the answer won't come eventually." The word "eventually" stuck in the air and Daniel had visions of Stacey arriving at work tearful someday. Clara put an arm around Blanche and led her away.

"Thank you," Oscar said, giving Petey a slight smile. He followed Clara and Blanche with his shoulders drooped.

"In a situation like this," Mary began, "ice cream is the best choice."

"Now that you mention it," Ruth Ann agreed, taking her lead, "I'm starving. Dinner seems like it was ages ago." Mary held out her hand for Petey, who took it without hesitating.

Daniel watched them leave, then pushed himself off the bench. The little smile Petey gave him earlier was unravelling the knot in his gut.

"Hey." Jonathan stepped out of the shadows and walked beside him.

"Go ahead," Daniel said. Jonathan's jokes and taunts were the last thing he was concerned about these days. "I know you like to see me fail. There must be some smartass remark you're happy to unload."

He shook his head. "Dude, I'm the opposite of happy. Ruth Ann hasn't even spoken to me since yesterday, not even a quote."

Daniel was startled by the heaviness of his voice. A few moments of silence passed, then Jonathan said, "How can I compete with what's outside? In here I'm the eternal stud—"

Daniel rolled his eyes.

"—but out there, I'm just a moron who likes movies. I can't take care of her if we leave. Once she steps foot outside,

I'll be dropped for the first guy who comes along."

There was another long pause before Daniel wrestled the courage to say, "Yeah, but you've been together for so long."

"Maybe that's the problem, though," he said. "She knows I can't give her want she wants anymore."

Daniel let this latest enlightenment sink in. They reached the grand staircase and matched each other's steps up to the fourth-floor landing. "Well," he finally said, "what would make you happy? To be inside without Ruth Ann or leave with her and take a chance?"

Jonathan didn't hesitate. "It doesn't matter. As long as I'm with her, I'm happy."

"Sounds simple to me," Daniel said. Jonathan's brows knitted together, then his face slowly relaxed.

In the kitchen, Ruth Ann was busy clearing away the dinner things with Petey lagging behind, helping at his own pace. Everyone moved around, making snacks. Daniel's stomach growled. Now that things had calmed a bit, he realized he too was starving.

Jonathan scooped three different kinds of ice cream into a cereal bowl for Petey, and drizzled it with chocolate syrup. Another dessert was off to the side, and Daniel suspected he was building a sundae for two.

Mary made a noise at the back of her throat. "How about sprinkling a little insulin on top? That's so gross. Petey can't eat all of that."

Jonathan nudged Petey. "Sounds like a challenge, huh?"

Mary opened the huge stainless steel fridge, trying to decide. "There's nothing but brownies and leftover ham."

Daniel looked over her shoulder. "Go sit down," he said, reaching into the fridge. "I'll make you a sandwich. Grilled cheese okay?"

She looked surprised at his offer, but in a pleasant kind of way. "Crusts off, if you don't mind," she said, pulling up a stool.

Daniel warmed up the grill and watched from the corner of

NIGHT SHIFT

his eye as Jonathan motioned to Ruth Ann with his own colossal bowl of ice cream, passing her a spoon. He slipped out the kitchen door and she followed behind surreptitiously. Petey, he noticed, was making his way around the counter to be closer to them.

He buttered the bread and placed the cheese on top, then added a layer of sliced tomato. "Tomato?" Mary scrunched up her nose.

He smiled at her expression. "That's mine."

"Interesting variation," she said.

Petey stared into his melting mixture of chocolate chip mint and rocky road. "That's how Virginia always made them for me."

A hush fell over the kitchen, then Daniel said, "It's much better than just the cheese."

"Yup." Petey stared into the bowl, using his spoon to swirl the flavours together into a brown goo. Daniel flipped the sandwiches, then took down three plates from the shelf and lined them along on the counter.

"One grilled cheese with the crusts cut off," he announced, handing Mary her plate. He looked over at Petey. "Do you want to share?" he asked, sliding half a grilled cheese and tomato sandwich toward him.

"Thanks," he said, pushing away the neglected bowl of dessert.

They ate in silence, getting used to being together again.

"I can't believe you cut the crusts off for her," Petey said through a mouthful.

"She's so spoiled," Daniel replied.

Mary played along. "It's just what I need!" She finished the last piece and cleared away her plate. "What are you going to do for the rest of the night, Petey?"

He used his finger to pick up the last few crumbs. "I'm pretty tired. I'll just go back to my display." He walked out of the kitchen, then paused at the doorway and turned back at Daniel. "Thanks for the sandwich," he said. "It's actually better

259

than I remember." Then he pushed through the swinging door.

A grin spread across Mary's face, matching Daniel's own look of surprised accomplishment.

She filled the sink with hot soapy water, then opened one of the drawers and threw a tea towel at him. Taking the hint, he stood beside her, letting the sounds of the water and the clinking of dishes fill the silence nicely. He was comforted, doing this daily chore with her.

Her fingers brushed against his, wet and slippery. He swallowed, remembering the dream on the leather couch—it was playing in his mind, stuck on the repeat button.

She said, "So, are you and Monique dating exclusively?"

Daniel almost dropped the plate. Where the hell did that come from? "It's the last thing on my mind, actually."

"Ignorance is bliss, I guess."

He refused to take her bait, and decided to play on her weakness. "Unless you're a curious person," he smirked.

Mary passed him the next plate, making sure to keep her eyes on the sink. He wiped that one, then reached for the next. She ignored his hand and instead slammed Petey's bowl down.

Part of Daniel did a little victory dance; the other part was getting tired of always being the bad guy. "You're the one who practically pushed me out the door to get the report," he said. "Maybe I didn't want to leave. You never considered that, did you?" He wanted her to lose her cool, he wanted her to slip up and admit she was jealous.

Mary glared back at him. "You said you wanted to go. Then you stayed away for the rest of the night!" She pulled the plug on the sink, and sent it tumbling along the counter.

"I don't have to clear any of my activities with you. Besides, in case you haven't noticed, a lot is going on with Blanche and Mr. Oliver, and—"

"And you're leaving soon," she blurted out. "You lied to me. You're not holding on, are you? I saw the resignation letter in your employee file."

A troubled stillness settled between them. He felt stupid

standing there with a tea towel bunched up in his hand. "I promise to stay and help Blanche," he said.

She avoided his gaze and wrung out the washcloth. "But you're only scheduled until the end of the month."

"Mr. Oliver will still keep giving me shifts."

"For how long?" she asked. Their eyes locked, and he couldn't breathe. His heart pulsed up to his throat, sending the usual rush of blood.

"As long as it takes," he said. He stepped closer, sliding his hand along the counter, until he touched her fingers. She looked at their hands for several heartbeats, and then stepped back, wiping her sudsy fingers on her jeans.

"I haven't told anyone," she said. "But maybe you should tell Monique. You two have enough secrets already."

"You mean like how my mother used to be a mannequin?" he said sarcastically. "That's a hard one to bring up over coffee."

"That's not what I'm talking about." Mary brushed past him and retrieved the roof key from inside the lower cupboard.

He tossed the tea towel in the sink. "Don't leave angry. I can't stand you—"

"—thanks so much. I can't stand you either sometimes!"

"No," he sighed, frustrated. "I can't stand you upset with me. I need you...okay? Everything is so confusing right now, but you're the only one I can really talk to."

Mary looked him up and down. "Sure, Danny Boy," she said, "don't worry, I'm still your friend." She walked to the steel door. "But even friends need time alone." She nodded toward the espresso machine. "I'm sure Mr. Oliver is waiting for his coffee."

Daniel stared at the rooftop door long after it shut behind her. How did she always manage to twist the situation and have the last word? He pictured her at the sink glaring at him angrily. Instead of teasing her about Monique, he should have pressed her up against the counter and kissed her.

261

He switched the espresso machine on. It was pointless, they could never have a life together, not the way he really wanted. He started to steam the milk, and worried about what kind of diagnosis the doctors would give him. Would he end up like Maureen, strapped to a bed and asking for Mary? He was sure there was a name for the freakish feelings he had.

What was wrong with him? Monique was sexy and funny. She usually hung on his every word. He should have been all over her, but when they met at the coffee shop for the report, he could barely keep track of their conversation. His mind was constantly wandering back to Mary, hoping she was jealous, wishing his attention to Monique would force her to notice him that way.

He looked down at the milk, now thick and frothy. Daniel made a perfect *W* in the foam, then turned the cup so that it became an M. "I'm pathetic," he mumbled.

In a depressed daze, he made his way to the ground floor. Staring at the closed security door, Daniel realized he hadn't seen Mr. Oliver all night. Preparing for a blasting, he reached up to knock when the sound of cursing made him stop. He pressed his ear against the door.

"It all has to fit together!" Mr. Oliver snapped. "What is he planning?"

Daniel slowly opened the door. Mr. Oliver was standing across from the opening of the secret room. "I don't know what to do," he cried again. "How do I stop him?"

Daniel craned his neck a few more inches and saw who Mr. Oliver was pleading with. An icy shiver ran down his body, and everything went numb. The coffee cup smashed to the floor.

# CHAPTER THIRTY-NINE

Stacey came into work earlier than usual and took Daniel aside as he was leaving the locker room. He was practically asleep on his feet and hadn't bothered to change out of his uniform.

"Have you thought anymore about what we discussed?" she asked in a hushed voice.

He blinked, trying to focus on her face, but the insides of his eyelids were made of sandpaper. "I need a little more time," he said. His latest discovery about Mr. Oliver had sent his mind on a one-way trip to *The Twilight Zone*.

She stifled a sob. "Last night Aunt Maureen fell out of bed again. She thought she was late for her shift. Her face is all bruised and she cut her forehead open. Please," she begged. "They've got her restrained now. She's so frail, and I'm worried she may not even make it to the weekend."

Daniel noticed the dark circles were still there under all her eye makeup. She looked as exhausted and desperate as he felt. How could he fix all of this? So many hearts were depending on him to do everything right. "I'm not giving up," he promised. "I'll have a plan soon."

She tried to smile, but the hopelessness bled through. He left Willard's with the strange sensation of being jealous of Mary. That maybe for once, he'd like to be the one stuck in pose, while the rest of the world struggled with its problems.

He collapsed on top of the hotel bedspread fully clothed. He didn't wake up for another ten hours, and by that time, he was already late for his shift.

He stood in front of Mr. Oliver. His hair was still wet from the shower. The pants were the same as the night before, but thankfully he had another shirt ironed and ready. Mr. Oliver moved back in his chair, making it squeak. "What do you have to say for yourself?"

Daniel stayed quiet. The image of Mr. Oliver fighting with a ghost was fresh in his mind.

A white eyebrow lifted, challenging Daniel. "Can you tell me why I shouldn't fire you tonight?"

"Because your bet is still in the bowl?"

"Comedian," Mr. Oliver grumbled. He gave Daniel another fifteen minutes of ridicule and put him on a strict hourly schedule.

Daniel hurried through the departments, checking his watch every five minutes. He rounded the corner into Sporting Goods and found Petey sitting on the floor, crying with his arms wrapped around his knees. He lifted up his tear-streaked face toward Daniel. "I know how Virginia left the store," he said.

It didn't take long for the others to arrive. Blanche flew down the aisle with her chiffon dress flowing behind. Petey was still on the floor, now with Clara's arms around him. "There, there," she cooed.

Mary moved closer to Daniel. "This is exactly the way we found him the day Virginia went missing," she whispered.

Blanche carefully knelt down. "Please, pigeon," she asked. "What do you remember?"

Petey took a deep breath, steadying himself, "I think it was the sandwich that did it. Or maybe it was the combination of that and the perfume. I don't know, but I dreamed about her all day." He looked at their concerned faces. "Only, it wasn't a dream. It was my last memory of her."

"Virginia told me there was something really important to talk about. I was scared because it looked like she'd been

NIGHT SHIFT

crying. We went to the kitchen, and she made me a grilled cheese sandwich with tomato." He glanced at Daniel. "It was my favourite, but I've never had one since that night. She told me something wonderful had happened—she had discovered her purpose."

"Her purpose?" Blanche asked.

"Yeah," Petey replied. "She said she had to leave the store. I asked if she was taking me, too. She said I had to stay, but someday each of us would have a chance to leave. Then she kissed me and told me she would always love me."

"How did she find her purpose?" Blanche's eyes were widening with each detail.

Petey's face lit up. "Mr. Willard told her."

Everyone exchanged confused glances. "She left over twenty years ago," Mary said. "He died not long after that."

"Mr. Willard knew about us?" Blance asked, breathlessly.

Petey said, "I was so upset I didn't bother asking about that part."

Clara nudged him gently. "Is there anything else you can remember?"

"I asked how she was going to leave, if Mr. Willard showed her a secret passageway or something, but she said she would walk out the main doors. I told her the outside wasn't safe. But she said the world was full of magic and beautiful things, and that everyone deserved to experience it. She asked me to walk her to the main doors, but I was too mad. She started to cry when I wouldn't let her hug me. Then she finally walked away."

A fist clutched Daniel's heart, its fingers digging in. He swallowed a few times, blinking hard.

"Oh, pigeon," Blanche sighed. "You didn't see her leave?"

"I thought if I didn't follow her, she'd change her mind and come back. But she didn't, and then I couldn't stop crying— that's when you found me."

Daniel knew exactly how desperate Petey felt, except he'd never had the chance for one last hug.

"But why did you lie?" Mary asked.

"I couldn't tell you the truth," Petey confessed. "I was so ashamed that she left me, I made up a story about not seeing her at all. And I guess I repeated it so many times, I started to believe it was true."

"What does this mean, though?" Clara asked, her diamond bangles tinkling against Petey's shoulder. "How can Blanche leave the store?"

Petey said, "All I know is that she left through the main doors. I'm telling the truth this time."

Blanche smoothed out his hair. "Of course you are, pigeon."

No one spoke. They were all thinking the same thing, to be so close to an answer only to come up with nothing again.

Daniel glanced at his watch. "I have to check on Mr. Oliver," he said.

Mary gave him a questioning look. "Don't you mean *check in?*"

"Not exactly," he mumbled.

Blanche walked over and took his arm, "I'll join you, Mac. You too, Mary," she called out, reaching for her hand.

The trio remained quiet as they made their way down the grand staircase to the ground floor. "At least it was something new," Mary finally said. "Each day we're learning a bit more, right?"

Blanche sighed. "But there's no Mr. Willard to help *me*."

Daniel wanted to say something to defend his mother, but wasn't sure of anything right now. They strolled along as if on a walk in the park. The glow from the display cases lit their way through the Beauty department. The only sound was the soft rustle of Blanche's gown, and their footsteps on the tile.

Blanche stopped by a makeup display and squeezed his arm. "Mac, please, is there anything from your childhood that can help me?"

"She told me it was important to get out and see as much of the world as possible. The more memories I replay, the more

NIGHT SHIFT

insight I'll have, but there's nothing I can think of that she did or mentioned that will help you, I'm sorry." Daniel wished there was more so Mary could finally see him as a hero and not some clueless guy, uncertain and afraid.

"Even that day in front of the window display as a young boy?" she asked, insisting he dig deeper.

Daniel winced. "She was terrified when I went into the store. After, she took me to a park. I ate a hotdog and chased pigeons, but she continued to look sad, sitting on a bench all by herself."

Mary focused down the aisle toward the main foyer. "Maybe it's as simple as Petey says. You have to find your purpose that will lead you out the doors."

Blanche inspected the eye shadows. "My purpose," she repeated. "Like a philosophy?"

"Think smaller," Mary said. "It could be a specific goal."

Blanche sighed and started up the aisle. Mary and Daniel shared a quick glance.

"What's the most important thing to you right now?" he asked, catching up to Blanche.

"Getting out to Maureen, of course," she answered. They made their way under the large archway that opened into the main foyer. Blanche began to discuss the history she and Maureen shared together. She practically glowed; it was a side of her that made Daniel warm to her. He was so attentive to her story that he didn't notice Mary slowed down.

"You don't know what it's been like for me," Blanche told him. "Having to listen to Maureen, knowing I could never answer or smile back at her. I used to watch the security tapes for hours, replaying her comments from memory. For years I waited for a miracle." Blanche gripped his arm with surprising strength. "I'm not sure how this is going to happen, but I have to see Maureen. She's my true love."

Mary cried out from behind. "Look where you're standing!"

Daniel and Blanche were on the white marble pattern

267

leading to the main doors—two feet beyond the black granite tiles of the main foyer. Blanche had gone beyond the invisible barrier effortlessly.

She screamed and ran back to Mary. "I can't believe it!" she said. Then Blanche realized what she'd done. "Oh no," she began to cry. "I was supposed to leave, but I came back!"

Daniel's heart raced; he looked to Mary for advice but she seemed to be awestruck as well. "Try it again," he said, holding out his shaking hand. "Come on, you can do it."

Mary patted Blanche's back and gave her an encouraging push. Blanche stumbled across the tile into Daniel's arms. They laughed nervously at each other.

"Wait," she said, panicked. "I'm not ready! I have to say goodbye to everyone. And I don't even know how to get to Maureen!"

He led her back to Mary, standing at the edge of the black tile. "No one is making you leave." His heart was easing back to its normal pace.

Blanche looked longingly at the main doors. "But what if this is my only chance?"

Mary smiled at her and said, "I don't think it is. Once you realized you were in love with Maureen, you became conscious of your purpose."

Blanche pressed a hand over her heart, breathing quickly. "Now what do we do?" She paced back and forth over the barrier, chatting nonsense about what dress to wear.

The toe of Mary's pink high tops were stuck at the edge of the barrier.

Blanche mumbled, "But the shoes should *complement* the outfit, not match too perfectly or stand out too much."

Mary took hold of her hand. "Don't worry," she told Blanche. "Stacey will help." She gave Daniel a serious look. "You're going to have to call her."

He knew this was unavoidable. "How do I even begin?"

"With the truth," Mary said simply. "Tell her that you'll be bringing Blanche to see Maureen."

NIGHT SHIFT

An expression of terror and excitement crossed Blanche's face. Daniel nodded. "I'll call her right after I check on Mr. Oliver." Blanche threw her arms around his neck, sobbing a thank you into his shoulder.

Mary and Blanche disappeared down the corridor toward the grand staircase, whispering excitedly. Daniel pictured the celebratory scene that would soon unfold without him. He scuffed along the main aisle, praying that Mr. Oliver was asleep.

# CHAPTER FORTY

He found them in the Matinee Room. Blanche looked up as he approached. "Come sit by me. What did Stacey say?" she asked anxiously.

Still shaking from his episode in the security office, Daniel sat on the edge of the booth. "She'll be expecting two visitors for Maureen tomorrow night."

Jonathan asked, "Two visitors?" Ruth Ann was tucked in close to his side, her hand lightly resting on his shoulder.

"I'll be escorting her," Daniel said, giving Blanche a small smile.

"Oh, Mac."

It was Oscar who said the one thing none of them could admit out loud. "I guess this makes it your last night with us," he said, his usual commanding voice wavering slightly. "Ladies' choice, whatever you want, it's up to you."

Blanche pursed her lips. "We don't have enough time to give everyone a makeover." She shot Mary a critical look. "You in particular, doll—"

"Whatever." Mary rolled her eyes.

"Since that's impossible, I'd like dancing and my favourite meal."

"Done," Clara nodded. Nervous smiles were shared around the table. The silence rested heavily around the booth.

Ruth Ann cleared her throat. "I'm glad you're going to

NIGHT SHIFT

finally be with Maureen," she said. "Nothing's more important than being with the one you love."

Jonathan put an arm around her and gave her a squeeze. "Especially if there's a hot tub."

Their jittery laughter became more natural. Daniel bowed his head and rubbed the back of his neck.

"Daniel?" Oscar asked, his voice full of concern. The unexpected gentleness touched him, but he was unsure how to tell them what he'd seen. "Is this about tomorrow night?" Oscar guessed.

"Are you having second thoughts?" Blanche asked. A look of horror crossed her face.

"No," Daniel said, easing her worries. "It's Mr. Oliver, he's really lost it. Last night I heard him arguing. At first, I thought there was someone with him in the hall, or even someone in the secret room standing in the doorway. But he was yelling at the picture of the Grand Opening! He was asking Mr. Willard for help. I stood there for at least five minutes," he told them. "He had a whole conversation with the wall. I couldn't make out everything, but he kept saying he didn't know what the plan was and how he had no idea what to do next. And then there was this really weird part about his whole life spent honouring a promise."

"He's taken care of Willard's for forty years," Mary reasoned. "It doesn't make sense for him to be—well, dangerous."

"But that's the thing, isn't it?" Daniel said. "Forty years is a long time. Maybe he's getting tired of waiting."

"Waiting for what?" she asked.

"What's the panic about?" Petey asked. "Finding out why Mr. Oliver is going cuckoo for Cocoa Puffs is the last thing on your to-do list, right?"

Oscar's smooth, commanding voice filled the room with authority. "I understand Mr. Oliver's actions are making you anxious, Daniel, but we know him best. It's not a man who is confused you need to worry about—it's a man who is desperate.

He acts without fear, without regard for the consequences."
Then he smiled. "That doesn't sound like our Mr. Oliver."

"No," Daniel said. Then he thought, not yet.

Jonathan stood up and stretched. "And I believe there's a
tray of martinis waiting to be mixed." Ruth Ann joined him on
his way to the kitchen. Daniel sat at the table watching the
others get ready for Blanche's going away party. Soon, it was
only him and Mary staring at the linen tablecloth.

"Martinis?" he asked.

"It's Blanche's favourite food," she explained. "Along with
shrimp cocktail."

Daniel slouched against the royal blue cushions. He gazed
across the room and focused on the hands of the antique clock,
perpetually marking the death of Mr. Willard. He gave Mary a
tired smile. "Things have been a little slow around here lately.
Do you think this is a good time to try winding the clock?"

"You'd be fired for sure," she teased. Petey's laughter
erupted from the kitchen.

"Seriously," Daniel said. "Am I the only one worried about
tomorrow night?"

Mary motioned toward the elevator. "Come on," she said.

They ended up in the Toy department. She led him through
shelves displaying action figures and remote-control cars.
Daniel looked up at the colourful kites suspended from the
ceiling. Their long tails seemed to fly in mid-air. It was pretend,
but it looked so real.

She stopped in front of a wall of plush toys. Choosing a
small stuffed puppy, she put her attention on retying the red
bow around its neck. "When I saw Blanche walk across the
barrier," she said, her head tilted downward, avoiding eye
contact, "I was terrified."

"You mean to finally get what she's been wanting for so
long?" Daniel guessed.

Mary nodded, concentrating on making the perfect bow. "I
wonder about the others, and what their purposes are. I guess
it's not enough to want something. Ruth Ann wants to start a

family with Jonathan, and he wants her to be happy. Petey wants to grow up. Oscar is...well, Oscar's too devoted to leave, and Clara just wants to sing." She retied the bow again.

He noticed she left herself out of the equation. "And you want to leave," he added.

Mary fidgeted with the ribbon. "What I want is irrelevant. Besides, love isn't the answer for me...obviously." She put the toy back on the shelf. "By the way," she continued, her voice a little higher than usual. "What exactly did you say to Stacey?"

"I asked if tomorrow night was possible, and not to worry, that I would handle the transfer personally."

"Good. How did she react?"

"She was grateful it could happen so soon and planned to let the hospital know that a visitor would be coming. She isn't going to tell Maureen, though. In case Blanche...can't make it." He didn't need to list all of the things that could go wrong. "Do we have a plan? How can I take her out the main doors if Mr. Oliver has the monitor on?"

"I can hack into the security files and put a continuous loop of video on the monitor." She said it offhand, but Daniel noticed the hint of pride in her voice. "It comes in handy with new guards who like to stay in the office, too."

Daniel glanced around, wondering why she'd chosen to bring him to this dark corner.

"About Monique," she began. Daniel braced for another confrontation, but what she said next surprised him. "If she hadn't hidden your wallet, you would have left and Blanche wouldn't have this chance with Maureen—and I'm grateful to her for that."

Daniel was torn. He was glad she wasn't upset, but the fact that Mary was no longer bothered by Monique proved she was content to see him as an experiment. He wanted to tell her the truth about how he felt, but what was the point? It wasn't as simple as Jonathan and Ruth Ann. It wasn't enough to be with Mary—he needed her to want him, too. He was so unsure about everything. What would *his* purpose be?

"You look tired," she said, reaching up and brushing a blond strand of hair off his forehead. "I'm worried that you're doing too much for us, that it's hurting you somehow."

Her unexpected touch sent a wave of adrenaline to every nerve ending. "I'm the only one that can do this," he said.

"You'd do it anyway, wouldn't you, Danny Boy?"

"I'm not as brave as you think."

She crossed her hands behind her back and leaned against the shelves in a way that made Daniel's pulse start to throb. "After you help Blanche," she asked, "how long will you stay with us? The others still don't know about your resignation."

He couldn't think straight at the best of times around Mary, let alone when she was so close. "Maybe some distance might be the best option," he offered. "It'll help give me some perspective on all this."

"Where will you go?"

"I don't know." His voice sounded wounded. "I threw away my Magic 8 Ball."

The little line appeared between her eyebrows. Daniel stepped closer. Suddenly, her arms were wrapped around him, and she was crying against his shoulder. He froze for a second, then hugged her tightly, almost lifting her feet off the floor. He buried his face into her hair, nuzzling her neck. "Mary," he whispered. "I wish it was you instead of Blanche."

"Don't," she sobbed. She pushed against his chest, then ducked out of the embrace and disappeared around the corner.

"Wait!" He followed her around a display of windup toys and promptly smacked into the chest of Mr. Oliver.

He stumbled back, glaring at Daniel. "You missed your last hourly round," he accused.

The sight of Mr. Oliver appearing in the dark was like something out an old horror movie. He had to think fast. "The Music Room," he blurted out, making a story up on the spot. "I thought it deserved a thorough check. I thought I heard mice or something."

As a result of his missed check-in, Daniel had to re-label,

274

NIGHT SHIFT

by hand, every switch in the electrical room, a task that took the rest of the evening. He emerged from the tiny, humid room with his shirt stuck to his back and eyes that refused to focus.

On the last hourly round of his shift, Daniel found a leftover martini glass half-hidden under a linen tablecloth. He washed it in the kitchen alone. It was too late to talk to Mary; the early morning staff had begun to arrive. She was already in her display, untouchable.

Daniel watched the golden arrow descend to the letter G. He unlatched the gate and walked through the jewelry counters like a zombie. He tripped over his feet and came down hard on the tile.

A hand was under his arm, helping him stand. "Are you all right?"

Daniel squinted at a pair of horn-rimmed glasses. "Mr. Travis?" he said, sounding a little drunk.

Mr. Travis made sure Daniel was standing on his own before taking his hand away. "Long night?" he asked.

"You could say that." Daniel opened and closed his mouth a few times, testing to see if his jaw was hurt.

Mr. Travis adjusted his fedora and glanced around the department. "It makes sense that security is across from the jewelry," he commented.

"Uh-huh." Up ahead, the door to the security office was closed. Mr. Oliver's voice was loud enough to make some of the jewelry clerks turn around.

Mr. Travis exchanged a glance with Daniel. "Mr. Hadley scheduled a breakfast meeting with me in the Matinee Room." On the floor, next to his feet, the familiar brown satchel was exploding with papers and several cardboard tubes.

"More things you'd like to change about Willard's?" Daniel asked, not even trying to hide his dislike.

Mr. Travis pushed up his glasses. "It must be a great advantage to be here at night, to go exploring without any distractions. I envy you," he admitted. "I've been studying this building for a number or years."

275

"Mr. Oliver told me."

Mr. Travis kept an even expression. "I almost wish it was the theatre again."

"That doesn't sound like something Consumers Plus would appreciate."

Arguing voices made them turn to the closed security door. Mr. Hadley's voice was hitting the high octaves. Mr. Travis reached for his bag. One of the tubes fell out. Daniel picked it up. "These are blueprints," he said, suddenly waking up. "To the original theatre!"

"Yes, of course," Mr. Travis said. "I told you, I take my research seriously." He read Daniel's expression and smiled. "Since Mr. Hadley is...ah, busy, will you join me for a coffee? I'd really appreciate your opinion on the new designs for the store. I think you and I share a unique appreciation for this place."

Daniel held the blueprints, hesitant to give them back.

"And I'll go over the original layout with you," he offered. "You seem attached to them. Your knuckles are turning white."

"Oh." He loosened his grip. "Yeah," he agreed. "Coffee is just what I need."

# CHAPTER FORTY-ONE

A waiter in the long blue apron and gold bow tie refilled Daniel's coffee cup. "Do you need more milk?" he asked.

"No thanks," Daniel said. "I take it black."

The waiter refilled Mr. Travis's cup, then took away their finished plates of eggs Benedict.

"And this area," Mr. Travis said, pointing to what Daniel guessed was the Confectionery, "was stage right, close to the wings, while the main stage extended to the middle of the ground floor."

"That far?" Daniel took a sip of hot coffee. "I had no idea it was so huge."

"Imagine the rows of blue velvet seats going almost to the last jewelry counter. Then there was the balcony and the private boxes along the sides." Mr. Travis looked at the blueprint as if a 3-D image of the theatre was rising from the paper.

Daniel squinted, trying to focus. The lines made no sense to him, but he knew Mary would pore over them until she figured it out. "Do you think I could photocopy these?"

"Of course." Mr. Travis sat back, looking pleased. "But if you want, you can keep them. I have copies."

"You have no idea how important these are," he said, rolling up the blueprints.

"You and I are a lot alike, I think."

Daniel answered with a snort. "Except I don't want to

change Willard's into a shopping zoo."

"Neither do I," Mr. Travis said. "In fact, I feel quite the opposite. I see it becoming a shopping oasis, something elegant but modern, more streamlined, with greater efficiency."

"It sounds like you're talking about a car."

"The store has to act like a machine, or else it will flounder. Look around the neighbourhood; Burlington Coat Factory, Frederick's of Hollywood, T.J. Maxx—these department stores specialize in marked-down high-end labels, usually seconds straight from the factories. People don't want to pay full price for anything these days. Barney's Co-Op is making a killing."

Daniel imaged Ruth Ann would have no problem spouting off business statistics to defend Willard's, but he was clueless and had no comeback. He stayed quiet, unable to refute the facts.

Mr. Travis continued. "An upscale store like Willard's belongs on 5th Avenue, but it's too small to compete. The grand staircase is lovely, but it takes up valuable retail space. The window displays bring lots of crowds to the front sidewalk, but they need to be running into the store, not pausing to look at the pretty mannequins."

Daniel could almost taste the eggs Benedict coming back up. He concentrated on counting the crumbs on the linen tablecloth. Mr. Travis added a spoonful of sugar to his coffee, content to let the silence linger. Daniel breathed in through his nose a few times. He had to say something. "It's not all about profit," he mumbled.

"You're absolutely right. It's about survival. And without the proper upgrades, Willard's will simply cease to exist." Mr. Travis played with the coffee spoon, clinking it against the mug. "How would you feel if you could never work here again?"

He swallowed, thinking of his upcoming resignation.

Mr. Travis pushed his coffee away and hit Daniel with a stare. "When a store loses profit, the first thing management does to recoup is redundancies. I understand you were just hired…but suppose you did keep your job. It's still only a

NIGHT SHIFT

matter of time before the store closes for good."

"You're lying."

Mr. Travis shook his head. "Trust me. I've seen it happen countless times. What I'm proposing to Mr. Hadley and the shareholders is to keep the original feel and style of Willard's but make it updated. Fix the elevator, repair the plaster, put in air conditioning. Because the alternative is—"

"I get it," Daniel interrupted. His eyes toured the restaurant. It looked perfect to him, but maybe it was better to embrace the changes if it meant keeping the store open. If the Muhlenberg Branch Public Library could be renovated with its classic architecture intact, maybe a few upgrades were...just what Willard's needed.

"You have to admit, I make a sound argument," Mr. Travis said. "Mr. Oliver is desperately clinging to sentiment. He'd let the whole store crumble on top of himself before he saw reason."

Daniel noticed a handful of waiters had gathered close to the kitchen door and were watching his table. He had an uneasy sensation. "Why do you care so much about what I think?" he asked Mr. Travis. "I'm only a night guard."

Mr. Travis lowered his voice. "I believe in thorough research, Daniel. There's a reason I spoke with you in particular the first time Mr. Hadley gave me a tour of Willard's."

Daniel glanced at the elevator, wishing he could escape this conversation. The eggs Benedict felt like a lump in his gut. "And why's that?" he finally asked.

"I know you have a special connection with Mr. Oliver, and I'm hoping you can persuade him to see things our way."

"Special connection?"

"Mr. Oliver has worked here for almost forty years. And in that whole time, do you know how many potential security guards he's interviewed?"

Daniel shook his head.

"Only one," Mr. Travis said. "You."

A coolness traveled down Daniel's spine, sending a shiver

279

over his skin. "That's it?" he tried to laugh, but it came out as a cough. He pushed himself away from the table and stood on shaking legs. "I think I should go," he stammered. "I'm overtired," he said.

"My apologies." Mr. Travis took out his BlackBerry. "Let me call you a taxi, it's on me."

Daniel managed to grab his backpack and get to the sidewalk, where a cab was waiting for him. Mr. Travis' words tumbled over again in his mind. *Mr. Oliver is desperately clinging to sentiment.*

Everything Mr. Oliver had ever said replayed with a warped meaning: using his full name as if to tease him, talking about protecting the store, and the other night, how he was crying to Mr. Willard's picture. *I don't know what the plan is, I don't know what to do next.*

Daniel thought he was confused, but now he realized his mistake. Mr. Oliver wasn't confused or afraid—he was desperate.

Daniel slumped in the backseat of the taxi, white faced and shaking. "And a desperate man," he whispered, "Fears nothing."

# CHAPTER FORTY-TWO

Tugging on his backpack, Daniel faced the long sheets of rain. The brightly lit window display illuminated the dark, wet sidewalk in front of the store. His loafers slapped through the puddles as he ran the last few steps. He stood in the light and looked up. All the blood in his head whooshed to his feet.

Mary was perched on the sparrow as Thumbelina. His backpack dropped to the concrete, forgotten. She turned her head and stared down at him. He raced to the window, and pressed his palms flat against the glass. "Hold on," he yelled. "I'm coming to get you."

He was frantic to save her; if anyone saw Mary move even an inch, she'd die. Daniel's hand was shaking too badly to fit the key into the lock. He saw Mr. Oliver on the other side of the glass door. The look of terror on his face matched Daniel's racing heart. Their images overlapped, and he couldn't tell if he was looking at Mr. Oliver or his own reflection.

The sound of screeching metal made him turn around. A massive wrecking ball hurtled forward, smashing him through the front of Willard's.

Daniel lay on his back, breathing heavily, blinking at the ceiling. He swore under his breath and kicked off the sheets. He couldn't even be a hero in his dreams. Still shaking from the image of Mary trapped in the display window, he took an extra

long hot shower.

He walked down West 18th Street, his anxiety building. Daniel went through a mental checklist for tonight. Mary made it sound simple, but there were so many things that could go wrong.

What if Mr. Oliver insisted on doing rounds with him? What if Mary couldn't override the security files? And what if Blanche dropped dead on the sidewalk or froze in mannequin pose forever?

His footsteps kept time with his racing pulse. He took a few deep breaths, trying to calm down. Mr. Oliver would take one look at him and know something was up. He had to purposely stroll into work tonight like he was counting down the days until his resignation. He glanced at the address on the corner building; he was getting close to Willard's. Daniel smiled and it felt fake.

That first morning he'd stood in the rain and stared at the entrance for over half an hour, trying to match up images of a childhood memory. The search for that faint moment in time had set all of this into action. He realized that even if he hadn't gone travelling, the inheritance would have brought him here…eventually. But that wouldn't have been soon enough for Maureen and Blanche.

This time, Daniel paused on the street, half hidden behind an ambulance parked across from Willard's. *Yeah*, he thought, *911 is right*. Hardly a good omen, but Daniel knew he had no choice. Everything had come down to this night; all of the loneliness, all of the searching, all of the dead ends, and all of the hoping with none of the rewards. He'd never been in charge of his destiny, he realized bitterly; it was laid out long ago.

He ran across the street and stopped in front of the window display. Thumbelina flew on her rescuer's back, ready to embrace a more beautiful life. Blanche was saving herself by finding her purpose. All he was doing was delivering her to Maureen. He wasn't the hero, he was the gofer—Daniel didn't need the Magic 8 Ball to tell him that.

He studied his image, mirrored in the glass. New haircut, new shoes, and cleanly shaven, but he was still the same pathetic loner who'd walked inside the store a month ago. Right now, part of him wished he'd never gone into the store. He whispered, "Walk through its doors and you will find, Willard's is just what you need."

Daniel squeezed his eyes shut, waiting for the urge to grab the next cab to the airport to subside. He kept his head down as he pushed through the main doors, taking the path to the grand staircase—he wasn't ready to see Mr. Oliver yet. He needed to see Mary, even if she was still in pose. He gripped the hand railing, smearing the shiny brass finish.

Blanche was in her usual display, wearing pajamas covered in bunnies. What was going through her mind all day, he wondered, knowing this was her last night inside the store? For the first time, he put himself in her shoes. How scared she must be, about to leave her only home and family behind.

Clicking heels came around the corner. Monique carried an armload of perfectly folded sweaters. "Hey, you," she smiled.

"I thought you weren't working until the weekend?" Daniel asked. He noticed she was limping a bit.

"New shoes," she explained, following her gaze to her feet. "Never try and break in heels when it's short-staffed. Stacey called in sick," she moaned. "I came straight from school."

Daniel guessed Stacey had spent the day at the hospital, trying to explain to the staff about the "delivery" tonight. He was grateful not to have be on the end of that conversation.

"But I can't rag on her too much," Monique said. "One of the girls heard she has a sick relative in the hospital." She hiked up the pile of sweaters and continued down the aisle. "I guess that explains the phone calls. You know, my Uncle Bernard was like that—talking secretively and being all paranoid, then funny the next minute and pulling quarters out of my cousin's ear. I was convinced he was a double agent for the government, but it turned out he was betting on the ponies." Monique dropped her voice and spoke out of the corner of her mouth. "Aunt Debbie

found out when the collection agency came."

She stopped in front of a long table and began arranging the sweaters in order of colour. "Seriously," she continued, "with all the crap that's been going on between Mr. Oliver and Mr. Hadley today, I would totally start working night shift."

Daniel did a double take. "What do you mean?"

"There was a big important meeting or presentation or something with a lot of important people."

He was too tired for this. "You're killing me with the specifics."

Monique didn't look up from her work. "Apparently Mr. Oliver came in early and crashed the whole thing. I was downstairs getting makeup samples from Helen when the yelling started."

"When was this?"

She shrugged, "Like half an hour ago, I guess."

It hit him like a slap in the face. "The ambulance," he said. Monique gave him a confused look, but he was already heading for the ground floor. He hurried down the steps, hearing Monique's heels click behind him. He ran down the aisle between the perfume counters—his eye caught a bottle of Chanel No. 5.

Up ahead, there was activity in the main foyer. He waited at the back of the small crowd, huddled outside the entrance to the Gift Shop. A stretcher was being pushed toward the main doors. He noticed several branches of the golden tree were bent out of shape from all the commotion.

The patient was wrapped in blankets with an oxygen mask covering their face. *Caucasian male…possible heart attack*, crackled on the paramedics' portable radio. Monique came up beside Daniel and touched his arm. "I've never seen Mr. Hadley so upset," she said.

Daniel looked down at her. "He just had a heart attack!"

"Mr. Hadley's standing over there," she pointed. The portly manager stood off to the side, fidgeting with the buttons on his vest.

Leaving Monique behind, Daniel squeezed his way through the crowd, pushing to get to the front. The stretcher paused long enough at the main doors for him to catch up. Mr. Oliver's gray face was barely recognizable without his familiar sarcastic sneer. Daniel grabbed at the side rail. A bony hand emerged from the blanket and covered his. Mr. Oliver's voice came out muffled. The paramedics motion for him to let go, but Daniel held on, gripping tighter. He brought his face closer to Mr. Oliver's.

"...protect them," Mr. Oliver wheezed, his eyes wide and terrified.

"How?! From what?"

Mr. Oliver mouthed something, but Daniel couldn't hear him. The stretcher lurched out of his grasp as the paramedics rushed across the street. The ambulance pulled away with its lights flashing. Staff that had collected on the sidewalk slowly filtered back into the store. Daniel didn't move until the last echo of siren faded into the traffic.

He turned and faced his reflection in the display window. This time he saw who he really was, a sellout. He had been swayed by Mr. Travis and his theories about survival and capital gain, leaving Mr. Oliver to fight for Willard's on his own—and it might have killed him.

The Little Mermaid perpetually gazed into the face of her sleeping, true love. "'To her he sent no smile,'" he said. "'He knew not that she saved him.'"

What if Mary hadn't lost the night-vision goggles, but instead saved him in the dark, and then quickly left before he could turn on the lights? He would have quit that first night for sure, convinced his rescuer had been a ghost. He'd be another weird story for Monique to tell the next night guard.

Would they be safe with the next guard? What if he was mean, or some crazy guy? Or worse, what if he was like him? But instead of running away, he stayed with them, and took care of them—took care of Mary?

He shuffled over in front of Thumbelina. "'Fly over

mountains, where there is greater beauty.'" Daniel took a deep breath. "'Willard's is full of magic and beautiful things.'"

Then he stared at the Tin Soldier, forever at attention on one leg, gazing at the paper ballerina. He remembered how Jonathan had remarked about the sad endings, 'doomed lovers from other worlds', he'd said.

"Not if I can help it," Daniel vowed. He stared at the window displays, feeling like he was on the wrong side of the glass. He gripped the brass handle of one of the main doors, letting his thumb trace the top curve of the *V*. He didn't need to pull out the black notebook this time. "'I've travelled the world looking for my heart's desire,'" he recited, "'and I looked inside myself and found home.'"

In the main foyer, several branches of the golden tree were lying among a few bags of crushed tulips, twisted and broken by the crowd. Daniel tried to bend one back into shape, but it snapped in two. He looked closer and saw each branch had a tiny green shoot painted over its rough texture of golden bark. It was pretend, but it felt so real, so vulnerable.

The door to the security office was open. On top of the desk, beside Mr. Oliver's flashlight, was a 3-D model of Willard's. Daniel's knees threatened to buckle. No wonder Mr. Oliver had had a heart attack.

Gone were the royal blue banners with the golden scrolling letters. The large window displays that stretched the length of the storefront were replaced with the large neon symbol of Consumers Plus. The brick facade and arched masonry were turned into windowless concrete walls, high and straight with perfectly sharp corners.

Even Mary's tiny oasis wasn't spared. The very top was encased with a plexiglass roof. The Consumers Plus logo blinked back at him from the computer. He touched the screen and the PowerPoint presentation began.

The piano music and articulate narration did nothing to soften the shock as Daniel saw the animated version of Mr. Travis's plans. The Matinee Room, with its art deco theme, was

NIGHT SHIFT

now a cafeteria-style restaurant, with white tables and chairs bolted to the floor. Gone were the archways and sunken rooms. Every level was a flat warehouse concept with rows upon rows of shelves. Even the aisles had kiosks placed in between, letting no free space go unused.

The grand staircase was replaced by four new elevators. There were dry-cleaning dropoffs, cheap souvenir stands, and even a one-hour eyeglass service. It wasn't the shopping oasis Mr. Travis had promised—it was a goddamn airport. It wasn't modern or efficient, it was cold and sterile. Even the mannequins, he saw with a jolt, were shiny, smooth—and headless.

Nowhere in the new store was there room for Mary and the others. Daniel closed his eyes. A ball of heat inside his chest started to grow. Mr. Oliver told him from the start.

*If you want to protect her, you've got to know all about her.*

Daniel's heart quickened but he felt calm. This was his purpose. His life—his real life—was on this side of the glass.

Sean walked into the office. "What are you doing here this early?" he asked.

The corner of Daniel's mouth curled up. "Because it's where I choose to be." He ignored Sean's confused expression and asked, "Where's Mr. Hadley?"

"Menswear, I think."

Daniel strutted down the main aisle feeling the ball of fire in his chest explode. He was like a gladiator about to enter the Coliseum, but this time the lion wouldn't win. He paused at the various rooms of Menswear, scanning for Mr. Hadley's red face. On top of the handkerchief table, he saw the familiar fedora. Mr. Travis stood in a three-way mirror, pleasantly chatting. One of the tailors in a blue vest and gold tie was crouched on the floor, marking the hem with a piece of chalk.

Daniel stood behind him, feet firmly planted. "You lying piece of shit," he said.

Mr. Travis met his gaze in the mirror. He lifted his chin and touched the knot in his new tie. "I never lied," he replied,

ignoring the shocked expression on the tailor. "You interpreted my subjective comments as facts. I simply told you the store is old and needs renovations."

"Renovations? You're destroying it!"

"I'm afraid that's a matter of opinion—yours, actually." Mr. Travis turned and faced Daniel. "This store is dying, financially and structurally. With its cracked ceilings and faded paint, the inside has grown stale. Today's shoppers want to feel energized and need impulse purchases to keep their high going. Willard's is a relic with more ghosts than shoppers. It's already dead. I'm doing the decent thing and putting it out of its misery." Mr. Travis put his attention back on his reflection, motioning for the tailor to return.

Daniel noticed Oscar in a blue suit along the far wall and tried to summon a commanding voice. "You're wrong," he said. Mr. Travis ignored him. "You're wrong," he repeated louder. Several shoppers stopped and craned their necks over the clothing racks. "Willard's isn't a relic, it's an escape. People feel it when they walk through the main doors. It's a chance for them to forget their outside lives. I should know, Mr. Travis, I'm proof."

"I've been alone for months," he continued. "I thought if I kept travelling, I'd find something that might explain why I'm still alive, and my parents are dead. But everything reminds me of how I will never be with them again; family reunions at airports, mothers telling stories to their sons, even music! The outside world is full of reminders of how much I've lost."

A few clerks nudged each other and motioned in Daniel's direction. He paused and took a deep breath. "I don't know why, but working at Willard's makes me feel like I'm not missing anything. And that I'm finally getting a life back."

Mr. Travis answered with a pitying smile in the mirror.

Daniel was aware of the growing audience around him, but he kept the speech going. "Imagine you've spent the last hour sitting on the bus, and you're walking home in the rain. Then you see the window display and it makes you smile for the first

time that day. When you get to the jewelry section, the clerks let you try on all the diamond rings."

Heads nodded in agreement.

"Then you spend the next half hour in the Confectionery. You're allowed to sample anything you want. And even if you only buy one little chocolate, the clerk wraps it up specially. You leave that night knowing that you'll be back to Willard's because when you're here it feels like...well, it does feel like a relic from the past, because it's stepping into the best dream you had as a kid." He smiled, thinking of Stacey.

"And how much would you charge for the one chocolate?" Mr. Travis asked. His voice cut through the air like a hot knife. "That one customer just took the attention of three clerks and two hours."

"You'll never understand," Daniel said. "Willard's isn't a building, it's a *being*, and it makes people feel alive. You want perfection, but that's impossible because nothing perfect can be real."

Business Attire had never been so quiet on day shift. Daniel continued to stare down Mr. Travis, waiting for him to reply.

"You're absolutely right," a voice sobbed from behind. Mr. Hadley mopped his red face with a handkerchief. He continued to cry, getting the attention of most of the clerks. Soon a tray of chocolates was offered under his nose. "Willard's will not end like this," Mr. Hadley said, between chews.

"Didn't you listen to anything I said during breakfast?" Mr. Travis pulled Daniel away from the crowd. "I thought I could count on you," he said.

Daniel wrenched out of Mr. Travis's grip. "Someone else asked me first."

Mr. Hadley recovered enough to take Mr. Travis back to the security office. Daniel waited, partially hidden by an archway.

Monique's flushed face appeared. "Wow!" she said, jumping up and hugging him. "That was like something right out of *Glee*! We should be doing a dance number or

something."

"Uh-huh," he said, looking over her head. She continued to gush as other clerks gave him pats on the shoulder.

After the longest fifteen minutes Daniel had experienced, the door opened and Mr. Travis came out, fedora in place with his familiar satchel in hand. Daniel followed until Mr. Travis was all the way outside. When the two main doors closed together to form the cursive W, Daniel smiled, and it felt real.

"—so maybe tomorrow?" Monique was still with him.

"Sorry?"

She rolled her eyes. "You never listen. It's like your mind is somewhere else whenever I'm talking to you."

"Look, I'm sorry but—" he paused. A familiar face watched them from the entrance to the Gift Shop. "What's the deal with Sean?"

Her cheeks flushed. "What do you mean?"

"Sean's always around when we're together, and he's standing over there, staring at you."

Monique whipped her head around. Sean dropped his gaze and turned away from them. "We, um…used to date. And I thought he was over me, but maybe he isn't."

Daniel realized Mary must have known all along. He asked, "Are you over him?"

Monique picked at a fingernail. "I'm not sure. I think…I think I kind of like the idea of him being jealous." She looked at him with big puppy dog eyes. "Are you mad?"

He laughed out loud. "No. But why are you standing here with me? Go talk to him."

"Really? You think so?" Her voice was a mix of hope and surprise, like she was trying to decide if he was serious or not. "Only if you tell your girlfriend the same thing."

"I don't have a girlfriend."

"Well, whoever you're thinking about when we're together."

"Is it that obvious?"

Monique gave him a half smile. "I should know; I was

NIGHT SHIFT

doing the same thing."

Daniel motioned with his head. "He's waiting for you."

She walked proudly in her new shoes toward the Gift Shop, no hint of a limp.

Daniel found Mr. Hadley on the leather couch in the security office, holding Mr. Oliver's trusty flashlight. He stared blankly at the display model. "Mr. Travis will have to come back and pick this up tomorrow," he said.

"What's going to happen now?" Daniel asked.

Mr. Hadley let out a puff of air from his cheeks. "Nothing."

"So, no Consumers Plus take over?"

"One of the anonymous shareholders was dragging their feet, anyway; it would have taken months."

"You sound disappointed."

Mr. Hadley's face became hard. "My main priority is to make sure this store stays open. Each day there are new shops in the neighbourhood. I have to be vigilant. Mr. Travis seemed to be offering a long-term solution."

Daniel's chest began to tighten. Had he screwed up again? "*Is* Willard's bankrupt?"

"No," he sighed. "But sales can always be better."

A day guard walked in holding a clipboard and looked sheepishly at Mr. Hadley. "Oh, yes." Mr. Hadley placed the flashlight on the desk beside the model. "Obviously you're the only night guard scheduled for this evening." He grimaced like he was about to pull out a painful splinter. "Do you need someone else?"

"Actually, Mr. Hadley," Daniel said, feeling invincible, "for tonight, I think I can handle it alone."

# CHAPTER FORTY-THREE

Daniel stood in front of the wall of monitors, smiling at every image, drinking up all the details. Mary and the others were still in pose. The screen for the main entrance showed the last group of clerks gathered in the foyer. He left the office whistling, shiny key in hand.

When Willard's was dimmed and locked up for the night, he took the elevator to the first floor, relishing the squeaks and groans of the antique machine. He stopped outside the entrance to Sleepwear and squinted into the darkness. Lying in a heap at the foot of Blanche's display were the hated flannel pajamas. Daniel wondered what kind of outfit she'd chosen for tonight.

"Hi," Mary said quietly from behind.

Daniel spun around. "Wow" was all he could say.

"Clara picked out the dress," she said, her hands nervously playing with the white fabric. "Apparently this strapless Valentino number is one of Blanche's favourites."

The soft glow from the counters made her look like an angel. Daniel felt like his skin was the only thing keeping him in one place.

"It's a surprise," she explained. "We're all dressing up for her." She touched one of the dark waves pinned up off her face; the rest of her hair flowed down her back.

"Oh my God," he breathed. "You look so—"

"Don't say it."

NIGHT SHIFT

"—uncomfortable."

Mary looked shocked, then started to laugh. "It's the shoes," she said, pointing at her foot.

"You're wearing stilettos!"

"Sergio Rossi, Mac," she mimicked.

He held her gaze, letting the moment last between them longer than usual. She touched her hair again. "Oscar said your speech was very impressive."

"Took me long enough to realize this is where I belong." The sudden blush on her skin made his pulse race. "Mary," he said, putting a hand over his heart. "You take my breath away."

Her expression fell. "Don't play with my feelings," she said. "You can't show up acting romantic and wonderful. It's not fair."

"Have you looked in a mirror lately?" he teased. "If anyone's not playing fair, it's you."

"You have no idea, do you?"

He heard the hurt in her voice and his smile faded.

"In my entire existence nothing compares to the butterflies I feel when I look up and see you watching me. For years," she said, "I've listened to clerks gossip about their boyfriends. I used to tune out, completely bored. But after we kissed, it changed everything. A whole new part of my brain began to rewire itself. And now I have these feelings."

Mary looked down and started to wring her hands. "I can't stop imagining us together, all over the store. The daydreaming is out of control." She swallowed and began to talk quickly, the words tripping on her tongue. "When I think about you and Monique, I hate you, but when we're together all I want to do is kiss you! It's actually painful. You make me happy and miserable at the same time—it's incredibly frustrating."

Daniel couldn't believe she'd liked him the whole time, and not as an experiment, but as a real guy, a boyfriend—a lover. He was terrified to say anything wrong that would make her run away.

She paced awkwardly in her shoes. "Ruth Ann keeps giving

293

me Judy Blume books to read, and it helps for a bit, but it doesn't make being your friend any easier. We'll never be together and I have to accept that. You want someone *real*...not someone like me." She stumbled. Daniel moved forward and caught her in his arms. She let out a long sigh, and he could feel the energy leave her. She pressed her forehead against his chest. "I wish we'd never had that first kiss," she whispered.

Daniel touched the small of her back and pulled her closer. He matched her breathing. In. Out. In. Out.

"I used to think I was a victim because of all the things that happened to me," he said. "But tonight, I finally understand. It's my choices that make me who I am." He tucked a finger under her chin, tilting her face up. "I choose to stay. My life is here, with you," he said. "You make me feel like I'm not lost anymore. And it doesn't matter that I threw away the Magic 8 Ball away, because you're all the magic I need."

Mary's eyes travelled over his face, "I thought you wanted Monique," she asked.

"I've been a complete jerk," he said. "I was only trying to make you jealous, to see if you felt the same way."

"But...?"

He pressed her open palm against his chest.

Mary's eyes were rimmed with tears. "Your heart is racing," she said.

"It always does that when you're close. I've never met anyone like you. You're brave but scared, beautiful but tough, and you drive me crazy because you're so perfect, but you can still be jealous and angry. You're flawed—you're human."

"But I'm not real," she said, her voice breaking as she began to cry.

Daniel caught her tear with his thumb, and pressed it to lips. "Salty, just like mine." He kissed the tear on her other cheek. Mary sighed and wrapped her arms around him. His lips moved along her jaw until he found the softness of her earlobe. "You make *me* feel real," he whispered. "I love you."

Before she could answer, he closed his mouth over hers,

NIGHT SHIFT

and kissed her in a way that erased any doubt.

Menswear was quiet, except for the whispering coming
from Business Attire.

"Mac, you're a peach," Blanche said, running up to him.
Instead of an evening gown she'd opted for a cream-coloured
fitted jacket and skirt, with several strands of pearls. Her hair
was wavy and tucked behind one ear. She'd taken extra care
with her makeup and nails. "Look what you're going to buy!"
she held up a suit.

"Blanche." Oscar rolled his eyes. "At least let him pick out
the tie."

"It's okay," Daniel said. "I trust Blanche."

"I know you can afford it, but I don't want you to feel you
need to spend this much money," Oscar said.

"I have an employee discount. Besides, that's what a credit
card is for."

"I love it when you talk retail," Blanche cooed. She
nervously flitted around, unaware of Oscar discreetly picking up
several garment bags and walking away.

Blanche was a fashion perfectionist. "Here," she said,
helping Daniel with the vest. "Leave the top button undone."
She stood beside him in the three-way mirror and her eyes filled
up. "You're so handsome I'm not even looking at myself."

"Thanks," Daniel said, trying not to laugh.

"See?" she said, smoothing out the shoulders of the jacket,
"I told you I'd have you in Armani by the end of the month."

"So you did," he agreed. Their gazes met in the mirror.

Suddenly she was in front of him, fixing his tie, fussing
needlessly. "Before we leave, there's something I need you to
promise."

He cleared his throat. "Of course."

"Whatever happens tonight, if something goes wrong, you
must leave me at once." She lifted her eyes and looked at him
seriously. "Can you promise me that? If I drop dead on the
sidewalk, I want you to run away. You can't be dragged into

any kind of police investigation. You'll have to leave me…do you understand?" "

Daniel nodded, unable to find the words big enough for this moment.

She gave herself one more critical look in the mirror, smoothing out the cream skirt. "I wouldn't trust this evening to anyone but Alexander McQueen," she said. Then she picked two flowers from a lavish bouquet on one of the cashier's desk, one was placed in her clutch purse, and the other in Daniel's lapel. "White roses are Maureen's favourite," she said, dreamily.

He offered Blanche his arm and silently escorted her out of Menswear.

The ground floor was completely quiet. Daniel smiled as they paused under the archway to the main foyer. Blanche put a hand to her mouth. The others were lined up under the golden tree. One by one they turned their faces as she walked toward them, trying to swallow her tears.

Blanche went first to Jonathan, who was dressed in a tuxedo. "You should be in movies, not watching them." He kissed her cheek, unable to think of anything funny to say. Ruth Ann stood beside him, wearing a flowing Dior gown. Blanche held up a hand in disbelief. "You're wearing a dress! I knew there was a girl in there somewhere," she said.

"In *The Wonderful Wizard of Oz*," Ruth Ann said, blinking back tears, "when Dorothy is leaving, the Tin Man who always wished for a heart tells her he finally has proof that he has one, because he can feel it breaking."

Blanche moved on to Oscar, who was wearing a sharp black suit with a silver tie. He gently kissed her hand. "I can't believe you're leaving me with all these fools," he teased. "Willard's will be less stylish and elegant without you."

She hugged him tightly. "Take care of these silly kids. They need you just as much as you need them."

Clara smoothed out her long black Oscar de la Renta dress. "I want you to know," Blanche began, "the only reason I can

NIGHT SHIFT

leave tonight is because you're back with us. It's no mistake that you woke up when you did."

Clara put a hand on her hip. "What's all this philosophical nonsense? What about my outfit, girl? Do you know how long we agonized over what to wear?" She laughed as a tear rolled down her face.

Blanche gave her head a light shake. "Of course, let me see the shoes. Jimmy Choo—perfect!"

Next was Mary's turn. "Thank you for being so brave, doll," she praised. "Without you, Daniel would never have come into our lives." Blanche reached out and touched her hair. "A French twist would be better, though." Then she squeezed Mary's shoulders and gave her a quick kiss on the cheek. "And pearls, too."

At the sound of a light cough, Petey peeked around.

Blanche reached for his hand. "The best of the bunch," she smiled. "I had no idea the store carried tuxedos that small."

"Cufflinks, too!" he grinned.

"Of course, pigeon." She stepped back and looked at all of them. "It's just like a *Vanity Fair* cover," she gushed.

Jonathan finally found his voice. "Except the most glamorous one isn't in the shot," he said.

"Don't be stupid, I'd have my own spread." She looked down at Petey. "I would like for you to escort me to the door, please." He took her hand and they walked to the main doors, where Daniel was waiting.

Petey stopped when his feet reached the barrier. "When Virginia left, I was so angry I didn't understand what was happening, but I do now." He let go of Blanche and took out a piece of paper from his jacket pocket. "I was going to give this to you to read later, but Daniel thought you should hear it from me."

He unfolded the note and cleared his throat. "Dear Blanche," he read, "you are the most beautiful and magical thing in the world, and it would be selfish not to share you with the outside. Love, Petey."

Blanche reached down and gave him the longest hug. Then she took his letter and kissed his cheek. He blushed and walked back to Clara's waiting arms.

Daniel led her across the white marble to the main doors.

"I'm counting on you to take care of them for me, Mac." She gripped his arm tightly, staring straight ahead as he unlocked the doors.

When Blanche's foot passed over the threshold, he glanced back over his shoulder. Mary and the others were huddled together with silent tears running down their faces.

# CHAPTER FORTY-FOUR

"Hello?" Stacey answered. Daniel could hear the panic in her voice.

"We're just around the corner," he said.

Earlier, he'd told her that Blanche was in his care, and that he would be bringing her personally. He suspected Stacey had been so worried about Maureen's deteriorating condition that she was willing to suspend disbelief and agree with anything he said.

*What exactly was she expecting?* he wondered. *That he'll pull up with a mannequin wearing one of her aunt's favourite dresses?*

Stacey said, "I don't have anything to help you take her up with. She'll be too heavy for us to carry."

Daniel glanced over at Blanche opening her purse and checking the rose for the fifth time. "You won't have to carry her," he said. "She's wearing Louboutins." There was only silence. "Everything is going to be all right," he tried to reassure her. "But you need to promise one thing."

"What?"

"Please don't faint."

"Okay," she said, weakly.

The limousine pulled up to the hospital. Daniel had never been inside one before tonight. He'd arranged it earlier, knowing Blanche deserved glamorous transportation.

She'd clung to his arm at first, eyes wide open and staring out the window. "There are no walls," she'd whispered. Then she remarked how fast they were going, and started to shake. By the time the car made the final turn though, she'd let go and had the window rolled down half way.

Daniel stepped out and saw Stacey standing alone, tightly clutching her raincoat against the wind.

He wasn't surprised to see the dark circles under her eyes. She looked him up and down, noticing the suit and tie. She moved to the side, trying to see around him.

A cream-coloured stiletto came out first, followed by a manicured hand reaching for Daniel. In one elegant movement, Blanche stepped out of the limo and stood before Stacey.

"Blanche?" she whispered. Stacey's eyes fluttered and she immediately dropped.

Later, at the nurses' station, Daniel and Blanche watched Stacey taking sips of water while sitting in a chair. After a few nervous glances their way, she stood up and motioned for them to follow her down the hallway.

Halfway down, Stacey paused by a door. With her eyes only on Daniel, she stepped back to let them enter.

"Wait!" Blanche whispered. "Do I look all right?" she asked.

He smiled. "You were never lovelier."

The small, bare room was nondescript and anonymous. Even the patient herself was void of colour or personality. Maureen's wiry black hair flared out on the pillow around her head. The bruise on her forehead from the latest fall was purple and sore looking.

Daniel had flashbacks to his father's cancer ward. He put a hand on the wall to steady himself. Stacey hadn't been exaggerating: Maureen look like she only had a few days to live.

Blanche let go of his hand, then took a few steps toward the bed. Her bottom lip quivered, and she turned her head away.

NIGHT SHIFT

Daniel worried she was going to run out of the room. She noticed the bedside table and her expression softened.

A plain, slim blue vase held a single white rose, now wilted and edged with brown. Blanche removed the dead flower from the vase and carefully replaced it with the one from her purse.

"Maureen?" she said, bringing her face close.

Her eyes opened and Maureen looked back with a vacant expression. Then slowly, her face squinted into a smile. A pale hand reached up. "My Blanche," she cried.

Daniel moved a chair over to the bed. Blanche sat down and held Maureen's hand. He left the room and found Stacey leaning against the hallway, her eyes red and swollen.

"Is it safe for them to be together?" she asked. "What I mean is…" She dropped her voice to a whisper. "Last week she was a mannequin, and now she's alive. If I go back in there, is my aunt going to be holding hands with something plastic?"

"Only Blanche can tell you for sure," he answered. Stacey stared at the floor, then she blew her nose and went into the room.

After a few minutes, Daniel felt a hand on his shoulder. Blanche was beaming back at him. "It's all settled," she said. "Maureen still owns an apartment uptown. I'm going to help move her back home, and take care of her. I can't believe I'm finally with her. I've found my purpose," she said. "I can never return to the store; my place is with Maureen now."

"Are you sure?"

"It's just like waking up in Willard's and intuitively knowing the rules without anyone telling me. I know it in my heart. The barrier will always exist for me now."

Daniel thought of his mother, watching him from the sidewalk, while he ran into the store. She was terrified because she couldn't follow him. Perhaps once they find their purpose, Willard's made sure they only moved forward, never returning to their old lives. He wondered what his mother's purpose had been.

Blanche kissed his cheek. "I'll keep in touch through you."

301

She gave Daniel one last critical look and fussed with his tie. "Now hurry up, and get back to Mary."

In the back of the limousine he tapped his foot and checked his watch every two minutes. He'd been away from the store for almost an hour. Finally, the Willard's royal blue banner came into view. Daniel slipped out of the backseat and ran to the main entrance while fishing for the key in his pocket. Only once he was inside with the doors locked behind him did he feel at ease.

*Honey, I'm home.*

The branches of the golden tree twinkled in the darkness, softly illuminating the foyer. Daniel loosened his tie and slung his jacket over his shoulder. He whistled while making his way to the security office. He stopped a few feet from the closed door. The frosted glass glowed from inside.

Daniel walked in and his stomach lurched. A familiar silhouette stood in front of the wall of monitors. "How did you get in?"

Mr. Travis turned. His huge smile made Daniel take a step back. "I've finally found it!" he said, clapping his hands. "All this time I thought I'd find the gold, but this is better!"

"What are you talking about?"

"The real treasure of Willard's, of course!" He waved a hand toward the monitors. "Is it some kind of biotechnology? It's fascinating!"

The floor dropped a hundred feet underneath Daniel. Mr. Travis was watching the tapes—the tapes he'd forgotten to turn off.

"She actually stepped down from the platform," Mr. Travis said, his voice high and breathless. He pointed to an image of Ruth Ann leaving Kitchenware, tossing her blue-and-white-striped apron back to the display.

Daniel's mind raced to come up with a plan. "I don't see anything."

Mr. Travis gave another one of those creepy smiles and wagged a finger at him. "I had a hard time figuring you out, a young man so attached to a department store. I was certain you

NIGHT SHIFT

were looking for the gold as well."

"Gold?"

"George Willard's missing gold bars," he said. "I came back here tonight to work out some kind of deal with you. Mr. Hadley was so taken with your speech, I thought we could make an arrangement."

"Nothing you're saying makes sense." Daniel tossed his jacket onto the couch. "You're not welcome here. Do I have to call Mr. Hadley?" He was expecting to be welcomed by Mary's open arms, not this. Mr. Travis was scaring him. He wanted him gone.

"Be my guest," he said. "We'll invite him down for some home movies." Mr. Travis pushed a few buttons on the monitor. "I think he'd find this one particularly interesting. Might help explain why you're the one night guard who doesn't mind exploring the dark corners of the store."

Daniel held his breath as Mr. Travis played the tape showing him at the entrance to Sleepwear. Mary arrived and they started to talk.

"She tried on a black dress earlier that I preferred, but I guess she knows what you like," Mr. Travis said.

"Turn it off," he said, through clenched teeth.

"No, the good part's coming up. Although, I have to say, it is a bit creepy. But I guess everyone has their fetishes."

Daniel wanted to lunge at Mr. Travis, but he couldn't, he was transfixed by the image of him and Mary together. When he watched them kiss, he could feel it all over again, how she'd trembled in his arms, and then kissed him back, saying that she loved him, too.

"This will change everything," Mr. Travis said, now staring at the model building of Consumers Plus on the desk. "A whole store employed by human robots. They'll never have to be paid, require breaks, or sleep—"

Daniel peeled his eyes away from the tape. "No," he said. "They're not robots. They're real."

"—we'll never have to close. We can be open twenty-four

303

hours, every day of the week." He put his attention back to the monitors, randomly clicking buttons. "But how do they work? What's the energy source?" He looked at Daniel. "Take me to them."

"No."

He grabbed Daniel by the shoulders. Beads of sweat dotted his forehead. "The profit margin will go through the roof. This building will be the flagship for Consumers Plus."

"There will be no Consumers Plus," Daniel said, shoving him hard. Mr. Travis stumbled backward into the desk. His hand came down and punched a hole through the model. He looked stunned for a moment, then he narrowed his eyes and lunged forward.

Daniel's back smacked against door, and the frosted glass cracked behind his head.

Mr. Travis stepped away. "You can't keep this a secret. People will find out—corrupt people. You're just a kid, you need me. Listen, together we can make millions."

"They don't belong to anyone. They're real," he said.

Mr. Travis ran a hand over his face. His glasses were knocked off and his hair was messed up. He picked up Mr. Oliver's flashlight. "Get out of my way," he threatened.

Daniel shook his head. "No."

The flashlight came down hard, then two more times. Daniel crumpled to the floor, seeing blasts of colour behind his eyelids. Then footsteps faded away. He pushed himself up on his knees, feeling a gush of warm blood run down his face.

He leaned against the wall and saw the black-and-white photo of Willard's Grand Opening. Daniel picked up the flashlight, still smeared with his blood, and staggered down the hallway to the electrical room.

His good eye wandered over the panels, now labelled in his own handwriting. He found the main power switch and pulled down hard. He was instantly swallowed up by complete blackness.

Daniel carefully navigated the ground floor, with the

304

NIGHT SHIFT

flashlight illuminating only a few feet in front of him. "Mr. Travis," he called out, trying to keep his voice steady. He stomped up the grand staircase, trying to make as much noise possible. His only plan was to warn them to stay hidden.

He reached the landing of the first floor. The flashlight swept over the racks of ladies' spring jackets. He stopped and listened—dead quiet. "I called Mr. Hadley," Daniel yelled. "He's on his way…with the police."

The voice was right behind him. "Who's the lying piece of shit now?"

He spun around and wobbled, fighting to keep his balance. Mr. Travis was holding a lighter in front of him. He grabbed the flashlight from Daniel and whacked him again. The pain was enough to make him gag. He clutched the side of his head, fearing it would crack open and spill on the tile.

Mr. Travis looked down at Daniel. "Mr. Hadley is sitting at home eating a box of chocolates. That bumbling fool is clueless. His trust was so easily earned it wasn't even a fun challenge. Who do you think gave me a key to the front door?"

"Why are you doing this?" Daniel struggled to stand. "Leave us alone."

"You owe me." Mr. Travis put a hand under Daniel's arm. He tightened his grip and made him walk down the aisle. "Willard's was supposed to be my golden ticket. It took years of research and working every weekend and holiday making deals for Consumers Plus. When head office finally noticed, I convinced them this store should be next."

"And this is your backup plan?" he said, trying to buy time. He tried to steer Mr. Travis back to the landing.

"No. *They're* my backup plan."

"The gold doesn't exist! I already asked them."

Mr. Travis grunted and pulled harder. "It's not about the gold anymore, you idiot. Come on lover boy, call out your girlfriend," he demanded. "I have a proposition for them."

"To be your slaves?" Daniel tried to tug his arm away, but Mr. Travis was stronger than he looked. "You'll never get away

305

with this. Mr. Oliver has information on you. He knew exactly what you were after. His lawyers have all the documents."

"Not much of a threat, considering everyone thinks he's crazy. I hadn't anticipated the night guard to be so onerous. Too bad he's probably dead now. Enough—call her out!" From across the department an engine revved. "What the hell is that?"

Daniel looked around, unsure. "Um, the store is haunted."

Mr. Travis moved the flashlight beam, trying to catch the source of the noise as it grew louder. Daniel's head whipped around, following the light in every direction. He saw the elevator gate was open, showing the greasy cables. Squealing tires make both of them turn around. Blinding headlights came straight at them. Daniel jumped backward into a clothing rack. There was an eerie silence, followed by the splintering crash of metal and glass as the car hit the bottom of the shaft. "Petey!" he yelled.

"I'm sick of this," Mr. Travis said. The flashlight shone under his face, distorted with rage. He grabbed Daniel's arm, twisted it behind his back, and forced his cheek to the floor. "Call her out!"

"Run, Mary!" Daniel's arm was contorted at an impossible angle. A foot slammed down hard on his shoulder.

"I didn't want it to come to this," Mr. Travis said, breathing heavily. "But you've given me no choice. A loved one's pain is a wonderful motivator." He gave a sudden jerk.

There was a snap as Daniel's arm exploded. He bit down on his tongue, tasting blood.

"Stop!" Mary screamed. The sound of bare feet slapping against the tile came closer.

"Yes," Mr. Travis whispered.

"No," Daniel grunted. Out of the darkness, the flashlight reflected off the strapless Valentino gown with Mary's long brown hair flowing down her back. Her perfectly still hand was in pose. "Oh, God," he breathed.

"Please," Mr. Travis pleaded, reaching out to touch her face. "Speak to me. I can give you a whole new life. Please!"

NIGHT SHIFT

Mr. Travis wiped his sweaty face with his sleeve. "Tell her, Daniel. Make her wake up," he demanded. He lifted the flashlight high above his head. "Make her wake up, or else."

Daniel lunged forward, but he was a second too late. The beam of light was eclipsed when it met her head. Daniel's shoulder smashed into the floor, sending hot streaks of pain to every nerve. Blackness crept into his periphery, making everything play out in slow motion.

He lay on his back, watching the explosion of brown hair, and skull fill the air above him. Particles swirled in the beam of light as tiny pieces of plaster landed on his face. Something hard rolled against his good hand. Daniel found the switch and turned off the flashlight.

There was the distinct sound of crunching and grunting. Bodies were falling around him. Daniel screamed.

Warm soft hands touched his face. "Oh, gorgeous."

"He's out cold, Oscar," Jonathan called out.

Daniel tried to sit up, but several hands pushed him back down.

"Is he okay?"

Daniel recognized the scared little voice. "Petey, I saw the car...I thought."

"It's okay, he's out cold," Jonathan repeated. The flashlight was taken from Daniel's hand, and turned on.

"Cover his eyes," Oscar ordered, his voice farther down the aisle. "Pull the jacket over his head, Jonathan. Make it look like it happened during the struggle with Daniel."

"The phones still aren't working!" Ruth Ann called from far away.

"Damn it," Oscar growled.

Daniel faded away, lost in a memory of the first time he met Mary. Clinging in the darkness of the elevator shaft, her breath washed over him. Wisps of her hair brushed against his cheek. It was so real.

"Clara! Why is there so much blood?" she gasped. "Ruth Ann! Make the call!"

307

"Mary?" he choked, opening his eyes. "I saw him hit you!"

"It was a decoy," Mary brushed the hair off his forehead.

"This phone isn't working either," Ruth Ann's voice called out.

"I turned off the main switch," Daniel breathed.

"What were you thinking, running after him?" Mary cried, her tears falling on his cheeks. "You could have died!"

"I had to save you."

"You're so stupid," she said, giving him light kisses all over his face, "and brave and wonderful."

Clara knelt beside them. "Hold this against the wound to stop the bleeding." Something pressed against his forehead. He arched his back in pain.

"Hold on, Daniel," Mary said, bringing her face close to his. "Please, just hold on."

"His cell phone," Jonathan said, searching Daniel's pockets. A pair of night-vision goggles were sitting on the top of his head, pushed back like sunglasses.

"Daniel should do the talking," Oscar instructed. "It has to be his voice." His stoic face replaced Mary's. "Tell them you had to struggle with an intruder," Oscar said firmly. "And that you need an ambulance."

Jonathan held the phone as the 911 operator came on. "There's been a break-in," Daniel began. Oscar nodded, silently coaching him. Within two minutes sirens were echoing down the avenue.

NIGHT SHIFT

# CHAPTER FORTY-FIVE

Their cab was stuck in traffic. The ride from the hotel to the hospital should have only taken fifteen minutes, but already Daniel's watch told him they were over half an hour late. Alice sighed heavily and crossed her legs. She drummed her fingers on the top of her carry-on bag, still upset.

"Just say it," he smirked.

"Say what?" She adjusted the brightly patterned silk scarf around her neck. "That you aren't old enough to be on your own, and next time, instead of finding you in a hospital, I'll find you in a morgue? Is that what you think I should say?"

The cab driver sneaked a glance in the rear-view mirror.

"You won't find me in the morgue," Daniel said. "Besides, I'll only have a cast for four weeks. I've had worse playing hockey."

"Hockey," she huffed. "You should be coming back with me. I can get you a job at the firm for a while." Alice paused and softened her voice. "I think that maybe it was too soon for you to go out on your own."

"Do I need your permission to stay here?"

"No, kid, you don't. But—"

"But," he interrupted, "it really means a lot knowing you're still going to be there, whenever I need you."

Alice looked defeated. "All right, I get it," she said. "You're all grown up."

"There are advantages," he said, flashing her one of his

309

dimples, "to my staying in one place for a change."

"True," she said, looking out of the window now that the traffic had started again. "I don't have to hold my breath listening to the news when there's a plane crash or bus accident."

He knew he was winning this argument, and it was exhilarating. "And I'm less than a three-hour plane trip away."

"Yes, that too."

"And you'll always know where I am."

"Hmm." She turned and studied him. "By the way, do you plan on living in the hotel?"

He lifted a shoulder, concentrating on stopping the blush. "There are some friends at the store I can crash with a few nights of the week."

Alice opened her mouth to protest.

"And I've already started looking for a place," he added quickly. The cab stopped in front of the hospital. Daniel gave her a one-armed hug as she patted his cheek roughly. "Thanks for coming down and taking care of me," he said.

"Don't be stupid, kid. A couple of days in a five-star hotel to give you pain medication was the least I could do." She made an obvious motion toward his sling. "I guess there's nothing else I can say to make you change your mind about coming home?"

He smiled. "I think I'm ready to make my own home."

"So independent," she clucked. "And you're sure about going back to that job? Do the doctors say it's all right?"

"We've already talked about this."

"I know...I know," She put up a hand.

Daniel leaned forward. "She's continuing on to JFK," he told the driver.

"Say hello to your boss for me," Alice said, giving him one last hug. He opened the door and stepped out of the cab. "And call in a few days," she ordered. "No more texts. I want to hear your voice to make sure you're not overdoing it at work."

After checking at the front desk, Daniel found the right

NIGHT SHIFT

room. He hesitated at the doorway, wondering what sight would meet him. The last time he'd seen Mr. Oliver, he had looked like a corpse.

"Step aside," a voice called from behind. "Lunch is coming, and I don't want to share my green Jell-O." Mr. Oliver was wearing a blue housecoat and being pushed in a wheelchair. A young woman in casual slacks and a white top brought him into the room.

"All right now, Albert," she said, one hand under his arm. "Like we practiced all morning." Mr. Oliver stood and pivoted into the bed. Soon his legs were up on a set of pillows. "Same time tomorrow?" she grinned.

"You're the boss," he replied.

Daniel waited until she left the room. "So," he began. "How's the heart?" It seemed the most obvious and least tricky question to start with. Mr. Oliver no longer resembled the gray, raspy version he still had nightmares about. In fact, he looked more rested than Daniel had ever seen him.

"Two new stents," Mr. Oliver said, pointing to his chest, "and I'm as good as an eighteen-year-old. I should send Mr. Travis a thank-you card. The surgeon said I was close to dropping on the spot if they hadn't intervened. Instead of having physical therapy with a pretty girl, I might be sitting in my apartment, stiff as a frozen trout, undiscovered for weeks until someone breaks down the door because of the smell."

"Nice visual."

He studied Daniel's face. "My flashlight did that?"

Daniel smoothed out the bandage above his right eye. "I'll have a thin scar."

On the windowsill, a large bouquet of flowers was still in its plastic wrap. "They're from Mr. Hadley," Mr. Oliver said. He reached across and pulled a newspaper off the bedside table. "Have you been reading about Willard's biggest fan?" he asked, motioning to a mug shot of Mr. Travis.

Daniel's eyes flicked away from the image, a face he never wanted to see again.

311

"From the looks of the news footage," Mr. Oliver said, "you really did a number on him." Daniel stayed quiet, knowing it was Oscar who'd delivered the massive blows. "I guess he fooled everyone."

"Not everyone," he said. "You knew what he was."

Mr. Oliver squinted at the article. "Roger Andrew Travis," he read. "Nice initials. Never trust anyone with three first names."

"Thanks, I'll remember that." Daniel tapped the end of the bedframe. He'd planned to apologize right away, but the conversation was taking another route.

"I visited you right after they set your arm. Your lawyer was at your bedside." He almost smiled. "She worries about you, being all alone in this big city."

Daniel looked uncertain. "How could you visit me? You had a heart attack!"

"I told you, I'm as good as a teenager now," he said. "Besides, the wheelchair does all the work."

"I don't remember you coming."

"Of course not," he said. "You were all drugged up. And I have to say, our conversations are much more interesting when you're asleep." Mr. Oliver returned his attention to the paper, trying to locate the crossword.

Daniel dropped his gaze and gripped the bedframe. "You know about them," he said, "don't you?"

There was a crinkle of newspaper. The air in the tiny room grew thicker. "Willard's has many secrets," Mr. Oliver said. "I have a few of my own. And maybe even you." There was a pause. "Do you know the best way to keep a secret, Daniel?"

"No," he said, staring at his white knuckles.

"Tell no one."

A whistling attendant whisked into the room and dropped off a lunch tray. It was like an intangible time limit had expired on his question. Mr. Oliver was keeping all his secrets—for now.

Mr. Oliver lifted the tray cover, and grimaced. "Not exactly

the Matinee Room's culinary fare," he said, looking at his lumpy stew.

"At least there's Jell-O."

Mr. Oliver dropped a tea bag into the cup of hot water and dunked it a few times with his spoon. "Think you can keep things in order as night supervisor, until I return?"

"Supervisor?"

"You'll need to interview someone for night shift," he said. "The day guards keep calling in sick, the morons," he grunted.

"I plan on returning tomorrow night," Daniel said. "I'll go in early for the interview."

Mr. Oliver raised his chin, and they stared at one another. "Can I count on you?"

Without hesitation he answered, "Always."

# EPILOGUE

The hotel digital clock read 11:59. Daniel stared out the window toward Willard's with his phone in his hands. He glanced at the clock again. Midnight. Finally, the phone rang.

"Mary?" he answered.

"Who else calls you in the dead of the night?"

He inhaled, picturing her lips close to the phone. "Where are you?" he asked, wanting to imagine it exactly.

"In the Toy department," she said. "At the counter by the board games."

"Is Twister on sale?" he teased.

She told him about two guards, now flipping a coin to see who had to do rounds. Roger Travis was in the forensic unit at prison, screaming about maniac robots who tried to kill him. That rumour, plus the fact the video footage the night Daniel had been attacked was mysteriously erased, only added to the reputation of night shift at Willard's.

"Mr. Hadley must feel like a jerk," Daniel said.

"Not so much. Gossip about the little department store that stood up to Consumers Plus has captured everyone's imagination. Sales are up. Long live retail," she sighed.

"Has Petey terrorized anyone lately?" he asked, feeling sorry for the guards.

"He's too busy sulking," she told him. "His car was completely wrecked. We're sure it got thrown out."

NIGHT SHIFT

"Maybe it's stored somewhere, I'll look around tomorrow night."

"I can't wait to see you," she said.

He smiled. "Should I pack for a sleepover? I never did get much of a chance to use my new bachelor pad."

"You mean the cloakroom." The edge to her voice was unmistakable. Since finding the blueprints in his locker, Mary had spent the last week meticulously studying the original layout of the theatre. To her disappointment, they revealed nothing spectacular. "I can't believe the secret room was just a closet."

"A closet that's big enough for a hot tub," he suggested. "I bet one could fit nicely in the corner."

"Two reasons why that will not work," she said. He imagined her counting it out on her fingers. "One, Willard's doesn't even sell hot tubs."

"I could order one online."

"And two," she continued, ignoring his comment. "There wouldn't be enough room to play naked Twister."

"You're bad."

She laughed. "How's Blanche?"

"They're bringing Maureen home next week. She's helping Stacey get the apartment ready. She sounds…content."

"I think that's the first time I've ever heard her described that way." Their laughter petered out, each waiting for the other to talk.

The words almost got stuck in his throat. "When I thought he killed you," Daniel said. "I knew I'd never be happy again. I was supposed to rescue you, but it ended up being the other way around."

"You *did* rescue me. I'm not the same girl who pulled you out of the elevator. I mean, all I used to care about was finding a way to the outside, but I've never thought beyond that, until now. I've changed because of you, and so have my hopes for a future I thought only happened in fairy tales."

His breath fogged up the window. Daniel let her words

315

wash over him; it was like she was reading his heart. His finger traced a cursive *W* on the glass.

"I can't wait to see you," she repeated. Her voice was laced with an urge that made his pulse pick up.

He told her, "Not being with you has been—"

"Excruciating."

"Exactly. You're the most important thing in my life, now. I'm going to the archives to start researching the store. I'll photocopy the whole damn library. James Willard knew about you. Maybe he has a diary or something. There's got to be a connection with the magician and the clock, I'm sure of it, all I need is time, Mary."

"I thought we decided time travel was a bad idea?" she teased.

"It's only one part; maybe it leads to the real answer about your past."

He heard her change position. "I don't care about finding out if I had a past. I want to move ahead, toward my future. Our future."

"Our future," he repeated. He smiled against the phone. "I may not be the smartest guy or even the strongest, but someday, I promise, I'm going to take you by the hand, and run out the main doors."

"And until then?"

"Whatever you want."

"Then be prepared to lose, Danny Boy—I'm wicked at Twister."

It was two hours until closing time. Daniel paused in the main foyer, letting the energy of the store revitalize him. Clerks kept asking about Mr. Travis. He gave the same short answers to everyone: "The guy was crazy," "Yes, he's very lucky," and "Yes, he's staying on night shift."

He ran into Monique on the first-floor landing. "Daniel!" she squealed, almost dropping the cardboard box she was carrying. "I heard you weren't coming back until next week.

NIGHT SHIFT

How's your arm? One of the clerks said it was shot clean off!"

"Not exactly," he said. "Um, anything interesting happen while I was away?"

"I won the glass bowl lottery!"

Daniel pretended to look confused. "Lottery? You mean the bets about me quitting?"

"Since you're crazy enough to stay on nights, they decided to pick a random name from the entries. I couldn't believe it," she said, bouncing on the spot. "I never win anything!"

"Was there enough to quit this job?" he teased.

"Not exactly," she laughed. "But enough to buy something totally indulgent and useless."

"Like new shoes?"

She shot him a look. "Shoes are never useless. I'm bringing in my mom to get anything she wants." Monique blushed a bit. "She works a lot and hardly ever spends any money on herself. She deserves a treat."

Daniel knew it was Mary and Ruth Ann who made sure Monique's name was on every piece of paper in that glass bowl. He'd even secretly added an extra couple hundred to the total winnings. He smiled and said, "Meant to be, then."

She grinned, shifting the box in her arms.

"Can I help?" he offered.

She stared pointedly at his right arm in a sling. "No thanks, Lefty." She blew a wave of hair off her forehead, the colour high in her cheeks. They traded embarrassed smiles. She nodded to the box. "They're waiting for this in Menswear."

Daniel stepped aside. "Don't lose your necklace again," he said.

Monique gave him a curious frown, then continued toward the grand staircase.

He found her standing with a hand on one hip, staring across the department. "You'd be surprised the things people try to hide in the displays." He tucked a wrapped caramel into Mary's perfectly posed hand. He also left a note folded over

317

many times, telling her he'd be waiting in the Confectionery by the chocolates. Then he walked away, whistling "Gymnopedie No.1."

An hour later Daniel sat behind the antique desk and read the name on the file in front of him. "So, Brian," he said, looking over at the slightly nervous interview hopeful. "Your resume shows you've worked in security before, and you have a lot of volunteer experience."

"That's right," he answered. "And I'm taking my third year of dental school."

"You'll be doing a lot of reading at night?"

"Well," he squirmed in the chair, making it squeak. "During my breaks, of course."

"Night shift at Willard's is perfect for studying. In fact, this room is ideal. It's quiet, there's good lighting, and a big desk. With the wall of monitors, you can keep an eye on everything right from this chair." Daniel tapped the arm rest for emphasis. "You seem like a great choice," he said, closing the file. "But there's one more question I have to ask."

"Sure."

Daniel put a hand over his cast, and fixed him with a stare. "Do you believe in ghosts?"

# ACKNOWLEDGEMENTS

Stories, or rather ideas for stories, are usually the conglomeration of images that at first, seemingly have nothing to do with each other. And that encouragement, no matter how casual, at the right moment can make all the difference.

While visiting Brenda, my sister-in-law who lives in London, I got lost in *Harrods*. I remember wandering through the sumptuous confectionery wishing I could have the whole store to myself at night.

Then one summer afternoon my sister, Cynthia, suggested I write a book. We were on vacation and dreaming up other ways to earn a living other than nursing.

I rolled my eyes at her, but the seed had been planted, and over the following months, an idea began to congeal. I've always loved a good ghost story with an unexpected twist, and the memory of getting lost in that famous department store was the foundation for Willard's.

Over the next eight years I wrote this story. It was molded and improved by many people.

Thank you to Naomi Hackenberg for suggesting I tell the story from Daniel's point of view. And also to Roseanne Wells who spent many hours polishing the rough bits.

A standing ovation goes to Penelope Jackson, editor of my dreams and overall awesome person.

Thank you to Emma Dolan for giving *Night Shift* such a sophisticated cover.

A warm nod of gratitude goes towards the readers around

the world who have fallen in love with this story on Wattpad. Their enthusiasm is partly responsible for this book being in print.

Thank you again to my parents, Eric and Ethel Bishop for all their support in my writing and my life.

High fives and hugs to my siblings, Cynthia Flack and Brad Bishop.

Always, I am wholly grateful for the support from my husband Ken, and our children, Ruth and Adam. And also, Cody, our loyal dog and full time giver of unconditional love.

Most importantly, I am honoured to give thanks to the very first readers of this story: Barbara MacDougall, Tricia Dauphinee-Bishop and Shannon Macgillivray. Their earnest excitement and staunch support made it possible for Mary to step down from her display. Without their enthusiasm the doors to Willard's department store would never have been opened. Thank you all, so much.

# ABOUT THE AUTHOR

B.R. Myers appreciates a design in her cappuccino, loves shopping for vintage jewelry, and dreams in colour. Always in the mood for a good scare, she spent most of her teen years behind the covers of Lois Duncan, Ray Bradbury, and Stephen King. When she's not putting her characters in compromising situations, she works as a registered nurse in Halifax, Nova Scotia, where she lives her husband and their two children. You can visit her online at www.bethanymyers.blogspot.ca.

*(Photo credit: Tanya Reynolds Photography)*

Made in the USA
Charleston, SC
19 May 2016

**Produced for DK** by WonderLab Group LLC
Jennifer Emmett, Erica Green, Kate Hale, Founders

**Editorial Partner** Angela Modany
**Design Partner** Project Design Company
**Cover illustration** by Rowena Blyth
**Internal illustration** by Aparajita Sen

**Publisher** Sarah Forbes
**Managing Editor** Katherine Neep
**Managing Art Editor** Sarah Corcoran
**Project Editor** Sophie Adam
**Production Controller** Isabell Schart
**Production Editor** Sachin Gupta

First American Edition, 2025
Published in the United States by DK Publishing,
a division of Penguin Random House LLC
1745 Broadway, 20th Floor, New York, NY 10019

Copyright © 2025 Dorling Kindersley Limited
25 26 27 28 29 10 9 8 7 6 5 4 3 2 1
001–345059–Apr/2025

All rights reserved.
Without limiting the rights under the copyright reserved above, no part of this publication may be reproduced, stored in or introduced into a retrieval system, or transmitted, in any form, or by any means (electronic, mechanical, photocopying, recording, or otherwise), without the prior written permission of the copyright owner.
Published in Great Britain by Dorling Kindersley Limited

A catalog record for this book
is available from the Library of Congress.
ISBN 978-0-5939-6149-0

DK books are available at special discounts when purchased
in bulk for sales promotions, premiums, fundraising,
or educational use.
For details, contact: DK Publishing Special Markets,
1745 Broadway, 20th Floor, New York, NY 10019
SpecialSales@dk.com

Printed and bound in the UK

www.dk.com

This book was made with Forest Stewardship Council™ certified paper—one small step in DK's commitment to a sustainable future.
Learn more at www.dk.com/us/information/sustainability

By following the CASEL Framework in this way, children reading this book are encouraged to learn critical character-building skills—from how to effectively communicate their emotions to how to be a thoughtful leader and problem-solver—in real time. Plus, they'll have fun while doing it!

| CASEL Framework competencies presented | Key questions to ask to relate to the characters |
|---|---|
| **SOCIAL AWARENESS**<br><br>Taking others' perspectives | When Sam reflected on the differences between his and Tami's interests, how could he have taken on Tami's perspective? How did he take on her perspective? |
| **RELATIONSHIP SKILLS**<br><br>Resolving conflicts constructively | When Sam and Tami couldn't decide between an 80s or 90s theme, Sam suggested a "through-the-decades" theme so people could make their own choice. How did Sam's solution resolve their disagreement? |
| **RESPONSIBLE DECISION-MAKING**<br><br>Identifying solutions for personal and social problems | On page 76, Tami and Sam discuss how they aren't on the same page. How did they identify some of the problems and solutions? |